P9-CMX-801

Harvesting Ice

by Lawrence Cirelli

To Jackie—
Thanks for your comments —
Lawrence Cirelli

Town Book Press
Westfield, NJ

Publisher's note: This novel is a work of fiction. Names, characters, places and incidents either are the product of the author's imagination or are used fictitiously, and any resemblance to actual persons, living or dead, events or locales in entirely coincidental

Cover Art: John Curch
Author Photo: Colleen Cirelli

Town Book Press

255 East Broad Street
Westfield, NJ 07090

Town Book Press is an imprint of The Town Book Store of Westfield, Inc., an independent bookstore established in 1934.

ISBN: 1-892657-09-0

Printed in the United States of America
First Trade Printing: August 1999

10 9 8 7 6 5 4 3 2 1

Library of Congress Catalog Card Number: 99-63778

To my children: Lisa, Andrea and Bryan

Winter

Mark dipped the blade of his wooden oar into the channel that cut through the frozen lake. He slapped at the black surface with an upward motion sending droplets of water into the cold, black winter air, watched as they turned to tiny ice balls that scurried across the top of the ice like miniature misshapen marbles. He couldn't recall how young he was when his father first showed him this magic. Maybe six. Maybe seven. His father's baritone voice hollered "Alakazam" as the water drops reached the apex of their flight before turning instantly to ice to the open-mouthed wonder of the boy.

The recollection brought little warmth to the young man. Pleasure once mined from such memories had hardened into a block of bitter irony. Mark sat immobile in the middle of the frigid water as the small row boat rocked gently from the jerking of the oar. He sighed deeply, watched his breath disappear quickly into the moonlit sky. He slapped at the lake again, this time with a downward stroke. The flat crack of the oar echoed around him, each reverberation progressively muted as the sound spread outward towards the darkened shores.

Mark's day started twenty hours earlier with the arrival of the heatless sun. The serenity of that first day's dawn made this his favorite time of the harvest. He stood in a wordless prayer as the wind ripped off the land across the bowled surface of the virginal lake. His solitude was short lived as men arrived from around Sullivan County to begin the annual ice harvest.

He spent most of that January day standing on the tail board of a horse-drawn scraper removing the dry snow ice from the frozen surface, repeatedly urging the resistant draft horse across the width and breadth of the lake. In years past, Daniel would have joined him driving another scraper, crisscrossing the lake like two misplaced charioteers. All that day Mark caught himself looking over his shoulder at the emptiness that made the day longer and colder. He would not let anyone else scrape alongside him, preferring to make an extra run himself rather than tolerate a substitute for his brother.

He started the draft horse down the center of the lake, clearing snow from an eight foot wide swath of ice with each pass. Steam from the horse's mouth hung over it like a cloud, partially obscuring the bulky harness. Mark halted the horse occasionally and walked to the front of the scraper stamping his feet on the hard surface to stimulate circulation. He put his hands in front of the horse's nostrils to thaw the collected frost, doing so as much to warm his own hands as to help the animal breathe easier. As soon as Mark made two passes with the horse drawn scraper, the ice men started cutting the channel. Two straight lines were run down the center of the lake, about a half inch deep, with a mule-drawn ice scorer. The clanging of metal bars and the chipping sounds of resistant ice reverberated continually along the lake until it was impossible to distinguish between reality and echo. A square was marked out and the first block of ice cut. There was a ceremonial quality to "sinking the header", as the first cutting was called. The foreman of the harvest cut through the ice using a five foot hand saw, careful to cut the block wider on the bottom than on top. All Mark's life, he had never known anyone but his father to fill that honorary role. His father's powerful circular motion buried the five foot saw into the ice, cutting almost a full inch with each stroke. The wooden handle reached the ice and with an involuntary groan, his father pulled it out again with a fluid motion that belied the effort. When he completed the square, the block was sunk, providing a starting point for the larger horse drawn saws. The other men stood in a determined quiet, each seemed to reflect on this annual marking of time in their lives.

The men worked with an economy of conversation. Like steam from factory machines, their breath hovered around them, stirred in eddies of mist by the robust motions of their arms, before disappearing into the frozen atmosphere.

By the time the afternoon's ebbing sun reached the leafless tree tops, a black scar of forbidding water branded the glass-smooth ice. For all but Mark, the first day of the winter harvest ended. Tomorrow the men would return to score the ice, forming a grid that turned the entire surface of the lake into a quilt of frozen threads. It was Mark's job to keep the channel open overnight with the motion of the rowboat until the men returned with breaking bars, pikes and draft horses at dawn. Mark would spend that day sleeping before rejoining the effort the following day, as the men pulled the ice cakes from the lake. He got paid an extra six bits for staying up all night. In the past, he'd have done it for nothing. As a young boy, the responsibility intimidated him, but as he gained the unspoken respect of the ice men, the repeated annual challenge became a source of pride.

But now he was tired. The night brought such a bitter cold that the moonlight seemed to offer a relative warmth. Mark rowed with his left hand, turning the small boat around. The bow scraped the ice wall that framed the channel. There was barely enough room in the hand cut avenue to allow the maneuver. Mark surveyed the white lake on the eve of its annual metamorphosis, rowed backwards away from the shoreline and watched as the ice house seemed to skate away behind him.

His life was rooted in the ice harvesting rituals that had persisted largely unchanged. For over a hundred years men had extracted ice from these New York waters. This lake was better than most. It was fed from a mountain stream on the west bank that exited on the southeast side, not far from the Pine Bluff house. The ice grew clearer and denser in waters like these, producing the best cakes. Stagnant waters allowed too many air bubbles to enter the freezing process, producing inferior ice less dense and quicker to melt.

Mark had always looked forward to the annual harvest. Although the workday was long, the work was not that difficult. The carnival atmosphere of the harvest days brought out neighbors he hadn't seen since fall as they emerged to help or to watch the carving out of the lake. He found a stabilizing satisfaction in being involved in an industry that had gone on year after year essentially unchanged. Oh, the tools had changed some. Most harvesters used horse saws that replaced the old hand saws, each horse saw doing the work of twenty men. Some of the larger harvests upstate used gas-powered saws that did the work of five horses at substantially more risk to the operator. More local ice men died with their original allotment of fingers once the hand saws faded into a rusty disuse. His father's nine-fingered grandfather had cut ice. Maybe rowed the channel as Mark did now.

The years before he was old enough to work the ice had gnawed at the boy. Each winter he begged his father to let him help, only to be turned down because he was too young. He had worn his youth as a badge of shame, impatient to be old enough to help. Finally, at age nine, his father let him ride the shine sleigh. It was his job to remove horse manure from the ice with a square ended coal shovel taller than the boy himself and paint the contaminated area with formaldehyde, leaving a shiny spot on the ice. Mark hated the strong chemical smell but embraced the opportunity to work alongside the men.

He first rowed the channel eight years earlier when he was thirteen and he still remembered the nightmares from those days about falling asleep in the boat. Tall phantom ice men arrived in a misty dawn to find Mark asleep at the oars, the channel they had cut the previous day covered over by new ice. An entire day's work spoiled. All his fault. Hundreds of dollars wasted. All his doing. He couldn't move. His arms locked as tight as the boat trapped in the ice. He wanted to holler out to the men that it wasn't his fault. That somehow he wasn't to blame. He screamed through lips bonded shut by ice, his mouth frozen closed. Always at this same point, he'd awake cold and shivering, usually wrapped tightly in bed linens that restricted all movement. A frightful dream to the boy, but as he grew older, it became just "the dream". The original terror made nostalgic by repetition.

He reached under the wooden seat of the row boat for his thermos of coffee. He fumbled for his cup, his gloved fingers wool fat and awkward. In ten years, he never once fell asleep. Over the years, that became part of the dream. The dream men shouted to him, some in tears, some in anger, "But you've never fallen asleep before! How could you let us down now?" He shivered. Raised his cup to his lips in a toast to what never was. The black coffee was tepid though it wasn't yet past two-thirty. He rowed erratically one handed, bouncing the boat gently off the sides of the channel. It was a good year for ice. The top of the boat was level with the fourteen inches of ice that walled the channel.

Mark finished his coffee and picked up the second oar. He raced down the channel as if he was in a crew boat like the ones he'd seen sketched in Harper's Weekly. But he stopped his sprint after covering fifty yards, wary not to break a sweat. There were still four hours before daybreak and he knew he wouldn't survive the night with a wet back. Nor would he want to. He had made that mistake before, when he was fifteen. He spent the remaining days of that winter nearing pneumonia, unable to speak with laryngitis and ague.

Mark rowed slowly along the edges of the channel. His oars broke the fragile skin of new ice, thin as butterfly wings, not yet fully hardened. He loved the sound it made, like glass breaking softly in slow motion. He liked how the bow of his boat creased and shattered the unstable ice layer as he inscribed his jagged course, until minutes later on his return from the other end of the lake, all traces of his path disappeared, smoothed over in the satin of tentative new ice.

A little past three, he rested in the ice shanty. He stoked the wood stove and made more coffee to fill his thermos and thaw his frozen body. But he preferred to not stop at all. There was no feeling that Mark hated more than reentering the boat after a break in the shanty. The air felt a hundred times colder and the night tenfold blacker after just a few minutes in the warm glow of the makeshift cabin. He had to adjust to the cold anew as his fingers cried out for warmth in a dull scream. He hated that the most: his fingers getting re-accustomed to the frost. Some nights they'd refuse to clutch the oars in silent mutiny. The cold all the more ponderous against the mind's memory of warmth.

A thunderous crack of contracting ice filled the air like the boom of a nearby cannon, even its echo loud. His grandfather used to tell him the frightening sound was the two faced god Janus striking the ice, a warning to all mortals of his power. But the young man had abandoned those notions of earth walking gods. God, he knew, issued no warnings. The Lord giveth, but He taketh away with such surgical precision that it took a leap of faith broader than Mark was capable of to believe that he was being watched over. He did not dwell long on thoughts of God, although the solitude and inherent beauty of the frozen lake lent itself to the task.

He felt old. Had said as much to his father that morning. Michael Lerner laughed, then stopped abruptly as his laughter was absorbed by the vacuum of his son's eyes. He stumbled to find words that might reach his son, to help him. But the words he had at his disposal were inadequate to the task. Michael drew on a lifelong reservoir of practice and said nothing to the boy.

"I'm not going to harvest ice anymore," Mark had said. "This is it for me."

He expected an argument. Crossed his arms in front of his chest.

"It's been a rough year," Michael said after a moment's pause. "No need in deciding already about next year."

Mark uncrossed his arms and put his hands in his back pockets. He knew his father's will was no match for his own, but the realization was disconcerting and unwelcome. The small part of boy left in him wanted to jump into his father's arms for comfort, but he had outgrown any comfort the man could have lent him.

It had been a difficult year. The kind of year that shot youthful optimism from the sky like an exploding dirigible. A year that would break a lesser man, and on that winter night in 1929, Mark could not say with any certainty whether he was, in fact, such a lesser man. 1928 had brought him more money than any Lerner ever accumulated. But the crooked numbers scratched in his ledger mocked him. He had paid too high a price for his fortune and, in the end, it could not purchase even a portion of what he truly wanted and once had.

The two most beloved people in his life were gone and he could not hide from the fact that his own actions were to blame. He stared at his guilt the way a fat man looks into a mirror, forced to believe what he saw, but wishing somehow it wasn't true and not quite certain exactly when it became so. The facts were cold on his exposed skin. He didn't do anything wrong, but everything he did turned out wrong.

Mark shivered from these recurring thoughts and turned his attention to the ice as he paddled across the lake. The frozen quiet was as thick as the ice that bordered the symmetrical scar of the channel ripped through its middle. He lifted the oars from the water and watched as tiny icicles formed and dripped weakly to the black pool.

He occupied himself with remembered stories his grandfather had given him. Mark's great-grandfather had sailed on the first ship to bring ice to the tropics with Frederic Tudor in 1810, sailing from Boston to Martinique with their ephemeral cargo in an attempt to fight the yellow fever. His grandfather spoke of sailors who refused to sail fearing the ice would melt and sink the ship. He laughingly told of the first time the ships arrived in Martinique and how the natives feared the ice. It burned their hands, and they cowered from it as though it belonged to the devil. Some braver souls purchased pieces of ice and complained bitterly of being cheated by the white-skinned captain when the ice inevitably melted.

"Martinique. Martinique," the boy said aloud. Even the word seemed out of place in the barren cold. His frozen jaw barely able to form the rich tropical word.

Mark felt foolish in his wooden dinghy when he measured it against the tall-masted sailing ships of his grandfather. He tried to conjure up the exotic ports whose names sounded like songs coming from his grandfather's lips. Barbados. Saint Croix. Bermuda. Mark looked at the small land that surrounded the lake. His only home. The only port he ever visited. What was it that propelled some men into the world and left others rooted in a sheltered harbor? Mark looked across the lake to Pine Bluff. The moon lit a path across the channel and up the shore to the imposing house. He knew then that he must leave. He'd tell his father in the morning. He vowed to himself that he would never return. He would harvest ice no more.

Pine Bluff

June 22, 1907

The table was set hours before Mark was born, the players all present. For most of his life, Mark was never more than passingly involved with anyone born after him. The women in his life were older. His brother. His friends. As though he was the final actor hired for a long-running play; the other actors in varying degrees of comfort with their roles by the time he was born.

Mark arrived at the Harrison table. Its sparkle and order welcomed the boy long before he knew the implications of its finery. Water shimmered in Waterford crystal catching and dispersing the light from the overhanging gas chandelier. Highly polished Gorham silver was set like sentries alongside Limoges dinner plates. Embroidered table linens lay rolled obediently in silver rings.

Foot high beeswax candles marked the boundary of a centerpiece of fresh flowers arranged in a pair of potbellied vases impeccably painted by Japanese artisans half a world away. Greens, reds and yellows from the overflowing vases bent nearly to the top of the crystal mimicking the china pattern. Pewter buckets of ice stood guard at opposite ends of the long table, unopened bottles of wine sunk deep inside. Color and light copiously filled the table.

The Harrisons were in attendance. Austin Harrison, serene in the turmoil of the exigent birth, pulled the chaise lounge from the corner of the dining room as Mary Lerner dropped to her knees amidst the moisture of her own water breaking.

"No sense in moving her now," he stated as he walked ceremoniously to the linen closet to fetch sheets and towels.

His wife, Lucretia, interrupted a running commentary on the trials suffered in the daily ritual of being herself long enough to act the midwife. She seemed almost grateful for the respite, and in truth, was indispensable.

And Emily– Emily was there, thirteen months old. She looked up from the cold stare of her porcelain doll to be entertained by the commotion of adults scurrying about in anticipation of Mark's arrival. His father scooped her into his arms and ushered her away unwilling to have her or himself witness the birth of his second son.

Mark was born twenty-two minutes later on the fringe of luxury and wealth. He grew up with it, close enough to recognize it and to know its pretenders. By the time he was twelve, he had polished the hood ornaments on the finest automobiles. He had helped prepare the choicest cuts of meat in the finest culinary sauces from recipes from around the world. He knew the weight of damask drapery lined in silk. Had poured imported brandies and liqueurs. Knew a good Cuban cigar from its imitators by smell alone. Had put a shine to beautifully crafted Italian leather shoes. Was as familiar with the finest ornaments in life as a librarian was to literary genius.

Mark lived with his parents and brother in the two bedroom apartment off the kitchen of the grand house called Pine Bluff. There was no sign so designating the place but it was rarely referred to in any other way. The Lerners had been the caretakers of the Harrisons' summer house since 1906 when Mark's brother, Daniel, was born. The stately house had a porch on two sides and gables on all four. It sat on a rise overlooking a lake near the Delaware River. Sloping east, the grounds ran down to a ten stall horse barn, and west, passed by an ice house before easing into the shallow waters of the lake. The Lerners small apartment was an addendum to the main house. It was a little less than thirty feet by thirty feet and could only be entered through the kitchen, a room nearly as large as the apartment.

A sprawling tin sink anchored the kitchen adjacent to a massive oak work table centered on its pumpkin pined floor. During the summer months when the house was filled with the Harrisons and their Manhattan guests, all eight burners of a heavy steel stove were often fired at once preparing the meals. An array of black frying pans and solid steel pots hung from a rack above the stove. A collection of ladles, spoons, whisks, and other kitchen utensils hung from another rack above the sink like spindly metal spaghetti. In spring and summer the breezes from the open door and three huge windows blew against the utensils and they banged together like metal wind chimes. It was a noise so subtle and such a part of the sounds of the house that it was only noticed when it stopped.

Part of Mark's delight in the coming of spring was the opening of the windows that started this seasonal symphony. Since he was tall enough to reach the rack, he climbed upon one of the wooden benches that surrounded the oak work station and rearranged the utensils to alter their sound. Maybe he'd put the grater next to the masher, or the soup ladle next to the dicer. He'd climb down, close his eyes and listen to the different tinny tappings. Then he'd turn and run out into the yard, the screen door banging behind him, content in his contribution to the harmonies of the house.

Nine months a year, all but the Lerner apartment and the shared kitchen was closed down. The front parlor sofas and divans were covered with linens, looking like stagnant white ghosts. Persian carpets were rolled up and covered with newsprint to save them from the fading rays of the oblique winter sun. Drapery and sheer curtains, packed in wooden crates, sat at the base of each window.

Fourteen chairs rested overturned on the dining room table. The linen shrouded silhouette seemed like the skyline of a ghostly city when seen through the French doors that led in from the front porch. Growing up, Mark avoided looking into those windows if his chores required he pass by. He knew he was born in that room, and feared the room as if it might also hold an exit from his life. The six bedrooms on the second floor and the two on the third floor were frozen in identical barrenness. The mattresses were rolled up and tied exposing the springs of the bed like machinery under the hood of an auto. No soaps rested on the pitcher and bowl tables. No matching towelettes, monogrammed PB for Pine Bluff, had yet appeared. The vases on all the night tables were turned upside down on the cotton runners that covered their marble tops. A cutting garden behind the kitchen provided the sacrificial flowers that filled the bedrooms with color and fragrance three months a year: the flowers changed twice weekly by order of Mrs. Harrison whether the rooms were occupied or not.

But now the house was reborn as it had been every May of Mark's life. Old linens pulled off the furniture were washed and hung out to dry before being packed away again until September. Furniture was waxed. Oil boxes were filled for the nightstand oil lamps and although Mary Lerner complained about the mess they made, Lucretia Harrison would not allow them to be retired to the attic. All but the third floor rooms were fitted with gas lights, installed at no small expense eleven years earlier, the year Mark was born. The formal dishes were pulled from the pantry and washed and set out to dry on the top of the tin sink.

"Why we got to wash these plates?" Mark's brother complained. "Ain't no one used them since we washed them last time."

"You aren't here to be asking questions all day," his mother answered. "Mark, when Daniel has all the dishes out of the pantry, you get to sweeping it out. Put fresh newspaper on all the shelves. I don't want to see even one mouse dropping when you're done. Step to it, now, or we'll never be ready in time."

Their mother stood at the kitchen table polishing silver, "Pine Bluff" engraved on every handle. She hummed while she worked. Sad songs that Mark had known since birth. Songs with no words. She'd try to sound cross with her boys if they took to wasting too much time. But it was an effort for her to be cross, and the boys knew it.

All the doors were opened. All the windows. The wooden screens pulled off and carefully numbered by Mark's father to be washed and replaced before the Harrisons' arrival. Fly carcasses dotted the sills trapped between screen and window since last September. Green seed pods, that looked and felt like caterpillars, blew in from the Black Walnut trees that stood along the driveway. The massive trees enveloped the house in shade all summer. Each May morning, Mark ran room to room sweeping the seedlings into a black metal dustpan and ran outside to dump them under the thick-trunked trees.

An urgency filled the air. The Harrisons were coming, like an annual comet across the Lerner sky. The house was awakened. Every corner swept. Every mouse trap checked. Every piece of crystal shined. For the Harrisons.

The Harrisons

Mark ran aimlessly alongside the driveway with his head down, his ankle-high leather boots kicking up a fog of dust with every step. Emily Harrison was running to escape a cloud of gnats that collected where she sat rocking on the porch. He ran to the corner of the house as she ran from the front. He never saw her as she rounded the four foot hydrangea that anchored the corner of the front garden.

They collided with a force that knocked them both backward. Emily hit the ground and rolled landing on her right knee. A dazed Mark pulled himself up to a sitting position and stared blankly at Emily. Her summer dress, a small Calico print, was pulled above her skinned knee. He sat embarrassed looking at her freckled face. She was twelve years old, a year older than Mark.

"I'm right sorry," he stammered.

She said nothing at first. She sat in the dirt looking at him, her young brown eyes sparkled below the unmanageable cluster of her reddish-brown hair. Her straw hat was knocked off so it hung sideways from her neck by the elastic of the chin strap.

"Your head's bleeding," she finally said.

"So's your own," he answered. He brought his hand to the warm spot above his eyebrow just below the fuzz of his short cropped haircut and brought it down red stained and wet. She started laughing, a giggle at first, until he joined her without knowing why.

"Aren't you a sight," she said.

"I'm right sorry," he repeated. His hand was cupped in front of him holding a tiny pool of his own blood. She wiped her own head. Her left eye had hit his right. They sat with matching red hands giggling at nothing. The sounds of birds and crickets drowned out the distant clatter from the kitchen. She took her own red hand and slapped his open palm as both sat there grinning.

"Now we're blood brothers," she said. Her eyes danced with the excitement of her own words.

"But you're a girl!" The pain of this lifetime arrangement causing him more discomfort than the open cut over his eye.

She looked at him as if that were exactly the point.

"Can't be helped," she said. She fixed her hat with her un-bloodied hand, still not standing. "You can't undo blood brothers."

He stood finally and dusted off his overalls with his bloody hand until he realized what he'd done, and switched quickly to his clean hand.

"It ain't right," he said. But he knew he couldn't argue against the time-tested rules of blood brotherhood.

"I'm as good a blood brother as any old boy. I can climb trees higher than you, and if you catch me running, it's only because I slowed down to let you."

He shook his head at this blasphemy and reached to help her up. She stood eye to eye with him and licked her finger to brush the blood from his eyebrow.

"Ow," he said.

"Ain't nothing," she said. Then with an impulse that nearly knocked him over again she brushed his cheek with a breeze of a kiss.

Mrs. Harrison appeared on the front porch.

"Oh Lord!" her mother screamed. "Emily! What has been done?"

"Ain't nothing, Mama."

"Blood brothers," she whispered to Mark as she turned toward her frantic mother.

"My word!" Mrs. Harrison said. "Not one day arrived and look at the trouble. You'll likely be scarred for life, my poor thing." She fluttered over to her young daughter. "And what are you doing with the help?"

Mark lost sight of Emily as her mother's imposing frame swallowed her from view. He watched as they went inside to have her cut forehead cleaned and bandaged amid Mrs. Harrison's concerned clucking.

He walked to the stable and drew a bucket of water from the pump to wash his head in the cold water. He held a torn piece of old linen on his cut until it stopped bleeding and sat with his back leaning against the barn staring at the house. Then he jumped upright and ran to the lake behind the ice house, a smile covering his face.

Mark continued around the lake about a half mile down the steadily sloping ground until he reached the river bank. Mr. Harrison stood in a clearing dressed in tweed knickers and sweater vest hitting perfectly good golf balls into the Delaware River.

"Morning, Mr. Harrison."

"Good morning, son."

He swung again hitting the ball ninety yards into the water, thirty yards short of the opposite bank.

"What brings you to the river so early?"

"Nothing, sir."

He watched Mr. Harrison hit two more balls into the river.

"Why you hitting all your balls into the river?"

Mr. Harrison's face reddened in lieu of a response and Mark watched as he swung his hickory golf stick again before realizing he wasn't trying to hit the balls into the river. Mark watched as a tiny white ball arched gracefully over the water landing on the sandy soil across the river.

"Just so!" Mr. Harrison called. He looked at the boy triumphantly. "I'll give you a penny for every ball you retrieve."

Mark's smile signed the contract. The river was no more than a foot or two deep here, and best he could tell, there were twenty-five balls or more to be mined. Mr. Harrison reached into the small canvas bag and chose a different hickory shafted club to hit more balls into the water, grunting with each swing. He swung harder and harder and the harder his swing the nearer the ball plopped into the shallow water.

"Well I must be off," he said as the last ball disappeared with a splash. "I have a match."

"I'll leave the balls on the porch," Mark called after him.

It made Mark laugh to see Mr. Harrison so uncharacteristically inept, but he would be certain to wait until he was safely out of sight before doing so.

Austin Harrison III radiated a presence that lingered at Pine Bluff long after he left for Manhattan each August. Mark had only a vague knowledge of the insurance business that he owned in partnership with his brother, Stephan. Its offices took up an entire floor of the Flat Iron Building that Mark had seen only in pictures and it employed over a hundred people. But that represented most of Mark's information about the source of the Harrison wealth.

Each year Austin arrived at his summer retreat at the beginning of June, in a black suit that was, in truth, several years out of style. As he unfolded his tall slender frame from his automobile he removed his hat and handed it to his driver along with his stick. He greeted Mark's parents on the front porch as if he was their guest. He removed his jacket and starched collar ceremoniously and put neither on again until he was ready to leave three months later to return to his Manhattan apartment. Mark's mother Mary, as always, had a pitcher of lemonade waiting for him.

"Ah, summertime!" he said and laughed mightily as if summertime was a joke that only he got. It wasn't actually summer yet. Temperatures in New York State that time of year often dropped into the fifties at night without so much as a raised eyebrow from the locals. But Mr. Harrison's arrival marked the beginning of summer as his departure marked its close.

If you asked the eleven-year-old Mark to describe Mr. Harrison, he'd be forced to admit that he knew him to be a liar. True was true, and everything in between a lie. The man lied about his height, often stating he was six feet tall, when clearly, he was several inches taller. He lied about his wealth, downplaying the size of his fortune if the subject was mentioned, and it was never introduced into any conversation by him. Nearly fifty years old, he denied his own speed and strength, often saying that he was no Olympian. But Mark never forgot the incident with the colt several years earlier.

The colt had spooked in a thunderstorm and had gotten itself hung up on a barbed wire fence that surrounded the paddock furthest from the house. At the sound of its pathetic whinnying Mr. Harrison leapt from the porch and ran the two hundred yards to the paddock. Before Mark, his brother, or his father could make it to the fence, Mr. Harrison reached the colt and with a powerful lunge brought it to the ground. He leaned heavily on the frightened colt and held it still. He began to remove the barbed wire entangled in its neck. The second Mark reached them he dropped to his knees in the mud and spoke softly to the colt telling it exactly what was happening. Mark put his hand to the colt's neck and never moved his eyes from its frightened eyes. He took the strand of wire from Mr. Harrison and passed it behind him to his father, handing off each barbed section as one might advance a pail of water in a bucket brigade. As Mr. Harrison carefully unwound it from the colt's mane and withers with one hand, he held the three hundred pound yearling to the ground with the other. When the colt was freed, Mr. Harrison told Mark to jump back, the first spoken word by any of them to one another. He released the colt from his grasp and sprang backward as fast as he could to avoid the bucking of the newly liberated horse. He thanked

Mark for calming the colt and allowing him to handle the "secondary" task of grounding and disentangling the animal. He engulfed the boy's small hand in a comradely handshake. Mark refused to wash the blood from his hands until bedtime, savoring the red brown badge the rest of the day.

As he grew older, he realized that most of the truths he held were truths he learned from that lying man, more so than his own father. He was the liege lord of this manor home and, with the possible exception of his wife, he answered to no one.

Mark learned at an early age that much of what happened at Pine Bluff was done to avoid a row with Lucretia. According to her detractors she only married Austin because he was a distant cousin to President Benjamin Harrison. She also had family in politics when they married, a cousin who was a senator or congressman or something. She could never remember which. Mark heard the story a thousand times about how she first met Austin, how she thought him a bit of a bore with little awareness of social convention and how she found his aloofness exasperating. She never hesitated to make riveting and humorous luncheon conversation out of the fact that she had the foresight to see the potential hidden in him. A kernel that she, and she alone, was able to discover and cultivate.

Mark remembered sitting on the stairs adjacent to the dining room with his brother Daniel eavesdropping on a Harrison dinner party.

"Yes," they heard Lucretia say in a story repeated to every summer guest like a mantra, "Austin was beastily crass when we first met. I remember the first time he sat in my father's dining room. His elbows were on the table and he proceeded in front of fourteen of New York's most lovely people, to blow on his soup." Daniel rolled his eyes and elbowed Mark in the stomach trying to get him to laugh. Mark peeked around the corner to see her raise her hand to cover her face, as if still embarrassed by this behavior. He watched as she issued a practiced chuckle while gazing endearingly across the table at her much changed husband.

"Of course, no one had the bad grace to remonstrate him, but came to love him as I did," she purred with a contented sigh.

She didn't seem to notice that Austin sat blissfully ignorant of her tired refrain with the weight of his considerable frame resting heavily on his elbow planted firmly next to the bread plate. Daniel snickered and Mark ran out the front door before their childish espionage was discovered.

Sometime during the first week of Mr. Harrison's annual arrival to Pine Bluff, he would summon Michael Lerner to his office to "have a go at the books". Mr. Lerner's entire year funneled to this one day. He felt the subtle pressure of a man whose livelihood depended on the caprice of another. Not a week went by that Michael didn't remind himself that this lifestyle could end at any time.

If the truth were known to Michael he would have been aware that Mr. Harrison was not all that concerned with turning a profit on Pine Bluff. Michael shared the inability of the lower middle classes to accurately gauge the wealth of the well to do. In fact, even if Pine Bluff cost Mr. Harrison several thousand dollars a year, he wouldn't consider letting it go. But he knew that the pressure felt by Michael Lerner kept the country place running efficiently. It never occurred to him to let Michael think the money was of no concern. It was just "good business sense" to encourage the man's obvious concern.

Michael's every decision about what to spend, and where, was based on that annual bottom line. He was able to show a small profit every year since Daniel was born, except 1913 when he lost thirty-five dollars. Every purchase was listed in "the book", a large gray ledger with red leather corners that was revered in the Lerner house as much as the Bible.

The Lerners sold eggs from their chickens and apples from the orchard. With this income Michael kept up the mechanics of house maintenance but his main source of income was generated from his carpentry skills. The Harrisons paid no salary for the Lerner services but provided them instead with a rent-free home. Michael hired himself out to work around the county, charging more than other carpenters in the area but still turning down more work than he took on. With Mr. Harrison's approval he also kept all the money made each winter harvesting ice. The majority of the local men were employed by the grist mill, and for the others the annual ice harvest provided winter's only income. Michael learned not to count on the ice money because the price was so unreliable and the winter weather too fickle so far south. Two years earlier the winter stayed so warm that the ice never thickened more than seven inches, too thin to support the horses, and the Lerners barely harvested enough ice for their own needs. A good year might bring Michael an extra four or five hundred dollars but even that amount seemed in jeopardy as the larger customers downstate were recruited by the upstart electric refrigeration companies.

Michael's life was comfortable and he knew it. He lived the life of a rich man, he often said, without any of the headaches. His house was the largest in town and although not all of it was at his disposal, he derived a measure of satisfaction from living there. He was able to pay $460 cash for a brand new Ford, bragging to Mary that he had no need of the new "pay as you go" fad.

He spent little money on himself, except for his weekly trip to The Shohola Glen Hotel, across the river in Pennsylvania. Even during Prohibition, he still enjoyed his weekly meeting at "the hotel" unaware of how much influence was leveraged behind closed doors to keep the taps opened. He'd occasionally drop a few nickels into the slot machine there but he preferred billiards. He was decent player and might have made a fair amount of pocket change doing that, but he never gambled on billiards. "That'd be changing a pleasure into a chore" he'd say.

Mary Lerner, for all appearances, sat like a matched bookend to her husband. Like most women, she sewed all of her own clothes except for the one or two packages that found their way under the Christmas tree. She was a mystery to her son, seemingly without wants or desires unrelated to his own well-being or his brother's.

Ever since Daniel and Mark were boys, the Harrisons kept two horses in their barn for their occasional riding pleasure, as well as the large draft horse used for ice harvesting. Mr. Harrison liked to ride once or twice a week, and as Emily got older, he sometimes brought her along. Hers was the colt that Mr. Harrison had rescued. Lucretia did not value the horses and never quite made it down to the barn. As Mark got older, it was he more than his father or brother who would tend to the stable.

Since he was nine years old he had sated his thirst for horses by wandering over to the Sheer barn, east of the lake about a half a mile from the Harrisons. Phil Sheer was an ornery round, bald man who insisted on spitting his chaw of tobacco wherever he pleased. If a man had the misfortune of placing his boots within Phil's target area, that was his business and of no concern to Phil. He had a scorn for every man who ever bought a horse from him. "If it was a good horse," he'd say safely out of earshot, "I wouldn't be selling him." But Phil Sheer was more than willing to teach his eager young pupil everything he knew about horses. Mark somehow mined the solitary sliver of warmth still left in the horseman.

Phil first took Mark with him to horse auctions when the boy was nine years old in 1917. If Phil was selling a horse, the spectacle of a nine-year-old handling it made the sale go easier. If they were buying, Phil had trained the young boy how to make the horse buck, to drive down the price. At the last auction Mark rode seventeen horses in front of prospective buyers. At the end of that day Phil gave Mark twenty dollars. It had never occurred to Mark that people might get paid to go to a horse auction. He had never seen a twenty dollar bill before and wasn't certain it was real. It was more money than Mark could spend in a year. He took it home with him and deposited it in the cigar box he kept hidden under his bed. Not for safe keeping. The money meant nothing to the boy, but as a memento of the day that he once got twenty dollars from Phil. It seemed after that day that Phil would sometimes turn his head and deliberately try to avoid Mark's boots when he spit.

But Phil taught Mark about horses only in the way that someone must have taught Mozart to play piano. It was truer that Mark learned about horses from the horses themselves. He listened to them. He heard them protest a command with the pinning back of their ears. He listened to their fears and annoyances as they bucked gently or violently and he filed away the information he got from them.

Since his tenth birthday, he'd ask his father if he could feed and turn out the Harrison's horses. His father disliked the job, and soon, Mark didn't need to ask anymore, but took on the job enthusiastically. It would have surprised Mark if anyone referred to the caring of the horses as "work". Michael could see that his son had a way with the animals and in 1919 purchased a new colt for twenty dollars from a widow in Port Jervis. He bought it after a particularly profitable porch renovation, and didn't need to dip into the Harrison operating capital. The eleven-year-old gladly incorporated the care of the colt into his daily routine. Mark knew from Phil that it did no good to train a horse that young. A lot of folks rode two-year-olds, but those horses broke down too often. By the time the colt was three, Mark had a saddle on him and walked him around the ring on a longeline often enough that the colt forgot about the saddle. He laid across the colt's back, while constantly telling it what he was doing, until the colt had gotten used to the weight of a person across his back.

With that success behind him, Mark decided to try to break him himself. He had never broken a horse, but had watched Phil. The thirteen-year-old didn't think his father would approve of his decision, although his father never mentioned the colt, so he waited until he was away on a carpentry job that March. Within a week's time he was trotting the colt around the paddock. In two weeks he was cantering. By mid-April he took the horse out onto the trails and was jumping fallen logs and an occasional coop by May.

Michael Lerner was approached by a neighbor at the hotel in May who asked if he'd be willing to sell the horse to him for forty dollars. Michael was shooting pool at the time.

He chalked up his cue stick as he asked, "Which horse is that?"

"The horse your boy's been riding all through the county," the man answered.

No one had told Michael the colt had been broken. He leaned against a stack of telephone books that took up a valuable corner of real estate on the crowded barroom floor. He walked to the table and tapped his cue stick on the low embossed tin ceiling while considering the stranger's words.

"Nine ball in the side," he said. As the ball dropped into the leather pocket of the table he said, "I'd need to get sixty dollars for that horse. It's a true and gentle horse."

He had no idea what kind of horse he was, but he knew if Mark trained him, he'd been trained right.

"I'll be around tomorrow noon," the horse buyer said. "Let your boy show me what he can do."

Michael returned near midnight from the club. He rose early the next morning and walked down to the stable before breakfast. He figured the boy'd be there soon if he wasn't there already. He shook his head in wonder when he entered the barn. The boy had the stable spotlessly clean. New hay was spread on the floor. The stalls were mucked clean. The Harrison's tack was polished and hung on hooks the way tack is hung at a fancy riding stable. A bridle and girth that

Michael didn't recognize hung next to theirs. The boy had taken over the barn without a word to anyone. Michael felt a little sheepish as he tried to remember the last time he'd walked down to the stable. It had to be nearly a year. Only then did he realize that he had completely ignored the stable as Mark took on more and eventually all of the barn chores.

He didn't know what to say.

"Where'd you get the new bridle?" he asked.

Mark sat on a bench watching his father inspect the barn.

"I bought it with my ice money." Mr. Lerner had always let his sons keep their share of the winter's ice money. "It weren't new when I got it," he added defensively.

His father nodded. He seemed uncertain of what to say next.

"You got a name for that horse?" his father asked pointing to the three-year-old.

"Matches," the boy said.

The father nodded again.

"You broke him already?"

The boy looked to the ground. He bent and picked up a loose stone in the hay and threw it off to the side. Nervously he answered, "Yes, sir."

"A man's coming later today. Wants to buy him."

The boy's face fell. Was he being punished for overstepping his bounds? For deceiving his father? Tears welled up in his eyes splintering the light coming through the barn window.

"I've got an idea," Michael stared at his son as if trying to solve a puzzle, "let's sell the man this here horse–"

"But, Pop, I trained that horse myself."

"Let me finish, son," Michael said tenderly. "Let's sell this man this horse. Next month, I'll talk to Mr. Harrison and tell him I bought the horse with his money. I'll tell him we turned a forty dollar profit and there's more where that came from. If I know Austin Harrison, he'll give us, you, I mean, the go ahead to do it again. Thirty dollars is more than your ma and I get from a year of selling apples."

"You mean we'll get another horse?"

"Hell, yes," the father said. He looked around at the seven empty stalls. "Maybe even before long we can fill all these stalls."

The boy smiled.

"We'll need a little up-front money," his father said. "Buy some new bridles, some halters. New brushes," he added as he picked up a sorry-looking curry brush from a shelf the thirteen-year-old had built.

The boy laughed. "I got about twenty dollars saved," he said, now eager at the new business prospect.

"Let me talk with Mr. Harrison first," Michael said. "I'm not sure that he won't be willing to front our, I mean, your little venture."

The boy answered with sparkling eyes and a wide smile. For months he had been lingering at the Feed and Grain daydreaming of buying new tack, new brushes, hoof picks, sheets, blankets, saddle pads. Never did he dare to dream he might have it.

"You eat breakfast yet?"

"No, sir."

"Well, I'm sure your mama's up by now. Let's go eat."

The boy walked up to the house shoulder to shoulder with his father. Nothing more was said.

They walked in the back door into the kitchen. Mr. Lerner said good morning to his wife, and continued inside to his desk in the corner of his bedroom. He pulled out the ledger. He went down the ledger column until he came to an entry that read "Horse pellets...$2.00" He crossed out the word "pellets" and added a zero behind the two. It was the only blotted item ever made in the ledger.

"The boy's fixed up the barn so you wouldn't recognize it," Michael said to his wife as he walked back into the kitchen.

"I know," she said.

"He's broke that colt," he added.

Mary looked up from the eggs she was fixing to her son's face.

"I know," she answered again.

"A man's coming today to buy that horse," he said.

She looked quickly up to her husband. "Oh, Michael," she said, "You can't sell the boy's horse."

"Whoa down now," he said. "We'll get ourselves another. Your boy's going into the horse business," he crowed.

She took the black frying pan from the flame and put her hands in her apron pockets. She looked directly at Mark as she said to her husband. "I'm sure he'll do well."

When Mr. Harrison called Michael in for "a go at the books" in June of that year, Michael had to work hard to sound calm. After going over the normal household account, he explained the purchase and the resale of the horse. Mr. Harrison smiled. Michael offered that he thought more could be done along those lines, and Mr. Harrison smiled again.

"How old was the boy when Emily's colt got hung up on the wire that time?"

Mr. Lerner thought a moment.

"He couldn't have been much more than eight or nine," he finally answered. Mr. Harrison stroked his mustache in thoughtful silence. After they spoke a while longer, Mr. Harrison said, "Better bring in the boy."

That was the first time Mark officially entered the office. He'd sat at the desk from time to time since he was tall enough to climb on to the desk chair, but never when the Harrisons were home. Mr. Harrison shook the thirteen-year-old's hand.

"Your father's explained about the stable." His fingers went up to his graying mustache.

"Yes, sir," the boy said.

"He tells me he has another purchase in mind."

The boy's eyes darted to his father. That was the first he'd heard of this.

"I didn't know," he said.

The boy's father stood with his arms folded in front of his chest. He stepped behind his son. Mr. Harrison asked Mark to sit down.

"He tells me that a man upstate has three two-year-olds that he came by from out in California," Mr. Harrison said.

"California!" the boy said, pronouncing the syllables as if he never dreamed he'd have any call to say the word.

"Ah, you know where that is," Mr. Harrison said.

"Yes sir, out past Ohio," the boy answered a little too hastily.

Mr. Harrison roared. "Yes. Yes. Out past Ohio." He stroked his mustache while looking warmly at the boy. "Let's go see those horses, say..." and he hesitated while running over an itinerary in his head, "...Tuesday. Are you free on Tuesday?"

"Yes, sir," the boy said. "Maybe I can get Daniel to feed that morning. I'll be ready at dawn."

"Tuesday it is then," Mr. Harrison said. "Maybe we should call the first horse 'Ohio'. That one will be yours. A horse trader needs his own horse. But by next summer, I want to see all three of them equally trained. Don't be spending all your time on your own."

By June 5th, five of the ten stalls were occupied.

Mark rode at least two of the horses each day so all the horses were worked at least three times a week. The hay purchase was doubled and soon the Narrowsburg Grain and Feed knew Mark on sight and no longer asked "Where's your Dad at, son?" every time he entered the store.

Mr. Harrison had given Mark a ledger of his own. "It'll help you with your arithmetic," he said. He told Mark that he didn't need to turn a profit, but that if he was going to have horses, he wanted good horses.

"Do what you think is best," he told the boy.

"I think we should shoe the horses more often. Maybe every six weeks," the boy said. "There's a farrier in Narrowsburg says he can shoe them for eight bits."

"Then hire him," Mr. Harrison said.

At age thirteen, Mark was in the horse business.

By the time he was fifteen, Mark had sold five horses and bought six new ones. He bought one for five dollars. The owner told him he couldn't be ridden and that Mark could sell it by the pound if he wanted. Mark knew about the horse meat traders, but the idea was repugnant to him. "Ain't no bad horses," he thought to himself, "just bad riders". But he said nothing to the man. The horse nearly broke him, but Mark eventually had him trained well enough to sell to a man from Peapack, New Jersey.

"Never trust him over a fence," Mark told the buyer at parting. "He'll run out soon as not."

"An honest horse trader!" the buyer laughed.

Mark smiled. "And stay off his mouth. He'll buck you right off if you're too strong handed."

The man thanked him and paid Mark the agreed upon sum of eighty-five dollars. Phil had taught Mark that a horse was worth whatever someone was willing to pay for it.

"I'll be back," he told the boy as they loaded the horse into the trailer.

Mark stuffed his hand into his pocket, his small fist clenched around his well-earned profit.

Turtle Rock

1922

Turtle Rock was a fifteen foot long oval rock so named because it looked like a great turtle shell breaking the surface of the water. It sat at the edge of the lake, maybe four feet from shore. When Mark was smaller, he'd follow his brother Daniel and his friends to the shore but he was unable to make the leap onto the rock without getting a boot full of water. He stood marooned on the land and watched as his brother and his friends sailed off into boyhood camaraderie without him on the stationary stone. Mark leaned between the two eight foot tall boulders that stuck upright in the sandy river soil. They looked as if they had been placed there by some mythical Lake Titan, and formed a natural gateway to Turtle Rock. His brother and friends spoke as if the four feet of water formed a sound-proof demarcation line that excluded anyone not standing on it. They never spoke directly to the younger Mark, clearly visible on the shore.

"Why's your brother tagging along for?" Billy asked.

"Leave him alone," Daniel answered.

"We can't talk with him standing there," Jackie said.

"He won't say nothing 'cause he knows we'll beat the crap outta him if he does," Daniel said.

"If you don't, I will," Billy said threateningly.

"Yeah," Daniel said, "you're a regular Lionel Strongfort," and he shoved the skinny boy backwards.

Mark was a good foot shorter than the three older boys back then. The summer he turned twelve he went alone to the rock. He tried to make the leap from shore but landed on his knee and opened a gash on his first attempt. He tried again and again until his knee was beaten and bloodied and his boots soaked through. But now, two short years later, he joined the other three boys on equal footing effortlessly making the leap from shore.

Mark and Daniel walked towards Turtle Rock in the summer of 1922 skipping stones in the hot midday sun. The two brothers wore equally short haircuts. They were both momentarily the same height, but the younger Mark had not yet grown to his full adult height. Both were broad shouldered and walked with the same gait so they were indistinguishable from behind. But face-on, their differences were obvious. Daniel's nervous green eyes touched everything, never apparently focusing on any one thing as if merely taking attendance on the world around him.. Mark's eyes were a penetrating blue that fixed on each object intently as if searching for the essence hidden behind the commonplace. As they neared the lake, they saw Billy and Jackie sunning themselves barechested. Both waiting boys were Daniel's age, sixteen. Jackie worked with Daniel at Mel's Station pumping petrol. Billy did nothing mostly, relying on collecting empty bottles to generate whatever pocket change he needed. He still got four bits a week allowance from home, much to Jackie's envy. But Daniel knew Billy's drunken father beat him often for the slightest infraction of his ever changing rules and would throw Billy pocket change to try to ease a sober conscience. Anyway, Billy spent no money from one end of the week to another so his lack of a steady income posed no real threat to his lifestyle.

"Hey, fellas," Daniel and Mark called.

"Well look who came outta the stables for air," Jackie said.

"Good to see you little brudda," he said as he greeted Mark with his outstretched grease-stained hand. Though two years younger, Mark stood several inches taller than either of them.

"What's the big pow-wow for?" Mark asked.

"Billy's got a telescopic glass. A good one."

"Where'd you get it?"

"It belongs to Mr. Hobbes. He lent it to my Daddy. I took it from his workbench but I've got to get it back before he comes home so this might be a once in a lifetime opportunity."

"To do what?" Mark asked. "It won't be dark enough for hours to see stars."

The other three boys laughed.

"It's just right to see the biggest star on this lake," Billy said. "The Ink Widow," he added in a baritone voice that imitated as best he could the voice on the radio.

Mark looked up instinctively to the house up the bank.

"You mean Mrs. Scott?"

The other boys laughed again.

"The very same."

Mark thought for a second. "How old you figure she is?" he asked.

"Old." Daniel said.

"Maybe fifty," Billy guessed.

"She ain't fifty," Daniel said, "but she's old."

"How old?" Mark insisted.

"Maybe twenty-nine or thirty."

"That's old," Jackie said, and the other boys agreed.

Mrs. Kristen Scott had captured the boys' imagination since she had moved into the Radclay house years earlier. She was the closest neighbor to the Lerners, situated a quarter of the way around the lake. Mrs. Scott provided most of the fodder for youthful conjecture in Sullivan County.

She first commanded their attention because she moved into the Radclay house even though everyone knew it was haunted. Billy and Jackie had personally witnessed the ghost hovering around the house that sat less than ninety yards from the lake. The ghost was recognizable to both boys as the ghost of Ray Radclay, a boy about Mark's age. He laid in a coma for most of the last year he lived there. He fell through the ice and had been fished out eight minutes later by Mr. Radclay in the winter of 1916. He refused to die, but he also refused to live. It did not seem to occur to any of the boys that a ghost rarely appeared before a person's death, a fine point of no consequence to the local boys. Daniel personally interviewed both boys after their ghost sightings in order to see if they were lying, and although each boy described the ghost in a completely different way, each had pinky-sworn to telling the truth. Daniel wrote off the discrepancies to fear. Billy had seen a white misty cloud with three-inch black eyes that swooped in and around the boy's second-story window. Jackie's ghost wore a beard and only the top half of a torso. It was discovered hovering over the boy's porch. Jackie said the ghost told him he was Ray Radclay grown up.

"You spoke to him?" Daniel asked, slightly suspicious.

"Heck no," Jackie said. "I was too scared. Ray's ghost swooped down in front of me and told me to stay away."

"How do you figure that Ray's ghost is so old?" Daniel asked him.

"Accelerated time," Jackie said with authority. "Everyone knows that being in a coma twists time. Every hour is like a day. So each day is like twenty-four days. You get old fast. Ray's been in a coma for near a year so that would make him..." The boy hesitated unable to do the arithmetic without a chalk and tablet. "...old. Old enough to wear a beard."

The other boys nodded in agreement.

"Where'd you pick up that accelerated time cow pie?" Daniel asked. "It sounds like a lot of applesauce to me."

"Well, it ain't neither. H.G. Wells wrote it in a book."

"That book wasn't real," Mark chipped in.

"Of course he had to pretend it weren't real," Jackie said defending both himself and Mr. Wells. "If he said it was real, they'd have to put him in the loony house with all the ax murderers like Lizzie Borden."

Daniel nodded. "I believe that's true," he told the other two boys thereby setting the story in stone with his confirmation. Any story sworn to by two boys quickly became truth. Anyway, facts were facts, and after hearing Jackie's description of the Ray Radclay ghost, Billy slowly altered his memory so that now both ghosts were almost identical in the retelling.

"I can't believe she's lived there two years with a ghost," Mark said.

"She's used to ghosts. Her husband died in the war and his ghost is probably there too. So if there's already one ghost, another ghost don't make it any scarier to get used to."

The boys nodded again at this indisputable logic.

Mrs. Scott deserved their respect for living with all the ghosts of Sullivan County and they showed it to her by crossing to the other side of the road anytime they saw her in town. She waved to them as they stumbled along watching their feet trying to ignore her. They'd always sneak a glance as she walked across the small street.

"Good morning, boys," she'd smile and wave, as if some big joke were known by one and all.

"Why do you figure she's so friendly?" Billy asked Daniel. "If I lived with ghosts I'd be too scared to talk to strangers in case one of us died and decided to join the other ghosts in her house. She's inviting more ghosts each day."

Daniel looked at Billy with a quizzical stare. The possibility of Billy stumbling on a truth every once in a while couldn't be totally dismissed.

"I guess she don't care about them," was the only explanation Daniel could come up with.

The second strange thing about Mrs. Scott was she always wore men's clothing. She wore men's trousers with suspenders and buttoned shirts without the starched collars and men's ankle high leather boots. "They was her husband's clothes," the boys had determined, but they couldn't account for the fit. The clothes covered Mrs. Scott as if they'd been tailored for rich folks.

"Where do you suppose she gets the men's clothes?" Billy had wondered aloud.

"She must order them from Roebuck's," Daniel said. "It's the postman's job to see that everyone on his route only orders what they're supposed to," he averred. "So she must be paying a bribe to him to keep quiet."

"Where'd you hear that?" Billy asked with a challenging smirk. "My uncle's a postman and I never heard him say anything about checking packages."

Daniel felt obliged to defend this new challenge. "It's a federal law. It's called tampering with federal mail and it's a felonious offense."

No one could argue with a fact lied on so authoritatively. And who among them could argue that a woman ordering men's clothes wasn't tampering?

"I could just bet how she pays off the bribe," Billy said and now the three older boys began punching each other on the arm and guffawing knowingly while winking so often you'd think they stood in a sandstorm.

"How?" Mark asked.

"You're too young to know how women bribe men," his older brother said.

"Oh, that. I know all about that," Mark said. "I seen the female horses bribing the males," he stated.

"Well it's different with people," Daniel said knowingly. "People like being bribed," he affirmed. The two other boys nodded in wistful agreement.

And that was but half of the Ink Widow's legacy. The boys sat on Turtle Rock discussing her mysteries as seriously as the archaeologists who had recently discovered the Egyptian boy king's tomb. There seemed to be no end to the secret rooms of her mystery. Sometimes as the boys sat talking about her, they'd see her come outside and sit on her porch rocking chair. Sometimes she'd have no shoes on and her bare feet perched upon the porch rail less than ninety yards away generally got the older boys to winking and punching each other's arms again. In the summer, the view to the porch was partially obscured by a wavering curtain of leaves and branches.

"Why do you call her the Ink Widow?" Mark asked on more than one occasion. His question was generally ignored.

But finally, on the day Billy showed up with the telescope, the boys decided to let Mark in on Mrs. Scott's darkest mystery.

"Before he died in the war, Mr. Scott was a typesetter," Billy began, "for some newspaper in New Jersey."

"His fingers were always black," Jackie footnoted.

"You can't get that ink off your hands," said Daniel who always felt called upon to verify any rumor with facts real or imagined. "Just reading the newspaper turns your hands black. You can imagine what his hands looked like."

"When he peed," Billy continued, "he got ink all over his thing."

The older boys nodded to one another in sympathy with the dead man's burden as the conversation momentarily degenerated into a discussion of whether you should hold your thing the whole time you peed, or just to pull it out and put it back in your undershorts when you'd finished. They could reach no consensus about proper hand placement. The conversation wandered back to Mrs. Scott.

"So every Saturday night," Jackie said, "when the Scott's consumed their marriage vows–"

"What the hell are you saying?" Daniel asked.

"He's saying 'when they fucked'," Billy said.

"That's not consumed," Daniel said.

"That's what the priest calls it," Jackie said. "A priest can't say 'fuck'."

And here the conversation dropped down another notch into the theological implications of a priest saying 'fuck', until it wound back around to Mrs. Scott's plight.

"Why do you say every Saturday?" Mark asked.

"Saturday night is sex night," Billy said with the experience of a lifetime of squeaking Saturday night springs ringing in his oversized boyish ears.

"It doesn't have to be Saturday," Daniel said. "Some people have marital consumption any day they want."

"Golly!" Jackie said, his brain boiling from the possibilities.

"It's a mortal sin on Sundays," Billy said, and as that made perfect sense to the other boys, no one said anything. For several minutes a youthful quiet filled the air above Turtle Rock, as each teenage boy traced an incomplete dotted line of sexual knowledge and experience back to the idea of Mrs. Scott having sex any day but Sunday.

"So after years of marriage obligations," Jackie finally resumed, "Mrs. Scott's private parts had turned to black."

"And anyone who touched her with their members," and here the boys laughed, "would have a black private until he died."

"Like a sailor's tattoo," Billy added.

"Yeah, like a tattoo," Jackie agreed.

"That way Mr. Scott always knew if his wife was consuming other marriages."

"Yeah," the boys agreed.

It was with that secret and awe-inspiring knowledge that the boys now reached for Billy's father's friend's once in a lifetime opportunity telescope.

Mark waited his turn as the other boys eyed Mrs. Scott and related her every movement.

"She's crossing her legs," Daniel said. "She has short pants on!"

"Oh my God," Billy said.

"I can see the bottoms of her legs. Wait– I can see above her knee."

The other boys were in a tither now, like puppies jumping around and atop one another in their excitement.

"She's reading a book," Jackie said on his turn at the glass. "She's putting a new comb in her hair," he sighed. "She does have short pants on!" he said confirming the earlier sighting.

"I saw her nude once," Daniel blurted out.

Jackie lowered the telescope from his eye, the specter of her naked more compelling than the reality of her clothed.

"You're a lying Kraut spy," he said.

"I saw her right there," Daniel said as he pointed to a sacred spot in the lake just beyond Turtle Rock. "She was swimming buck naked."

The boys closed their mouths one by one as if savoring the taste of the vision. They knew Daniel never lied to them, especially about anything as important as this.

"What did she say when she saw you?"

"She didn't see me."

"What did you see?"

"Mostly her shoulders."

The six eyes of the other three boys were fixed to the spot on the lake as if collectively they could summon her mirage.

"Until she got out. Then I saw her whole backside."

The boys sat mesmerized like cobras under an Indian mystic's flute. Mark took the telescope from Jackie's unwary hand.

As the boys pumped Daniel for more details, Mark lined up Mrs. Scott in the telescopic sights. She wore her hair short, clipped above her ears with some sort of decorative hairpin that exposed her high forehead. Her hair was a brownish blond color straight on the top and curly on the back and sides. She was a slender woman and as pretty as a girl in a newspaper advertisement. As he watched her, she rested her book on her lap and seemed to look directly at him. He lowered the glass for an instant, embarrassed, until he realized she couldn't possibly see him through the trees that obscured the rock from her view.

He replaced the glass to his right eye as she languidly stretched her right arm over her head. Her hand lowered to her neck as Mark stood breathless. Her hand absently drifted down into the open collar of her shirt. As her hand continued its descent her shirt opened, briefly exposing her bare breast. She had no undergarments on.

"I can see her breast," Mark whispered, his voice so quiet it was almost drowned out by the lapping of the water on the rock.

The other boys instinctively and simultaneously lunged toward the telescope knocking it from Mark's hand. As the glass loudly hit the rock, shards of glass scattered around them. Mark looked towards Mrs. Scott's porch.

"She must have heard that," he said. The boys heard her screen door bang shut as she stood up and entered her house.

"I'm a dead man," Billy finally said as the boys stood transfixed amid the tiny pieces of glass that lay shattered among their bare feet.

"Now look what you've done," Billy said to any one of them hoping for a volunteer for his blame. "You all act like you've never seen a woman's titty before."

This hit the boys' pride hard, although each was fairly certain that no one on that rock ever had. Billy picked up the telescope. The chrome end was dented and the bottom lens had been reduced to two fingernail-sized shards of glass. He felt like he held an enormous chasm in his hands. A pit large enough to swallow him whole.

"I might as well go home and start whipping myself to save my old man some time."

The other boys winced at the thought of Billy's hide being made into a payment for the broken telescope.

"I didn't even get to see her," Billy said.

The boys left the rock with a mixture of sexual excitement, apprehension and guilt churning around in their stomachs.

They marched towards their homes silently like defeated soldiers.

"I've got some money if you need it," Mark whispered to Billy.

Billy looked up quickly into his friend's eyes.

"Thanks," he said. "I'll let you know."

"Money well spent," Mark thought as he ran ahead to catch up to his brother.

Throwing Gliders

During the war years, Mark spent most of his time playing soldiers with his friends or with the horses over at the Sheer barn. He saw Emily once or twice a week after the summer of '21 as she started coming to the stables with her father. Mark would tack her horse for her and un-tack when she returned. In '23 she did not come at all, opting to spend the summer in Rhode Island with friends. For the most part, Mark and Emily rarely saw one another. He was forever running to Phil and his horses and Emily was usually visiting with any one of a dozen little girls invited to Pine Bluff for her company. For three months a year they were like brother and sister. That is, they orbited the same house but they rarely shared time together. When they did, however, they were always able to reach a comfort zone in a matter of minutes. No matter how much time had elapsed since their previous meeting, they always seemed to pick up where they had left off, completely avoiding the awkward fumbling of re-acquaintance. Mark hit his stride with Emily. He hit it quickly and effortlessly. Occasional guests who happened to see them together were forever commenting on how close they were, a mistake certain to draw the scornful eye of Lucretia Harrison. No one ever repeated the mistake in her presence.

His encounters with Emily were sprinkled in the ocean of Mark's life like islands of an archipelago. Most were small, almost inconsequential when considered alone but together were enough to form a bond between them. Mark would have asserted that he didn't care one way or another about Emily. That is, until 1923. It was the worst summer of his life, and although it might have only been coincidental, it was the only year that Emily did not summer in Pine Bluff.

They had their adventures, as children will. One summer they became stranded on bicycles in a lightning storm in a flat wheat field that stretched out to the horizons. The lightning surrounded them, striking so near that the hairs on their arms were raised. They believed themselves to be safe because of the rubber tires of the bicycles and found out years later that it wasn't true and that luck alone prevented them from being struck.

Another summer, when they were ten or eleven, they found $1.85 in a change purse on the street. They decided not to turn it in and ran for miles convinced that the FBI was in hot pursuit, stopping finally to buy ice cream, a couple of sarsaparillas and two wooden gliders. They tossed the planes into the summer air while they walked and chased the erratic flight trying to catch the fragile planes before they crashed to the ground. Oblivious to their direction, they were soon hopelessly lost miles from Pine Bluff. They met an older boy, maybe thirteen years old, who promised to lead them back home if they gave up the gliders and ten cents each. Emily cowered from the boy's leer and grabbed Mark's arm as he turned over their money and toys to the prematurely bearded boy.

When Emily was fifteen, she shared a stolen cigarette with Mark behind the barn, but they caught the hay on fire with the live embers and damn near burnt down the barn. To this day, three boards under the west side window remain scorched.

But by far the biggest island in their archipelago was the letter Emily sent Mark in the late fall of 1924, when he was seventeen. Mark was building a new ice house with his father and brother. The older house was smaller and the bottom boards rotted. The supply of ice it stored lasted barely into September. They had chosen a perfect site for the new house along the lake free of trees and exposed to an inimpeded circulation of air. The house was twenty by thirty and eighteen feet high. The brothers had spread ten inches of sand along the bottom of the house and had set drains in the sand to let water flow back into the river. This ice house was twice as large as the old one they tore down and could hold over three hundred tons of ice. The inside of the house was hemlock and the outside was pine.

It had taken the three men nearly two weeks to complete. Mark and Daniel stayed on the ground cutting the boards with measurements called down to them by their father. Daniel complained in time with the saw, his epitaphs sprayed the sunlight like the sawdust from the wooden-handled saws. He worked best when he could complain and both Mark and his father long ago learned not to listen. Mark always measured the lumber twice before marking the boards with the flattened carpenter's pencil. Daniel refused to follow his brother's lead and would tell Mark as he handed him a board, "I cut it twice and it's still too short," echoing the only joke they ever heard their father utter.

They had spent the previous day packing the side walls of the completed building with twelve inches of wood shavings and were done except for the painting. Mark was white washing the outside of the house when Daniel came running down the hill.

"What's wrong?"

"Nothing's wrong," Daniel said. "You got a letter today from Italy."

"Italy?"

"Who do you know in Italy?"

"No one."

"Someone knows you."

"Where is it?"

"Mother has it."

When Mark got to the kitchen, his mother was at the work table cutting and dicing vegetables. Her red hands mechanically chopped with the heavy butcher's knife, her wet fingerprints visible on the dark handle. Mark sensed her agitation before any words were spoken.

"Why is that girl writing to you from Italy?"

"What girl?"

"Emily Harrison is what girl. How many girls do you know in Europe?"

"Why'd she write to me?" he asked, effectively deflecting his mother's suspicions.

She reached into her apron pocket and withdrew the letter. The envelope corners were bent, the ink of his name blotted. Mark sensed that the letter had taken the brunt of more wear since its arrival than it had during the Atlantic crossing. He wanted to read it in the privacy of his bedroom. His heart was beating hard against his skin. He took the letter and left the kitchen unaware of his mother's worried expression or its cause. He ran his finger carefully over the black letters of the purple stamp. "*Italia*" it read. He carefully slid his pocketknife into the transparently thin paper of the envelope and sliced it open.

My Dearest Mark,

Italy is wonderful. Mother and I arrived with Uncle Stephan. Daddy is, of course, home working. We stayed in Florence in a horrid pension but left after two weeks arriving today in Venice. At least now we are in a decent hotel, although I think it comes at a dear price. This country is so filled with art and history that it becomes quite a burden for me. Mother and Daddy expect me to remember every artist and every cathedral, for what purpose I cannot imagine. It is all so beautiful, but I cannot seem to remember who painted what or where. Daddy says Europe is essential to a well-rounded education but Mother sees it merely as a requirement for good luncheon conversation.

We passed through the most beautiful countryside on the way to Naples. There are motorcars here, but they are quite unreliable so Uncle Stephan hired a coach. It was all so romantic traveling the way that Mother did, or even Grand-Mama. We passed a man ponying horses across a field in the midst of blue-green hills. The sun was setting behind him and in silhouette (and I'm certain, because of fatigue) I truly believed for the briefest moment that it was you, and I felt so homesick, and I so wanted to be at Pine Bluff and I hope you're taking good care of Abbey and I hope– Well, listen to me! I am so silly. Anyway, I only wanted to tell you that Italy reminds me of you and if the Maharishis are correct and we have had past lives, I am certain that you and I once lived here together. Please forgive me my presumptuous and rambling letter, but I'm certain you'll understand.

Yours truly,
your blood brother,
Emily

PS We may arrive in Pine Bluff in June or we may forego our visit this year. It is all so uncertain.

Daniel barged into their shared room as Mark folded the letter and placed it in his cigar box under his bed.

"What did she want?" he asked.

"I have no earthly idea," Mark answered.

He wondered at her last sentence. He did not understand. He did not even understand what it was he was supposed to understand. But he felt no need to.

"Girl stuff," Daniel said, intoning the universal explanation for all things unexplained.

When Daniel left the room Mark reached under his bed to retrieve the letter. For no reason he could put a name to, he reread it before placing it into his shirt pocket.

The Ink Widow

1926

Mary Lerner pulled the leftover Thanksgiving ham from the oven, hoping to feast on the remnants of the holiday sentiment. She tended to overcook on holidays, always with the idea of a repeat performance. It seemed as her boys grew older it was more and more difficult to corral her family long enough to have a full meal together. On Thanksgiving she had uncharacteristically borrowed white table linens from the Harrisons and had set the kitchen table to resemble the finery she had seen at their normal summertime suppers. She had placed dried flowers in a waterless vase on the center of the round table. As Mark entered the kitchen, he watched his mother standing proudly in front of the table.

Mary loved a holiday. It was a time to take full measure of her family and to reflect on the growth of her boys. To Mark, Thanksgiving was just another Thursday. Daniel balked at having to wear his Sunday clothes twice in the same week. But both boys participated in the holiday without serious complaint. Michael Lerner seemed unmoved by any holiday, although he was a difficult man to read. It seemed to Mark that his father stored emotion like pennies in a glass piggy bank. Then for no clear reason, he would spend it all in a lavish outburst that embarrassed the recipient in its relative excess. As a family, the Lerners spent emotion frugally until the boys had learned that it was a luxury not usually in the annual budget. A vocalized 'I love you' was rarer in the Lerner house than a five-course dinner, but yet it seemed that no one ever hungered for the want of one.

On that late November afternoon Mrs. Lerner brought the leftover ham to rest on the round oak table as her family sat noisily. Michael asked Mark about the horses. Daniel discussed rumored ice prices for the upcoming season. Mary Lerner sat, mostly in silence, listening to the music her men made.

As Mark finished second helpings he leaned his armless wooden chair back on its rear legs. A shot rang out from near the house almost sending him backwards off the precariously balanced chair. No one spoke at first. They sat listening until a second shot cracked the silence.

"It sounds like it's coming from the Radclay's," Mary said.

"You mean the Scott's?" Michael asked.

"She don't hunt," Daniel said.

"I think I'll go and see if there's a problem," Mark said.

"I have peach cobbler," his mother said. "I'll wait until you return."

Mark put on his coat and threw a knitted scarf around his shoulders. He walked out the back door leaving the screen to bang a miniature reply to the gun shot blast. An early dusting of icy snow crunched loudly under Mark's boots. He debated saddling Ohio, but decided instead to walk off his supper in the crisp late autumn air.

He took the path that ran along the lake, past Turtle Rock turning right up the small hill to Mrs. Scott's porch, calling out as he neared the house.

"Mrs. Scott! It's Mark Lerner."

He hoped she was finished shooting for the day. He clomped up the porch steps making as much noise as he could, so as not to surprise anyone. Before he knocked on the door, it swung open. The Ink Widow stood shotgun in hand. She had two cartridges in her left hand and seemed intent on using them.

"Is everything all right?" Mark asked.

"No it isn't, but by God it will be," Mrs. Scott said in a loud voice.

Mark entered the unfamiliar house. Mrs. Scott wore her usual men's trousers, but the suspenders hung down uselessly against her thighs visible under her unbuttoned plaid parka. Her blue cotton shirt was buttoned to the neck. Her hair was longer than Mark had remembered and hung below her collar in tight curls.

"Are these the right cartridges for this gun?" she demanded of Mark.

"Let me see," he said calmly as he took the gun and cartridges from her thin hands.

"No ma'am," he said. "These are thirty gauge."

"Damn it all! I told Peterson what gun I had and he sold me a whole box of these shells," she said pointing distractedly to the open box that she had emptied onto the kitchen table.

"You aiming to fix a late-season turkey?" Mark asked. He still held the gun.

"I might at that," she said, a smile coming to her face for the first time.

She had the whitest teeth Mark ever saw but they looked softer than the ice blue of her eyes. The last time Mark stood close to her, they were the same height, but he had grown several inches in the intervening years. She spent her smile quickly and tried to return to her anger.

"It's the Morgans," she said. "They're out on the lake staking out an ice field. They think I don't know my rights." She spoke in short spurts as if out of breath. "But I do." She crossed her arms in front of her chest defiantly. "That's my ice!"

Mark turned to look out the open door behind him to the lake clearly visible through the leafless trees.

"Well, you either scared them off or killed them," he said.

Mrs. Scott put her hand to her mouth as if the possibility of killing anyone never occurred to her. She was thinly built and even up close did not look twelve years older than Mark.

"I was just trying to scare them off," she said. "That's my ice." she repeated with much less venom. She walked out onto the porch searching the lake surface for any sign of the two men she had targeted moments before.

"I aimed for them," she said. "I figured that would be the best way to miss 'em," she added, a smile returning to her lips.

She walked to her bookcase and brought down a rolled piece of paper and carried it to Mark, still standing in the open front door.

"It says right here–" she browsed down the legal copy of the New York state law that governed ice cutting, "'the owner or lessee of lands bordering upon the river or lake shall require the ice formed on said water between the center thereof...'" She interrupted her reading. "There's more about ice houses here. Wait a moment. Here– 'such owner or lessee of said lands and ice houses shall have the exclusive privilege of cutting and harvesting all the ice so formed'"

She exhaled a deep breath. Looked at Mark proudly as if she had just defended the Union in congressional session.

"I already hired out two colored men to harvest that ice for me. The Knickerbocker people already agreed to a price for the harvest." Mark knew that the Knickerbocker Ice Company was the largest ice company around and usually bought all the ice they could through small regional offices. The Lerners sold their ice independently, gambling on a larger piece of the profit at a bit more risk.

"How did you know it was the Morgans out there?" Mark asked. The Morgans lived on the other side of the lake. They kept to themselves as most of the locals did, and Mark never had any call to deal with them directly.

"Bill Morgan came here last week, telling me he intended to expand his harvest this year. Asked me, told me really, he'd be coming further out the lake this year. I warned him to stay to their own stake. I told him I wasn't interested in selling any rights to anything. He got all 'well missy this', and 'well missy that' and I well missy'd him right out the door."

"I'll go speak with him tomorrow if you'd like."

She relaxed visibly. The creases of her eyes softened towards Mark. She knew the Lerners carried the Harrison weight behind them and that no one in Sullivan County would have the temerity to offend the Harrisons.

"Well, that might save the Garrabrants some bother," she said referring to the local undertakers. "Come in, Mark," she said suddenly, although Mark had been standing in her open doorway for nearly five minutes already. It was unusual to be invited into a Sullivan County home. In all the years Mark knew Billy and Jackie he had never seen the inside of their houses. Visits were held on front porches and a man's presence on his own porch represented an open invitation to friends and neighbors to come and sit. But rarely did a visitor pass through the front door.

"Take off your coat," she said as she removed her own parka. She winced a little as she rotated her right shoulder out of her jacket.

"How can you men shoot these contraptions?" she said. "I darn near separated my shoulder for my effort."

Her hand reached into her shirt popping open the two top buttons. She pulled the blue cotton slightly off her shoulder revealing an already dark purple bruise around her collarbone. She had the tiny shoulders of a young girl. Her collarbone protruded skeleton-like through her white skin.

"That's a lot of gun for a small person," Mark answered.

"I suppose," she said absently. There was no more anger in her voice. "But it's the only gun I've got."

Mark nodded.

"Would you like a cup of coffee?" she asked.

Mark sat on the flowered armchair that faced the window out onto the lake. He looked around and took in Mrs. Scott's house for the first time. The walls of her parlor were lined with bookshelves, filled with more books than Mark had ever seen in one place before. The books were stacked helter-skelter, some horizontally, some placed with the bindings facing inward. As he looked more closely, he noticed that most had scraps of paper sticking out from their pages.

"You read all these books?"

She looked up from her kitchen sink where she was preparing the coffee and looked at the books as if noticing them for the first time.

"Most," she answered.

She had more books than the traveling lending library wagon that stopped monthly at the lake. A Lerner instinct forced him to quickly estimate the cost of such a collection. She had hundreds of books.

"Where do you get 'em all?"

There was a bookseller in Port Jervis, but Mrs. Scott would have worn a path in the road if she had purchased them all there.

"I buy most for pennies at auction sales," she said. "They list auctions in the newspapers. I enjoy going to them. I bought most everything in this house from auctioneers," she added. "Except the bed." She pointed with her thumb towards the only other room of the two-room cabin. Mark could make out the heavy wooden frame of a massive bed through the open door.

"Some I get from a new club in New York City. It's called 'The Book of the Month Club', and every month, they send a new book by post. I just love it," she said.

Mark noticed the abrupt change in her mood. Her anger had been eclipsed by a genuine excitement over her books. Mark figured he would have been unable to read all the books in her house even if he had started reading nonstop at birth.

She stood before him with a steaming metal cup of coffee.

"Thank you ma'am," he said automatically.

"Call me Kristen," she said.

She sat on a haggard divan across from Mark. The pattern on the arm rests was nearly worn off. She sat quietly watching him drink his coffee until he started to feel uncomfortable in the silence.

"You have a nice place here," he said.

"Thank you."

"I think you'll have no problem protecting your ice field. You've probably got a week or so before you'll need to stake it out. I'm surprised Morgan was out on the lake already. The ice can't be more 'en three inches thick. Last year we was staked out by now, but it's been a lot warmer this year."

A threatening silence hovered before Mark. Kristen didn't seem to mind if they spoke or not.

"Do your colored boys cut with a mule saw or by hand?" he asked.

She smiled, but Mark couldn't guess as to why.

"I don't know," she said. "I didn't ask."

"Hmm," he said, as if he was thinking about her answer. But he wasn't thinking of saws at all. It had struck him all of a sudden that he was actually sitting alone having coffee with the infamous Ink Widow. He just wished he could think of something to say. She didn't seem to share his discomfort, but he was feeling mighty self-conscious at her steady, penetrating stare.

"Do you like to read?" she finally asked him.

"You mean books?" and immediately wanted to kick himself for such a stupid question.

She laughed.

"Well, I read some," he answered.

"Who's your favorite writer?"

"I like Ernest Henning," he said. "I read 'The Sun Almost Rises' a while back."

She smiled at his effort.

"Hemingway," she said. "I should have known. He's a real man's writer."

Her response embarrassed him a little, but again, he couldn't say why. They returned to the silence for several long seconds.

"How about you?" he asked, anxious to hold onto the thread of conversation that connected them.

"Oh, it changes really. For a while I read nothing but the Brontes and Galsworthy. But lately I like Somerset Maugham. I got 'The Moon and Sixpence' from the book club."

Mark never heard of her. Or him. He thought that if they were going to keep talking, he'd have to come up with something a little more intelligent to say, and he couldn't for the life of him figure out what that might be.

A man's voice called from the porch rescuing him.

"Kristen? Mark?" It was his father.

"Oh Jeez," Mark said. "I forgot they were waiting on me for peach cobbler."

"I'm sorry I interrupted your dinner," she said as she stood to open the door.

"Hello, Kristen," he heard his father say.

"Hello, Michael. I'm so sorry I've set everybody off with my little 'Battle of Pine Lake'."

Mark was a little surprised at the easy way they addressed one another.

"We thought when Mark didn't come right back something might be brewing."

"No," she said. "I tied him down and forced him to make polite conversation," she said laughing.

Mark hadn't felt like she made him do anything.

"I'm sorry I took you all from your dinner table," she said again. "Can you stop to visit a moment?"

"No," Michael said. "Mary will be anxious if we both stay on too long. Everything's all right then?"

"Thank you. Yes." Kristen said. "But if you don't mind, I've asked Mark to help me tomorrow."

Michael shrugged in reply.

"You coming along soon, son?"

"In a few minutes. Start without me if you will."

Michael left Mark to fend for himself.

"So you think I'm correct in my claim?" she asked the boy as she returned to her divan. Mark sat back down on the armchair and wasn't too hurried to leave, peach cobbler or not.

"Yes, ma'am," he answered. "Would you mind if I took that lawyer paper along with me though?"

Kristen handed it to him. Mark breathed in her scent as she stood close to him.

"I'll let you know what Morgan says tomorrow," he said, standing to leave. He re-rolled the document carefully.

"I would be much obliged," she said. "I'll put on a new pot of coffee. After supper hour then?"

Friday morning Mark took Ohio around the lake to the Morgans'. He debated ringing Bill Morgan to announce his visit but decided a surprise might be more to his advantage, and besides, he wasn't sure if the Morgans were "on the phone" yet. There was history between Mark's father and Bill Morgan that started a few years back. Mark wasn't sure what it was about except that it had involved Mark's mother. He took his father's dislike of the man as his own.

He tied Ohio to a low branch of a maple and walked up the frozen dirt path to the Morgan's front porch. White paint was chipping off the door in a few sections exposing a black undercoat from years before.

Bill Morgan opened the door and crossed his arms in front of his chest as he recognized the boy. He was perhaps an inch shorter than Mark but outweighed him by a hundred pounds. His blue flannel shirt sleeves were rolled up revealing the dirty red sleeves of his undershirt.

"Mark Lerner," he said without warmth. "What brings you to the poor side of the lake?" He made no move to invite the boy in from the cold.

"I understand there was a misunderstanding with Mrs. Scott."

"What business is that of yourn?"

"It's my business when a lady asks me for help against someone intent on taking advantage of her."

Morgan laughed a joyless laugh. "That what she told you, son?" He rubbed his hand across his unshaven face. "That weren't my gun shooting wildly across the lake," he said. "I'll tell you what now. If she took my offer to gather her ice, it'd been her taking advantage of me."

A raspy laugh forced its way out of his small mouth. "I must have been fool out of my mind to offer her so much money for doing nothing. I'm glad she said no, son. She saved me from an unfavorable contract." He walked to the edge of his porch and spit brown tobacco juice over the rail.

"Now, if you don't have nothin' further to say, I got chores to do." He slammed the door without looking at Mark or waiting for any response.

Mark remounted Ohio. He felt like spitting himself. The entire episode left a bad taste in his mouth. Part of him had hoped for a physical confrontation. He pictured himself going back to Mrs. Scott's a black eye in tow, like a wounded knight returning to his damsel in distress. But Morgan's rude and quick withdrawal seemed anticlimactic. He had steeled himself for a confrontation since last night, and now felt foolish and unnecessary.

After supper, Mark walked back to his room in the stable. He had unceremoniously moved himself out of his parent's small apartment a year ago, on a night when Abbey had colic. He gradually spent more and more nights in the barn, until his departure each night was unnoticed. He expected a protest from his parents that never came. He had running water, a toilet and a wood burning stove in his new living quarters. The stove had been used infrequently in the past, kept stoked just enough to keep the stalls from freezing, but now Mark kept it fired up all winter. He worried originally that the horses wouldn't grow a sufficient winter coat with the barn kept warm, but Phil assured him that their coats grew according to the amount of daylight and had little to do with temperature.

He still took most of his meals at the house, but liked the illusion of independence his own room gave him. After about a month, he returned to his new quarters to see that his mother had come down and hung curtains on the two small windows, and placed an old Harrison braided rug on the rough floor. She never said a word about it.

Mark washed his face and wet his hair. He went searching for a mirror that he thought he had, but couldn't find it. He debated a change of clothes and settled for a clean shirt. The cool flannel felt good against his skin and was not the source of his discomfort.

He walked the half mile to Mrs. Scott's while running over a roster of possible subjects to talk about. Except for the towering pines that dotted the area, all was gray and brown in the rapidly approaching twilight. The temperature was a cool forty-four degrees but Mark's palms were sweating as he rounded Turtle Rock.

She opened the door before Mark knocked.

"I was hoping you remembered our date," she said.

Mark wondered at her choice of words.

"Come in out of the cold. I've got a fire going."

Mark entered and removed his coat. Kristen took it and hung it on a brass hook on an otherwise empty coat rack. A warm glow spread out from the open hearth of the stone fireplace. The corners of the room were in darkness.

"I made a cake," she said. "Did you have your supper?"

"Yes, ma'am," Mark said.

"Kristen," she corrected.

Three chairs surrounded the porcelain topped table that sat in shadow in the corner of the room that served as a kitchen. One chair was piled high with books, Collier's and Saturday Evening Posts. Mark took the chair that faced the fire. Kristen put a fat slab of cake on a heavy white plate in front of him.

"Coffee?" she asked.

"Thank you," Mark said. "I went to see Bill Morgan this morning."

Kristen ignored his comment and sat down at the small table with her own coffee. Mark struggled in vain to come up with one of the topics he had rehearsed all day. He couldn't remember one. He bit into a forkful of the cake.

"Do you like the cake?" she asked.

The apples were hard and the cake dry with the texture of sawdust.

"Yes ma'a–Kristen. It's good cake," he lied.

"I'm not a very good cook," she said.

Mark sipped the coffee. It burnt his tongue but helped him swallow the cake.

"You're supposed to protest vehemently at this point," she said.

Mark blushed. She laughed.

"You don't have to finish it."

He said, "Oh, no. It's good cake," and took another bite that he tried to swallow without such an obvious effort.

"You should have no more problems with Morgan," Mark said. And that was that. Eight words. The only reason for his being there. He thought he should have spread them out a little. Embellish the non-event of the morning somehow.

"I didn't think so," Kristen answered. "Thank you, Mark."

He looked around her house as if searching for an exit. His eyes stopped on the gilded framed portrait, similar to the one of Mr. Harrison hanging in Pine Bluff.

"Is that your father?" he asked.

"No," she said. "My grandfather. I didn't really know my father all that well."

Mark sat staring at the portrait. The man had Kristen's narrow nose and steel blue eyes, or she had his. They looked more fitting on a woman, he thought. The man seemed delicate.

"He was in the brewery business in New Jersey," she said. My father managed to squander most of what Grandfather made. About the only thing left was my trust fund, and only because Grandpa protected it from Daddy's tampering. It's not much, only four thousand a year, but enough to live on out here."

Mark answered with an awkward boyish silence, impressed by the fortune, but pleased more that she felt enough of him to tell of it.

She stood and went to the armchair where Mark had sat the day before, and picked up a stack of three books. They were tied with a purple satin ribbon, like a gift.

"I thought I'd lend you these. I think you'll like them." She paused a moment. "But then again, I thought you'd like the cake," and she laughed at herself. She took the half-filled cake plate from Mark's placemat and brought it to the sink.

"The books are easier to swallow than the cake. Promise." Her eyes danced as they reflected the jumping flames of the fire.

She took a box of matches and struck one against the porcelain table top to light a candle centered on the table. The candle smoked a little in a flare of light, then settled down into a warm glow softening the dark corners of the kitchen.

"You lived at the Harrison's long?" she asked.

"My entire life."

"Good people," she said. "Austin Harrison was the one who told me about this house. He helped me keep it after my husband died. He had an insurance policy that, of course, wouldn't pay off on a wartime death. But Austin bent the truth a little. He said that because Rob died six months after discharge, the policy would still pay even though he died of war injuries. I owe a lot to that man."

Mark thought about Mr. Harrison. It was just like him. He used the truth when it served justice and abandoned it when it didn't. He seemed larger than life to Mark and this story from Kristen added to his biblical proportions. Even at his young age, Mark realized that this was the power of money. Not the cars, the china, the crystal. This was money. It let a man make rules. He did not feel any great pull to it nor did he covet the trappings, but he was fascinated by it nonetheless. He liked watching money in action. Liked to see the way it was treated by those who hungered for it.

Kristen asked Mark about his daily routines and Mark told her about the stable. Words came easy to him when he spoke of his horses and this time Kristen seemed relieved by his rush of conversation. She seemed willing to let Mark ramble on. And he did.

"Do you ride?" he asked after a time..

"Oh, no," she said. "I'm a transplanted city girl," and she laughed. "When the city empties out in summers, I still like to visit old friends. Most of them still live on the West Side down by Greenwich Village. Sometimes I think of going back."

These were magical words to Mark, who despite the geographic proximity, thought of Manhattan as a faraway, romantic place like Rome or Persia. A place in books, populated by a breed of people different from himself. Like the Harrisons and their parade of friends.

Kristen reached between the books and magazines on the third chair, and fished out a pack of Chesterfield's. Mark knew women smoked but had never met any who did. She offered him a cigarette which he refused.

"Are you always so polite?" she asked.

He felt challenged by the question and reddened in response.

"Nope," he said. "I'm a cussing, tobacco-spittin' mean son of a buck most days. You just caught me on an off day."

Her mouth smiled at him, but those hard blue eyes of hers never softened. She raised the back of her hand to her forehead in mock dismay.

"Oh, what's a poor helpless girl to do?" she said and they both laughed.

Mark had the sensation of being in a maze as their conversation veered around unspoken walls that formed the invisible boundaries between strangers. He stayed that evening until her mantle clock chimed ten.

"Come back when you've finished the books. I've got more," she said as she swept her arm around the room. They said a polite goodnight.

"Stop by anytime," she said.

And he did. He read the first three books in eight days. He liked the Somerset Maugham, but couldn't stay awake through Norman Douglas. They spoke of the books and whatever flowered from the seeds of those conversations.

Mark found himself thinking of Kristen more often. There was a tension he felt in her house that he never knew before. A good tension. He returned to it often during the winter of 1927. As they drifted into an uneven friendship, he thought of her as more of an enigma than anything else. She rarely mentioned her husband. Mark would often look up to find her staring intently at him. But it was like she had two sets of eyelids. One set that opened so she could look out, and another set that let other people look in. That second set was never opened though and left Mark with precious few clues about what went on behind them.

In early March, Kristen came down unannounced late one afternoon to his stable. It seemed odd to see her outside the walls of her own refuge. She seemed vulnerable there, almost frightened as she raised a tentative hand to his horses' necks. She flinched every time they moved and she refused to enter any of the stalls.

"They'll crush me against the walls," she said.

"I knew someone who had three ribs cracked that way," he said, cementing forever her refusal with that hard fact.

She watched him care for his horses. Watched his hands comb out their manes. Brush out their coats. Pick their hooves. She watched with apparent fascination his mundane tasks of cleaning or repairing bridles and saddles. She prattled mindlessly when she was nervous and she was nervous often in his barn. He would describe an idiosyncrasy of Abbey's or Ohio's or the others and she'd ask how he knew so much about them. He never had an answer for that question. She seemed so small in his stable as if she were the younger of the two.

He found his way to her house more and more evenings. She had a comfortable presence about her there that he found contagious. By the early days of spring, Mark walked or rode to her house as thoughtlessly as he entered Pine Bluff. He found himself struggling to read faster to finish his "assignments"; sometimes staying up until almost eleven reading by the steady light of his kerosene lamp. He saw Kristen almost every week.

On March 16th, Mark brought Ohio around to Turtle Rock on his way back from his daily ride. Kristen was sitting on her porch as he passed. She called to him and waved.

"Come visit," she called.

Mark hollered that he'd be back in a few moments and trotted Ohio back to the barn. He didn't take the time to clean his tack. He brushed Ohio down quickly, threw a light sheet over him and headed back to Kristen's. This was the first time he had visited without the pretense of borrowing or returning books.

She was still camped on her porch when he returned. She was rocking slowly in a large green wicker chair huddled up in a heavy wool sweater. Her heels rested on the edges of the chair and her knees were drawn up to her chest. Most of the day had been unseasonably warm, but it cooled off quickly as the sun fell behind the trees. There were two small Ball jars on a wicker table that sat between the two rockers. Both were filled with a purplish liquid that came from a crystal decanter as well cut as anything Mark had ever seen on the Harrisons' table.

"Would you like to join me in a blackberry brandy?"

"What's the occasion?"

"No occasion," she said, "unless you absolutely need one. Then we can drink to spring."

"All right then," he said picking up his glass. "To spring."

The new taste of the illegal liquid was pleasant and warmed his throat. He sensed a change in Kristen and wondered how much of the nearly half empty bottle of brandy was in that day's work. He finished his glass and she poured him another without asking. They sat a half hour or so on the porch and watched the sun disappear behind the distant tree line.

"I'm cold," Kristen said. "Let's go inside."

He followed her into the house and watched as she skillfully started a fire in the stone fireplace. He sat on the faded divan and poured them each another brandy. She walked to the back of the divan and leaned across him to reach her glass, brushing his face lightly with her shoulder as she did.

She stepped around to stand in front of him sipping the warm liquid, staring intently at his face the whole time.

"Would you like to kiss me?" she asked.

Mark reached up and grabbing her shirt lapels firmly, pulled her face down to meet his lips. Her kiss was hard and passionate, but Mark sensed that her passion was only partially a response to him. She kissed him full on the lips. Kissed his top lip. Then his bottom lip.

Mark felt like he was embarking on a train. As he and Kristen passed different sexual mileposts, he thought of different girls he had taken to the same stops along the line. When Kristen deftly put her tongue into his mouth, he thought of Eileen, the first girl he had done that with. When he unbuttoned her blouse, he thought of Bonnie, the lumberyard owner's daughter. When he reached under her silk camisole, he thought of Susan, that summer night when he was fifteen.

Kristen had small boyish breasts with hard long nipples that he noticed many times before pressing against the cotton of the inside of her shirts. His fingers touched them now with a youthful hunger. Her bare skin on his hand quickened his heart to a faster pace as if more coal had been shoveled into the steam engine's fire. The train he was on showed no signs of stopping as he passed through stations never visited before. When Kristen bent to unbutton his trousers, and kissed his navel, he realized he was in an uncharted sexual county. Still the train rumbled down the track. When she stepped out of her own trousers his head was spinning. She removed her undergarments and stood before him in brilliant nudity. As he sat unmoving on the divan, he again felt that contagious comfort she exuded, even more so in her nudity, and he lost any inhibitions he might have expected himself to feel. She took his hand and walked him to her bedroom. She walked backwards never taking her eyes from his. He wished he could see them better in the dark. He wondered if he would have seen both sets of her eyelids open.

A large oaken headboard and footboard framed the soft mattress. She laid down, his hand still in hers, and wordlessly pulled him lightly down on top of her. When she took him into her hands and slipped him inside of her all thoughts drained from his head supplanted by pleasure. Pure pleasure. The train had reached a heretofore rumored station. At that, the train came to a screeching climactic halt, and it took far less time than Mark would have wanted. They laid together, still in silence. She smiled warmly at him, her face mostly in shadows. He didn't know what, if anything, to say. He said nothing until less than ten minutes later, his youthful member was summoned for a return engagement, and he had her again. This time he was able to stay longer than a minute and her excited and climactic spasms brought him to a fevered pitch he could never have dreamed of.

Afterwards they lay together side by side. He nestled down to kiss the flatness of her stomach. She seemed to have dozed off and he might have also, but it was difficult to tell. The previous experience was so like a dream that he couldn't be certain if he had momentarily crossed the line into sleep. Less than a half hour later, he took her again, this time more slowly. He was amazed at how quickly they fell into each other's rhythms. Then they slept. Both of them in an exhausted heavy sleep.

He awoke that evening as the unfamiliar chime of her clock rang out eight times. He opened his eyes to see her leaning on her elbow studying him.

Before he could speak, she said, "You must be starving. Let me fix us something to eat."

He smiled an agreement and went to use her water closet.

As he returned to her parlor, she stood at the ice box wearing nothing except his flannel shirt. It barely reached her mid-thigh. She was smiling like a school girl who had just enjoyed her first off-color joke.

She started to laugh. "Is it–?" she started to say, but interrupted herself with laughter. She struggled to collect herself. "Is it still pink?"

She covered her laughing face with both hands, as if she just uttered the funniest four words in the English language.

He knew immediately what she was asking and turned his now red face sideways trying to get a better vantage point to see her. She was still laughing, her shoulders shaking with the effort.

"You knew?" he stammered. "How?"

She moved to him quickly, and took his hand.

"Come here," she said and walked him outside onto the porch. He wore only his trousers. She slid one of the rocking chairs over in front of the stairs, lining it up carefully with the edge of the front door.

"Sit exactly here, and don't move," she said.

She ran down the stairs toward Turtle Rock stopping halfway down the dirt path. She turned to him again and said, "Don't move!" She spun around and ran the rest of the way to the lake leaping onto Turtle Rock effortlessly. She stood facing him ninety yards away, and said without shouting, "The Ink Widow lives there in that haunted house."

Then she bowed.

He heard her perfectly. She half skipped and half ran back up the porch still giggling, and out of breath. The sight of her barefoot and half naked in his shirt excited him all over again.

As she bounded up the porch, Mark asked, "How–?"

She cut off the rest of his question. "I don't know," she said. "But I think it's those two upright stones. I always picture them like hands alongside a shouting mouth." She put her hands in that position to demonstrate. "If you move a foot in either direction, you can't hear a thing. I discovered it quite accidentally."

"I'm really sorry," he said "we were just boys."

"Don't be sorry," she said. "You've all entertained me for years from that rock. Anytime I'd see you there, I'd turn off the radio and sit down for some real entertainment."

"You are the devil," he said, and stepped to her again.

"And by the way, mister. I'm only thirty-one now. Golly. You boys had me one foot in the grave already."

He smiled. She hugged him and kissed him in between grins and looked down at his trousers. She backed up half a step and put both hands out in front of her chest palms out and fingers up.

"No more," she said laughing. "I surrender."

Lindbergh

"I bet he'll quit now," Daniel said.

"I don't think so," Mark answered. "I don't think he's a quitter."

"I'm not saying he's a quitter," Daniel said, fully aware that in May of 1927 there was nothing more insulting to say about a man. "But it might just not be possible. And besides, the money won't do him much good if he's dead."

"I wasn't talking about the money. It's just sometimes a ball gets rolling down a hill and you can't stop it no matter what you do. And anyways, I bet he doesn't even know those French guys died."

"Everybody knows," Daniel answered.

The two brothers floated down the middle of the Delaware River, baking in the sun in Billy's borrowed canoe. Daniel sat in the rear, occasionally using his wooden paddle as a rudder to steer around river rocks. But mostly the boys were content to let the current take them downstream. The dark early morning clouds that had caused Billy and Jackie to go back home to bed had blown east taking the threat of rain with them. The plan was to paddle from Narrowsburg to Pond Eddy. Mark was not disappointed when their friends decided to abandon the trip that morning at dawn. A fairly steady drizzle covered the area. The river was still cold and fast from spring runoff. Jackie couldn't convince the two brothers to postpone the outing for another week.

"I can't go next week," Mark said. "It's today or it's forget it."

"But it's gonna rain all day," Jackie said.

"Then we'll get wet," Daniel said.

"We ain't going."

"Bye," Mark said.

He hadn't intended to be so abrupt but he was tired of Billy and Jackie backing out of plans. Besides, he wanted to talk with his brother alone. They had been canoeing for almost four hours. The sun still two hours from being directly overhead. When they spoke at all, they talked mostly of Lindbergh. And who didn't? Nothing since the end of the Great War had electrified the area like Charles Lindbergh. Kristen was consumed by Lindy fever. She begged Mark to ride to the train station early each morning to get the Times or the Herald-Tribune as soon as they arrived from the city. In early May, only one or two people waited on the platform with Mark. Over the past two weeks, the number had grown to nearly twenty every day as the freight train dragged itself through the station depositing mail bags and wired bundles of newsprint. It's hard to say why everyone was so caught up with the twenty-five year old barnstormer.

"He's so brave," Kristen had said. "So young and handsome."

And maybe that was it.

"He'll get a $25,000 prize if he makes it," Jackie had read.

Maybe that was the fascination.

Mark's father said he'd never make it alive. He'll disappear into the Atlantic like a moth into the sun and never be heard from again. Maybe it was that promise of grim failure that was so riveting.

"What do you think was going through those French guys' heads when they started falling out of the sky?" Mark asked his brother. He leaned back in the canoe with his hand dragging alongside, leaving a tiny wake that was dwarfed by the path of the water settling behind the canoe. For the past two weeks, everyone was buzzing about Nungesser and Coli crashing to an early death trying to cross the Atlantic from Paris ahead of Lindbergh.

"I don't know," Daniel said. "Vooley-voo, Holy Sheet?"

The brothers laughed. Mark pulled his hand out of the cold water.

"Do you ever wish you could fly?" he asked Daniel.

"Hell, yes. I think on it almost every day. I feel more strongly pulled to it than I did about driving."

Mark watched Daniel look up to the sky longingly, as if he was hoping to see himself flying overhead.

"If I hadn't 'a been born so darn late, I'd of signed up to fly in the war."

"Kristen's husband flew in the war," Mark said.

And there it was. The subject broached. Mark's back was to his brother but he could feel his eyes hot on the back of his neck.

"Yeah. Kristen," was all Daniel said.

Mark pointed out an eel trap coming ahead on the river. Daniel steered them away from it. Mark turned halfway around in the canoe, so he could face his brother. His hand, cool from the river, went absently to the back of his neck. The canoe rocked gently from this motion. He looked Daniel in the eye.

"Yeah, Kristen," Mark mimicked.

Until a couple of weeks ago, Mark thought his secret rendezvous with Kristen went unnoticed. That was when Daniel had casually asked: "You going over to Mrs. Scott's again tonight?"

"Dunno," Mark said.

And that had been the sum of the discussion on the matter. It wasn't like Daniel to let his brother's life go without his personal review and commentary. Mark figured he'd just wait until his brother asked him directly. But he hadn't asked. Mark was bursting to tell as much as Daniel was bursting to hear. Like mental arm wrestlers, neither boy backed down from his proud silence.

"Are you? You know?" Daniel said.

"What?" Mark asked.

"You know." And as Daniel made a circle with his thumb and index finger of his left hand, he pushed and pulled the index finger of his right hand through it.

Mark smirked. Looked away from his brother across the river's surface to the dark woods along the shore. He lowered his chin to his chest looking down at his wet canvas shoes in the canoe. He shook his head back and forth slowly. Smiled in spite of himself.

"You're unbelievable," Mark said.

"Maybe," Daniel answered. "But that doesn't answer the question."

"This–" and Mark imitated his brother's finger gestures, "is not a question."

Daniel laughed. "It's the only question."

Both brothers laughed.

Mark retreated into a momentary quiet, calculating how much to tell Daniel. He weighed the vulnerability of Kristen's reputation against the implicit trust he had for his brother. Daniel started paddling. Mark watched himself float by in the mirror-topped water as the canoe cut across the river.

"It's not always about sex," Mark said.

"Yes it is," Daniel said. "Sometimes it's flowers and sex. Sometimes it's a little hooch and some sex. But all roads lead to sex."

Mark's head nodded agreement while his thoughts formed a denial.

"You're so cynical," he said.

"Are you saying you're in love with the woman?"

"No. Maybe. I don't know. No. I guess not."

"Good," Daniel said. "There's nothing more boring than listening to somebody in love. And if you ain't in love, then it's just the sex."

Mark was silent again. Daniel obligingly went along wearing the smug look of a pinochle player who just scored his nine of trump.

"I don't think I want it to be just about sex," Mark finally said.

"It either is or it isn't," Daniel said. "A person doesn't have much say in the matter." He stopped paddling. "And anyway, why not?"

Mark squirmed on the hard seat of the canoe.

"It's starting to feel wrong," he said.

"Wrong? You mean God wrong? Hellfire damnation wrong? Hell's bells little brother. I ain't never heard a sermon leaning toward the virtues and graces of unmarital sex with a widow. But come to think of it, if I was running the sermon mill, I might throw one in every now and again just to spruce up attendance."

Mark laughed, but his laughter halted abruptly like a leave floating downstream getting hung up on a rock.

"No. Not hellfire wrong," Mark said. "It don't feel wrong like that." He looked down and spoke to his brother's reflection in the water. "It's just that after all that sex, we'd get, I don't know, a little closer. Like me and–" he started to say.

"It's just sex with a widow," Daniel said. "Now give me the details. Don't leave out any important stuff."

"Not a chance," Mark said as he violently rocked the canoe west then east knocking his unwary brother into the cold water.

"You sum-bitch," Daniel hollered as his head came up from the river. Mark was already fifteen yards downstream.

"At least tell me if she's got a nice caboose," Daniel called.

"I'll wait for you at Pond Eddy rock," Mark answered. He knelt into the bow of the canoe and paddled furiously in a sprint the final two hundred yards to Pond Eddy. He turned to see his brother floating downstream behind him. The tops of his canvas shoes sticking out in front of him as he floated on his back in the current spouting water from his mouth like a contented whale. Daniel seemed unconcerned at being left behind. Already Mark was losing clear sight of his brother, as he paddled on ahead.

The way the Lerners spoke of personal matters was not unlike the patterns set by the popular weekly serial films. A topic was introduced. Looked at. Laughed on. Addressed circuitously and then left to set for a couple of days often hanging like Pauline off a cliff until reintroduced days later when maybe a bit of advice might be offered. Maybe it would have been expected that the brothers would resume their Kristen conversation when Daniel finally floated into Pond Eddy.

Daniel carried one of his canvas shoes limping noticeably as if the quarter inch of absent rubber on his one bare foot was throwing off his ability to walk.

"I don't think the glue on this rubber's gonna hold up to all this water," was all he said.

"I wear mine all the time in the water," Mark said. "Put some newspaper in them and leave them in the sun. They'll be jake by morning."

Daniel caught up to his brother as he walked up towards the road to where Mark had already dragged the canoe. He put his arm easily around his brother's shoulder.

"You going over to the stable?"

"In a while."

It wasn't until the following Wednesday that they spoke of Kristen again. After finishing work, Daniel walked down to the stable with two bottles of Hire's.

"You got an opener down here?"

"Hanging by the light switch," Mark said.

Mark threw two bales of hay down, taking the one closest to the door for himself so his back faced the opening. He knew that Daniel couldn't clearly see his expressions with the late afternoon sun bright behind his back.

"You straighten out that Kristen stuff?" Daniel asked.

"Some."

"She looking for more than you're willing to give her?"

"Nope."

"Why you feel you got to come to a solution where there ain't no problem?"

Mark shrugged.

"You ain't gonna tell me about the sex, are you?"

"Nope."

"One of these days I'm gonna stop telling you too. Then you'll know what it's like."

Mark said nothing. Daniel pulled out a pouch of Bull Durham and some papers and rolled two cigarettes. He could've bought pre-rolled, but he liked the ceremony as much as the smoking. He handed one to Mark and struck a match against the concrete apron leading into the stable.

Mark inhaled deeply and blew out a cloud of blue-grey smoke. The smoke expanded in the slanted rays of the sun until it seemed impossible that so much volume could have come from only two cigarettes.

"So what's the problem?" Daniel asked.

"Didn't say there was a problem. Everything's all right. Unless that's the problem. Everything's just all right."

Mark leaned toward Daniel on his bale of hay and lowered his voice to little more than a whisper.

"Last week we were laying in bed," Mark began. "We were talking about how brave Lindy was. I asked how she felt when her husband left for war. I meant was she proud of him and all that."

Daniel nodded.

"She told me he left long before the war."

"What did she mean by that?"

"At first, I didn't know. She hadn't so much as spoke his name since I've, you know, known her. Then all of a sudden, it's all she wants to talk about. Him or Lindbergh. Something about Lindy is driving her crazy. I don't know if she knows what it is. I don't, I can tell you that." He took a long swallow from his cold root beer leaving his fingerprints on the sweating glass. "Her husband flew in the war."

"Yeah. You already told me that."

"Something happened before then that hurt her. Hurt her bad."

"What?"

"I think he cheated on her."

"With who?"

"She said she didn't know."

"How did she find out?"

"She found a note the woman sent to him. It was tucked into his Bible. She knocked it accidentally on the floor and the note fell out. She showed me the note."

"What it say?"

"Said 'If you don't leave, you'll never forgive yourself.' Something about him not being responsible for Kristen's happiness, and that her love for him shouldn't be a prison. Then it said there was no future for them, and that he should go and follow his dreams."

"Wasn't it signed?"

"It was signed 'M'."

Mark paused for a reaction from Daniel but got none.

"Kristen said she cried and cried all that day. Never got out of bed. She said she thought they had a perfect marriage. A perfect love. Said she felt so betrayed."

"What the hell is a perfect love?"

"I've got no idea," Mark shrugged.

"What did you say?" Daniel asked squashing his cigarette butt under his heel.

"I said maybe they didn't have sex. I was just trying to make her feel better. She gave me a look that made me feel like a stupid kid. Said it made no difference. It was the secret confidence that so betrayed her. Said it was being so wrong about something that shook her so badly. She asked me how I'd feel if I walked into the Shohola and heard you telling someone how much of a burden I was to you."

"She said that about me?" Daniel asked.

"Yep. I told her it wasn't possible. That you'd never say something like that. 'Exactly', she said. 'Exactly how I felt.' She said it wasn't possible. But there it was. Everything she ever believed in, her whole life. Everything she thought she had. I remember her exact words. She said 'Everything I thought I was turned to black by a bunch of words scrawled on a piece of paper.'"

"What did she do?"

"Nothing. Said she laid in bed all day wondering what to do. She thought of going to her mother's in Ohio. Thought about going to her friends in Manhattan. Contemplated the 'grand gesture', as she put it. Throwing all his clothes into the lake. Smashing all the glass in the house. Burning down the house. Said she thought this kind of thing all day. Never got out of bed. Until it was evening and he came home."

"What she do then?"

"Nothing. Never did nothing. Never said nothing. A week later he told her he'd enlisted. She said she already knew. Said she let him make love to what was left of her, but that he knew something was seriously wrong. She said that was her way of getting even. Letting him wonder forever what was wrong. She never told him."

"Why'd she tell you?"

Mark looked at him closely.

"I don't know. Sometimes I feel like she's trying to teach me something. But I don't know what. She tells me as if she's trying to explain something that has something to do with me. I don't want her to stop the telling though. It makes me feel good when she tells me about him. Strange. Ain't it?"

"Yeah," Daniel said, a confused expression on his face. "But I still don't see your problem."

"Didn't say it was a problem," Mark answered. "It's just a thing."

"Want another smoke?" Daniel asked after a few seconds.

"No."

Both boys stood up as if their meeting had been officially adjourned. Neither was real strong on what was accomplished by all this quiet talk, but both felt better for the telling of it.

Speculation

On May first Lucretia Harrison sent out twelve invitations for a surprise dinner party to celebrate Austin's upcoming July birthday. She also sent an invitation to her cousin Charles Dawes as she had for every event and near event of her marriage since he was first elected to the Senate. He had yet to accept a single one, but Lucretia always saved his polite letters of regret and circulated them among her guests during the festivities, making certain that no one would forget who she was. Now that the man was Vice President she held little hope of acceptance.

On May 16th, a letter postmarked from the District of Columbia arrived. She didn't open it until the 17th presuming it was yet another polite regret.

Dear Lucretia,

I am in receipt of your letter of invite for the planned festivities of my cousin's fiftieth birth date. I will be en route to Saratoga for the August season, and would be honored to remake your acquaintance at that time.

It was signed Charles Dawes. Lucretia's scream woke Austin who had fallen asleep while reading in the adjoining room. He ran into the parlor where Lucretia had nearly collapsed into a brocaded armchair.

"What is it, my darling?"

"Oh my–! It was–it was a mouse. Nearly crawled up my leg, it did. Oh my–! "

Austin frowned a response. He made a perfunctory search of the room and returned wordlessly to his book in the front parlor. Lucretia fanned herself with the letter still clutched in her fist, confident that she had successfully deflected her husband's suspicions, but nearly overwhelmed at the immensity of the task before her. It would simply not do to have the Vice President of the United States greeted by such a humble gathering as the one she had planned. Lucretia calculated the implications of Mr. Dawes' acceptance. His presence demanded an extravagant gesture and after recovering from the original shock she dedicated herself to the project in the grandest style she could summon. This could be her crowning moment, insuring forever her place in New York society. She also thought it a chance to be accepted for her own bloodline, and not just because she married a Harrison. But she had barely two months to accomplish six months work.

On May 27th, before the Harrisons left Manhattan for Pine Bluff, Lucretia sent engraved invitations to ninety people, eight weeks to the day before the planned party. On many of them she added a handwritten note, "Of course, the Vice President has promised his attendance, and I'm certain you wouldn't want to miss this opportunity to see him again." She wondered about the "again", thought it might be supercilious. After all, none of her friends had met the man before, but he had been invited to parties they attended, and she reasoned that was almost as good. In fact, Lucretia had only met him once, at her wedding twenty-six years earlier and was not certain she would recognize him in a crowded room. She closed the invitations with a polite *Respondez S'il Vous Plait* in the bottom left corner and signed her name "Lucretia Dawes Harrison".

During the next several days, she went to work as soon as Austin left for the office. She telephoned Stephan and told him the news while unfolding her plan. "I must count on your assistance," she pleaded. "I have invited all your business friends. If you could persuade Mayor Walker to accept, I am certain his crowd will join." She read him her roster of invitees. "Did I leave anyone out?"

"Lucretia, where are you going to house these people?"

"The important people can stay with us at Pine Bluff. The rest of you will be taxied to the local hotels. I've already booked all available rooms."

Stephan ignored the slight, accustomed over the years to nothing less. It took him fewer than three seconds to realize the beneficial business implications of "*le grand soiree*".

"I have called Erie and hired a dining car that will be added to the Port Jervis line out of Penn Station. It will be a hoot. Please, Stephan, I need you to campaign for this party. I've invited the young people too. Surely you can persuade the old folks you know with the prospect of rambunctious young flappers?"

"The things you say to ingratiate yourself are just too kind," Stephan said. He was silent a moment and Lucretia could hear the tapping of a pencil on the other end of the line. "Invite Frank

Schwartz from Morgan. If he comes, you'll have a success. If they know he's coming, they'll come."

"But isn't he a Jew?"

"Lucretia, darling. If you want people to travel four hours for a weekend in July, you need to entice them with more than the prospect of dancing flappers. Frank has been known, after a few drinks, to drop an occasional market tip. Everyone knows that. They follow him around Valentino's like rats follow cheese waiting for a morsel of financial wisdom to fall from his plate. I'll start a few rumors that Morgan is up to something big in August. Let it be known that Schwartz is coming. They'll come."

"Are you certain?"

"Lucretia, Lucretia. This is what I do. Trust me."

"And what if the Vice President finds out there are Jews present?"

"For God's sake, Lucretia. The last time I looked, he was the Vice President of the Jews too!"

She laughed. "All right, Stephan. I'll do as you say."

"Thank you."

"Oh, and Stephan–the caterer needs a minimum of three days to get things ready here. I was able to persuade Monsieur Coutreau to take on our little gathering. You remember he did Alfred Smith's cotillion for his eldest daughter? It'll be grand! I must count on you to get Austin back to Manhattan on July 24th."

"How am I to do that?"

"Must I think of everything? Surely you have the wherewithal to summon your business partner back to the office. Isn't there something that he does there?"

"He'll be unwilling to leave Pine Bluff in mid-summer on any account."

"Invite him to play golf."

"He won't drive four hours to play golf."

"Oh Stephan," she said. "You're being difficult. Do this for Austin."

"Austin will hate this. If you've invited ninety people, he will be busy all evening avoiding eighty-eight of them."

She released an exasperated sigh.

"He'll be so flattered," she said. "A party will make him so happy."

"Yes," Stephan said in that tone of voice Lucretia had come to recognize but never fully understand. "I have seen him very happy as he was leaving a party."

"So I can count on you?"

"As usual."

"And you'll take care of the authorities about this prohibition thing?"

"Yes, my darling. If Jimmy Walker is there, it should be no problem."

"You are just so wonderful," Lucretia preened. "And I really mean that. I'll have a big kiss waiting for you upon your arrival."

"I'll do it anyway," Stephan said with a disarming laugh.

She rang off feeling much more optimistic than she had when she called.

The Lerners were told in June about Lucretia's surprise celebration but rumors had already reached them before then. The planned party was a boulder dropped into the Sullivan County pond. Barryville was accustomed to a brisk tourist trade. The little town of six hundred people swelled in season to nearly six thousand, most making the hundred mile journey by train, stopping across the river in Shohola, Pennsylvania. The Shohola Glen Hotel was no stranger to Manhattan's high society. Zane Grey lived nearby and was a frequent guest of Arthur Rohman's bar downstairs. Smokey Joe Wood lived in Barryville not too far from Pine Bluff and Babe Ruth stopped by on a few occasions to visit his teammate from his Red Sox days. But the rumored party was bigger than that, poised to be the grandest event ever seen in the area.

As soon as Lucretia had booked two guest houses, word went out and the other hotel owners raised their nightly rates seventy-five cents to two dollars and fifty cents in anticipation of her call. Gossip flew through the stagnant early summer air like feathers in a tempest. If a man was told a rumor, he felt obligated to see the rumor and raise it with one of his own. "The President is coming to Pine Bluff!" some had said. "Charles Lindbergh might fly in" others countered. "Charles Mitchell is coming" was advanced with "Andrew Mellon's son is taking a train in from Pittsburgh!" This last was told to Michael Lerner by the town's only councilman himself, although neither knew if Mr. Mellon even had a son. The mayor of Barryville took the opportunity to let his constituency know that it was his doing that promoted the party. He warned the locals about price gouging and let everyone know that this singular event could be the beginning of a Renaissance in the area. If the famous and powerful people of Manhattan enjoyed themselves, then surely they would return year after year. Barryville would be placed prominently on the social map. Property values would soar. Tourism was neck and neck with the grist mill as the largest source of income to the area. Scores of people sought out the cooling breezes of the Delaware, or dropped their children off at the summer camps that sprinkled the riverside. The small hotels and guest houses turned a modest profit most years. But this was bigger than all of that. Boom time was on the visible horizon.

Sullivan County had been plowed and sown like a fertile cornfield for exactly such an event. A steady pounding from downstate daily newspapers had softened the skeptical underbelly of the county mind set. Daily reports from "The World", "The Sun", "The New York Times", "The Daily News", and occasionally "The Brooklyn Daily Eagle" dropped stories of unprecedented newly acquired wealth on the railroad platforms of the local towns in a steady litany that had been accepted, reluctantly at first, by the local populace. Magazines reached the New York State towns with dizzying frequency, until articles like "The Ladies Home Journal" story of last September 3rd entitled "Everyone Ought To Be Rich" were accepted and repeated as fervently as sermons. The question for many Americans, with the exception of the farmers who were mired in an inexplicable recession, was not "if", but "when?" would prosperity reach town limits. In small towns throughout the country, a new word had been introduced and seized on. Speculation. As the decade of the Twenties sprouted into full bloom "speculation" had usurped the "right to bear arms" in the hierarchy of The Bill of Rights.

Newsprint greedily reported the private details of the lives of Rockefeller, Mellon, Vanderbilt and the like who were revered as modern day Titans. Their arrival at an opera or Broadway play was reported down to a description of their attire and the company that they kept. They, and not Presidents or film stars were the consuming subject of American journalists. They were the heroes. The rich were expected to make money, but now that The Great War had ended, prosperity was no longer just for the wealthy. And what had made this possible? Speculation. Was there a man in America sitting comfortably in a six thousand dollar house who did not know what was happening in Florida? A man who had not heard of relatively poor folks just like themselves selling his six thousand dollar house for ten thousand dollars, and having the rights to that house resold again for eighteen or twenty thousand dollars weeks later? And those rights sold again within the month for thirty thousand dollars. Thirty thousand dollars! Was there a man in America who did not believe that he was just as deserving as his poor counterpart in Florida? There were some, surely, but in the summer of 1927, they were huddled in the silence of the infidel. These were not foolish men. Unschooled perhaps, but educated by the unending stream of success stories that they read daily over morning coffee. They could, and did, read all the details of speculative deals every day in every newspaper in the country.

And if this could happen in Florida, imagine what might happen in "a nice place". Even Florida, filled with mosquito-laden swamplands was booming. Even a place like Florida, that was essentially uninhabitable four months a year with paralyzing heat, was firmly immersed in the nouveau religion of the nineteen-twenties. Speculation. Men had their ears vigilantly posted for the sound of opportunity knocking, and no one could really blame them if they mistook the sound of their own excited hearts pounding for the sound of opportunity begging to be let into their lives. A poor man is his own economist. It is a simple calculation for him to see that money being spent is the opportunity for money being earned. And in Calvin Coolidge's America everybody made money.

On June first, when the Harrisons made their annual trek to Pine Bluff, they could have no way of knowing of the wave of optimism that accompanied their brand new 1927 Dusenburg down the dusty roads of Sullivan County.

Within an hour of their arrival, Daniel came running down to the paddock where Mark was schooling Keystone, a chestnut brown thoroughbred. Although it was barely ten o'clock, the temperature already surpassed eighty. The back of Mark's shirt was dark with sweat as he rode the shimmering horse. Keystone saw Daniel before Mark did and backed up quickly in fear of the running boy. Mark struck the horse sharply with his whip until the horse moved forward.

"Sorry to startle you," Daniel said breathlessly.

"That's all right," Mark said. "Actually, it's good that you did. Her first reaction is always to move backwards. She's dangerous like this. I gotta retrain her."

"When did you get her?"

"Yesterday. I told you I was going to the auction with Phil."

"Oh yeah. I forgot."

"I outbid Phil for her."

"That must have gotten the old geezer's goat. What did he say?"

"He said," and Mark lowered his voice to sound like Phil, "'You overpaid for that horse. She ain't worth a damn dollar more than I bid. That horse is afraid of her own shadow'"

"Did he spit on your shoes?"

"Darn near."

"What did you say?"

"I told him she'd be worth it when I got done with her."

Daniel howled with delight. "That's telling him! I wish I could have seen his face." Daniel did not share his brother's regard for the man. He scratched his ear in thought. "If she's so bad then why'd you buy her?"

"'Cause Phil wanted her," Mark said laughing at himself. He shrugged at nothing in particular. "What brings you down here this morning?"

"The Harrison's are having a party here in July."

"So?"

"So, Mrs. Harrison is hiring damn near every man in town."

"What for?"

"For everything. There's gonna be over a hundred people here. She'll need men to drive people back and forth to their hotels. Some to help set up tents. Some to help clean up the place before and after the party. She even wants to hire some girls to help with flowers and take wraps and other girl stuff."

"So?"

"She wants me to organize it. I have a budget. I get to hire anyone I want. I'll have the guys kissing my behind all summer for a chance to work. And the girls! They gotta come to me if they want to be hired! Think of the possibilities!"

Daniel obviously had. His voice raised in pitch and speed as he ran off the news. Mark started to trot Keystone around the ring to a jump he had made out of old fencing. As he trotted around to where Daniel stood, he asked, "How much of a budget?"

"That's the beauty. It's unlimited. It'll be hundreds of dollars!"

"Are you kidding?"

"Nope. I told her if I gotta hire twenty or thirty people for three or four days, it might run up a bill of three or four hundred dollars a day."

Mark halted the horse.

"What did she say when you told her that?"

"She just asked how much I'd pay them for an hour. I told her I'd need to pay the men a dollar and a half an hour and the girls maybe seventy-five or eighty cents."

"Why so much?"

"That's the beauty here, Mark. It don't have to be so much. But I was, you know, trying to think up the highest price."

"What she say?"

"All's that she said was we probably wouldn't have to pay the men who drive so much because they'll make money in gratuities."

"What's 'gratuities'?"

"Tips. She said the people they pick up will tip the drivers with a nickel or a dime. They're used to that in New York."

"Sounds like you're in for a lot of work," Mark said.

"Work?" Daniel said. "Don't you see what's going on here, Mark? I'm gonna own this town all summer! I'm gonna make a fortune. Maybe enough to buy Jackie's father's old model A. This is gonna be e-e-easy money." He moved his fingers as if knocking the ash from an imaginary cigar.

"How much you gettin' paid?"

"From Mrs. Harrison, I don't know. But I'll get paid from everyone I hire."

"How you gonna do that?"

"You're so stupid. You think Billy's smart enough to ask me for a dollar an hour to drive some swells to a hotel? I'll tell him I'll give him twenty-five cents a run and he'll get tips from the swells. If he gives me a hard time, I'll tell him I'll buy his ethyl too."

"So how you gonna make money doin' that?"

Daniel knocked on the fence he leaned against and said, "Hello. Is this your head soundin' so hollow? If he works four hours, I'll charge Mrs. Harrison five dollars. I'll pay Billy a dollar, plus maybe thirty or forty cents for the ethyl. I'll make three or four dollars a day on each guy!"

Mark looked down on his brother as he sat the sweating mare.

"Sounds like stealing."

"Stealing?" Daniel put his hand over his heart and squinted into the sun facing Mark. "You wound me, my innocent little brother. This is business. Mrs. Harrison already agreed that a dollar or a dollar fifty an hour is all right. If I am able to hire people for less, I should be awarded for my business savvy."

"Rewarded," Mark corrected.

"That's what I said."

Mark legged his horse forward and rode around the ring again.

"Will you stop riding that stupid animal for five damn minutes?"

Mark circled the ring and again halted Keystone in front of his brother.

"I'm thinking," he said.

"Well, think sitting still."

Keystone moved forward and backward a step or two as if answering Daniel.

"She don't like standing still," Mark said. "I can't believe Mr. Harrison is gonna spend a thousand dollars to have a party."

"That's the beauty. He doesn't know. It's a surprise birthday party for him. The Vice President of the United States is coming. Mayor Jimmy Walker, too. Business people from J. P. Morgan."

"They're coming here?" He looked at his brother and they both started laughing.

"They can go anyplace in the entire world, and they're coming here?"

"The mayor said this is gonna be only the start. He said this town is gonna be like the French Triviera."

The boys laughed.

"I reckon I'll need to learn to speak French," Mark said, and the boys laughed again, giddy with the improbable situation.

"I'm gonna be Napoleon," Daniel said.

The boys sat smiling at one another. "So what you want to be?" Daniel asked. "A taxi driver? A circus tent builder?"

"Whatever it is, it's gonna cost you full price."

"I figured you'd say that. That's why I told you it was only a dollar-fifty an hour."

Mark shook his head in feigned disbelief.

"Mr. Harrison is gonna have a full blown shaking fit," he said.

"Yeah, well– I got other things to worry about."

"I can't believe the President is coming."

"Vice President," Daniel corrected.

"What's his name?"

"I dunno," Daniel said. "Listen, I gotta go. I'll talk to you some more after dinner. You going to Kristen's tonight?"

Mark shrugged. For reasons that arrived from outside the normal path of his thoughts, he found himself thinking of Emily. He wondered what she'd look like dressed up. Who she'd dance with. Kristen seemed distant. Small.

"Maybe," he said, as he waved to his brother.

Night Shadows

Kristen was restless the weeks surrounding Lindbergh's crossing. May became June. The trees fuller. The crickets more plentiful, filling in every crack of hot summer silence. Fireflies arrived some nights in such abundance that the dark green curtain of woods mirrored the star-filled nighttime sky.

On May 20th, the day Lindbergh took off, Kristen sat on her porch all day. She waited, as it seemed everyone did, minute by minute awaiting news of his landing. She sifted the sky's every dull noise for a metallic drone that might be him. She had read that he was heading north to Newfoundland before turning east, and hoped that he might fly over her little hamlet. Her small life. She was being irrational, she knew that. Mark told her repeatedly that Lindy would be at least eighty miles to the east, but still she hoped to see him.

"You never know," she said.

On June 1st, the day the Harrisons arrived, she sat alone on her porch. Kristen found herself thinking again about Lindbergh. She held a three-day-old newspaper that carried a photo showing him in an ill-fitted suit, with holes in the back where souvenir seekers had ripped at his clothes for a memento. "Imagine that," she thought, "meeting presidents and ambassadors in your shining moment of glory with a torn coat." The story had reported that Lindbergh met with Mme. Nungesser in London. She wondered what he might have said to her. She marveled that Mme. Nungesser would want to meet with him. "I don't understand people," she said to herself, and laughed at the glimpse she caught of herself as people sometimes do, when they see themselves objectively for a brief moment.

She had celebrated Lindbergh's landing with Mark, a bottle of Chardonnay, and a dinner they never did quite get to. She wished she somehow could have traveled to Long Island to witness his departure. She wanted to wave to him one last time. She actually said that to herself, in those words. "Wave to him one last time," and as she said the words, she understood everything. She understood her nightly dreams of her husband, Rob. Understood the excitement she felt at every Lindbergh radio report. Her understanding brought no comfort.

That night she listened to the Philco Radio Hour at nine o'clock and had just switched stations to listen to the tenor, Al Chaskin, at ten when a tube popped in her radio. The soothing baritone voiced companion that she relied on nightly went silent in mid-sentence. The quiet echoing in her rooms was overwhelming. Kristen lit a cigarette and paced her small kitchen. She put the cigarette down and went to the radio. She wrestled with the heavy mahogany cabinet and managed to pull it away from the wall. She unscrewed the heavy cardboard back. There it was. One black clouded tube amidst a board of unintelligible wiring and dimly candescent orange tubes. She lit another Chesterfield and walked back to the kitchen where she found the remainder of her first cigarette burning a black fingerprint on the edge of the wooden table where she left it.

"What is the matter with me?" she asked silently as she squashed the stub of her cigarette. Her eyes darted around the room as if searching for an ear for her jumbled thoughts.

She threw on a sweater and half skipped, half ran down to the lake. She decided part way down the path to go to Mark, but with little resolve. "He's probably sleeping," she said to herself. "He'll be awake in what?, six or seven hours? What can he do anyway? Maybe he's got a tube. Maybe he's awake."

Her pace was as erratic as the words she spoke aloud. She stopped for a moment and tried to organize her thoughts. "You're acting like a lunatic. Go home and get some sleep." She started walking again in the dark around the lake to Mark. As she neared his room at the stable, she passed Pine Bluff. The main house was in shadows blending at the edges into the night. A lamp was burning in the Lerner apartment. She cowered from it, walked a wide arc away from the house avoiding the light as if its meager flicker would reach her in the darkness and expose her irrationality. Kristen prided herself on her invariant self control, and she shivered noticeably as she felt it fly past her like a blind bat in the darkness. "What am I doing here?" she asked.

She reached the barn and opened the wooden door, perspiration heavy on her neck although the night was mild. She edged down the center of the stalls in the dark stable. Blacker here than outside. Her hands defensively waved in front of her for fear of bumping something, but she could not see her own fingers. The acrid smell of ammonia filled the barn. The noise of the horses seemed ominous. An occasional snort. A kick of a stable wall. The swishing of tails chasing flies. Even the sweeping sound of hay being tossed sounded threatening.

She walked to the end of the row of stalls, and turned right towards Mark's room. She had been down here before, twice, but never into his bedroom. She tapped lightly at the inner door as if afraid to wake him. She unlatched the door. The click of the metal latch sounded loud as thunder to her ears. The hinges creaked out her fears. Mark did not awake. She stood at the foot of his bed seeking him in the darkness, her hands grasped the wooden footboard. A hint of moonlight oozed through the gauze of his curtained windows. She turned to leave, her eyes adjusting to the darkness, but abandoned her escape in two steps, returning to the foot of the bed.

"Mark," she whispered. "Mark. It's me, Kristen," she whispered louder.

She felt foolish. "Leave here now," she commanded to herself. "What are you doing here?" But she turned away from that rational alternative and touched his foot gently. Mark leapt from bed, startling her. In one motion that seemed to take no more than a second, his eyes opened and his feet landed with a slap on the hard floor. He stood bewildered.

"Mark. Oh, my. I'm so sorry. Mark, it's me, Kristen."

He relaxed slightly. His shoulders, arched defensively like a cat, dropped to their normal position. He rubbed his eyes.

"Kristen," he said slowly as if recognizing a childhood friend. "What's wrong?" His reflex of alarm had dissipated and was replaced by concern. "What's the matter?"

"Oh, Mark," she cried. She stepped to him and wrapped herself around him, surprised by his nakedness.

"What's wrong?" he asked again. He put his arms around her.

"Nothing. I don't know. Nothing's wrong. A tube burnt out on my radio. I almost burnt my house down. Nothing's wrong. I don't know why I'm here. I'm sorry. I'm sorry."

She was sobbing loudly. Mark felt her warm tears falling on his bare shoulders, as she shook in a paroxysm of release. Mark squinted through pieces of incomplete dreams struggling to focus on this incongruous event.

"Nothing's wrong?" he asked quietly.

"No. I'm sorry, Mark. I don't know why I've come. Let me go. Go back to sleep." But she made no motion to leave, or to ease the strong grip she had on him.

"What time is it?" he asked.

"I don't know. Maybe eleven," she said noticeably calmer.

"Let me turn on a lamp."

"No, please don't. They'll see it from the house. Please."

He sat on his bed. Rubbed his calf muscles that had tightened in a spasmodic contraction when he was startled awake.

"That was quite a wake up routine," she said as a tiny laugh escaped from her parted lips. Her nose was running and her cheeks were wet with tears. "I'm sorry I startled you."

Mark leaned back against the headboard, supporting himself with a rolled-up pillow. Her attempted laughter diffused the inherent threat of her late night arrival.

"Well, if a tube burnt out in my radio I'd probably do the same to you," he said in the most serious voice he could muster.

"Oh, Mark. Must you always tease me so?" She was smiling. Her crying ceased. "Go on though. Surely I deserve it."

She wanted him to keep talking.

"Come and lay with me," he said.

"Oh, I mustn't. It's my– I have to–"

He reached from his bed and offered his hand. Kristen removed her boots, sweater and trousers, wordlessly letting them fall to the floor. She crawled under the blanket in her shirt and undergarments, letting the boy embrace her.

"I feel such a fool," she said burying her face in his shoulder and cried again, more softly now.

"Don't," he said.

Her hand was on his heart. She felt it beating. Pulsing. Steady. Young. Alive. She lowered her hand and held his erection. She held it lightly as if it was an egg.

"I'm sorry Mark," she said, and fell asleep almost instantly without removing her hand.

Mark lay awake, uncomfortably trapped between tumescence and concern. He watched Kristen as if trying to read her until sleep finally returned.

When he awoke in the morning, she was gone. His recollection of her leaving was as vague as his understanding of why she'd come.

Summer Storms

The light of day made Kristen feel sheepish about her intrusion the night before. She drove into Narrowsburg for a new radio tube. Order returned to her life as the four prongs snapped snugly into place. She decided to explain herself to Mark, although she wasn't certain what that explanation might be. Her ill-defined need embarrassed her.

After a restless morning, she started down her porch steps, stopped and returned to her parlor and grabbed a book. Better to have a reason for her visit.

She walked crisply down the trail to Pine Bluff watching her shadow dart in and out of view. She stood at the double doorway of the stable and called his name. The stable's serenity mocked the terror she had felt the night before. She hesitantly went inside to await his return. Half of the stalls were empty. Some of the horses must be turned in, or turned out, or whatever it is he always does, she thought. She didn't understand his passion for horses but liked to watch it displayed on his face. Loved the excitement of his voice when he spoke of them. The smell of horses, leather, hay and wood all melded together into an aroma that she had come to associate with Mark.

She pulled down a rectangular bale of hay from the stack by the door as she had seen Mark do effortlessly on several occasions. The weight surprised her. She sat for a while until restlessness compelled her to pace around the barn. She touched all the things the names of which she was ignorant. Bridles. Halters. Lead lines. Draw reins. Mark's things.

After waiting a half an hour she stood to leave. She went to his bedroom to see if she might find a pen and ink to leave him a message. The room was tiny, maybe ten feet square. A 'Narrowsburg Grain and Feed' calendar was the only thing hanging on the whitewashed walls. There was no wardrobe, his clothes hung on a makeshift rack. A few books were stacked on a small end table next to a silent clock that had stopped ticking earlier that morning. Two pair of riding boots were thrown on the floor next to a boot jack in the corner. She stood at his bed and picked up his pillow drawing it to her face breathing deeply the smell that she had grown so accustomed to in such a short time.

She found a pen and an almost dry inkwell on his desk. "Sorry I missed you. Wanted to apologize for last night. Thank you, Mark." and she signed it "K". She left it on the table that held his pitcher and bowl. She picked up his shaving brush. His steel razor. Kristen closed the razor and pretended to shave, peering into a tiny mirror that fit easily into her small hand. As she ran the razor down her smooth cheek, she heard him enter the barn.

She hurried out of his room, and stood at the end of the long stable. She knew his eyes needed a few moments to adjust to the semi-darkness and she wanted to say something before she startled him. She did enough of that last night, but as she was about to shout to him, she heard him speak and knew he wasn't alone. She instinctively ducked back into the doorway. Where had she placed the book? That would explain her presence. But in his bedroom? She suddenly craved the sanctuary of her own house. Mark's companion came into view. It was the Harrison girl. She had forgotten the Harrisons had arrived. What was her name? Rebecca? Sarah? No. Emily. And suddenly the quarry became the hunter. She peeked around the doorway, her eyes caught by the girl's horse. Its coat was shimmering in sweat. A white film of dried lather stood out starkly against the blackness of the mare's muscular chest.

The girl was laughing. "Oh, you, Mark," she said. "I can't believe you did that. I could have fallen off!"

Kristen's eyes shifted to the smile lighting up the girl's face. She thought the girl spoke with exaggerated excitement. Kristen knew their eyes would have adjusted to the light, and was panicked at the prospect of being caught. But she couldn't seem to speak out. Emily never took her eyes from Mark who stood with his back to Kristen just inside the entrance to the barn.

Kristen watched as Mark unhitched the girth from Abbey. As he did, Emily bent under the cross ties and stepped to the right of the horse where Mark stood and started to undo the horse's throat latch. They were standing so close they could have shared a pair of boots. Kristen stood frozen as she watched Emily's breasts brush against the back of Mark's muscular arm. Still neither of them noticed her as the seconds piled into minutes. She knew the look on Emily's face. Knew it instantly, as any woman would. She wanted to see Mark's face. Wanted to see its response.

Kristen stepped back into the bedroom, leaned against the wall, her eyes closed. She remembered her book on the bale of hay. Her eyes ran to Mark's water closet and she crossed the small room, reached up, and pulled the chain of the toilet. After waiting a few seconds she noisily unlatched the open door, collected herself and walked boldly into the stable.

"Oh, Mark!" she said.

Both Emily and Mark jumped visibly. Emily bumped into the side of the stall kicking the wall with the heel of her boot. Her face flushed a deep red. Mark seemed nonplused.

"Hello, Kristen," Mark said. His hands were filled with tack. "Give me a minute to hang this up."

"I just stopped by to, um, bring you a book," Kristen said lamely.

She hadn't taken her eyes from Emily. The girl was desperately trying to regain her composure, not knowing where to stand. She shuffled back and forth alongside her horse, making it nervous. She didn't seem to know what to do with her hands, crossing her arms in front of her chest, then putting them to her sides before crossing her chest again. Kristen saw that the girl's discomfort would protect her from any suspicion. At last Emily reached behind her for a brush and started grooming the horse.

Mark returned from the tack room.

"Kristen," he said, "Do you know Emily?"

"We met years ago," Kristen said. "But I'm certain I wouldn't have recognized you." Her eyes still fixed to the young woman's face. Kristen had remembered a face full of freckles, but they were mostly gone now. She had grown into quite a lovely young woman. Her thick hair was cut short in a bob that Kristen recognized from the latest Collier's. She was about Kristen's height, maybe four inches shorter than Mark and thin as a flapper.

"Emily, this is Kristen Scott," Mark said.

"Hello, Mrs. Scott. Yes I believe we have met."

Kristen bristled at the Mrs. Scott.

"Let that go, Em. I'll get it later," Mark said.

Kristen's eyebrow arched at the Em.

She turned to Mark. If he was uncomfortable at all, he didn't show it.

"What are you doing down here so early?" he asked.

She wondered if he intended that to be a private joke, a reference to last night. She would have none of it.

"It's almost four o'clock," Kristen answered.

"Oh my goodness," Emily said. "I'm late. I have to leave. Judith is waiting. I'm really late."

"Go ahead, Emily. I'll put Abbey out," Mark said.

Emily picked up her helmet and whip that she had placed unwittingly close to Kristen's book on the bale of hay. She saw the book and looked quickly and inquisitively at Kristen.

"Good bye. I don't mean to be rude, but–"

"It was nice to see you," Kristen said. "Another time–"

Kristen joined Mark in watching Emily run from the stable. Both watching completely different things.

"Bring Judith next time," he called to her, then turned to Kristen. "I can't believe it's four already," Mark said as Emily escaped their view. "I haven't fed the other horses yet."

He seemed flustered.

"What time did you think it was?" Kristen asked.

"I don't know. One or two, maybe."

"When did you leave here?"

"I don't clearly know. About eleven."

"Eleven? You've been gone for five hours?"

Mark's face reddened in response. They stood suspended in silence as if they occupied the space in a movie between reels.

"Well, I came to apologize for last night."

"No need."

"And to invite you to supper tonight." That was a momentary inspiration.

"Sure. What time?"

"Seven."

"All right," he said.

Again she left that barn, for the second time in twenty-four hours. She was confused, and glad she had three hours before Mark came over. She needed that much time to find her composure.

Kristen started home as the late afternoon sun began to wane. It hit the path along the lake in a mosaic of light and shadow. The bright patches under the trees were like stepping stones leading her back to safety. As she neared her home, she relaxed, her heart stopped pounding and she slowly regained the control she felt so essential.

Something had changed. Kristen wished again that she could have seen Mark's face as the girl stared so intently into his. She was fascinated by the naive candor of the girl's desire. She wondered if he was he aware of it or if he returned that desire.

Kristen recalled her initial forays into his world. He was oblivious to her subtle flirtations at first. She thought it endearing. His deferential treatment made her feel he would never hurt her. His reluctance to speak about his past girlfriends made her believe she could trust her fragile situation to his discretion. She enjoyed watching him struggle for conversation. It made her feel safe. In control. And although the woman in her craved the relationship, the wounded animal inside her desperately needed to be in control.

But today in the barn she felt threatened by the Harrison girl. The emotion troubled her more than the cause. She didn't love Mark. Well, maybe she did love him in a way, but she wasn't in love with him. She had promised herself she wouldn't do that again. And he wasn't in love with her. That thought brought a wry smile to her face. She found it amusing that the young boy felt that somehow he "should be". As if sleeping with her required it. But that obligation came from his own upbringing and from no implied demand from her. She preferred it the way it was.

She noticed that now, three months into their relationship, he struggled with conversation after he bedded her. It was better this way. She was no flapper, but she was well aware that the charade of morality that dominated her teen years had been exposed for what it was in this last decade. She wasn't as licentious as the silly coeds that filled Life magazine each week collecting men like trinkets. But the men she did kiss, she kissed well.

She traded with Mark in good faith. As he lost the clumsy hard corners in his lovemaking, she took a measure of pride in the lover he was becoming. She taught him well. He owed her that much. And more than that she did not want. But the mysterious purpose of last night's episode still troubled her.

Kristen reached her house and went to the icebox for a bottle of beer. She rubbed the brown label-less bottle on her face and neck, then moved to the porch and sat in her favorite rocking chair looking down at the lake. Dinner could wait a few minutes longer. She had some leftover chicken on ice. Maybe she'd make a pot pie. It was the one meal she could handle with relatively good result. She smiled to herself. No one would ever marry her for her cooking.

She finished her beer and rocked herself to sleep. She awoke moments later with a start. An elusive dream slipped away from her like a boat from the shore. Mark was in it. Emily. Horses. But the dream shattered like thinly blown glass and the pieces she remembered did not add up to a coherent image. She wondered how long she had slept. It was cooler and she wrapped her arms around her shoulders. She tried to remember where the sun was when she dozed off. It nearly reached the tree tops high on the mountain across the lake. It wouldn't be dark for hours, but her position in the valley left her with a cooling shade well before nightfall.

She walked around her house to the vegetable garden in back and pulled some carrots from the dark earth. She un-tucked the front of her shirt from her trousers and piled the carrots into it. The breeze felt good as it kissed the bare skin of her stomach. She thought she might encourage Mark to make love to her outside tonight. It made her feel so sensual to be naked outdoors. So wanton. But the planned moments of intimacy served only to remind her of the contrast with Rob and their impulsive and greedy lovemaking. She wondered if there would ever come a time with Mark that she wouldn't think of Rob. She wondered how many more years remained in the sentence of pain he left her as she moved from day to day in the prison of his memory.

She dropped the carrots into the sink. Cut and filleted the chicken. She forcefully rolled dough into a thin crust and placed it into a pie plate filling it with the carrots, potatoes, peas left over from yesterday and the chicken in a passable white sauce. She placed it in the oven. Mark would be punctual, but she had enough time for a bath.

He arrived just as she returned to the kitchen, his hair still wet. She stood at the sink as her hand went to her own wet hair and she smiled. He kissed her in greeting, as had become his habit and stepped to her radio to turn down the volume. Mark leaned on the back of the divan watching her as she set the table.

"Did you get the horses fed?" she asked.

"Yes."

"And the Harrison girl, did she get home in time for whatever it was she ran off to?"

"I suppose," he shrugged.

She looked for a flicker in his eyes when she mentioned the girl but didn't find one.

"Do you ride together often?"

"No. Maybe three or four times a month."

"Is she a good rider?"

"Not really," he answered.

"Was that black horse hers?"

Kristen surprised herself with her pertinacity.

"Yes," said Mark patiently. "It was her colt that got hung up on the fence when I was a boy," he said. "I told you about that."

"Oh yes. I remember now."

She was setting the table and monitoring dinner as they spoke.

"Pour us a glass of wine," she suggested.

Mark handed her a glass and took his own to the front door. He stood with his back to Kristen and leaned against the door frame looking down at the lake.

"A storm's coming in," he said.

On cue, a bolt of lightning split the sky in a jagged golden line that touched the lake, followed almost instantly by a loud house-shaking thunderclap. She loved a storm. Loved the way it enveloped her home insulating her from everything outside.

Mark walked back into the kitchen and stood behind her at the oven. He lowered the strap of her suspender enough to move her shirt from her shoulder. He kissed her bare shoulder, then her neck. She purred contentedly, reached behind her and pulled him closer to her. He lowered his hand from her neck and cupped her breast.

"We can't be skipping another supper," she said, and they both laughed at their conspiracy.

"I'll behave," he said, breaking away with his arms held up in surrender.

"Don't behave too long," she said.

Mark returned the playful look in her eye. He stepped to the divan and laid himself down so he could watch the approaching storm roll towards the front windows.

They sat through supper inside a promise of sex that is sometimes more stimulating than the act. The buttering of bread carried a hint of sensuality. The biting of a roll a tease.

"Does the Harrison girl cook?" Kristen asked.

"I doubt it," said Mark. "They bring their own cook whenever they come. I think toast might prove too great a challenge."

Kristen laughed.

"Much like yourself," Mark added, smiling all the while.

"Oh, you!" she laughed and threw a roll at him missing him by two feet. "Perhaps, Mister, we should bring you into the kitchen to test your cooking skills."

He rolled his eyes, and they sat for some time without speaking.

"She better marry well," Kristen said after several minutes.

"Who?" he asked. "What are you talking about?"

"The Harrison girl."

"The Harrison girl. The Harrison girl," he mimicked. "Her name is Emily and I'm sure Mrs. Harrison would hire Al Capone to remove any suitor not to her own liking." He stared at Kristen as if trying to measure an ingredient unfamiliar to him. Her eyes, as usual, revealed no further clues.

"Sounds like you've given it some thought," she said, her smile gone.

His own smile disappeared like water sucked into the blotter of her stare.

"Are you jealous?" he asked with unforced incredulity.

"Don't be silly."

"Yes," he said. "Don't be." All the warmth gone from his voice.

They sat for what seemed like a long, long time. Mark with the obstinate silence of a man guarding a door that he refused to open. Hers the silence of a woman weighing and sifting words, choosing them carefully that they not be wasted. She sensed an advantage she didn't want to relinquish.

"She's in love with you," Kristen said finally.

Mark frowned. "That's ridiculous," he said sharply. "We could never be together," he added.

The corners of Kristen's eyes wrinkled at his dissent. A part of her hoped for a denial on a different front. She marched forward.

"That's the most dangerous kind of love," she said. "Love for someone you cannot have never dies. Never grows old."

He pushed back in his chair. The legs scraped harshly on the wooden floor. He walked to the front door, raking his fingers through his scalp, resting them at the back of his neck. He turned to face her. She hadn't moved.

"Why are we talking like this?" he asked.

She had been thinking the identical thought. She took a sip of her wine. What was this argument of theirs? It lacked substance. Tactility. They were shaking a stick at ghosts.

"Sit down, Mark," she said, her voice softening.

He walked back to his chair and stood behind it holding the soft, round curve of the wood. His knuckles were white. He picked up his wine, drank it while looking at her through the top of the glass. She looked suddenly ugly to him through that parabolic glass.

"Is this the wisdom of 'The Great Ink Widow'?"

The anger in his voice shocked her. He had never referred to her in that way before. Clearly she had unearthed a vein richer than she had intended.

"Are you saying the only love that lasts is for someone you cannot have?" he persisted.

She didn't know why this generated such an intense response in him.

She met him head on, not willing to back down from the fight. He had stumbled onto the core of what she reluctantly had come to believe. What her marriage had taught her. If for no other reason than self-defense, this was precisely the conclusion that she had come to accept. She stood and carried her half eaten dinner to the sink. He followed behind and, grabbing her shoulder, turned her to face him.

"Is it?" he demanded.

The rain had started. The pounding on the roof forced them to speak louder. She took his hand from her shoulder and held it in hers. She raised her hands, as if in prayer, his still in her grasp.

"It seems to be," she said. Her voice barely a whisper. The implications of her own words stung her, as if believing the words was all right, but the speaking of them too harsh.

"It seems to be," she repeated. She did not like the words she had spoken. They were buried in the darkest rooms of her thoughts and she hated that she believed them. "It's like the Negro blues music," she said, trying to summon allies for her defense. "Like all these books," she said, her eyes fixed on his. He glanced at the rows of books behind her. "I've read every one of them searching for one story about two people happy to have each other in their lives." Tears started to seep from her eyes though she made no crying sounds.

"Every one of them is about someone hopelessly in love with another. Living a life of torment in search of the other. Believe me, I've read them all."

She dropped his hand and stepped to the bookcase.

"The Brontes. Every one. Edith Wharton. Lily Bart," she said waving Forester's "Room With a View" in front of him. It was the book she had randomly grabbed to bring to the stable that afternoon. Her cold argument seemed less ignoble as she summoned the written defenses the books provided.

"Boy loves girl. Girl doesn't care. Girl loves boy. Boy doesn't care. Not one book in a thousand any different. If they come together at all, the book ends. They go riding into a purple sunset with the promise of a full happy life together." She walked back to Mark, taking his hand again into hers. " I want to see the promise fulfilled. I want to know it exists. Can you tell me it exists?"

She was crying now. She punched his chest with her fist.

"Of course it does," he said, his own anger cut by her declaration. He put his arms around her shoulders as he had done last night. It seemed so very long ago.

"Does it?" she asked with a tearful defiance that challenged him to prove it.

"Doesn't it?" he asked weakly.

She shook herself from his grasp. She stood motionless, like a child lost in the forest, then ran to the front door. She escaped into the storm, blinded by her tears. As fast as she could run, she bounded into the rain.

"Kristen!" he called. But he made no move to follow.

Mark poured himself another glass of wine, but drank instead from the bottle. He went to the door. He saw nothing but gray sheets of rain blowing onto the porch, almost reaching him behind the screen. An occasional drop touched his face. Cold. Ice cold.

Discordant notes reverberated in the darkened room. He sat heavily into the arm chair trying to replay their conversation from the flirtations at supper to her hasty departure. Tried to make sense of it. But he couldn't. Nervous energy overtook him. He turned to the kitchen. Cleared the table. Washed the dishes. She still did not return. He dried the dishes and put them into the cupboard. He put two clean wine glasses on the table next to the empty bottle.

He stood in front of her bookcase like a man in front of an altar of an unfamiliar religion. "These are her gods," he thought. "and I don't believe them."

Mark sensed her presence and turned to see Kristen standing in the doorway. He hadn't heard her return over the drumming of rain on the roof. Her clothes clung to her outlining every curve of her figure. Her hair hung straight, dripping a reservoir of rain around her. Water pooled below her stocking feet, black from mud.

"I'm cold," Kristen said, barely audibly. "Hold me, Mark. I'm cold."

Invitations

Mark learned more about the upcoming party listening to Emily and Judith than he would ever have cared to know about anything. It was all they talked about. Who was going to sit at the table with the Vice President? Whose table was going to be next to the table of the Vice President? Who would be offended if they weren't within two tables of the Vice President? Who would be slighted? Who did they want to slight? On and on it went as if nothing had more importance since the Treaty of Versailles. Mark had never heard the term "seating arrangement" and would never have dreamed it would warrant more than five minutes attention.

"Why don't you just let everyone sit where they want? he asked.

The girls laughed. "You're so funny," Judith said. "Emily always says how funny you are. Can you imagine?"

June fifth was the third consecutive day the girls came down to the stable to ask Mark to take them trail riding. If they mentioned the party inside the house Mrs. Harrison threw a fit. They felt no such constraints in the open air. Mark never rode with Judith before that week. He had seen her sporadically since they were all children, but had never spoken much more than a greeting to her. She was like a sister to Emily and had spent at least part of every summer with the Harrisons since her father started working for Messenger Life sixteen years earlier. Emily always told him how quiet she was, but it wasn't something that Mark ever noticed. She was a pleasant girl, not as pretty as Emily, but if she wasn't standing close to Emily, Mark thought she looked better. She had just turned twenty-one, like Emily, a year older than Mark. Her hair was short, cut like Emily's, but it wasn't as thick, and looked– Well, Mark couldn't say how it looked. It just didn't look as good as Emily's. She was an inch shorter than Em, maybe a little thinner. Daniel had always liked her. He told Mark that he thought she was more "real looking" than Emily, but he conceded that he thought Emily had nicer breasts. Daniel thought it was stupid that Emily always looked like a girl in a magazine. "I know for a true fact that it takes her an hour to get dressed every damn morning. Not just Sundays, but every damn morning." It puzzled Mark that it bothered his brother enough to mention.

It had rained again all night of the fourth, and the horses had to negotiate mud and puddles all morning. Judith only knew how to ride sidesaddle, something Emily refused to ever do, and as Mark had no saddles she could use, he and Emily decided to teach her to ride astride. Mark liked having Judith come along, except that when she did they rode slower. They walked their horses for the most part, maybe threw in a short trot now and then and mainly kept to a fairly flat terrain. If it was just he and Emily, they would trot more and take a slow canter when Mark thought they were in a place where Abbey wouldn't gallop off. Mark let Judith ride his horse confident that Ohio would never do anything to put her in any danger. He felt certain that the two girls spoke of things other than the party, but nothing he had knowledge of first hand.

The girls waited for almost five minutes before returning to the topic of choice. As they started, for the thousandth time, to talk about seating arrangements, Mark's thoughts drifted to Kristen. He hadn't seen her since the second. He couldn't remember the last time he'd gone five days without being with her. She would be leaving soon for a few weeks visiting her friends in New York. Or maybe it was a month. He couldn't recall. He didn't think she'd make another nighttime visit now that the Harrisons had arrived and he knew he eventually would go see her. But he hadn't and he couldn't exactly say why. Partly because he didn't know what to say to her. He felt something change in their relationship that night. Something fundamental. He felt that somehow during the months he'd known her he had reached something inside of her, that he had somehow cut a channel through the ice that protected that part of herself that she hid from him. But when she came back to her house wet and cold, he saw that the channel had been iced over. He realized he was unable or unwilling to keep rowing to keep that channel opened. As he plodded along, his thoughts drifted to that night five days earlier. Kristen took off her wet clothes and they went to her bed, but they did not make love. She nestled close to him seeking his warmth and he held her until she fell asleep, then left her to return to his room. He thought it unlike him to become so angry at what she said. What difference did it make what she believed about love or about Emily? He felt foolish that he had made such an issue of nothing.

As he rode silently a few feet ahead of the two girls, he shrugged.

"What are you thinking?" Emily asked, a laugh in her voice. "You haven't spoken for ten minutes!"

The girls rode side by side and glanced at one another, smiling broadly. Mark's face turned a bright crimson.

"Nothing," he said.

"You think on nothing harder than any man I've ever seen," Judith said. "You didn't hear a word we said, did you?"

"No, I didn't," Mark said softly. "But I imagine you were talking about the party." He stood in his stirrups and turned to them. "What did you say?"

Judith gave Emily a knowing look and the girls giggled.

"I said 'Where are we?'"

Mark sat back into his saddle and looked around. He didn't know exactly where they were. He looked over his shoulder at the sun, and quickly figured it out. "I think if we cut through these woods we'll be at Kristen's," he said.

"Who's Kristen?" Judith asked.

Emily said nothing.

"Mrs. Scott," Mark said. "We're about a mile from Pine Bluff."

Mark led them on an extended trot, until he heard Judith shout to them to ask them to halt.

"You're going too fast," she hollered while bringing Ohio down to a walk.

"I thought she was right behind us," Mark said to Emily apologetically. She shrugged her shoulders in response. Her boots were splattered with mud. Teardrops of muddy water had flown up and clung to her cheek and Mark fought an urge to wipe them away. As they waited for Judith, Emily reached over to him and leaning on her horse's withers, touched his wrist. "Are you all right? You seem so far away today."

Mark smiled. "Yes." he said. "I'm fine."

She blinked at him with both eyes.

"Why do you always do that?"

She seemed embarrassed. "Do what?"

"Blink like that."

She laughed with a childlike nervousness. She edged Abbey closer to him, leaned forward in her saddle and whispered, "Because I can't wink."

"What do you mean 'you can't wink'? Everyone can wink."

"I can't." As Judith neared, she said, "Shh. Don't say anything. It's so embarrassing."

"What's embarrassing?" Judith asked. "Are you talking about me?"

"Yes," Mark said laughing. "Emily was just saying it's embarrassing how slow you ride that poor horse."

"Oh, Mark!" Emily shrieked, but she couldn't help laughing along with him. "Don't believe him, Judith. I was just saying how pathetic he was acting, like a schoolboy in love. That's what's embarrassing"

Mark blinked, momentarily speechless. He wished he could think of a clever rejoinder, but her joke had knocked him off stride. "You don't play fair!" He winked at her, smiling broadly.

"No, I don't," she said. Her smile had somehow left her lips and flashed in her eyes.

"I'll go first this time," Judith said. "That way I won't get left behind."

They trotted through the mud all the way back to the stable, the squishing sound of horses' hooves accompanying them back. As they took the last turn and reached the Pine Bluff property, Mark and Emily bolted past Judith in a spirited canter, but she either didn't mind or didn't want to complain about being left behind again.

As Emily passed Mark she called over her shoulder, "I'll race you to the barn!" He followed her a few strides and then pulled up and circled to wait for Judith. He was covered in the mud that splashed in Emily's wake.

"Aren't you a sight!" Judith said as she came up on him. "I can't believe you let her win. I'll never hear the end of it."

Mark couldn't go anywhere in town without being interrogated about the party. July 27th was circled on the calendars of damn near every resident as the day their fortunes would begin to turn. The town had gone berserk. Rumors were rampant that Mr. Morissey was offered fifteen thousand dollars for his twelve room hotel, but Mark suspected that the rumors were started by Morissey himself. The mayor, it was said, had gone into the town's emergency budget to hire coloreds to clean all the streets between the train station and Pine Bluff, and along the avenues that led to the hotels and guest houses. A gazebo was built in the vacant lot that the mayor insisted on calling Memorial Park. Mark's father was given that two hundred dollar contract, and he postponed his other jobs to ensure a timely completion. New saplings were planted around the rock where a brass plaque listed the names of all the town's war veterans. Shop owners were "encouraged" to clean up their storefronts. Miller's General Store sold their entire stock of paint and forty more gallons had to be trucked in from Port Jervis. All this was taken as omens of better times ahead.

Mark didn't see Emily or Judith again until the ninth. He hadn't been back to Kristen's either and was amazed at how easily he fell out of that habit. Except for a brief encounter outside the granary, he hadn't seen Kristen in nearly two weeks. She seemed to accept his excuse that he was busy accompanying Emily and Judith and he thought he sounded convincing when he complained about the extra "work".

The girls hadn't been down to ride during the past week, and that was usually the only opportunity he had to see either of them. The issue of seating arrangements for the party was apparently settled, and Mark was happy to take a break from the subject. Conversation went down a more meandering path, but tended not to stray too far away from a general subject of marriage or marriageable people the girls knew. It was then he learned that the girls would leave Pine Bluff from June twenty-third until the fifth of July.

"Where are you going?" Mark asked.

"We're going to New Jersey someplace. I'm not sure exactly where," Emily said. "Our friend is getting married."

"Marigold is your friend," Judith corrected.

Emily shrieked a laughing protest. "You're so horrid to that girl," she said.

Judith turned to Mark and said, "I call her Marigold because that's what she's trying to do."

Mark laughed. As he had come to know her better, Judith revealed a biting wit that always made him laugh. He liked being included in her confidential asides even though he never knew who she was speaking about. He found himself repeating the things she said to Daniel, who enjoyed them as much as he did.

"She calls herself an artist, but she seldom draws the line."

"Judith!" Emily looked quickly at Mark. "You're embarrassing me!"

"Oh, Emily! You sound like your mother," she said, but let the subject drop.

"We've become the 'old spinsters' in our group," Judith said turning her attention to Mark. "Everyone at the wedding will be asking if we're next. You're lucky you're a man. No one pressures a man to marry, but God forbid a woman reaches her twenties unattached!"

"Well, I, for one, am in no rush to marry," Emily said.

Marriage had become an uncomfortable subject for Mark. It was as though as soon as he neared twenty, everyone expected that he'd find a wife. But he felt no different about being married then he had a year ago. It was something that was always lurking on some vague horizon, and it surprised him that he had arrived at it already. Almost no one he knew was married. Daniel had a girl, and his mother had mentioned marriage, but Daniel hadn't. Billy got married last year, but only because he got his girl in a family way. Jack always talked about getting married, but he never lasted more than two weeks with any one girl. "And who would I marry?" he thought. Kristen was the only woman he saw.

"Let's trot," Mark said. "Judith, are you ready for a canter?"

"Let's give it a go!" she said.

On June 22nd, Emily and Judith came to the barn early to ride. They never told Mark they were coming, but he didn't need much of an excuse to stop his other chores and take them out whenever they wanted. There was a tacit understanding that his job included escorting Emily on her rides, and besides, he was acutely aware that they were leaving the following morning and had hoped they would come riding one more time. Emily was carrying a basket, wrapped in a checkered blue table linen.

"We decided to have a farewell picnic!" she said. "Can you fasten this to your saddle?"

Mark went to find a piece of rope, and when they were all tacked and ready to ride, he tied the bundle over a blanket to the back of Ohio's saddle. "I better ride him today," Mark told Judith. "I don't know if he'll like this. You can ride Piper. Just stay behind and he'll be all right."

As they started out, Emily halted. "Oh, no. Mark. I forgot the most important thing. We need a canteen. Do you have one?"

"Somewhere, I suppose. What do we need a canteen for?"

"I can't tell you. It'll ruin the surprise. Please, Mark?"

He rode back to the barn and rummaged around until he found an old tin canteen and filled it with water. The girls were walking circles in the paddock, waiting.

"Let's go," he said.

"Let's go far!" Emily said. "Let's stay out for hours!"

"Take us someplace new," Judith asked.

He took them around the lake past the Morgan's cabin. Mark watched as Emily appraised the rundown shack, but she said nothing. They slowly climbed a steep ridge along a stony path littered with pieces of slate that had fallen from the precipice above them. The horses stepped slowly through the uncertain footing. The riders were mesmerized by the hypnotic sound of iron horse shoes clattering over the loose and broken slate. They reached the summit of the ridge, and left the shadowed woods. No one had spoken since they passed Morgan's cabin.

"Oh," Emily said in an almost breathless gasp as she reached the top of the hill. "Oh, Mark," she said. "This is perfect."

The back side of the ridge stretched out before them in a green and golden carpet. They sat at the top edge of a vast bowl of a field surrounded by a distant tree line.

"Oh, my," Judith whispered as she reached Emily and Mark, and was met by the view. A brook snaked down the middle of the field, meandering through the downside of the bowl until disappearing over the far lip into the unseen. The sun was high but there was no humidity. Sun rays slanted visibly through bulging clouds down onto the hill inviting them to enter. A cooling breeze hit them with the precision of an oscillating electric fan. As they rode down into the valley Judith began singing a song called, "I'm in the Market for You", a song Mark had heard on Kristen's radio. Emily joined in, and after a while, as Mark picked up the lyrics, he joined in on the chorus. Judith had a beautiful singing voice. Emily sang as though she thought she did too. Mark knew enough about his own singing voice to keep it low, and was content in singing a baritone accompaniment to the girl's melody. They passed through acres of barley grass. The golden reeds hissed and waved in the summer breeze, swishing through the horses legs. They cantered along a long row of pine trees that marked the edge of the field. Mark looked around at the girls. Judith was smiling broadly. Emily, too. They caught up to him, and they rode three abreast in a silent reverie that the summer day demanded.

When they reached the back edge of the field's bowl, they turned and looked at the mile of ground they had just covered.

"Let's picnic here," Emily said. Mark loosened the girths of the horses and hobbled them loosely with pieces of rope so they wouldn't run off. The horses stretched their necks burying their heads in the tall grass.

Emily untied the basket from the back of Mark's horse and unwrapped a pitcher she had carefully packed in newspaper. She took a small brick out of the basket and asked Mark to hand her the canteen.

"What is that?" he asked.

She handed him the brick. It was labeled "David's Burgundy Wine Brick".

"Who's David?" Mark laughed.

"I think it's Da-veed," Judith joked, and taking the wine brick from Mark, she read aloud a warning in small print along the bottom of the package. "Adding water to this brick will result in an illegal violation of the Volstead Act of 1923." She giggled as Emily dropped the brick into the pitcher mixing it with a wooden spoon. The result was a surprisingly passable wine. Mark watched Judith swirl the red liquid around the inside of her glass before sipping it.

"Amos made this," Emily said, as she pulled cold fried chicken from the basket wrapped in opaque waxed paper. Judith spread the blue cloth on the ground and Emily produced buttered rolls, a slab of cheddar cheese, something she called pate that looked barely edible, apples, a bowl of potato salad, and a jar of pickled asparagus spears. She handed out plates and glasses and three tiny bundles of silver utensils she had tied with ribbon. She turned the basket upside down shaking out linen napkins that matched the cloth they sat on. And so they feasted.

As they ate, Mark listened to the incessant easy bantering of the two girls. He closed his eyes and focused on the rhythm of their voices without giving ear to the words. Emily poured more wine, and Judith began singing again, this time making up the words as she went along.

She stopped singing and said, "I want a cigarette."

Emily laughed. "You don't smoke," she said.

"I don't ride either, but here I am!" she said stretching her arms out wide.

"I have some," Mark said, and went to his saddle bag where he had tobacco and papers.

He rolled them each a cigarette. Emily inhaled enough to initiate a coughing fit.

"No, no. Like this," said Judith, and she sipped the end of her cigarette between sips of wine. "Blow smoke rings," she said to Mark. "Can you?"

Mark inhaled and puffed out perfect circles of blue smoke. Emily gazed at them as they hung in the air before breaking up and disappearing into the wafting air.

"Men are so lucky," Judith said. "I want to blow smoke rings in public."

Emily laughed and covered her mouth with her hand. "Oh, Judith. Can you imagine?"

They sat and drank more wine. Mark sat and leaned back on his hands, his arms stretched out tautly behind him. Emily knelt and reached for the pitcher, and poured the remainder of the quart into her and Judith's glass and topped off Mark's almost full glass. Instead of returning to her spot next to Judith, she laid down perpendicular to Mark and rested her head on his lap, facing Judith.

"Do you mind?" she asked.

"No," Judith said. "By all means, " and the girls giggled and laughed until their sides ached.

Mark's head was spinning. A result of the wine, perhaps, but he only had two glasses. He tried not to stare at Emily. Tried to act as natural and comfortable as she seemed. She continued to speak and to laugh and to joke, as if her head was resting on no more than a pillow. After a while, he found his voice, and joined in all the mindless prattle that could fit in a carefree summer day field in the summer of 1927.

After he got over the shock of Emily's proximity, he relaxed and consciously tried to stop grinning lest he appear a complete mindless idiot.

Heat thunder rolled from the distant sky. They sat and watched the clouds roll by as the horses snorted and grazed nearby. The breeze had disappeared and they sat together huddled in the still heat. After a long spell of silence, Judith said, "Should we be getting back?"

"Probably," Emily said, but nobody moved for a spell just as long. Mark laid back, giving his arms a rest. Emily's head stayed where it comfortably rested as thunder roiled nearer. Mark closed his eyes and tried to distinguish between where he was now and a dream. He opened his eyes and was surprised to see the girls packing their things back into the picnic basket. He had dozed for a second. He jumped up and walked to the horses stretching his stiff muscles as he walked. The girls seemed nervous.

"What's the matter?" he asked.

"We all fell asleep. It's almost four o'clock. Mother will be worried."

Mark helped them mount and they rode back down into the field's bottom and back up the other side. As they neared the woods, a deer sprang out of the tall grass in front of Emily. Abbey wheeled, but Emily held on. Piper bucked, frightened more by Abbey than the deer. Judith did not hang on. She flew off the horse and landed in the high grass in less time than it took to say it. Mark quickly turned and rode back to Judith. He dismounted as her frightened horse bolted past them.

"Are you all right?"

"I think I had too much to drink."

Emily laughed, relieved. Mark stood up as her frightened mount disappeared down into the woods.

"My wrist hurts," Judith said. "How are we going to catch Piper?"

"We might not see Piper until we're back at the stable door," Mark said.

He looked up to see her frightened horse galloping over the ridge.

"What are we going to do?" Emily asked, suddenly alarmed.

"I'll tie the basket on Abbey. Judith can double up with me. We'll have to walk all the way back. Maybe Piper will stop running along the way, but I doubt it."

"It'll take hours," Emily said.

"Well then, let's get started."

They rode back the way they came. Judith sat behind Mark, her arms around his waist, occasionally leaning her head on his back. "I think I broke my wrist," she said.

"Of all the bad luck!" Emily said.

"Yeah," Mark agreed, wishing it was Abbey that had run off and Emily's small fist was clutching his shirt instead of Judith's.

It took them over two hours to walk back. They caught up to Piper about a mile from Pine Bluff. He was standing on his rein and was blowing hard when Mark caught him. Judith didn't think she could ride, so Mark ponied the horse behind him. As they climbed the last hill that overlooked the stable, they saw Mr. Harrison saddling up a horse. Emily gasped when she saw him.

"Em, ride ahead and tell him we're all right," Mark said. "Quickly, before he leaves."

As Emily galloped off, Judith rested her head on Mark's back and squeezed his waist. "Thank you, Mark. I don't know what we would have done without you there. Emily's lucky to have you."

Mark had barely run through half of the implications of that sentence before they reached the barn. Mr. Harrison rushed to the boy, and extended his hand.

"Thank you, Mark. I was so worried when it got so late. I only prayed that the girls had the good sense to bring you along."

He stepped to Judith, and helped her dismount. Mark looked at Emily and her eyes locked onto his. She said nothing, and he could not decipher the meaning fixed in her eyes. She followed her father and Judith as they headed to the house. Before she had gone too far, she turned and silently mouthed two words to Mark.

"Happy Birthday."

She blinked and turned away.

Jumping Fences

Daniel told Mark that he thought Emily had returned to Pine Bluff on the evening of July sixth, but he hadn't seen her. She didn't come down to the stable until the ninth, sixteen days after their picnic. She found Mark in the largest paddock taking Abbey over several jumps he had fashioned out of logs, and another from river stones. She watched him for several minutes from the barn entrance before going out to greet him.

"I didn't know she could do that!" Emily shouted. "She's beautiful!"

"Hey, Em! I didn't see you coming." He trotted over to the fence where she stood shading her eyes from the sun. "She can do a lot better than this. If we had some real jumps, I bet she'd go four feet or more. You want to try?"

"No," Emily said, "I don't think I'm ready for that."

"Someday," Mark said. "Are we riding today?"

She wore her usual riding habit, tan jodhpurs and white blouse, but Mark noticed the blouse lacked its customary crisp starched appearance, and her hair was unpinned.

"Could we?"

He dismounted, and raised his irons.

"Is Judith coming?"

"She's not here yet. Won't be back until next weekend."

"How's her arm?"

"It's badly sprained, but not broken. She's been in a sling. She had to drink all weekend one-handed."

Mark laughed. "How was your trip?"

"All right," Emily said unconvincingly.

"Did you–?"

"I don't want to talk about it now, Mark."

Mark looked at her and frowned.

"Why don't you try riding Ohio? That way I can just throw your saddle on him and we'll be off in a few minutes."

"I've never ridden anyone but Abbey, but if you think he'll behave–"

As they rode off, Mark asked, "Where do you want to go?

"Anywhere. I don't care."

Mark rode behind Emily watching her weight shift in rhythm with her horse.

"How's Ohio behaving?"

"Wonderful. I just think of a command, and he's already moving."

She seemed distant. Something in the cadence of her voice was different, as if she wasn't thinking of what she was saying, and he noticed her eyes did not meet his when she spoke.

"So, have we decided who's going to sit with the King of England at the party?

Emily let go of a tiny laugh. "What do you mean?"

"If you listen to anyone in town, you'd swear every famous person in the world is gonna be here."

She smiled politely, then sighed.

"It was strange being here in the summer without you here." Mark caught himself in mid-thought. Maybe he shouldn't say things like that to her. "Not that I see you that often, but–" He trailed off afraid he wasn't making himself clear.

"What's it like here in the winter?"

"It's a completely different place. You wouldn't recognize it. You can see all the other houses around the lake when the trees lose their leaves."

"I don't think I'd like that," she said. "I wonder about it sometimes. I try to picture everything at Christmas covered with snow. I hate Manhattan when it snows. Everything gets so dirty."

Mark couldn't imagine ever hating Manhattan.

"What do you do all winter?" she asked.

Mark explained his routines certain they sounded excruciatingly boring to someone like Emily.

"Do you ride?"

"If it's not below twenty," he answered. He explained that if a horse was too active in near zero temperatures, he could damage his lungs. "It's a fine line," he said. "They get jumpy if they're inside too long, but if they start going crazy when I let them out, they can hurt themselves. I have to watch them all the time."

He had the impression she wasn't listening, so he stopped talking.

"Are you all right?" he asked after they had walked for several minutes.

She inhaled deeply, her nostrils flared. She exhaled without looking at him.

"I'm just a little out of sorts." She shook her head as if trying to chase an annoying fly. She still did not look at him, her eyes raked the stony path. "Tell me about the ice harvest."

He told her all there was to tell, which wasn't much, but she seemed interested.

"It sounds dangerous," she said.

"Not really. Sometimes there's an air hole hidden under a thin surface, and a horse might fall through. But it's rare. I've only seen it happen once, I must have been about nine or ten"

"Did the horse die?"

"Oh no. It's not like that. Each morning, we fasten thick rope around the horses neck, with a slip knot on one end. You've probably seen the ropes hanging in the empty stall. We hang the rope over the hames of the harness. When the horse fell through the first man to reach him pulled on the rope. It shuts off the horse's wind so he won't struggle too much in the cold water. I remember the men running to help. Everything else stopped. Within minutes, men appeared with planks that they laid along the edge of the hole. They slid the longer boards under the horse and everyone helped pull him out."

"Oh my. How horrid! What happened to the horse?"

"Nothing. They covered him with blankets and walked him around a while until he calmed down and started breathing normally. But he was shot for the day. We had to get another horse after that."

"I should think so. How terrible! Did Abbey ever do that?"

Mark laughed. "No. We use Sleeper, the draft horse. These other horses couldn't pull a sleigh."

"No wonder I never see anyone riding that horse. He must be tuckered out for a year after that. How horrible!"

They rode for nearly an hour tripping over pieces of disjointed conversation. Emily jumped from topic to topic and then seemed to lose interest immediately and fell into gray silences. Mark had never seen her so distracted, and he thought it had something to do with her weekend away. She refused to talk about it.

A hawk's shadow crossed their paths and they looked up to watch it soar effortlessly above them in the cloudless sky.

"I wish I could fly like that," Emily said.

Mark looked around, wondering why the hawk lingered above them.

"Look. Do you see that rabbit over there by the pine tree?"

They halted the horses. She squinted in the direction Mark pointed as the hawk swooped down and speared the rabbit with its claws. It shuddered and went limp almost immediately. The hawk bounded back into the air with one powerful sweep of its wings but dropped the lifeless rabbit. Emily grunted as if it was she who had been dropped to the ground. The hawk seemed distracted by their presence and abandoned the dead rabbit rising to the top of a tall pine waiting for them to leave.

"You never want anything from me, do you, Mark?"

He felt he missed something, as if a page in a novel had been removed and he had skipped from page thirty to page thirty-three. He thought about her question. Who was he to want anything from her? And yet, in a rarely visited, barely acknowledged room in his heart, he knew vaguely that what she said was not true. Mark's face reddened.

"Why does that make you blush?" she asked.

He hoped she hadn't noticed. He shrugged.

"Why don't men ever show their feelings?" she asked.

"I think I show them too much." He couldn't feel more uncomfortable if he were the rabbit. "Let's ride," he said and cantered off.

"I hate it when you do that!" she screamed.

He rode down the path until he realized she wasn't behind him and he circled Abbey and returned to where she sat.

"Why is it that men–" she started to say with an anger she had never shown him before.

"Do you trust me?" he interrupted.

"Of course," she snapped. "I wouldn't be–"

"Then stop talking and follow me. Keep Ohio right on Abbey's tail. I won't go too fast. Keep your heels way down."

"Who do you–?" she started to protest but he narrowed his eyes and raised the fingers of his hand to silence her. She dropped her heels.

"More than that. Bury them in the air. Like that. Now follow me closely. Stop talking and stop thinking and relax. More than that. Take a deep slow breath and relax."

"But I–"

"You're talking again," he said struggling to sound stern. "Relax. Don't talk. "

He trotted up the path and veered to his left across a wide field. The field was separated from the next by an eighteen inch high hedgerow. Mark eased Abbey into a canter. He looked behind him. As he expected, Ohio had also started to canter. He slowed Abbey almost imperceptibly closing the distance between the two horses. He headed straight for the hedgerow and fired another quick glance over his shoulder. Emily was right there. As Abbey left the ground, he shouted "Heels down!" Ohio lifted his front legs over the hedgerow and with a fluid grace and ease landed in full stride. If Emily had been holding a glass of water, not a drop would have spilled. An excited short scream broke her silence. Mark looked back. She was still right behind him, a determined look of concentration on her face. He didn't stop. "Relax," he shouted. He quickened Abbey's canter and rode along the tree line. Halfway around the field dipped like a swell between waves in an ocean. Normally he would have walked down the hill for Emily's benefit. Mark called to her, "Hold the reins higher. Help him down the hill." He watched as she followed his lead. As they approached another hedgerow he looked behind him calibrating the distance between them and slowed Abbey again. He jumped the hedgerow and shouted, "Heels down." He turned to see Emily land the sweating horse again in full stride. He watched as her arms instinctively followed the horse's head. Her shoulders were relaxed, her heels down. A smile took sole possession of her face. Only then did he stop. He slowed Abbey to a walk and let Emily draw alongside of him. Her eyes teared from the wind in her face. He blinked at her the way she always did to him.

She started to speak, but changed her mind. They rode back to the barn in an embracing silence. Once or twice, for just a moment, she stopped smiling.

The following morning, Mark had Abbey and Ohio tacked and ready to go when Emily arrived at eight, even though she hadn't said she was coming. She met him at the barn door.

"It scares me how well you know what I need," she said.

They stood less than a foot apart, a distance Mark usually found uncomfortable with other people. He felt no instinct to back away.

"What do you need today?" he asked.

She looked at him squarely and said without facetiousness and without a smile, "You tell me."

A strange sensation overcame Mark. He felt as if he and Emily had leapt over a rocky chasm hand in hand and landed in a soft field. He looked at her and squinted.

"What's the matter?" she asked.

"Nothing," he said, nodding his head slowly as he spoke, and he smiled.

Mark's thoughts raced to Kristen and back again as he stood bewitched by Emily. He realized that he and Kristen had reached a similar chasm the night she ran into the rain and they had not leapt over it. For a hundred possible reasons, some that had nothing to do with Kristen, he had decided not to follow her. He tried to picture, for a moment, what he would have done had Emily been Kristen that night. He couldn't say with any certainty, except that he knew he would not have let the same thing happen. Had Emily repeated then what she had said to him the day before about him not wanting anything from her, Mark would have known that she was wrong. He did want something from her. It was deep inside of him, barely formed, but it was contained in that moment like an oak tree is contained in a tiny acorn. He wanted more. More carefree rides, more picnics, more conversations. The protective ice that he and she instinctively used as a shield to protect their vulnerability had in that moment, and possibly for only that moment, melted. He had never even kissed Emily, probably never would. But if he slept with Kristen a hundred more times, she might never touch him the way Emily did now. He knew then why he did not seek out Kristen when Emily was around and it had nothing to do with Kristen and everything to do with Emily.

"Yesterday when you asked me about the ice harvest reminded me of something I hadn't thought of in years. When I was a child, I used to think that under the ice, the water was always as warm as it stays all summer."

Emily smiled, sat and leaned back on the stacks of bundled hay as if preparing to enjoy a rare concert performance.

"I was maybe four or five, when I got scarlet fever. I was very sick. I think that might be the closest I ever came to dying. After I recovered, I did recover in case you were wondering how the story will turn out–"

Emily laughed. Raised her eyebrows and dropped them again quickly but said nothing to interrupt him. He lit a cigarette he didn't particularly want. He wished he hadn't started the story, but he had nowhere to go but forward.

"My mother told me I couldn't go outside and run around until winter was gone, that I had to give my body a chance to get strong again." He looked to her to make sure she was still listening. "I asked her if she would ask my father if he could move the winter early. I remember she looked at me like I was maybe a little crazy. Kind of the way you're looking at me now–"

Emily laughed.

"Every year, after the ice harvest, spring would arrive. You see, I thought my father moved winter by taking the ice away so we could use the lake again–that unless the men moved the ice, winter would never go away."

Emily laughed at his story. "You weren't a very bright child, were you?"

"No," he laughed. "The problem is I haven't learned much since then."

"Mark," she said, and hesitated for a moment as if selecting from a thousand different responses, "the hay is on fire."

"What? Oh jeez," he said and quickly stamped out the flaming strands of hay under his feet.

Emily mounted Abbey and led her out towards the lake, turned and watched as Mark poured water over the floor, making sure that the tiny fire did not spread.

When he caught up to her, she said, "I talked to Judith over the telephone today. We want you to come to the party."

"But I–"

"Just wear your suit. It's black tie, but all of the young people will just wear suits."

They rode an hour but the horses were jumpy, and Mark brought them back to Pine Bluff disappointed that he was unable to find the place they were the day before.

Emily's invitation threw Mark into a quandary. How could he go to the party? He already told Daniel he would help chauffeur the guests and had helped him make charts with different color wax crayons that paired guests from different hotels with drivers. As Daniel expected, most of the men in town offered their services, but half of them didn't have cars. Jackie's friend Pete insisted he could transport ten people at a time in the back of his father's Ford pickup and Daniel got into a hell of an argument while declining his ill-conceived offer. As it was, he ended up with twenty cars to transport eighty people, besides the dozen or so who would be staying on at Pine Bluff. Mrs. Harrison made it very clear who needed to be picked up on the first run, and who could wait for the return trip. She let it be known that all cars had to be washed, waxed and inspected by him before they would be let out. Mark heard the grumbling about how Daniel had gotten a swelled head from this party and he could just imagine what they all would say if they knew Mark was invited to attend.

Mrs. Harrison spent the month of July barking orders to Daniel for a host of jobs she needed to have done. Most of the work could not be started until Mr. Harrison left, but Daniel lined up workers who were poised to invade Pine Bluff the moment his car left the driveway. She insisted that all the fencing around Pine Bluff be whitewashed, including all the fencing around Mark's paddocks. She threw a hissy fit when Daniel told her there was no paint to be found, and he ended up killing an entire day driving twenty miles each way after he finally located some of the precious liquid up north. Mr. Harrison ran out of his house on the day Daniel and eleven hired boys started to paint the fences.

"What is the meaning of all this?" he asked.

"Mrs. Harrison wanted it done, sir."

Austin stormed back inside and his bellowing voice could be heard all the way down to the fence line.

Lucretia took to the party as if she were born to it. No detail was too small. She told Mark that she wanted horses placed in the paddock adjacent to the tent that was to be set up after Mr. Harrison was summoned back to Manhattan. She hired a professional photographer for the evening and she thought it would make a delightful photo to have horses in the background. Every night at supper, Daniel reported the newest whim of Mrs. Harrison. With each detail his mother asked the cost and become progressively agitated as if she was the one who had to pay the bills. "She's spending a year's salary for a one-day party," she complained to her husband as if he was a co-conspirator, "and she'll be asking me in two months why I only made thirty dollars selling her apples." Michael sat in a quiet derived from years of experience. Daniel said nothing. He had already made $43.90 on his cut from the eleven fence painters and he wouldn't want to waste all his time on apples either.

By July eighteenth, Mary had all she could take, and after arguing with her husband, took a train to her sister's house upstate where she vowed to stay "until this ridiculous party was done with."

Mark debated telling everyone of his invitation, but decided against it. Kristen was gone until August. He didn't even tell Daniel. He figured he'd have enough time to taxi the guests, return home to change into his suit, and go to the party before leaving early enough to return the guests to their hotels and no one needed to know he'd ever been there. His primary concern became his suit. He could only hope it arrived in time. Embarrassment prevented him from admitting to Emily that he didn't own a suit, and he was childishly flattered that she assumed he did. He shopped through the pages of his mother's Sears & Roebuck searching for the perfect suit, but he hadn't a clue about what kind to get. They all looked about the same, and they all looked good to him. The prices ranged from $6 to $12 and he couldn't tell from the pictures what made one any different from another. He decided on a $9 linen suit, and decided to splurge with another two dollars to purchase a straw hat. He had a hell of a time trying to measure his inseam, having to bend down and still get an accurate measurement. He mailed out his order the morning of the eleventh and realized that afternoon that he needed a dress shirt and shoes. The dress shirt was another dollar seventy-five, so he debated going without new shoes, figuring it would be dark and no one would see his boots. "In for a dollar, in for a dime," he decided and included four dollars for a new pair of black patent shoes. As an afterthought he ordered a black tie for twenty-five cents just to be on the safe side in case all the young people did not only wear suits, as Emily had said. He added a note with his order, "Please speed this along as I am going to a party on July 27th." For nearly sixteen dollars, he thought, Mr. Sears should hand deliver the damn things himself.

Called Away

July twenty-third arrived and Emily had still not told her mother about inviting Mark. She went downstairs to breakfast as Otis was serving Lucretia coffee and toast.

"Good morning, darling," Lucretia said.

"Good morning, mother," Emily said. "Just coffee for me, Otis."

Lucretia licked the point of her pencil and crossed an item from her list.

"Mother, I've invited Mark to the party." She put both hands on the table as if preparing for a quick escape.

"Mark Cabot?" Lucretia asked absently. "Such a fine young man."

"No, mother. Mark Lerner."

Lucretia stopped and squinted as if unable to quite place the name. "Mark–Lern–Oh Emily! How could you?"

"Judith asked me to. She said she'd have no one to talk to at her table. You placed her all the way at the back table with–with–nobody!"

"That girl has not yet discovered silence. She has the impropriety to speak to a street peddler. I have put her in between Richard Kinlaw and Frank Hoying who will be most eager to entertain her. Oh, Emily, how could you?"

"Mother, I asked you not to do that. That is a prison sentence for Judith. They're still in school, for goodness sakes. And it's not even a good school."

Austin Harrison walked into the dining room, newspaper in hand, interrupting the discussion.

"What's not a good school?" he asked.

Before he could open the paper, the front door bell rang.

"I'll see to that," he said.

Lucretia started in as soon as Austin left the room. "I've never heard of such a thing. Are we reduced to inviting the help to fill tables? What will everyone say?"

Emily started to protest as her father returned.

"That was Western Union. Stephan has wired from home," he said as he unfolded the yellow paper. His lips formed the words as he read the telegram silently to himself.

Small fire in office stop No one hurt stop Need you here to recreate contract stop Urgent you return today stop

"What is it?" Lucretia asked.

"It seems there was a small fire at the office. Stephan wants me to return today, but I think it can wait until Monday. I've a golf match today."

Lucretia gasped.

"Now don't fret," he said. " No one was injured. I'm sure it was nothing."

"Stephan would not have wired for nothing. If I know him, he downplayed the incident so as not to unduly alarm you."

"Perhaps you're right. Maybe I'll leave tomorrow."

Tomorrow would be impossible. Monsieur Coutreau was already en route, with a caravan of trucks behind him.

"Why, Austin, that's so unlike you to be so irresponsible!"

He sighed. "Perhaps you're right. I will telephone him."

Austin walked to the front hallway and picked up the telephone. As with all of Sullivan County, the Harrisons shared a party line with half a dozen other phone subscribers. He picked up the line and interrupted an ongoing conversation.

"I'm sorry, this is Austin Harrison. Please have Gertrude ring me when the line is available."

He walked slowly back into the dining room.

"What did he say?" Lucretia asked.

"The line's in use. I'll try him later."

Lucretia frowned. "I'll try the line myself," she said.

Lucretia shot Emily a reproachful look as she excused herself from the table.

"It appears I won't be playing golf today," he said to his daughter. "Could I entice you to come along. We'll be back by Friday or Saturday."

Emily stared at him blankly, as if he'd asked her to walk all the way to Manhattan.

"I'm sorry, Emily," he said. "That's selfish of me. Never mind."

"I'll go if you want," she said.

"No, no. You stay here and keep your mother company. I'm surprised we haven't any guests. You know how she gets when she's alone. She's been on edge for weeks."

Lucretia reentered the dining room. "The line is available," she said.

"Have Otis bring some juice and coffee," he said and returned to the phone. Lucretia muttered something under her breath about the inconsiderateness of "those people" on the party line, and drummed her fingers.

She lowered her voice to an angry whisper and said "I did not think I needed to explain to you, of all people, that there are some things that just aren't done. I declare you will be the death of me yet!"

Emily sat silently for a moment. "I'm sorry, Mother. You're right. I don't know what got into me. But what can be done now?"

"I will speak to the boy. Don't worry. I'll be diplomatic."

Emily drummed her fingers on the table, unconsciously mimicking her mother. The sound was muted by the white tablecloth. She rested her chin in her other hand and stared out the open window onto the porch.

"I suppose I must return," Austin said as he sat back down to the table. Have Otis bring the car around."

The women looked at one another. How had they overlooked Otis? Lucretia's hopes for a successful dinner rested largely on his talents in the kitchen..

Lucretia stammered. "We need Otis here!"

"Why dearest, surely you haven't completely forgotten how to fix a meal?"

"But he's working on an order that was delivered from the butcher today. He has meals partially prepared," she said. "If you take him along, we'll have to forfeit over twenty dollars worth of meat." She thought she could rely on her husband's disdain for waste.

"Perhaps Mark would like to drive you," Emily said. "I'm sure he'd love the time off."

"He's needed with the horses," Austin said. "Maybe Daniel–"

"Daniel's away," Lucretia blurted out as she looked quickly to Emily for help.

"Judith and I can feed. We've watched Mark do it all summer. I'll go speak to him now," and she rushed away from the table.

"Why is everyone in such a hurry this morning? I'm sure this is nothing that warrants getting the entire house in an uproar over!" he said. "You haven't touched breakfast," he called to the sound of the front screen door banging.

"I'll pack your bag," Lucretia said and left Austin alone in the dining room dazed by the speed of the women of his house.

Emily ran down to the barn, but Mark was out. She called his name from the open door and waited on the mounting block until he rode into view on a horse she did not recognize. Her hand shielded her eyes from the morning sun as he reached her and halted a black mare.

"We have a small emergency," she said.

"What is it?"

"How would you like to drive Daddy to New York?"

His eyes widened. "Are you serious?"

"You're the only one available," she said and explained their dilemma.

"What about the horses?"

"Tell me what to do. Judith and I can feed and turn them out."

He could not remember the last time he hadn't fed his horses. But what a spectacular opportunity! He had never spent more than one night away from Pine Bluff. Never. It was a nearly overwhelming prospect.

"Sure!" he said. "When?"

"Now," Emily said. "As soon as you can get ready. I'll help you pack your bag, if you'd like."

Mark blushed. He didn't have a bag. And then he remembered his suit. It would arrive by post in the next day or two. Who would accept the package?

"I don't have a bag."

"I'll go get one of Daddy's. I'll be back in a moment."

"I don't need one," he said. "I'll use this," and he waved a sack as she turned towards her house.

He realized he had to tell Emily about the suit.

"Hey, Em?" he called to her.

She spun around, and he noticed the wrinkle on her brow.

"I need a favor back. I have a new suit coming– I– I need you to accept the package, and maybe bring it to my room."

"Oh, Mark. How sweet. You didn't need to get a new suit."

He couldn't begin to explain why he felt so small at that moment, and enormously foolish. His shoulders sagged involuntarily as Emily ran toward the house.

Manhattan

Mark was ready in five minutes. He hastily wrote instructions for feeding his horses on an empty feed bag and hung it on a nail on his bedroom door. After checking to make sure there was enough pellets and grain for three days, he threw a change of clothes into his sack along with his toothbrush and comb, and stood at the main house porch before Mr. Harrison appeared. As he packed his extra pair of trousers and two shirts he tried to remember if he ever saw Emily wear the same outfit twice. She even had four or five riding habits best he could tell. He sat on the porch step and studied the Harrison's Dusenberg. It was quite a bit different from the Model A's that provided all his prior driving experience.

Austin Harrison arrived with a small leather grip and after a businesslike smile and a perfunctory "good morning" entered the car taking a position in the back seat. Mark looked to the porch hoping to see Emily before he left, and climbed into the driver's seat taking the keys from Mr. Harrison.

He sat puzzled for a moment. He felt the fool, but was dazzled by the chrome and wooden appointments of the auto. 'The Spirit of St. Louis' probably managed with fewer gauges.

"Where do they go?"

Mr. Harrison took the keys from his hand and leaned forward slipping them into the ignition.

"Are you certain you're up to driving ?" he asked.

Mark swallowed hard. The car seemed enormous, but he assured Mr. Harrison that after a few moments, he would be fine. He put the car in gear and lurched forward. A look of concern flashed on Mr. Harrison's face in the rearview mirror but he crossed his legs and drew the newspaper between them like a curtain. It took several miles before Mark could smoothly shift the column mounted stick but before they reached Main Street he was changing gears smoothly. He hoped someone might see him driving that beautiful green machine, but no one was about that morning. He fought a horse-riding impulse of squeezing his legs together to make the car go forward, but after five miles or so he was gliding along evenly in the proud machine.

"When's the last time you've been to Manhattan?" Austin asked the boy.

Mark's eyes met the man in the mirror, then flashed back onto the road.

"I've never been, sir."

Mr. Harrison's eyebrows popped a silent response, and his face reddened in an apparent embarrassment that made Mark even more uncomfortable.

"Emily's told me so much about it, that I sometimes think I've been, though."

"There's no substitute for being in New York. It's not like being anywhere else. Least of all Barryville. I'll see if we can't set up a bit of a tour for you. We might not return until late Thursday or Friday. You'll have your fill by then, I should say."

"How soon do we arrive?"

Austin laughed. "The entire trip is one hundred and six miles. I dare say five hours, six if we hit traffic crossing over from New Jersey."

"Do we take the Holland Tunnel?" Mark had seen pictures of the tunnel construction and had dreamed of driving through some day.

Austin laughed. "Seven years of building and it's still not finished. Should be soon. Maybe by the end of the year. We'll have to content ourselves with the Bear Mountain Bridge. We'll drive down along the East River, through Harlem. It's lovely this time of year. A lot of Emily's friends have summer cottages there, but the Negro population is growing rapidly and I'm afraid some day the countryside will be swallowed up into the city."

They drove through the pastoral monotony of New Jersey. They'd go fifteen or twenty minutes without passing anything save an occasional farm tractor. As best as Mark could tell, more cows lived there than people. The rhythmic thumping of the tires on the concrete roadways made Mark drowsy and they stopped three times in the hills of New Jersey for pop or coffee. Mark liked walking into the roadside stores with all eyes on him and the Dusenberg. He reveled in being a stranger, comforted somehow, in the fact that no one knew who he was. He wasn't Mark Lerner here. He was anyone he wanted to be.

It wasn't hard to pass the time with Mr. Harrison. He read his paper part of the way. Slept some, and would intermittently tell Mark what to expect from the city. Every twenty minutes or so, like a scheduled radio broadcast, Mr. Harrison began speaking on a topic totally unrelated to his last. They covered a lot of ground. He told Mark about the rivalry between the nearly completed Chrysler building and the Empire State building. The Empire State building opening was delayed when a corporate spy discovered that the Chrysler building was going to be taller. The architects went back to the drawing boards and added more stories. "It's a race to the sky," Austin said with no little awe.

He told Mark about Wall Street and the little artist colony downtown. He warned him to be wary of the speakeasies.

"A cocktail might cost you a dollar," he said. "But a bottle of water could cost you twice as much. You'd be better served to avoid them altogether. While I'm thinking of it, there are nickels in the glove box. Be sure to take a handful for the subways. You can ride all day for a nickel," he said, "but you have to pay every time you reenter."

Mark suddenly tired of the journey and was impatient for the New York skyline to appear onto his windshield. Three hours into the trip and it seemed they were on a treadmill passing the same farms, climbing the same hills and passing the same roadside service stations over and over again. He felt the sun beating on his arm hanging out the open window and the wind blowing through the car. Heat from the engine blew onto his reddened face.

Without warning, trees began to dwindle in number and for every absent tree ten cars appeared in a mystifying urban ratio. The streets seemed to narrow and cars passed on all sides of Mark at dizzying speeds. The cars coming toward them in the northbound lanes passed within a few feet of Mark, and he pulled his arm from the window ledge lest he lose it to a passing motorist. Each car that passed took his breath away and he slowed with each one until the line of cars that had suddenly appeared behind him started an impatient growling of horn blasts. He had maintained a safe speed of nearly twenty-five but the cars around him must have been going thirty-five, maybe even forty miles per hour. They crossed over the Bear Mountain Bridge with Mark fighting every impulse to shut his eyes. He felt the bridge shake as he crossed and sped up hoping to be on the other side in the event of a collapse. As they exited the bridge Mark followed Mr. Harrison's directions around the narrow curves of the mountain. Cars behind him would not be content until he reached the speed of an airplane and tried to help him along with their horns. He watched helplessly as the exit ramp Mr. Harrison had pointed out flew past.

"That's all right. We can take the Harlem River Drive."

"Mr. Harrison–" he said, trying to quell the panic he felt.

"Why don't you pull over here, Mark. I know these streets a little."

Mark hand signaled out the open window and pulled onto the gravel shoulder as the line of cars passed him with a chorus of reviews about his driving skills. Once in the safety of the passenger seat, Mark took his eyes off the road and saw that they already were in the midst of the city. Tall buildings flanked the multi-laned highways. He looked behind him to see if he had missed a gate or some marking of the entrance to the greatest city in the world.

"That is the Bronx," Mr. Harrison said. "Coming up on your left will be the brand new Yankee Stadium. Are you a baseball fan?"

"I follow it some," Mark answered. "I read that Grantland Rice thinks Babe Ruth might break his own record for home runs this year."

"I wish we had more time. I'd love to bring you into the stadium for a ball game. It's truly something to see. Having only a daughter–" he started to say, but interrupted himself. "Following a game in the papers is a poor substitute for seeing it in person. Maybe another time."

His words barely registered as Mark sat with open mouthed awe at the gigantic bowl shaped stadium passing slowly on his left. So many times he had read the words "Yankee Stadium", and suddenly it was as real as Turtle Rock. Mark was surrounded by a hundred sights any one of which would have been amazing on its own. Together they shaped a confusing visual symphony that provided a colorful kaleidoscope more riveting than a newsreel. They entered Manhattan, the buildings grew taller still. Every store imaginable was lined up next to one another and then, in just a few short blocks, the same type of stores repeated themselves. Clothing stores, haberdasheries, restaurants of all kinds, some so crowded that customers were forced to sit outside. Milliners, tailors, shoemakers, enough to cater to the world. More stores in fifty yards than were in all of Sullivan County combined. Mark was astounded at how serenely Mr. Harrison took all of this. He seemed to hardly notice a thing. They drove down First Avenue, the view of the East River passing in and out of sight like the sun through the trees of a forest.

Mr. Harrison looked over to Mark, as he halted the car in front of a large canopy that stretched out from a building whose roof Mark could not see from the curb.

"You can start breathing again," Austin laughed. "We're here."

A uniformed man rushed to the car door opening it for Mr. Harrison as another opened Mark's door. They greeted Mr. Harrison by name and called Mark "Sir". He looked at the epaulets of their coats, like majors in Napoleon's army and figured he should be calling the doormen "Sir". What a strange place! What an exhilaratingly strange place.

They took an elevator to the twelfth floor, and as the elevator operator opened the brass accordion gate, Mark lifted his sack and Mr. Harrison's grip and followed him into the corridor. The doorman who rode with them took both from Mark's hand giving him a leering look in exchange. There were two doors on opposite ends of the long hall. The elevator operator took a key from Mr. Harrison and opened the nearest door. The corridor was the single nicest room Mark had ever been in. The walls were covered in a green velvet and gray wallpaper and gold sconces shone every few feet splashing the hallway with arcs of flickering light. Molding a foot wide edged the ceiling, and portraits in wide gold frames hung every ten feet or so from picture molding that rimmed the room. Islands of carpet cushioned the walk across white marble floors.

As grand as the hallway was, it was but a Spartan mimicry of the inside of the Harrison apartment. Mark felt as if he was entering the palace of an Arabian sheik. Dark rich woods, flowing heavy drapery, gold and silver lamps, Persian carpets displaying every color in the spectrum. Paintings of pastoral scenes in heavy gilded frames, oval mirrors with beveled glass edges, walls lined in fabric, deep cushioned sofas hidden by an array of pillows. Tables that held leather books, photographs, vases and glass statuary of every conceivable shape and color. Mark saw instantly that everything he had come to know as luxury, all the Harrison rooms in Pine Bluff, were rustic in comparison to the winter residence that the Harrisons thought so little of that it was never even mentioned in passing. He pictured Emily floating through the rooms in long flowing gowns, pictured servants bringing her eggs in little glass egg holders like he'd seen in films and he suddenly and inexplicably felt as deflated as last year's balloon.

Mr. Harrison went down a hall into another room and when he returned Mark had not yet moved.

"Make yourself at home," he said, waving his arm in a sweeping gesture.

"How?" Mark thought.

"Do you need something to drink?"

"No, sir." Mark felt overwhelmed, his senses overloaded. "Do you think I might rest a few moments?"

"Yes, of course. How thoughtless of me. You've been driving all day. Take the guest room. It's the third door on your right. Please, Mark, help yourself to anything. I'm afraid there's no food, but I called Benjamin and they'll send something up shortly."

Mark entered the guest bedroom already desensitized to the luxury. He took off his shoes and laid down on a bed topped by the most comfortable coverlet he had ever touched. He sank into the softness of the bed and fell asleep instantly.

He awoke less than an hour later in a momentary state of confusion. Nothing was familiar, and a splash of panic passed over him like a cold breeze. He went to the window, drew the curtains and stepped back involuntarily. He was higher than he had ever been before. Higher, by a ways, than airplanes flew. He leaned forward without moving his feet closer to the window and looked down to the East River. Barges floated by, some pushed by tug boats, in such quantity that Mark was certain a collision was imminent. Miniature cars flew by on the street running alongside the river below and it took several seconds for Mark to realize what made the sight seem so eerie. He was above the sound, encased in a silent ether that added to the dreamlike quality of his surroundings. Where was everyone going in the middle of a workday?

He walked back into the parlor finding a note for him by his sack.

Dear Mark,

I need to go to the office. I have told Benjamin to get you whatever you need. He is the building manager and will get you a taxi or direct you wherever you wish to go. Take his telephone number and call him or me if you need. Save a nickel for the telephone booth. Remember, you are on Sutton Place and 54th Street. The streets run east to west. The avenues north to south. Enjoy the city, but don't wander too far today. Tomorrow I will find you an escort to show you around.

A.H.

He was momentarily paralyzed by the choices he had. He was in New York City and he could do anything he wanted to do. Anything. Anything at all. He had absolutely no idea what that should be. He walked around the apartment, touching everything. He entered Emily's room as he would a shrine. A canopy enveloped her bed that sat so high off the ground that it had a step stool at the side to help her climb in. There was a doll house on a corner table filled with miniature furnishings like the ones in the apartment, complete in every breathtaking detail. There were dolls on a shelf. A small porcelain faced doll was holding hands with a boy doll much smaller. The girl doll wore a gown and a tiny toy horse rested between them. He took it from the shelf and a hind leg fell off, apparently broken for years, but saved nonetheless. He replaced the horse moving on to the next item as if he was in a museum of Emily. There were hats everywhere. He caressed the rich velvet and ran the satin of ribbons through his fingertips. He picked up her atomizer and smelled the fragrance that he had come to recognize as hers. The closeness of her suddenly felt very uncomfortable and he left her room hurriedly.

There was no part of the afternoon that did not strike Mark either with its novelty or absurdity. He was aware that no one around him shared his awe of the commonplace and their callousness to the subtleties of city life was just another ingredient of his amazement. Within the Harrison's Sutton Place building he could do nothing for himself. Doors were opened for him, elevators summoned and operated. Caps were tipped and cars offered. Once he stepped from under the awning of the tall building his stature plummeted quicker than the elevators that brought him to ground level. Outside he was an inconsequential ant in the army that he had watched chaotically marching from the twelfth floor window.

He walked in circles across 54th Street down Second, left on 52nd back to Sutton. Then larger circles. Across 57th all the way to Fifth.

Down to 45th and back again. He passed an endless array of buildings, many with wrought iron gates and some with canopies that stretched out to the curb of the cobblestone streets. Mark read the names of the buildings on brass plaques. Most buildings had doormen poised like soldiers ready to step to the assistance of the building's residents.

The streets were cluttered with double-decker buses, the open air upper tiers the preferred location on such a summer day. He passed the recently completed Hotel Dorset, its bricks still clay colored and new. Walked along the Hotel St. Regis and stood across the street watching the pretty people coming and going, the women in long gowns, the men with sticks and top hats. There was apparently no shortage of wealthy people in New York. Mark wondered how many knew the Harrisons. Or Emily.

Mark was glad he wore his Sunday cotton trousers and best collared shirt. No one dressed in the overalls or heavy denim cotton work pants he wore at home. He started out greeting everyone he passed until it became impossible and he walked by returning the blank stares of strangers in a rudeness that would have been unthinkable at home. At every corner he stopped and watched the parade of automobiles and trucks that stuttered past him at breakneck speeds often weaving around horse-drawn wagons that plodded down the cobblestone streets. Mark wondered about the effect of the hard stones on their hooves until, upon closer inspection, he realized shoes were the least of their problems. The horses dragged over-laden wagons displaying their rib cages in gestures of surrender, but were ignored or beaten. He spoke to a Negro rag man, his cart filled with discarded refuse, who told him his horse was seven years old. Mark would have guessed twenty-two or twenty-three.

The man laughed. "I ain't known a horse to reach eight years 'round these parts."

Mark winced. Abbey was ten and fit enough to go out for two or three hours at a stretch.

He stopped in several shops along the way. He wanted to purchase another shirt and some penny postcards for home. He found a shirt he liked but it cost three dollars so he closed his two silver dollars in his hand and left the store. After passing a half dozen storefronts with the European sounding "Antique Shop" printed below their awnings, he entered one, but it was only filled with used old things and he left again.

The sun left the streets early blocked by a phalanx of buildings to the west and Mark returned to the relative familiarity of the Harrison apartment about six.

Mr. Harrison was home and they shared a dinner supplied by Benjamin. Mark told him about the horses.

"There won't be a horse anywhere on this island in a few years. Mark my words," he said. "It'll be better for everyone. Perhaps one day people will travel throughout the city on a monorail."

Mark had read about monorails in Jules Verne, and had a futuristic drawing of New York in the year 2000 safely tucked away in his cigar box at home. Dirigibles floated over monorails in a pristine concrete landscape. What had seemed so fanciful in the drawing seemed nearly possible to him now.

Mark listened to the radio with Mr. Harrison until nine, and returned to his room. He was awakened several times during the night by the heat trapped between buildings and the unfamiliar sounds that bounced off the tall silhouettes all night. He watched barges passing in the river or autos on the road, their lights creeping in front of them as they blew through the streets like tumbleweeds in a paved desert. He could not imagine where people were off to in the middle of the night, but every time he awoke lights were visible somewhere. Sleep came at uneven intervals, but Mark did not care, relishing the opportunity to spy on this sleepless city.

After breakfast Mr. Harrison taxied Mark with him to his office in the Flatiron Building on 23rd Street. They rode down Fifth Avenue until it intersected with Broadway. Once inside, small armies of smartly dressed people greeted Mr. Harrison every step of the way.

He entered his inner office and said, " Send in the Smith boy."

"Pardon me?" Mark said.

"I was speaking to my secretary, Miss Harms."

Mark looked over his shoulder seeing no one.

"On this," Mr. Harrison said. "It's an intercom."

He pushed a button on the brownish-green machine and asked, "Is Stephan in yet?"

"No, Mr. Harrison," a squawking voice answered.

Mark stood speechless until a young man about his age entered the office dressed in a white shirt and collar, black pants and a green shade.

"Mark, this is Quinton Smith. He will show you about today, and I'll see you this evening at home."

Mark followed the young man out to the elevators and down into the street. No one greeted them as they had several minutes earlier. Quinton said nothing until they reached the sidewalk.

"This is the best spot in the city for watching dames," he said. "Because of the triangle shape of this here building the wind rips up Fifth and blows the girl's skirts like crazy. You're apt to get an eyeful at any moment. Even on a calm day."

Mark nodded, but said nothing. Within minutes Quinton's prediction unfolded as girls' skirts swept up revealing stockings and garters amidst the whistles from appreciative men loitering nearby. Mark thought the girls might be embarrassed, but they seemed to mind only a little. Quinton winked at Mark.

"I know all the best places to see girls. Stick with me, kid."

Mark nodded again although he was several steps behind Quinton. He took Mark to a dozen of the best places in the city to watch girls. He jingled nickels in his pockets incessantly and shook like a tambourine player when a particularly pretty girl passed by. He took Mark down into the catacombs of the subways with the practiced agility of a rat into the hold of a ship. They lingered at Macy's on 34th Street where Quinton informed Mark, in a conspiratorial whisper, that they were likely to see uptown girls. This meant nothing to him but he thought he would seem a little more worldly if he nodded a silent approval. They went up Broadway to the brand new Roxy theater where Mark took one of four thousand seats to watch his first movie extravaganza. A piano player played along with the film. Mark's eyes barely made it to the screen so impressed was he with the palace that surrounded and humbled him. After the show, they continued along Broadway past the Capital Theater, the Palace and the Criterion. Each grander than the last. Quinton took quickly to Mark and showed him all the ropes.

As they passed yet another theater Quinton said, "See that sign? Air cooled for your comfort?.

Mark nodded.

"The old crook what owns it heats the lobby all summer. Makes you wait ten minutes before going in. That's how he cools the theater, the old bastard."

Mark laughed.

"You think I'm joking?"

"No," Mark said, not wanting to offend.

"Where you from, anyway?"

"Upstate. Four or five hours away."

"Got nice looking girls there?"

Mark smiled, relieved that Quinton didn't ask him about Sullivan county. What could he possibly say that would mean anything to someone who roamed the streets of Manhattan with the expertise of J. Pierpont Morgan walking a bank. Mark took the bit and rambled on about the girls back home, trying his best to sound like Daniel. He embellished a little, the way Daniel would. He wished his brother were here now. He and Quinton spoke the same language and Mark would have preferred to listen to them.

"You ever get a girl in a hay loft?" Quinton asked.

"Sure," Mark lied.

"Damn. I always wanted to do that. I hear tell Mr. Harrison's got a daughter who's a real looker."

"Yes, she is. I mean, he does."

"I bet she wouldn't give guys like us the time of day."

"She's not like that," Mark said, but wondered all the same if Quinton was right.

Mark crossed Broadway with a bit of a strut after that. They parted ways on Third and 54th. The clock centered on the traffic light tower read half past six. Mark shook Quinton's hand enthusiastically.

"Thanks for the tour," he said.

"No problem, Country. Save me one of them hay-loft girls. I may just come on up one day."

Quinton hailed a cab, and Mark spun towards home feeling every bit the New Yorker.

Despite the miles he covered during the day, Mark was unable to sleep. He looked down at the barges and poked his head out of the window to try to listen to the sounds. There was a steady breeze twelve stories up, but it was incapable of penetrating the opening of the windows. He looked to the sky searching for a familiar constellation, something he might recognize. New York did something to him. Made him look at himself in a funny way. Made him feel small, like he wouldn't be missed at all if he fell into a manhole. But alive too. Like he was a part of something grand. He looked again to the stars, so dim compared to the lights on Broadway.

The next morning Mark woke alone again in the Harrison apartment. There was another note informing him that he should return no later than two for the return trip home. He wondered about this as Emily had made it clear that her father must be detained until Saturday afternoon. When he went to the lobby, Benjamin informed him that a messenger had arrived for him.

"For me?"

"Not ten minutes ago."

A message from Stephan Harrison asked for Mark's assistance in delaying their return to Pine Bluff. Mark called him using the telephone on Benjamin's desk. It was one of those new phones with the speaker and receiver in one piece and Mark felt self-conscious using it. Mark suggested they call the garage and bring the mechanic into their confederacy, which Stephan agreed was a "capital" idea. Stephan spoke to Benjamin a moment and returned to Mark with instructions about where to bring his brother's car.

Quinton was not provided because Mr. Harrison expected an early departure and the day hung enticingly before Mark. He decided to venture into the subways himself, start downtown and work his way back determined to cram in as much New York as possible.

He walked to Fifth Avenue and took the subway tunneling eventually to the lower East Side. The city that greeted him as he climbed the stairs back to the surface was substantially different from the one he left uptown on Fifth. There were no gentlemen with walking sticks. No women in gowns. This was not a postcard view that Mark could send back home. He felt as if the city had been flipped upside down and he had exited the subway in its underbelly as disconnected from glamour as the engine room of a steamer is from beautiful ocean views.

"Immigrants," he said to himself feeling a fear that surprised him. He didn't feel physically threatened by anyone, but realized after weaving through a congested block that he feared the hollow look in the faces of so many people. No light came from their eyes and Mark shied from that seemingly contagious blank stare as if they were coughers in a tubercular ward.

He thought of Kristen living here but could not summon a clear image of what that might have been like. She had said that she once lived "downtown". Surely she did not mean a place like this. She seemed far too vulnerable for this city.

Women wore long skirts of coarse fabric that looked entirely too hot for a summer's day. Men wore baggy pants, damp sleeveless undershirts and suspenders under ratty sweat-marked caps of browns and blacks. Mark was not ignored as he had been uptown, but spoken to harshly, often in foreign tongues, and pushed aside as he stood in the middle of this tepid wave of swarming humanity. He walked east and decided to take the first bus that was heading uptown. He did not want to return to the subways past the threatening gang of youths hovering by the stairway like vultures. Sidewalks were packed with peddlers selling bruised fruits and limp vegetables that would have been thrown away at home. Dead animals like suicide victims hung from string, covered in brandy-colored sauces that failed to camouflage their vileness. The combined smells baked in the morning heat creating an olfactory cloud that he could not escape. If he stopped to find his bearings, he was jostled and pushed along, and he tried to maneuver around best as he could. Mongrel dogs ran through the legs of the passers-by, ignored by everyone. The noise was cumbersome. It seemed that the smallest commerce resulted in vigorous arguments in unintelligible words.

Buildings were clustered together like broken down crates in a railroad yard. Not the majestic buildings of uptown, but stubby structures, three and four stories tall, with fat old women squeezing out of nearly every window. It seemed that all of the ragged people were speaking at once. Rope clothes lines sagged from building to building as though the rope alone held the dirty brick buildings upright. Gray laundry hung limply from every line like the flags of defeated nations. Amidst the tumult children ran, shouted and played in ill-fitting clothing that made them look like dwarfish adults trapped in a momentary youth. He attracted a choir of young children who pestered him for pennies. Once he emptied his pocket they multiplied like maggots until finally, a block away, convinced no more pennies were forthcoming, they released him from their clamoring. He was forty blocks from home. A hundred miles from Pine Bluff.

He saw a bus and ran towards it, pushing his way clear through the crowded streets, but he missed it. He planted himself at the bus stop sign, donning his newly acquired impervious mask of passivity. Once he stopped walking, the people did not look quite as menacing. Individually they looked almost normal. He watched a poor European woman reach into her deep pocketed skirt for a piece of red candy and watched the universal joy in her child's eye. He walked further north to the next bus stop, the streets marginally less crowded.

A horse-drawn ice wagon passed and he watched closely as the ice man donned a leather apron and hoisted a large block onto his back. He wondered if it was his ice. He felt a camaraderie with the man and he wanted to run to tell him that he had provided that ice. He exhaled deeply as he recognized his role. Never had he given any thought to where his ice ultimately arrived. He felt proud that he played a part in that great New York machine, but was vaguely dissatisfied that it was such a tiny part. He watched the ice man look upwards at cardboard signs displayed in the apartment windows that flashed instructions as to how much ice should be delivered that day. The man made notes in a tiny pad, and pulled ice tongs from the side of the wagon. The huge blocks Mark pulled from the lake in January had been reduced by thirty percent or more. They seemed small as the ice man pulled them from the back of the wagon. Mark watched as children chased the wagon diving for splinters of ice that sometimes fell like shards of glass onto the cobblestone streets. He thought of the ice house back home and the ice stacked twenty feet high in a depository that now seemed an embarrassment of riches. He followed the wagon for several blocks until another bus rescued him twenty minutes later.

He sat on the upper level in the back and looked behind him. He expected to see the immigrants rushing behind him to attach themselves to the only visible means of escape from their squalor. Why didn't they? Didn't they know what life could be like? The bus weaved along the streets that no longer followed Mr. Harrison's rules of east and west, north and south, and it occurred to Mark that Mr. Harrison had no idea what was down here. He stayed on the bus for hours, feeling safe in his height as it passed through the various villages that coalesced into this metropolis. When the bus returned several hours past noon to the market area he arrived at earlier, it didn't seem quite as threatening.

He marveled at the proximity between opulence and poverty. There seemed no overlap, it was all or nothing and he wondered where he fit in this grand scheme. To the men in top hats and sticks was he anything more than a dirty stable boy, a common laborer? To the ragged penny-seeking children was he not a wealthy outsider who, had they only known, lived on horses in a virtual Eden? And again his thoughts ended at Emily as it seemed all his thoughts had that summer. What was he to her? In his mood of candor, he hastily admitted to himself that, yes, he had thought of them being together. But only briefly and he quickly banished the thought. Ashamed, almost, that he was naive enough to believe it was remotely possible–and afraid that someone might see that thought in his eyes and justifiably ridicule him for it. What was he to Emily?

A craving overtook him and he wished he was riding Ohio with Emily behind him on Abbey galloping through a field blindly towards the sun. West. Away from New York.

Dancing

Mark walked toward the tents with the grace of a tone deaf dancer. An eerie light from the flicker of gas lanterns hovered over the gathering of guests. The white stripes of the tents shone iridescently in contrast to the dark green stripes that swallowed the feeble light. A hum of voices echoed off the high tent ceiling like the sound of geese under a low cloud cover. A warm summer gust blew under the tent and billowed the canvas like a wind-filled sail. He saw Ohio and Abbey running and kicking in the paddock closest to the tent and heard their distressed whinnying as they tried to make sense of the aberrant carnival. They would be a handful tomorrow, he thought, and fought an instinct to return them to the sanctuary of the barn. Mark lingered in the safety of the shadows. He noticed that none of the men at the party wore straw hats and he took his off and flipped it into the darkness. An orchestra that he could not see began playing a lively number and the buzz of conversation rose like the crest of a wave. Ohio kicked at the plank of the fence sending splinters flying dangerously close to the tent and Mark decided to fight his instinct no longer.

He walked through the middle of the tent glad to have a purpose for his entrance. More than a dozen round tables formed a half circle around the orchestra, and Mark felt that every eye followed his deliberate march to the horses. Under the tent, the smell of hundreds of fresh flowers permeated the festive air. Large overflowing centerpieces dominated each table in sprays of Stargazer lilies and Queen Anne's Lace in a blend of whites, pinks and burgundies that commanded attention even in the flickering light of the lanterns. There was so much to see that he saw nothing. Extraordinary color intertwined with abnormal sounds overloading his normal sensory reactions. He saw his surroundings as if through tear filled eyes. As he walked through the tent his foot hit the hard surface of a portable wooden dance floor and slipped out from under him. No one seemed to notice his stumbling because Ohio chose that moment to kick the bottom plank of the fence creating an unimpeded gateway to the crowd. Mark arrived at his horse as the city dwellers screamed and collectively moved to the far end of the tent. The orchestra stopped playing in mid-song except for a closed eyed flutist blissfully unaware of the turmoil. Mark reached Ohio, glad to see that Emily had left his halter on.

"Ohio, it's me, Mark," he said and grabbed a hold of the halter. Ohio threw his head back, but Mark did not let go. The horse's ears were pinned to his neck, and the whites of his eyes flashed a silent alarm. He noisily exhaled a nervous breath through vibrating lips as he recognized Mark. "It's all right, Ohio," he said and took his hand and cupped it around the horses nose above the nose band of the halter to calm him. He stood motionless with his left hand on the horse's neck until the terrified horse calmed to a manageable state of fear. Mark backed Ohio away from the tent toward the gate, and untied the lead line wrapped around the fence post. Emily's horse, Abbey, reacted to the unfolding events by dancing around the paddock in wide high-stepping circles and only now decided to follow Mark and Ohio to the darkened corner of the paddock.

As Mark regained control of his horses, a man's voice hollered "Good show, old chap!" and the crowd broke into a spontaneous applause. The band hastily began a rendition of "For He's A Jolly Good Fellow" and the revelers sang out in great relief. As the orchestra resumed its program, Ohio and Abbey sidestepped away on lead lines like dancers pirouetting around Mark's outstretched arms.

He talked to the horses all the way back to the barn. They calmed to his familiar voice. "If you didn't want to go to the party, you should have said something," he told them. "I don't know what you're complaining about. At least you didn't have to wear a suit." The horses stopped blowing, and Mark delivered them to the safety of their stalls. He threw an extra bale of hay on the floor and closed the door of the stable behind him, hoping to shield them from further evidence of the party. He returned to the tent feeling relaxed for the first time since he left for Manhattan earlier in the week.

"Ah, it's the man of the hour!" a stranger said as he reentered the tent. Someone else offered him a drink as yet another pressed one into his hand. His buttonless cuff erupted from his jacket sleeve as he raised the glass to his lips. He took a long swallow from the amber ice filled glass but the burning liquid did nothing for his thirst. He coughed as his eyes teared.

"You've lost your cufflinks in the fracas," a jacketless man said. "Here, take mine. I'd be honored," and he proceeded to undo his own silver links and forced them on an overwhelmed Mark before he could offer a refusal. Mark had not lost his cufflinks, merely forgot to order them with his suit, and had tied little pieces of wire together to hold his cuffs together. The man rolled his sleeves as the young woman he was speaking to moved to Mark and wordlessly took the cufflinks from his hand. She placed the links in her mouth, as his mother held pins while sewing, and expertly folded his cuff over once and inserted the silver links through four newly aligned buttonholes of his shirt. Mark hoped the light was insufficient to reveal his blushing face, but the young girl noticed and flashed him a smile.

"That was quite an entrance," she said. "The Vice President will certainly be jealous."

Mark looked at the girl for the first time. Her short black curls peeked out from a wide brimmed hat. She wore a long plain silk dress, and the light behind her silhouetted her figure. Mark got the impression that she was not unaware of the effect. Her lips were painted red, and her cheekbones were heavily blushed.

"Has he arrived?" Mark asked.

"Not in your grand style," she said. "He's over there standing by Austin Harrison."

Mark looked over to where the girl pointed. Charles Dawes anchored the end of an impromptu receiving line. Mark stared at him a long moment. He was every bit as imposing as Mark imagined. His silver hair parted in the center topped a stern unsmiling face as a long queue of guests awaited his handshake and personal greeting. He was shorter than Mr. Harrison who stood beside him sliding his finger in his collar as if it was too tight. Mark scanned the room for Emily, but did not see her.

"I'm Patrice," the girl said and extended her hand to Mark confidently. "Who are you with?"

"Mark," he said. "I mean I'm Mark and I'm not really with anyone. I mean, I was invited, but I don't really know anyone, except Emily and Judith. And the Harrisons, of course–"

"Well, we'll need to correct that, now won't we," she said. "Martin, Jonathan, come meet Mister–" she paused and looked at Mark.

"Lerner," he said.

"Mister Mark Lerner."

He was certain no one had ever called him that before. It sounded foreign to his ear. The men moved to them and shook his hand. They were followed almost immediately by two other girls, and an older man with a dreadfully crooked nose.

"Are you a Saratoga Lerner? Martin asked him.

"I have an aunt who lives near there. In fact my mother is there now."

"Oh splendid! I know your aunt. I clerked in her husband's law office."

Mark was about to explain that there was some mistake, that his aunt was a widowed seamstress, but Patrice came back with two drinks in her hands and insisted Mark take one off her hands.

"I had a boyfriend a moment ago," she said in an actress' loud voice. "But he's left me alone too long. I shall have to recruit another," and she raised the back of her hand to her forehead while the others laughed.

Mark felt exhilarated. He had spent weeks dreading a solitary vigil while strangers silently eyed him, or worse, ignored him completely. And here he was, surrounded by new friendly faces, pretty girls, and an unending supply of illegal refreshment. He stretched his arms forward as if pushing away those childish fears. His eye caught the sparkle of the silver cufflinks on the end of his wrists. He gulped the better portion of his drink. The liquid not quite as harsh as it was the first time.

A short man in a splendidly tailored black tuxedo rang a tiny brass bell in front of the orchestra, and waited as the music stopped and the voices simmered.

"Mr. Austin Harrison and Mrs. Lucretia Dawes Harrison cordially invite you to join them for dinner, " he said with a heavy French accent.

The orchestra left the staging area in front of the dance floor and was replaced by a woman harpist and a male violinist. The guests scattered to their appointed tables.

"Where are you sitting?" Patrice asked.

Mark laughed, thinking of the hours of riding he had spent listening to seating arrangements. Had he only known, he could have lobbied for a prime location.

"I don't know," he said. "How do you–? where is the–?"

Patrice laughed. "Men!" she said. "Over there," and she pointed at a table over by one of the two bars set up in the tent.

Mark walked self-consciously to the table. Only one card remained. His name was typeset on the small card folded like a tiny pup tent. He had never seen his name in print before. He ran his finger over the raised black letters. Mr. Mark Lerner Table Fourteen. He took the card and placed it in his jacket pocket.

As he searched for his table, Judith caught his eye, waving from a table at the back of the tent. "Mark," she squealed in unabashed delight. "We're over here."

He walked to Judith, and to his surprise, she kissed his cheek in greeting. She introduced him to the other eight people at the table, and he greeted them warmly before taking a seat to Judith's right.

"You look dashing," she said. "You dress up well."

He assumed she meant that as a compliment, and thanked her and told her she did too.

"I see you've met Patrice Johnson," she said.

"Yes," Mark said. "Is she an artist too?" he asked in a feigned innocence.

"Doesn't own a pencil!" Judith said, and they both laughed at their little inside joke.

"Where's Emily?" Mark asked. "I haven't seen her all night."

"I'll tell you later," she whispered.

"Is she all right?"

"Shh," Judith said and nodded. "Not now."

Mark looked at the table spread before him. The three people sitting opposite him were partially obscured by the imposing flower centerpiece. A white and silver china plate sat before him, flanked by two knives, two spoons and three forks. Two crystal goblets sat behind the plate, one filled with water. He was glad Judith was there and he decided that whatever she did, he'd follow. A salad was set on a small plate set on top of a larger matching plate. It held several kinds of leaves and grasses that Mark could not distinguish from the greens of the flower arrangement. It looked beautiful. It just didn't look like food. He picked up another card that sat propped against his water glass:

Menu

Appetizer

Tasting of House Prepared Salmon

featuring gravlax, tartare and smoked with osetra caviar

and traditional accompaniments

Entrees

Grilled Certified Prime Sirloin Steak

dry aged and heavily marbled

crisp buttermilk onions and thyme sauce

-or-

Classic Water Club Maine Lobster

simply steamed or broiled with hot lemon butter

with famous Mashed Potatoes O'Keefe

Most of the meals in his home were one pot meals except for holidays when the budget was spared and something resembling an entree or an appetizer might appear. But nothing in his lifetime had prepared him for this. He had never seen a "famous" mashed potato and the ones he did see did not have surnames. If this was food, he could safely say that he had never eaten a meal in his life. He was clearly alone in his awe. No one else seemed to give more than a perfunctory notice of the menu card before them.

A foreign man walked to the table dressed in a black suit cut nicer than Mark's and, with his hands folded in front of him, asked "Loobstare ooh Stay?" Mark looked at Judith in a small panic. She watched him expectantly, and when he didn't answer, she said, "I'll have the lobster." The other guests recited their preferences and when the foreigner came back to Mark, he said, "I'll have the steak." A crisis averted.

That same feeling that had accosted him at Emily's Manhattan home attacked him again. He was an impostor. His life was a poor replica of hers. It astounded him that they spoke the same language and could communicate at all.

He turned his attention to Judith. "I was surprised you invited me," he said.

"What do you mean?"

"Emily said she was talking to you over the telephone and you both decided you wanted me to be here."

"I haven't spoken to Emily since the wedding," she said, "but of course I want you to be here," she said leaning toward him and patting his arm with sisterly affection.

Mark sipped his drink, but only a taste of the watered-down amber liquid remained. A very short, very thin man walked across the empty dance floor that was in the center of the tables. As he reached the center he held his hands out as if he was dancing with a partner and did a little spin before continuing across the floor. People laughed politely, someone hollered, "You still dazzle them, Jimmy," and more guests laughed.

"That's Mayor Jimmy Walker," Judith whispered to him.

The foreign waiter returned with two bottles of wine, and stood expectantly again in front of Mark. "Why not try the red?" she said quietly to Mark. "I'll have the chardonnay," she told the waiter.
The other table members ordered, some asking questions about the wine. Mark felt like he was back in school taking an examination that he had not studied for. He downed the glass quickly and the waiter returned almost immediately and refilled his glass.

"What happened at the wedding?" he asked Judith.

She rolled her eyes in her head, and shook her head. "It was horrid," she said. "Didn't Emily tell you?"

"I've only seen Emily once or twice since then. She wouldn't talk about it at all."

"She broke off with her fiancé," Judith said.

Mark hit his tooth with his glass and winced.

"Her fiancé?" he asked. "I didn't even know she was engaged."

"Well, she wasn't formally engaged. But he asked her to marry him and everyone assumed she would. Everyone but me."

"But why?"

That wasn't the question he meant to ask. He meant to ask how was it possible that he didn't know she was engaged, or why had he been so stupid to think that he– He meant she– He didn't know what he meant to ask. "Why" was as good as anything.

"They had a terrible row over riding. We were all invited to ride with Mr. Andrew Bryant. He knows you, by the way. Said he bought almost every one of his horses from you–"

Mark did know him. He had bought the first horse Mark ever sold. The bay he first trained when he was thirteen and Mr. Bryant had been back almost every year since. Mark knew the man was from New Jersey, but had never made the connection that the wedding was in his home town.

Judith continued. "Walter, that's his name, Walter Preston, was appalled that Emily and I were willing to ride with their little group even though Mr. Bryant clearly stated that he was not equipped to have us ride sidesaddle. Emily told him we could ride astride, and Walter threw a fit. None of the women from New Jersey ride astride. He told her privately that no wife of his was going to embarrass him in that manner and that he wouldn't have it.

"Emily ignored him and went anyway without him. John Wanamaker was there and Charles Scribner. Emily wanted to meet him. You know how she loves to read. Well, Walter stormed off and Emily refused to run after him. You know how she is."

Mark didn't know "how she is". Apparently he knew nothing about the girl at all.

"Anyway, that was the second argument they had in two days. She wanted him to take her on a picnic the day before and he refused. 'I'm not going to eat on the ground like a common animal,' he told her. She was furious."

The appetizer arrived. Mark had barely touched his salad, but the waiter took it away. "I didn't know there was a time limit," he said to himself as much as to Judith.

She resumed her harangue without waiting for the intermezzo.

"This all started back in Manhattan. Emily thought Walter had challenged her reputation, 'She said, he said' kind of thing. You know how sticky that sort of talk gets. He couldn't have possibly done anything worse as far as Emily was concerned. She will hold no quarter with anyone about her reputation. She would lie and cheat to protect her name if she had to."

Mark wondered if the first part of that sentence belonged with the last as he tried to sort out all the things Judith assumed he "knew".

"Don't tell her I said anything to you. She's already annoyed with me."

Someone at the table asked Judith where she was from, and the conversation drifted away from Mark. He silently ate his whatever it was and was prepared when the waiter returned to take his empty dish. A hush fell over the gathering of tables as the violinist stood and performed a solo in between courses.

"I love this adagio," Judith said to no one in particular.

Mark assumed she was talking about the wine.

The soloist sat to a hearty applause and Mayor Walker stood and proposed a toast. He spoke for several minutes and a couple of times had the party breaking up in laughter, but Mark couldn't hear him very well from where he sat. He sat looking for Emily whose absence had become distracting. Stephan Harrison stood and welcomed the Vice President and proposed a birthday toast to his brother. He, too, sat down to loud ovation. The men stood and applauded and Mark joined them. Mr. Harrison stood and politely bowed as an army of waiters appeared from the darkness with large trays filled with silver metal-covered plates. Mark sat back down and surveyed the room trying to picture himself exactly where he somehow was at that very moment. He was certain he would wake at any moment. He felt someone watching him and turned to see Patrice staring at him. She winked and smiled.

From the corner of his eye, he saw Emily arrive from the shadows behind the head table and sit quietly in one of two conspicuously empty chairs next to her father. He watched her as she greeted the Vice President and acknowledged the others at her table. She looked radiant, and he wondered how she thought she could sneak into the tent unseen. His was not the only eye that followed her. She wore a wide hat, with flowers around the band, and he noticed the flowers were the same pinks and burgundies of the centerpiece. Her sheer flowing gown seemed less ornate than the other dresses that evening, but somehow more elegant. He could see her smile from across the room, but her face looked vaguely different. He tried to make eye contact with her, but she did not see him. She had missed half the meal, and he watched as she politely shook her head to the questions of the Frenchman who had announced dinner. A tuxedoed man came and sat beside her. He looked substantially older than she. His hair was parted toward the center of his head with a stylish little puff as if a breeze had blown it awry. He had a protruding Adam's apple that moved when he spoke, and a prominent paunch. Mark watched as he sat and rested his folded hands on his substantial vest.

"Is that him?" he asked Judith. "Is that Walter?"

"Oh, no," she laughed. "That's Thomas DeSouza. He's just a friend. Walter arrived earlier today, but she sent him away. She gave him back the necklace he gave her last Christmas and asked him to leave. They're quite finished."

As dinner ended, the orchestra began anew and the Vice President rose and escorted Lucretia to the dance floor. Mark was astounded at her effortless grace as she floated through the air in her cousin's embrace. For some reason, halfway through the song, the seated crowd started a polite applause as Mr. Harrison and Emily walked to the floor. Austin cut in on the Vice President, who bowed to Lucretia and proceeded to finish the dance with Emily. All this was done without apparent direction, but it had a practiced, formal air about it. As if on an unseen cue, couples from every table stood and walked to the dance floor, swallowing Emily and Mr. Dawes in their midst. Judith stood and asked Mark to join her.

"I've never danced," he said.

"Easy as riding a horse," she said. "I'll lead, you follow."

Mark took to the floor half as clumsily as he would have expected. He followed Judith's steps as he would a horse. He listened to her movements and reacted to them instinctively. He stepped on her toes only once, and she did not comment on it at all though he saw her wince.

"I thought you said you never danced," she said.

He smiled, and spun her around copying the steps of the men around him.

"I declare, Mark Lerner! You can cut a rug!"

He smiled proudly. At one point they danced within a few feet of Emily who was already dancing with a man other than the Vice President. He saw her hand dance past him resting on, but barely touching, the shoulder of her partner. He thought she blinked at him, but it was so subtle, he could not say for sure.

"What's DeSouza like?" he asked Judith.

"He's as dull as day old snow," she said. "Everyone thinks he's so intelligent because he rarely says anything. But I think his silence comes from a strong instinct towards self defense."

A song ended and the dancers stood and politely applauded. Another began immediately. Mark and Judith danced around the outskirts of the floor, until they passed Patrice and her escort.

"Hello, Jimmy," Judith said to him, and they changed partners wordlessly as if by pre-arrangement.

With Judith gone, Mark felt like a novice skater on ice. She had led him so effortlessly she had fooled him into thinking he could dance. He stumbled awkwardly, and apologized to Patrice. She moved her hand from his shoulder to the bare skin of his neck, and drew him closer to her. "You're doing just fine," she said.

When the music ended, he bowed to her slightly as he had seen Mr. Dawes do to Lucretia and returned to his table like a landlubber returning to port. As soon as he sat down a waiter walked by with a tray of drinks. Mark took another and listened as snippets of conversation danced by him.

"...I hear he's going to marry Dwight Morrow's daughter...." Mark loosened his tie, and stretched his legs under the table. The plates had been cleared away leaving only half empty glasses scattered about. "...I'm telling you what I saw. They were knee high trousers and they were definitely from Paris...." He sipped at his drink. Martin, who he had met seemingly days earlier sat at one of the empty chairs and offered Mark a cigar. Mark leaned back on two legs of his chair and blew huge clouds of smoke toward the top of the tent. "...He left the Coconuts bar well past three. He said it was three, but the sun was almost up when I saw him. He was the only married man there...."

Judith came back to the table, grabbed her purse from her chair, and said, "Having fun yet?"

Mark smiled and waved as she ran off towards the facilities. "...For the same price you can visit Italy for sixty-six days. And you aren't stuck in a horrid little pension. I'll have my agent ring you this week...." Mark watched Emily dance. She had not sat out one, and at that she never finished a dance with the same partner she started with. "...She was furious. She gave a luncheon for all of his people, and not a mention of it in the Times..." He watched Thomas DeSouza, wondering about him and Emily. "...Mark..." He studied the way he looked at her. It did not seem to him to be the look of a "friend". "...Mark!..." He looked at Mrs. Harrison and wondered how many of the people here she knew. Wondered. "...Mark Lerner!..."

He snapped forward in his chair. The front legs sunk into the grass as he landed. Judith was along side of him laughing.

"I have been shtanding here calling your name for five minutes!"

He laughed. "You said 'shtanding'."

She giggled a surrender to that possibility. She slapped his arm in a playful protest and the momentum of her swinging pulled her into him.

"Hello, Martin. Did she say shtanding?" Martin did not hear him. "She shertainly did," he answered himself and joined Judith in laughter far in excess of what was called for.

"Well, at least I was not in a near coma." She remained leaning against his arm.

"This is a truly swell party," he said, suddenly serious. "Thanks for inviting me."

"That was all Emily's doing," she said. "But I'm glad she did," and leaned over to Mark and kissed him again on the cheek.

He wiped a bit of saliva from his face with the back of his hand.

"How much have you had to drink?" he asked.

She held her arms out wide. "Thish mutch!" and they laughed again until Martin could stand no more, and he left them alone at the table.

Judith sat down beside him, and leaned into the back of her chair. Mark moved his chair closer to hers and rested his elbows on his knees.

"So why is Emily annoyed with you?" he asked.

"Because of you, silly!"

"Me?"

Judith leaned toward him and whispered, but her whisper was almost as loud as her normal speaking voice.

"She said I flirt with you. I told her 'I do not' and I told her she flirts with you shamelessly."

Mark sat silently, hoping she would continue.

"I told her 'What about the picnic?' She fell asleep on your lap, for goodness sakes." She shook her head slowly. "She talks about you constantly. I have known Emily my whole life and I have never seen her act like that with any other man–and she says I flirt."

Her hand fell to his arm as she steadied herself.

"I told her she would never marry Walter because he wasn't anything like you. She got so angry, I thought she might slap me."

"Did she?"

"No. Of course not. But she stormed back into the house and has hardly spoken with me since, until today."

"What did she say today?"

Judith sat back. "Are you taking advantage of my party mood, Mark Lerner? I fear I've said too much already!"

Mark looked for Emily and spied her at the far end of the tent laughing in a circle of guests. He wondered how it was that she was always in the center of every gathering.

He looked back at Judith sitting alone at the empty table.

"Poor Judith," he said. "Are you all right?"

She stood up as if to attention. "I have only now–just now begun to fight!" and she saluted him and walked back into the crowd.

He watched her wobble off, and turned to see Patrice standing beside him.

"What's a girl to do to get a second dance?"

He smiled broadly, and extended his arm to escort her to the dance floor. His head was spinning. The music sounded far away. Or maybe the music was spinning and his head sounded so far away.

Dangerous

Mark awoke with a start. He still wore his suit, and only vaguely recalled the walk back to his room. He did not remember anything much past dancing with Patrice. He promised her something, but he couldn't focus in on what. The sun was shining through the window of his room. "Oh crap," he said. "The horses." He had never stayed in bed long enough to see the sun reach his window. He sat upright too quickly, and his head rang like metal pots clanging on a concrete floor. He groaned and staggered to his water closet and retched. He crawled out of his wrinkled suit and threw it in the corner.

There was a pounding in his head and it took several seconds for him to realize it was someone knocking on his door. Daniel stood before him wearing a familiar straw hat.

"Hey little brother. You dead?"

Mark wondered why he was shouting.

"I saw the horses, or actually I didn't see the horses and thought you must have died. I hear you crashed the party last night. Ain't you the Doozey! Just when you think you know someone–"

"Yeah, well, I'm sorry I wasn't able to help you out. How did it go?"

Daniel reached into his pocket and pulled out the largest wad of money Mark had ever seen. He fanned the money in front of Mark and smiled at the reverence his brother paid to the impressive display.

"How much is it?"

"Seven hundred, sixty-eight dollars."

"How much is yours to keep?"

"Two hundred, twelve."

"Damn!"

"I just bought me a brand new Ford. Only three and one half years old."

"I get first ride. Shotgun." Mark's enthusiasm ran head on into his hangover and he winced a smile.

"Done."

"Where we gonna go?"

"Anywhere in the great forty-eight!"

The brothers laughed.

"All right," Mark said. " I just got to be home by morning."

"It needs new rubber but I can get some used tires for a couple of dollars. I still have over fifty dollars left."

"Damn," Mark said again.

"So tell me about the party. Why did you decide to sneak in?"

Mark debated a full disclosure and shrugged. He dressed as his brother sat down on his bed.

"I drank too damn much, that I can tell you." For a moment he felt like a young boy being called on the carpet by his father, but he didn't know why. "Where'd you get the hat?"

Daniel grinned. "Some swell lost it. I found it outside the tent. Looks brand new don't you know." He waited. "Well?"

"What the hell," Mark grumbled, and reached into the pocket of his jacket still buried in the pile of clothes on the floor and pulled out his name card. He held it out for his brother to read.

The smile dropped from Daniel's face.

"She invited you?"

"Yep."

"Who? The Queen or The Princess?"

Mark frowned. "Why you gotta call her that?"

Daniel shrugged. "Cause that's what she is."

"Not to me."

"'Course not." Daniel said. "Y'all gonna be the house nigger," he said in a bad southern accent.

Mark stood up and stepped to his brother.

"You're just jealous because she didn't invite you," and he knocked the straw hat off his brother's head.

Daniel pushed his brother aside and retrieved the hat.

"Like hell! I don't have any stocks and bonds and servants to talk about all night."

"It wasn't like that. They're nice people. I drank some hooch. Danced some."

"With who? That girl that just left here?"

"What girl?"

"Some skinny moll with short black hair."

Mark's head snapped up summoning the headache lurking under his furrowed brow.

"Where'd she go?"

"I dunno. I passed her as she was leaving. She said you were supposed to meet her here and take her riding. She asked me if I knew where you were staying and I told her you lived here. She left in a huff."

Mark shrugged.

"Yeah. Her. Patrice. We danced some." He paused a moment and laughed, "best I can remember."

"Ain't you the Valentino." He leered at Mark. "Not the Princess?"

"I'm not gonna tell you again. Why you got such a burr up your ass about her. What's she ever done to you?"

"It's just the way she is. You don't hear her like I do. She collects men like they were tin soldiers. Sets 'em up and knocks 'em down. Sends them reeling across the room with a flick of her finger," Daniel said taking the opportunity to flick his own finger at his brother's shoulder.

"Kind of like you, then." Mark said. "Too much like kind?"

"It's different, my innocent little brother. I'm a man. She ain't supposed to act like a man. There's rules about this stuff."

Mark shrugged off his brother's preaching.

"How do you know what she does?"

"I hear her on the telephone back to New York."

"You eavesdrop? What are you, a peeping Tom?"

"Not exactly." Daniel stopped talking and looked over his shoulder as if someone else might have joined them in the tiny room. "You promise not to say anything?"

"About what?"

"You gotta promise first."

"I'm not gonna promise on something I don't know." Mark's headache flashed a stubborn reminder. He rubbed his temple gently.

"Then I'm not tellin."

"All right. I promise."

Daniel paused. Sat back on the bed.

"I got head phones like the telephone operators wear."

"So?"

"I can listen to anyone up and down the party line."

"That's wrong. I don't want to hear this." Mark held his hands up to ward off his brother. "There's not even a piece of right in that. That's all wrong."

Daniel let himself fall back on his brother's mattress. His legs stretched out straight from the bottom of the bed as he looked up to the ceiling and said, "Yeah, I know. But it's like snuff. It's plenty hard to stop."

They sat in a dirty silence. Mark noticed the sole of his brother's shoe was almost worn through. Specks of dirt spilled to the floor like sand in an hourglass from Daniel's cuff.

"I wish you hadn't a told me that," he said.

"Don't be such a baby about it. It ain't all that wrong. Nobody gets hurt. You're always doin' that. Setting some high and mighty standards for everybody and then you act all personally put out when they ain't as perfect as you. Grow up. Anyway, Jackie did it. He wired it all together."

Mark said nothing.

"She's been engaged six times."

Mark didn't know if Daniel said that to take the heat off himself or not. But it had that effect.

"I don't believe it."

"I'm tellin' you. Six different men asked her to marry them."

"Well that's not being engaged."

"What do you call it, then?"

"It's not her fault if men keep asking her to marry them."

"There you go. Taking her side again."

"I'm not taking any side. What difference does it make to me how many fellows ask her?"

"It shouldn't make any."

"It doesn't."

Daniel sat up on the edge of the bed and narrowed his eyes.

"Don't let it, Mark. I see the way you look at her and I know how you get. You're always seeing the good in people and ignoring the way they are. That girl's trouble gift-wrapped with a ribbon and a bow. Leave it alone. Stick to the widow."

Mark didn't know what to say. Anyone but his brother would have been laid out half an hour ago for saying any one of the things he just said. Daniel had a way of patting him on the back that always left an oily hand print on his shirt.

"I gotta go," he said to Daniel. As he walked out the door he added, "Get your shoe fixed."

Mark set to working the horses trying to sweat out his hangover and to wash away the meeting with his brother. He hid in his work letting himself get lost in the details of the horses while ignoring all the extraneous noise in his head. He rode three different horses for an hour each in the ring. He worked on their leads. Ran tight circles and serpentines and set up a jumping course that required lead changes at every jump. After several unbroken hours of work, he sat on his bay watching contentedly as sweat dripped off his forehead leaving little marks in the dust beneath him.

After he took the last horse back to the barn he heard a familiar sound coming from near the main house, but he couldn't quite place it. He walked slowly toward Pine Bluff and was halfway up the hill when he recognized the sound of ropes rubbing on the fat limbs of the black walnut tree. He jogged to the top of the rise and saw Emily swinging on the old long roped swing. She leaned way back as she pumped and was going high enough that each thrust forward ended with a bump and a snap of the ropes before she retreated backwards. Her thin legs flashed white on each pass forward. As he walked to her she smiled him a greeting.

"You're awfully trusting of those old ropes," he said. "No one's been on that swing in years."

Mark fielded her smile and wondered what he had just said that might be funny.

"Did you come up here to ask me to dance?"

Mark blushed. Her flower-printed smock swirled around her and her slip winked at him on every pass. She wore canvas tennis shoes. He had never seen a woman wear canvas shoes except in newspaper ads.

"Because I simply can not recall you asking me for a single dance last night." Her words sounded like a song.

"Do you mean in that eight or nine seconds at about eleven o'clock when you weren't otherwise engaged?"

She smiled.

"I saw you dancing with Patrice Johnson." Her eyes flashed like heat lightning. "But you didn't join in on the Charleston or the Lindy."

"I didn't want to hurt anyone."

She laughed again. A short laugh.

"Did you have fun?"

"It was swell. Thanks for inviting me." He wanted to see if she "blamed" Judith. She didn't.

He watched her swing. She pulled the smell of honeysuckle toward him with every pass, her movements stirring up the sweet aroma that hung in the air. She closed her eyes as if he wasn't there and leaned far back as she sailed through the bright warm air.

"Patrice was quite impressed," she said with eyes still closed. "You're all she spoke of at breakfast. She told us all about your grand entrance."

Mark felt oddly uneasy, as if he was on stage.

"I'm sure Tom DeSouza spoke only of you this morning too."

She opened her eyes and sat up straighter on the swing. She didn't pump for a couple of passes and moved her head back and forth so the line from her eyes to his was unbroken.

"I see Judith's been at it again." She pushed backwards on the swing stiffening her legs and sat braced in that position studying him. He did not know why she always looked at him as if searching for buried treasures, but he found himself wanting to hide things behind his eyes so he wouldn't disappoint her.

To his surprise, Mark could feel his face flush. There seemed to be no refuge from Emily's stare.

"What does he do?" Mark asked trying to deflect her gaze. "I mean, what does he do for a living?"

"His father owns a real estate development company uptown," she said. "On sixty-fourth street."

She started swinging again.

"How come every time I ask one of your friends what they do for a living they tell me about their father's job?"

Emily laughed, but said nothing. He thought of what his brother had said earlier.

"Are you going to engage him?"

"Mark Lerner! That's a very personal question."

She dragged her feet kicking up dust as she slowed.

"And that's not how you ask. The question is 'Will we be engaged?'"

He bowed deferentially.

"Will you?"

She stopped swinging altogether. Again that look. He turned to face her squarely as if to prevent the question that stood corralled between them from brushing by him unanswered.

"He's just a friend, if you must pry." She scanned his face thoroughly and hesitated for a moment. "I could never be with someone that I wasn't..." and she stopped speaking momentarily as the crimson on her cheeks seeped to her neck, "...attracted to." Her last two words were almost whispered.

"Want a push?"

Without waiting for her answer he grabbed the swing and ran her backwards high enough to allow room for him to run under the swing before she started forward. She squealed with delight. He positioned himself out of the way so that she was between him and the sun and every time she passed, sunlight splashed on his face as if it was her wake. Mark sat down with his back against the tree listening to the ropes rub out a hypnotic wordless chant. Emily flashed in and out of his sight as she had the night before.

After several minutes, she asked, "Do you remember the letter I sent you several Christmases ago?"

Mark rose to stand in front of her as she pumped higher and higher on the wooden swing. He stood maybe an inch outside of the arc of her feet, and did not move. He saw her trying to stretch out a little further each time she neared him but he pretended not to notice.

"I don't remember any letter from Italy," he said innocently.

"It was–" and her head snapped to his in recognition. She smiled broadly.

"Oh, maybe it wasn't to you. I get so forgetful at times. I was writing about a man I saw in the hills–"

"I don't remember any letter about a man riding a horse," he said.

She cast her eyes to the ground unsuccessfully suppressing a smile.

"But if I did–? What about it?"

Her smile was a canopy shading them both under its cover.

"Oh, nothing–" she said.

He forgot to pay attention and eased into the orbit of her swing and had to jerk his head out of the way of her feet as she pumped higher into the crystal blue sky.

"...I was just wondering if it is true."

Mark stepped back into the shade just as they heard Judith calling her name.

Emily let go of the ropes from a height that would have intimidated Mark and flew through the air landing in the dust of his recently planted footprints. She did not waver as she landed. She put out her hands to brace herself from falling into him, but she didn't sway.

She leaned forward and whispered in his ear, "You're a dangerous man, Mark Lerner."

She was so close that when she formed the "M" in "Mark" her lips touched his ear in an electric connection that made him glad she wore rubber-soled shoes.

He snapped his head to see if Judith had seen her, but Emily did not seem to care if she did or did not. She waved good-bye to Mark the way girls sometimes do, moving only her fingers, and ran to meet Judith. The swing still moved through the air and he turned to look at it as if she was still there. He did not feel jolted by her sudden departure. He had the sense that she had merely ended, like a song that he heard on the radio. One that he felt he would be able to tune in again if he needed to hear it once more.

Mark saw Emily four more times that summer, but they never were alone together. It seemed like he saw her a lot more than that. Each visit seemed to linger for several days in his mind and just when her previous visit was wearing off, Emily appeared like a cavalry with reinforcements.

He remembered the day in September when she left. She waved to him through the open window of her father's car, a look he did not comprehend on her face. He wondered a moment if she had borrowed something of his that she forgot to return. The green car swirled a cloud of dust behind it as it drove away. Mark stood a long time and watched the dust settle. When it did there was nothing in his line of sight save the narrow brown ribbon of road. Still he had a nagging feeling that he lent her something and she was leaving with it. But he couldn't imagine what it might be.

Darts

A crust of snow made the roads too icy to drive though the night was pleasant enough for December. Mark figured he could walk the two miles across the bridge to the Hotel as easily as drive. He was late and he knew Daniel would be bitching, but Kristen hadn't wanted him to leave so soon. He promised her he'd see her the next day for Christmas Eve, and this seemed to mollify her somewhat.

Daniel was throwing darts as Mark entered the crowded bar and he threw a dart playfully at Mark that caught in the wool and dangled on his coat as Mark wedged it onto one of the laden racks. The smell of damp wool, beer and cigars melded together in the popular saloon as waves of loud talk and robust laughter floated through the smoky clouds.

"You're late!" Daniel squawked. "I've had to take everyone's money while I waited."

The other young men gathered around the dart board laughed.

"It's true," one of them called, "He's beaten almost everyone in the room."

"Yeah," Daniel added. His face was red and glowing in the steam heat generated from oversized radiators under the steamy windows. "And now my arm's probably too tired to beat you."

"There you go already, making up excuses for the whupping you haven't even got yet."

"The next time you give me a whupping will be the first time," Daniel said and walked over to his younger brother putting him in a head lock and mussing his short hair.

"What's the stakes?"

"I'll play you for beers," Daniel said, "and let me tell you, I'm thirsty tonight."

They played three games. Every time Daniel threw a double, Mark threw a triple, until his brother surrendered noisily, moaning like a bootlegger in a bottle smashing raid.

"Arthur!" Daniel called to the bartender. "Keep my brother's glass full. His money's no good here tonight."

The brothers raised their glasses in a silent toast.

"Is there anywhere to sit down?" Mark asked. "I've been riding all day."

"Yeah. I've got a table over there with Meghan and her friend Elvira," he said pointing with his thumb across the room.

Mark raised his eyebrows at the mention of Meghan. Daniel had been seeing her since June, far exceeding the longest stint he ever had with any one girl. She was a pretty girl, in a way, a little plump and a bit too loud for Mark's taste. But Daniel liked her. Daniel liked her just fine.

They exchanged greetings all around. Elvira graduated a couple of years behind Mark, and her high pitched whining voice reminded Mark instantly of what he didn't like about her. She had a crooked nose, but a real pretty smile. If only she wouldn't open her mouth, she was pleasant enough company.

"How come Arthur lets you boss him around like that?" Meghan asked Daniel. "All I ever get from him is a scowl."

"Arthur prefers the way this bar used to be when women weren't allowed past the dining room. And besides, I used to run glasses for him," Daniel said.

"Run glasses?" Elvira asked.

"In the summertime when the trains come up from Manhattan, they'd stop here to get drinks," Daniel said while pointing towards the door.

The train station was less than thirty feet from the bar entrance and a train's arrival would shake the building so even the deaf would know when it arrived.

"Later than that," Mark added. "Folks come out right up to the end of October to see the leaves turn color."

"Arthur paid me two bits to go along to the next stop and bring back the empty glasses. I've been running glasses since I've been ten. God bless Prohibition!" he sang out, and all the men within earshot raised a glass to Coolidge's folly.

"How's Mrs. Scott?" Elvira asked Mark as the boys took empty chairs from other tables and dragged them to the girls.

The atmosphere changed as if the door had been blown open. Mark looked quickly at his brother who flinched and directed his gaze over to the pool table.

Meghan squealed "Ellie!"

Mark fumbled red faced. "Who?"

"How the hell would he know?" Daniel said as he thumped his beer glass down on the cardboard coaster.

Elvira was flustered, unaware perhaps of the indelicacy of the question, but certainly aware now that it was an unwelcome gambit.

"I– I just thought– Excuse me," and she left the table knocking a chair over in her haste.

Mark, Meghan and Daniel sat as if separated by bars of silence. Meghan excused herself, "I better go see if she's all right."

As soon as she'd gone, Mark leaned toward his brother and glared. "Did you tell everyone in town?"

"I swear on Momma's life, I never told a soul. I'm not lying, Mark. I've told no one. Not even Meghan."

"Shit."

"I swear. I told no one. But I've been meaning to tell you, anyway. I think Mom knows–"

"She couldn't possibly– Dammit. Everyone must know. How the hell–?"

"It's a small town, Mark."

Mark nodded, but said nothing. He felt an emptiness in his stomach and suddenly felt real bad about leaving Kristen alone.

"Shit."

"I'll talk to Meg tomorrow and find out what she knows," Daniel offered.

Mark nodded. They sat in silence, letting the din of the holiday crowd envelope them, their eyes occasionally scanning across the crowded smoky room for any sign of the girls.

"What do you think of Ellie?" Daniel asked.

Mark shrugged.

"She's nice. Pretty, kind of."

"She walked six miles to be here. Meg told her you were coming and she wouldn't stay home. She didn't even ask me for a ride."

Mark looked to the chair she just left, but said nothing.

"...in case you want to start seeing someone your own age."

Mark didn't answer. Daniel traced his finger through some of the names carved into the table.

"What did you get her for Christmas?" Daniel asked after a while.

Mark's head jumped backwards an inch at the question.

"Nothing. I sent for something and it didn't come. I forgot–"

"Jesus, Mark. You've got to get her something. You know she'll have something for you."

"Yeah, you're right. I didn't–"

"Listen. There's a book on the front seat of my car that I bought for Dad. You can give her that."

"What'll you do about Dad?"

"I'll get Arthur to wrap up a bottle of brandy."

"Yeah. Thanks. Yeah. I should do that," Mark nodded.

Daniel looked across the bar searching for the girls.

"Meghan's really something, huh?"

"She's no Emily Harrison," Mark blurted out.

He did not know where the words had come from. They erupted from his lips like an untimely burp. He looked red-faced at Daniel hoping he wasn't offended.

"Hell, no!" he said jubilantly, as though Mark had just paid the highest compliment, "That she ain't."

Mark smiled, happy to have scored with his brother on a point that landed so far from its intended target.

He was still nodding silently when the girls returned to the table. Elvira squinted a crooked apology to Mark and his mouth smiled an acceptance. She exhaled deeply.

"If we go upstairs, we can dance," she said.

"Swell!" Daniel said, and he jumped up to leave.

"I'll be along in a minute," Mark said.

Meghan sat back down.

"I'll wait for Mark."

Daniel shrugged and walked off with Elvira towards the music.

Mark sat across the table from Meghan. Their eyes met and he quickly looked away. When he looked again, she was still staring at him, and he settled under her gaze.

"Does everyone know?"

"No," she said. "Ellie's father is her milkman. He saw you leaving one morning before dawn."

Mark exhaled deeply through his nose, but said nothing. He felt something rub on his ankle and he reached under the table and scratched his leg absently.

"You must be quite experienced," she said in a low voice.

"Hmm," Mark said before her words fully registered. His eyes flared and snapped to hers. Something rubbed his ankle again and he named it this time. Her stocking foot rode down his calf. He shook his head in a controlled violence.

"I'm certain I have no idea what you're talking about."

His indignation was for Daniel. He really liked this girl, and here she was flirting with someone before his shadow made it to the threshold of the room, and his own brother at that! He had enough outrage left for Kristen. He couldn't care less what Meghan thought of him, but the thought of this little whore judging her made his blood boil.

"I imagine I'm the least experienced person at this table," he snarled as he scraped his chair backwards across the floor rising in a near leap.

As he turned he bumped into his brother.

"What's going on?" Daniel asked. "Where you going?"

Mark didn't answer.

"It's too crowded," Elvira said. "We'll try again in a few–"

Her eyes went from Meghan to Mark and back to Meg.

"What did I miss?" she asked.

To avoid a scene, Mark sat back down across from Meghan. He would not look at her face but watched as she wrapped her arm through Daniel's as though nothing had just happened. He looked at his brother who sat like a jockey on a winning mount.

Ellie's eyes darted around the table.

"Did you hear what they were playing upstairs?" she asked. "That song Isadora Duncan always danced to. You know the one–I can't remember the name. It's so sad! Especially at Christmas!"

Mark found it difficult to concentrate on what she said, her piercing voice so annoying.

"That had to be the most horrible way to die!" Meghan said.

Daniel took his scarf from the back of his chair and threw it over his shoulder pretending he was choking. The girls laughed as he pantomimed Isadora's accidental strangulation, protesting in between shrieks of laughter at Daniel's insensitivity. "You're so horrid," Meghan laughed, but her words brought only more laughter.

As the laughter fell away, Mark raised a glass.

"To 1928!"

"Here, here."

"May all our dreams come true!" Elvira squeaked.

"May our scarves keep clear of all wheels!" Daniel toasted and the laughter rolled again.

"Is nothing sacred to you?" Meghan asked Daniel between gulps of air.

He raised his eyebrows and smiled at her.

"No." He laughed again. " No. I don't think so." Daniel cleared his throat. "Happy New Year." He looked directly at Meghan.

The conversation danced like blinking lights through the spectrum of 1927. Pola Negri, Clara Bow, Jolson, Valentino, Pickford and Fairbanks. The brother's knew little of actors and actresses and their conversation sang of Notre Dame, Knute Rockne, Army and Yale.

"How 'bout the Yankees?" Mark said.

"Aren't they in the World Series?" Ellie asked.

Mark started to tell her the series was two months over, but Daniel caught his eye and winked.

"Do you think they'll win?" he asked Elvira.

"Who do they play?"

"The Pittsburgh Pirates," Mark said.

"My father's from Pittsburgh," Meghan said.

"I think the Pirates will win," Ellie said. "Pirates are mean and tough and, and what is a Yankee anyway?"

Meghan laughed hiding her mouth with her hand.

"Yeah, what is a Yankee?"

"Let's bet," said Daniel. "I'll wager that the Yanks will win in–" he paused as if in deep arithmetical calculation "Five games. No. Four. I'll bet they'll sweep."

Ellie turned to Meghan and didn't see the brothers winking again.

"Do you know what they're talking about?

"Nope, but I'll bet the Pirates."

Mark and Daniel laughed.

"Me too," said Ellie.

"What'll we wager?" asked Daniel. Mark's smile turned into an evil chuckle. "I know. I'll wager you this. If the Yankees win the '27 Series in four games, you have to kiss whoever I choose."

Ellie looked quickly to Mark. "What if they don't?" she asked.

"Name it," Daniel said.

The girls looked at one another and giggled with a virginal depravity. "Give us a minute. Get us more drinks while we decide."

The brothers left the table arm in arm and worked their way to the bar. Mark pulled down one of the wrought iron bar stools and sat with his head in his hands in mock dismay.

"I don't believe this," he laughed.

Daniel slapped him on the back as they made their way back to the table spilling drinks in a trail along the way.

"We decided if the Pirates beat the Yankees even one game–how many are there?"

"Might be seven."

"If the Pirates win even one," Meghan said confidently, "You both have to kiss whoever we choose."

"Heads we win.." Daniel said to Mark.

"Tails you lose," Mark answered.

"Wait a minute. Something's fishy about this," Elvira squealed. "When do we find out?"

"The series will be over by New Year's Day," Daniel said.

Ellie looked at Meg for support.

"Are you telling the truth?"

Daniel turned to the table behind him. "Hey fellas, isn't the World Series over by New Year's Day?"

The men looked puzzled.

"Sure." said one "It's over long–"

"There you have it," Daniel said. "New Year's Day. They'll be some kissing going on for sure!"

They drank past midnight and stumbled to Daniel's car. The alcohol blurred Meghan's pass and Mark was not certain if it had happened the way he remembered at all. He watched from the back seat as she snuggled up as close as a girl could get to Daniel. He watched her hand go to the back of his neck and then disappear under his coat as Elvira fell asleep on Mark's shoulder. The snow skimmed roads slowed the drive to Ellie's house to a crawl. Mark woke her at her door and she kissed his cheek in farewell.

"Will you come see me?" she asked.

"Maybe sometime," he said wondering if he meant it even a little.

Mark stared out the window as a winter's sliver of moon stalked him through the twisting roads to Meg's house. He sat in the idling car as Daniel left Meg with an extended farewell on her porch. He returned to the car running and sliding like a schoolboy at recess.

"That was too rich," he said, and with the speed of an electric light, he turned serious. "Listen, I didn't want to say anything in front of Meg until I'm certain but I met someone who might be able to get me into the navy."

"The navy?" was all Mark could muster.

"Yeah. I want to learn to fly."

Mark closed one eye as he tried to focus on his brother, but could not get a clear image. He fumbled through blurred thoughts looking for the right thing to say. Or anything to say.

"Don't you need to go to college for that?"

"No, I don't think so," Daniel said. "I think they need stupid people to fly some of those rat traps." He tried to laugh, but it sputtered unanswered.

Mark looked at Daniel as if he was Ray Radclay's ghost. He knew he should feel happiness for his brother's opportunity, and he did for a moment until the image of his brother's flying overhead faded into a picture of himself without him.

"The navy?" he asked again.

"The navy."

"That's great!" he said using all the energy left in his body.

Mark stared out the window hoping to see something familiar. The cold of the glass felt good as he pressed his forehead to its blackness As they crossed the road that passed Kristen's cabin he thought he saw a tiny glow of light through the woods.

"The navy?" he asked the reflection in the window.

Air Hole

January 1928

"I'll tell you what. I can't tolerate that know-it-all son-of-a-bitch a moment longer."

Mark couldn't recall ever seeing his brother so angry.

"You mean that blond fellow?"

"Yeah. That Swede son-of-a-bitch. Come down from Maine bragging on the ice harvests up there and treating us like we were a bunch of kids playing with blocks."

"Well it did sound interesting, especially the part about the mechanical saw."

"Well damn you straight to hell too. If he's so damn interesting, go talk to him."

Daniel prodded his draft horse forward jumping on the wooden scraper as the horse hit stride.

"You can both have him, for all I care!"

So that was it. For two weeks he'd heard that Meghan had thrown him over for someone else, but on three separate occasions Daniel deflected Mark's questions about the matter.

Mark stood on the northern edge of the lake where they'd decided to pile the snow they plowed off the ice surface. Already the pile stood four feet high as he and his brother crossed the ice with their horse-drawn scrapers. There was a good six inches of powdery snow atop the ice and another three or four inches of snow ice under that before the twelve inches of good clear ice could be reached. It would take him and Daniel the rest of the day to clear the surface before the entire crew could start pulling the ice cakes from the water. Mr. Lerner wanted to try to get all the ice in within a week as the Almanac called for a major thaw after that.

Mark turned to his father just as the man flipped the ice scorer over on its side. The middle adjustable blade had loosened and was scoring the ice deeper than the other two blades causing the scorer to bind. The mule stopped every time the blade caught and Michael was having a hell of a time making any progress at all. He didn't need to score very deep. An inch would do, but every forty feet he had to stop and pack the groove with snow so it wouldn't freeze over again. Normally, he'd hire a boy for that chore but there were no boys willing to work in the near zero temperatures. One boy, Billy's next door neighbor but one, turned down an offer of $1.80 for the day. Mark's father was too stunned after that to keep looking.

"If one dollar eighty means nothing to a boy, I guess I was born too late. I ain't Rockefeller settin' out to hand out dimes for doin' nothing."

Mark moved his horse into the snow pile and dumped his load of snow from the scraper bed. He turned his reluctant horse back across the ice and looked for his brother who was already returning from his pass. The soft snow piled up quickly in the eight foot wide scrapers. Mark waited for his brother to return to the pile.

"I'm sorry about Meghan," he said. He wondered if he should tell his brother about the pass she made in December. Maybe it would make Daniel feel well rid of her, but he wasn't really certain it was a pass after all and decided against it.

Daniel shrugged. "Makes no damn difference to me what the girl does. She's a suffra-God-damned-jet and I suppose she can do whatever in hell she pleases."

"Why'd she leave?" Mark asked. "Did you tell her about the navy?"

Daniel exhaled loudly through his nose. His breath swirled between them.

"Can't you see I'm working here? Look at my arms. They're moving all the time." Daniel waved his arms around like an off-centered windmill and shouted, "This ain't no sewing bee gossip club. We got work to do," and he rode off again after dumping his load of snow.

Mark could hear him complaining as he rode off but the words were muffled by the sound of the horse's large wooden ice shoes. He laughed in spite of himself. Daniel was nuts over Meghan. He begged off last week's poker game to be with her knowing full well he'd have to take a rash of guff for his absence. He even started using hair grease because she liked the way it looked. Mark jumped off the scraper and tightened the u-bolt that kept the round wooden ice shoe on the horse before turning his scraper back towards the middle of the lake.

For the better part of the next hour he and Daniel carried on a conversation of intermittent sentences delivered as they passed one another moving to and from the snow pile.

"How do you know Meghan's with the Swede?" Mark asked as both boys arrived simultaneously at lake edge.

"The little strumpet was flirting with him all night at the Winter Social," Daniel answered. "I ain't blind."

Daniel's anger appeared to wane but flared up at every one of Mark's questions like a fire being splashed with bacon fat. His horse paid for his anger, as Daniel refused to stop at lake edge and rest. Ten minutes later, the brothers passed again.

"Just because she talked to him at a dance doesn't mean she's taken to him," Mark said.

Daniel frowned but said nothing until they crossed paths again several minutes later.

"I can tell when a girl's lost interest," he said. "She's gone. Believe me, she's gone."

"Maybe she'll come back," Mark said hopefully.

His brother scowled but never halted his scraper. He seemed to purposely avoid his brother for several passes. Mark thought he saw him slow his horse if they were about to meet. A half hour later, Daniel met Mark at the snow pile again. The lake was only about one-quarter cleared.

"Nobody ever comes back," he said.

It wasn't so much the words but the look in his eye that let Mark know the conversation was ended. Mark had never been thrown over by a girl and had a morbid fascination in watching his brother struggle with it.

He turned his attention to the lake. The channel had been cut two days earlier, but yesterday's unexpected snow delayed the cutting. If they weren't able to break off a couple of floats by nightfall Mark would have to row the channel another night. The temperature hadn't crawled much past zero in three days and Mark was not looking forward to another twelve-hour shift keeping the uncompromising channel opened.

Nothing had yet gone well with this year's harvest. It was a lot harder for Michael Lerner to organize a crew than it was when Mark was a boy. The summer of '27 saw a huge drop in demand for ice downstate, and prices had fallen drastically. A lot of the large food companies had made the costly move to electric refrigeration, as had just about all of the breweries. The breweries were big customers. Their demand often controlled the volatile price of ice, and it was impossible for the ice sellers to get a good price for the thousands of tons that went unbought by breweries alone.

A lot of the men who normally harvested locally went north to Utica where the big ice houses were. The Swede told them the ice house up there was thirty feet high and bigger than Palmer Stadium in Princeton where the Tigers played. They had a gas-powered conveyor belt elevator and a mechanical shaver. The northerners cut the lakes into floats of ice, some as large as twenty feet by fifteen feet, and piked them along the channel into the shaver that automatically took off the top three or four inches of wasted snow ice.

Another crew of men hammered through the scored ice with breakers and broke off cakes three feet long by a foot and a half wide. The blocks were usually twelve to fifteen inches deep.

"Each cake must weigh three hundred pounds!" Mark said. But what impressed him more than the size was the fact that one man did not have to work at all the facets of the harvest. Some men were just sawyers. Some were breakers. Some worked the conveyors. Some older men just piked the ice from place to place along the lake. Not like their little operation where the Lerners did it all themselves.

"The weight ain't nothing," the Swede told them. "The mechanical lift can bring them to the top of the ice house as fast as the crews can run them through the chutes."

"That must be one helluva lot of ice," Mark said.

"I hear that grass don't grow within fifty feet of the ice house because it doesn't know winter's over."

"How can they stack the ice so fast?" Mark asked ignoring his brother's scowl. "How many fellows work the top of the elevator?"

"Two, the times I was up there," the man said. The cakes come off the conveyor so fast that all the men got to do is guide them to the next available space with their pikes. They got another five or six guys to hand the cakes off to. The ice don't slow down until it gets to the top of the pile."

Mark thought he'd like to try a big harvesting operation like that. They didn't even have a conveyor at their little lake. They piked the ice themselves along the channel and put a hook on the back end of each block and pulled it up the ramp with a rope by hand to be loaded into the sleigh and driven to the ice house. He'd especially like to see the mechanical shaver. The worst part of his work was turning every other row of ice cakes over before stacking them in the ice house. He used metal tongs to flip the hundred pound cakes. The ice had to be stacked snow ice side to snow ice side with saw dust only between the layers of clear ice. It was back-breaking work flipping hundreds of heavy cakes in a week. By the end of spring, the snow ice melted and the stack of ice compacted by several inches each row in the storage house. So besides being easier, the mechanical ice shaver saved enough room to add several more rows of ice. More money for everyone. Mark shook his head wistfully.

"I wish we had one of those shavers," he said to the Swede, but he had already left.

As the morning went on, Daniel said less and less. It bothered Mark to see his brother without his usual swagger. The brothers stopped for a lunch of stew Mrs. Lerner had made with stale biscuits that had to be dunked into the gravy to be edible at all. With the weather this cold, the men stopped and ate every two or three hours. This time the brothers were joined by their father and two other men, but at any given time of day the shanty contained someone hoping for a respite from the impassive cold. The conversation did not linger over the weather or the expected price of ice. Both subjects were too depressing. One of the men had been to Narrowsburg to see the moving picture show and the other said he heard they were making talking movie films in Hollywood, California. Mark had read that, too.

"Charlie Chaplin says adding sound to pictures is as stupid as putting words to Beethoven," he said.

He looked at his brother for a comment. Daniel hated Chaplin, but he said nothing.

"It's a fast-changing world," Michael Lerner said as he picked up his pike and opened the door onto the cold lake officially ending lunch break. Mark swallowed the bottom half of his coffee and followed his brother out the door.

"You all right?" he asked.

His brother looked at him with a bewildered expression but said nothing. He shrugged his shoulders and walked to his scraper. They took the feed buckets off their horses and coaxed them back onto the ice. Mark did not want to leave his brother alone. Instead of running perpendicular to him as he usually did, he flanked him so his scraper picked up where Daniel's left off. The nose of his horse was about even with the back of his brother's scraper. Daniel looked over his shoulder nervously.

"What you doin'?" he shouted over the squeaking and scraping of the plow. "Get away! You're too close!"

Mark ignored him. That might have been the first lunch in his life that Daniel didn't either ride him about something or try to take half his food and Mark didn't like it a bit. He figured he could aggravate his brother enough to shake him out of his foul mood. He didn't know why, but he didn't want his brother across the lake from him. He wanted to stay close even if he tried to chase him away.

Mark looked up at the gray sky looking for the sun.

"Damn, it's cold," he said though he knew his brother couldn't hear him.

He craned his neck straight overhead where he figured the sun ought to be but saw no discernible brightness through the cloud cover. The cold took the opportunity to sweep under his scarf. He shivered and put his gloved hands under his arm pits one at a time. He was too cold to take off his gloves and fish for his pocket watch, but he figured it must be near one o'clock. They had three and a half or four hours of daylight left, not enough time to finish clearing yesterday's snow. Mark wanted to stop scraping and break off a row of floats so he wouldn't have to spend the night clearing the channel again. His brother was about eighteen feet in front of him and he pushed his horse forward so he could tell his brother his plan.

"Daniel!" he called.

He didn't hear him.

"Daniel!"

His brother turned around just as the strange noise began. At first it sounded like a sheet of paper being ripped directly under his ear. Then a tinkling like tiny pieces of glass breaking and falling around him. The noise lasted only a few seconds followed by a confusion of

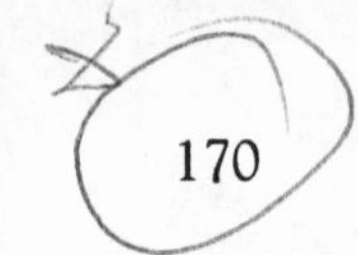

light and noise. Mark knew instinctively what it was although he only personally witnessed one. Air hole. That deep hole that lurked under a false crust of ice indiscernible even on close inspection.

Quick flashing sights and pieces of sounds cascaded in front of him like cards being riffled in a deck. He could see each sight, could hear each sound clearly like individual cards unnaturally suspended in air before falling to the ground. He heard a rush of air. Daniel's large horse neighed in panic. Water splashed. The tinny sound of the metal scraper brake dug into the ice. Wood splintered. Pieces of footboard floated eerily through the air before bouncing along the top of the ice. Mark could not understand why everything had slowed so. He looked at Daniel and watched him blink. The single blink stretched into minutes. His brother's mouth opened in a scream shaped oval but Mark could count seconds before the sound reached him. Leather reins snapped like a whip as they slackened and stiffened against the hide of Daniel's horse. Remnants of his scraper were swallowed into the black hole that had erupted through the frozen serenity of the virginal white ice. The scraper splintered like a door kicked through. He saw his brother flying ahead towards him as wooden pieces dropped into the black hole. Mark's horse shied and jerked left trying to avoid his flying brother. From far off he heard his father's voice. "Air hole! Air hole!" He heard the sound of pikes and breaking bars clanging as they were discarded along the surface of the ice by men rushing to the aid of the two brothers. The sound had nowhere to go under the low gray sky except to bounce and echo across the width of the lake. Mark heard all these things clearly and separately like instruments in a deadly orchestra.

As Daniel's scraper disappeared into the water, his horse was pulled backwards into the black gravitational field of the hole. The horse struggled to move forward or at least to yield no ground. Daniel was thrown almost clear of the hole. He might have cleared it altogether if Mark's horse did not arrive at the precise spot his head was going to land. As Mark's horse inadvertently kicked Daniel's head, he staggered throwing Mark through the air over his brother like a two man acrobatic team. Mark dropped his reins, but they caught his boot as he flew past his horse. He felt his arm fold painfully under him as his face scraped the rasping crystals of surface ice. He saw his brother's open-mouthed face intermingle with the front legs of his horse, but he heard no scream other than his own. He saw his brother's body fly left towards his horse and then whip around to the right like a sawdust rag doll back toward the black hole in the ice. Mark saw no awareness in his brother's eyes as his limp body slid towards the hole. He wondered why his brother made no sound. Mark's leg twisted in his reins and he was suddenly wrenched left in an excruciatingly painful lunge as his horse struggled to rise and pull itself away from the hole that had just swallowed his brother. He felt his head banging against the ice surface as he was pulled by his terrified horse. He saw the gray sky bounce and spin above him. Pain filled his head. He struggled to lift it from the ice until blackness eclipsed the painful gray of the vibrating sky above him.

Mark awoke some minutes later to his father kneeling over him with an expression so twisted that Mark barely recognized him. He looked at his brother lying next to him. Ice covered his hair like a diamond studded cap. Mark wondered what he was pointing at, his finger unmoving and ungloved.

"I'm all right," he said, but he passed out before his father could utter a protest.

He awoke again and recognized that men were carrying him on a plank like a war casualty.

"Tell Emily not to chase the chickens," he said in a delirium that brought no laughter from the stone-faced men. He passed out again.

The next four days were cut out of Mark's life like the core from an apple. He remembered vague sensations more than events. The feeling of warmth that seemed to usher in waves of pain. The sensation of being pushed and prodded. Strangers touched his eyes and face in nightmarish dreams. Someone kept calling his name. He regained consciousness several times a day, each time he awoke to someone standing over him. It took all his energy to open his eyes and sharp throbbing daggers took the opportunity to rush in each time so he closed them quickly hoping to shut off the gateway to all that suffering.

By the fourth day, he stayed awake for longer periods of time. Sometimes ten or fifteen minutes at a spell. He realized he was in his brother's bed.

"Where's Daniel?" he asked, or he thought he asked. He wasn't certain because no one answered.

At another awakening he realized his left shoulder was wrapped tightly and taped to his side. His other arm was encased in white plaster bent at the elbow. On another excursion to the surface he felt the same hard white plaster on his right leg.

"I'm thirsty," he said and immediately someone placed a wet cloth to his lips.

His face burnt. He didn't know if he'd slept minutes or hours. He was hungry but the light of day hurt his eyes and made them tear. He closed them and slept another day.

On one of his trips to consciousness, Mark awoke to Doctor Kenney speaking softly to his mother. Was she sick? She looked haggard and worn with dark circles under her eyes. The doctor was not summoned capriciously to the Lerner house and Mark realized someone must be ill.

"How is Daniel?" he asked.

Mary Lerner rushed to his bedside. She put her hand to his forehead. The Doctor held a light to his face and asked Mark to follow it with his eyes without moving his head. Could the doctor have been sent for him?

"I must have fallen asleep," Mark said. "What time is it?"

Mary looked at the doctor.

"I dreamed the Harrisons were here," he said. "With Judith, but not Emily."

Mary sat at the edge of her son's bed. She caressed his head and absently fixed his hair.

"They were here. For Daniel."

"Why am I in his bed? Where is he?"

Mary put the palm of her hand to her mouth and looked to the doctor.

"Mark," he said. "Your brother did not survive the accident. He died almost instantly from severe head trauma."

Mark did not understand.

"No," he said. "I mean Daniel."

Mary Lerner looked to the floor and sighed.

"Mark," the doctor continued. "Do you remember anything about last week? About the accident?"

What a strange question. What accident? What about Daniel? Why was his leg so heavy and why couldn't he move his arm?

"I don't understand."

He started to panic. His eyes widened and his breath came in spurts.

Mary looked nervously to the doctor.

"Everything is all right. Try not to get excited. The worst is over."

Mary put a cool cloth on his forehead. She asked if he wanted more to drink and she placed a half filled glass to his lips and let him sip tepid water.

"What is the last thing you remember before the–before you fell asleep?"

He thought for a moment. It was hard to say.

"Daniel didn't finish his stew. He didn't eat his egg at all. I ate it."

He thought longer. Why was it so hard to remember?

"He was upset, I think, about Meghan. I'm sorry. That's all I can–did you say Daniel was–what did you say?" Silent tears ran from his mother's eyes in channels that seemed cut into her face. Mark did not remember seeing them before. The roots of her hair were gray. He didn't remember that either.

"Why can't I–? Why is it so hard to think?" he asked the doctor.

"You have suffered a severe concussion. You have been unconscious for the better part of five days. You awoke occasionally and spoke. Do you remember any of this?"

Mark started to shake his head 'no' but it hurt to move.

"Doctor?" Mary said. "Is this–?"

"This is all quite normal after a severe concussive experience accompanied by shock. It will take a while for him to put thoughts together." He reached into his bag and retrieved a stethoscope. "He may never remember the accident."

Mary sighed. Mark wondered why the doctor spoke as if he wasn't there.

"You broke your arm in two places, son. You suffered a compound fracture below the knee. You had a class two separated shoulder and scraped most of the skin off your face. You're fortunate to be alive, young man." The doctor turned to Mary. "He will need to eat.

Something light to begin with. Soup broth perhaps. Then work up to farina. Plenty of liquids. I don't think you need to keep trying to wake him. He is out of the woods, I believe. Let him sleep. Sleep is the best restorative medicine we have."

The doctor packed his bag and patted Mark's good shoulder.

"Take it a little at a time, son."

He nodded to Mary and left not waiting to be shown to the door.

Sentences began to connect for Mark.

"Daniel is dead," he said more as a statement than a question. As if he had known all along. As if he had always known.

"Yes, dearest. But you mustn't dwell–" Mary could not finish.

Mark sighed deeply. He turned his head and focused on Daniel's dresser. A white doily hung from the sides. A bottle of hair grease showed itself twice. Once in the mirror. A small metal airplane sat on the doily. One of the propellers was broken and paint had chipped off one wing.

"Is he–gone already?"

"Yes. We buried him yesterday," his mother said as if she was trying the words on to see if they fit.

Mark nodded.

"A lot of people there?"

"Most everyone in town. The Harrisons."

Mark nodded again.

"Meghan Harrington?"

"Yes," Mary said.

"I'm sorry, Mom. I'm sorry."

Mary bent over her surviving son. A single tear fell on his face.

"I know," she said. "Let's concentrate on making you well. Your father will be relieved you've awoken. He's been a wreck."

"The horses?"

"Your father's been feeding. We've figured it out. I don't think we'll lose any before you're ready to get back to it," she said with a weak smile.

Mark tried to sit up, but dizziness overwhelmed him.

"Take your time," Mary said. "We've got lots of time."

Within a week Mark could sit up and could manage his crutches well enough to make it to the toilet and back. On his first day out of bed he went to his brother's closet where he found the headphones Daniel told him about. He had hoped that they weren't there, that his brother was lying to him. He didn't want to think about him eavesdropping on people's conversations. He pressed his back to the wall and slowly slid down to a sitting position. his cast thumped solidly on the floor as he carefully unraveled the wire splices that tapped the headphones into the phone line. He had no idea why that was so important to him to do that, but he felt a great sense of relief when it was done.

By the end of the week, Mark negotiated a trip to the front parlor window and looked down onto the lake. No one had removed the ice. He thought of his childhood fear about winter never ending but did not smile at the memory.

Windfalls

In June of 1928, a week after his arrival, Mr. Harrison asked Mrs. Lerner at breakfast if she would ask Mark to meet with him in his office before lunch. The Harrisons' annual arrival had been awkward. They had stopped by Pine Bluff briefly after Daniel's funeral in January, the only winter visit in anyone's memory. Normally a time of joyous, welcoming hellos that subliminally ushered in summer, this year's arrival had been a skeletal walk-through of previous year's rituals. It had been a cold spring and the garden flowers were only now approaching full bloom. A pitcher of lemonade awaited Mr. Harrison as it did every year but Mrs. Lerner was nowhere to be seen. Mr. Harrison greeted Mark's father solemnly and awkwardly orchestrated the unpacking of the auto, leaving the lemonade untouched.

Mark had no way of knowing about the row Lucretia had with Austin in March about their annual sojourn.

"We couldn't possibly summer at Pine Bluff this year," she said to Austin.

"Of course we shall."

"We should leave the poor Lerners to their grief. The proper thing to do is to write them and say we shan't be coming this year."

While it seemed to Austin that Lucretia was acting out of genuine concern, the truth was she had already spoken to the Minors and had tentatively inquired about summering with them in Cape May.

"Exactly what the Lerners need is for life to return to normal. Can you imagine how ghastly this past winter has been for them? You saw that house. Every stick of furniture linen covered. Every shrouded chair must have seemed a ghost to the distraught Mrs. Lerner. We owe it to them to go and put on our best faces."

"I cannot agree that that is the proper thing to do," she said emphatically.

"I believe it is." But he knew he would need to sweeten the deal for his wife's cooperation. "And I think you should invite the Kinslows."

"But you always disliked Mrs. Kinslow," no small surprise in her voice.

"And I still do. She is loud and crude. But I think that is exactly the ticket needed to enliven that household."

Lucretia reflected for a moment. A summer with the Kinslows would certainly prove to be entertaining. Mrs. Kinslow was a competent tennis partner and could play bridge for hours. It was a concession, she knew, on Austin's part to invite her at all.

"And maybe the Fosters?"

Austin groaned. It was Patricia Kinslow he disliked, but he got on quite well with her husband William. He liked neither of the Fosters.

"Oh, damn it all, yes. Invite whomever you bloody please." As Austin stormed out of the room, Lucretia wondered at how he was ever able to negotiate a satisfactory contract at the office.

By the time Mrs. Lerner had managed to locate Mark, it was eleven-thirty. He hurriedly ran to wash unsure what to expect from the meeting. He inherited his father's nervousness in personal meetings with Mr. Harrison, although for no defined reason. His mother had given him no clue as to the purpose of the meeting.

"Good morning, sir," Mark said. He extended his hand and firmly shook the hand of Mr. Harrison.

"Good morning, Mark. Come in. Sit down, please," he smiled weakly.

Mark looked around the stately office. Mahogany block paneling covered the ten foot high walls. There was a personal water closet off the office, its door craftily incorporated into the paneling, so only the presence of the brass door knob gave away its location. Mr. Harrison was silhouetted by the late morning sun as it rushed in from the double French doors behind him, and it was difficult for Mark to see his face. Mr. Harrison's golf clubs rested on a stand alongside his desk. A wooden model of "The Morgan" whaleboat sat suspended in a glass case on the mantel over the never used fireplace. A vase of roses sat on the corner of the massive desk providing the only splash of color to the shadowy office. This room alone remained untouched and unshrouded all winter. Mark often snuck in during the fall and spring months since he was a young boy, and sat behind Mr. Harrison's desk wondering what it must be like to captain a ship the size of Mr. Harrison's.

Mark sat in the large leather arm chair across from the desk.

"Do you smoke?" he asked, while offering the twenty-year-old a cigar.

"No, sir."

"Good. No sense in rushing into that," he said. "Mind if I light one up?"

"No, sir," Mark said, a little surprised by the question.

"Mark, I wanted to tell you personally how sorry I was to hear of Daniel's death. I am sure it is a crushing blow to you and your family. Your mother looks like she hasn't eaten since."

"Yes sir. She's taken it quite hard," Mark muttered, his eyes looking to the worn carpet.

"When we were wired that one of the Lerner boys had drowned, I can't tell you how upset we all were. I feared at first it might be you," he said but then coughed and rushed to add, "I mean, of course, that we were devastated that either of you might come to such a demise." He fumbled uncertain if his intentions were being understood. "You seem to have come around nicely to form. All the bones mended, are they?"

"Yes, sir."

"Yes, well, this is all a terrible business."

He paused and picked up his cigar, re-lit it with a thick blue tipped wooden match until the sweet smell dominated the small room. Mark said nothing. An uncomfortable silence wafted in the smoke filled air. Mark knew that he was Mr. Harrison's favorite. Daniel, in fact, was the person who pointed that out at every possible occasion. Daniel hadn't resented the favoritism shown to Mark. He seemed to accept it as the normal course of events as if, given the choice, Mark would be his favorite also. He joked about Mark being "the favorite surrogate" only because it made Mark uncomfortable. Daniel had delighted in seeing his usually unflappable younger brother squirm under flattery. He never told Mark that he loved him. That just wasn't something a Lerner man did. But Mark felt the warmth hidden like a soft walnut in the hard shell of all his brother's barbs.

Mr. Harrison handed Mark a large manila envelope trying to bully his way through the discomfort that he too seemed to share.

"Mark, this is something I did against your parent's wishes, or your mother's wishes, at any rate. I had mentioned to her several years ago that I had written an insurance policy on both you and your brother. Your mother would not hear of it. I thought at first that she had misunderstood, thought that I expected your parents to pay the premiums. That was not her concern at all. 'Blood money', she said emphatically. 'should a woman prosper at the death of her son?' she asked me. That was the only time I have ever seen your mother indignant. She doesn't understand, Mark, the modern ways of life insurance."

"'It isn't a question of prosperity,' I told her. 'It is a way to compensate for the possible loss...' She cut me off abruptly. She made the sign of the cross and told me in no uncertain terms that her wishes were that I cancel the policies. She excused herself and left the room. The subject was never broached by either of us again."

"I'm certain that she thought I respected her wishes, as a gentleman would, but–" and he coughed again uncomfortably, "I did not. I expected, as I guess we all did, that she and your father and myself, for that matter, would all be with the Lord long before the insurance issue would surface again. But, as we see now, He works on his own timetable.

"I hope you don't think poorly of me for ignoring your mother's wishes. But, I am not completely sorry to say I merely changed the beneficiaries of the policies. Had you died Daniel would have been issued a recompense, and now that he has passed long before–" He stopped and sighed.

"Mark, you have in that envelope a draft for seven-thousand, eight hundred, seventy nine dollars. The policy was for seven thousand, five hundred, but with reinvestment of dividends– Well. That doesn't matter now. The check is yours, Mark. To do with what you will."

Mr. Harrison rose and poured himself a whisky from a crystal decanter on the lowboy that sat in readiness across from his desk.

"Mark?"

"Yes sir. Please. If you don't mind."

Mark drained his glass with one quick motion. He sat waiting for a kick to jolt him from the cloudy stupor he had fallen into. Mr. Harrison refilled their glasses. Mark had never tasted scotch whisky before and he couldn't have laid claim that he had tasted it now.

"Perhaps I could use it to repay your generosity in the cost of the horses," Mark said.

Mr. Harrison put both his hands in front of him, fingers pointed upward, as if trying to fend off an evil spirit. "Out of the question, young man," he said. "One thing has nothing to do with the other. I certainly have no desire to be repaid. Besides, the money you've made me with the stable has certainly surpassed the startup costs of that situation. If you were an older man, I might be insulted by your suggestion."

"I didn't mean–"

"Of course not. I only mean to say it is completely out of the question. Besides, the impropriety of my receiving a benefit check would surely bring the insurance commission bastards down my neck."

He smiled as if he had just joked. Mark had never heard Mr. Harrison swear before and was further disoriented to hear it now.

"I started you in that business because I wanted to, and I would have done the same for Daniel if he had shown the initiative. You Lerners are a headstrong lot, I must say." He laughed again that hearty laugh that Mark had never learned to associate with humor.

"Mark, it is a fast changing world out there. And I would say this to my own son if I had one. A wise man can build a respectable fortune if he were to invest a sum of money this size wisely. That is the payment you can offer me, Mark. Your success will be a reward that would far surpass the few dollars that I contributed to it."

Mark cleared his throat, uncomfortable with such an outpouring of emotion.

"Thank you, sir."

"You might need to find a competent broker. I know some fellows at Hoagland, Allum & Company or at John Muir's who are quite capable. You must be careful, Mark. I know this seems an enormous amount of money to you but people lose this much money in a single day."

A slight nod backwards of Mark's head let Mr. Harrison know that Mark had heard him.

"What a lot of fellows call investing today is nothing more than gambling. Selling and buying short is a fool's game, in my opinion.

You cannot sell what you do not own, I always say. But I'll say no more. This is your money, Mark."

Mark thanked him and sat in silence uncertain if there was more to their meeting.

"I'm sorry I have put you in a moral dilemma with this draft," Mr. Harrison said. "I see that I have put you in an uncomfortable position of deceiving your parents or of telling them the truth and possibly causing more pain. All I can say for my part is that I have told no one of this matter. Not even Mrs. Harrison. Whatever you decide will have no confirmation or denial from me."

"Thank you, sir. I haven't determined what I'll do."

"Nor should you have," he said. "A decision like this cannot be made over a quick shot of whisky."

Mark began to rise.

"There is one more thing, Mark, though it has nothing at all to do with this matter."

"Yes, sir?" Mark sat back down.

"Emily has it in her head to ride with a hunt club next winter. I am not in favor of this but you may have noticed how intractable that girl is."

He smiled. Mark returned his smile with his own.

"In my opinion, her teachers at the Riding Academy in Manhattan are a lot of fools. They may know about horses dancing around in a ring, but they know precious little about horses running in a pack in wide open country. Do you think you could find the time this summer to school Emily? Make a hunter out of her?"

A genuine smile filled Mark's face. There seemed to be no negative aspect to this arrangement.

"Sure," he answered, trying not to sound too enthusiastic. He thought for a moment before adding, "But we have no jumps. I'll need to start her off in the ring."

"I have taken the liberty to order some from New Jersey. I expect them to arrive today or tomorrow. Is Abbey up to the task? Or do we need a different mount?"

"Abbey's capable."

"Good," Mr. Harrison said. "I told Emily I would speak to you and only if you agreed would I allow her to pursue this whim of hers."

"I'll be happy to."

"Only if you tell me in September that she is ready, can she continue. She understands, and has agreed to those terms."

Mark smiled.

Mr. Harrison stood and extended his hand. Mark shook it firmly. Each man looked into the other's eye. What Mr. Harrison saw in Mark's he approved of with a quick, almost indiscernible nod of his head.

Mark left the office and walked to the barn saying nothing to anyone along the way. He started to tack up his horse, Ohio. But he changed his mind and decided instead to saddle Emily's horse, Abbey. He needed time to think. As he saddled up he reminded himself of the bank draft. As momentous an event as that was in his life, Mark found it only the second most remarkable event of the day.

Lessons

"Are you ready for me this morning?" Emily asked Mark as she entered the barn.

Nearly a year had passed since he last saw her. Her beauty seemed to arrive seconds ahead of her announcing her arrival. He smiled. Said 'good morning' and watched her walk through the stable in the middle of the stalls. She started haltingly to offer condolences and to ask after his health, but Mark waved her off as politely as he could. She walked uncertainly, almost like a bride walking down an aisle past the stalls that flanked both sides of the center walkway. The dark wainscoting that ran along the bottom half of the stalls and on the ceiling absorbed whatever light that might have pierced the dark stable from outside. As she walked she grabbed the cross-ties wall-mounted at the doorway of each stall and let them slide through her hands dropping them when she reached the next, so that by time she reached the end of the stable all the cross-ties were swinging and banging against the wood. Mark blew a silent whistle.

"What are you all dressed up for?" he asked as soon as he could summon his voice.

She looked down. She was wearing a new spring riding habit that she had purchased at Macy's before she left Manhattan. The jodhpurs fit tightly around her inner thigh. Her white blouse, buttoned to her neck, was topped with a large Cameo brooch. The rusty brown plaid of her riding jacket seemed to match perfectly her reddish brown hair. Her knee high black leather boots were highly polished and Mark wondered who had put the shine to them.

"Well, I need to make a good first impression on my new teacher," she flirted, curtsying slightly in his direction.

He smiled again. "Well, Emily, as fine as you might look, you're overdressed for the occasion. Or I am woefully underdressed." She brought her hand to her face in mock horror.

"Oh my, no," she said, then she laughed aloud.

"The way I see it," Mark said suddenly serious, "we've got three months to get you comfortably over four-foot fences. How often can you come?"

"Why, everyday." The smile had gone from her lips if not completely from her eyes. "I'm quite earnest about this, Mark. Daddy has made it very clear to me that the road to hunting goes through this barn."

"All right," he said, pleased by her determination. "My intention is this. You should warm up in the ring for fifteen minutes. Then we'll school Abbey over the jumps for a half hour or so. Then I think we should ride out on the trails to help build up her stamina. She's fit, but not fit enough for a hunt. Do you have that much time?"

"Yes."

"What about your guests?"

"Hmm," she sighed. "I forgot about them. Judith is here most of the summer. Then Andrea might come the end of July. Maybe Lisa in August."

The summer that stretched out before them seemed too finite to Mark, as she sectioned off the days.

"Maybe they can join us on our trail rides some times. Perhaps we can start earlier in the day," she said. "Are you an early riser?"

"I'm down here before dawn most mornings," Mark answered. "If you can get here by six we'll be done before the heat gets too high. We should ride at least four times a week." He paused thoughtfully for a moment. "Have you had many lessons?"

"I've only jumped a few times at the academy and that time with you last year."

"Good," he said. "Then I won't have much to un-teach."

She seemed completely focused on his every word.

"All right, then. Let's go."

"All right, then."

They stood face to face maybe eighteen inches apart. Mark was now about four inches taller than Emily. In the time it took him to blink an eye, he thought of their introductory collision. She was taller than he then, nine years ago. A few seconds passed. Emily never took her eyes from his. Warm pockets of air passed between them in their silence.

Mark had Abbey tacked up and ready.

"If we're going to start so early it'll be best if you tack Abbey yourself," he said. "I'm still feeding that time of day."

"I've never done that before," she said. "At the academy the horses are tacked when we get them and you've always had Abbey ready for me here."

She seemed embarrassed. She started walking her horse with her stirrups long so they bounced against her girth as she walked.

"All right. It'll take a few times until you get the hang of it. We'll start that tomorrow." He watched her approach the mounting block. "Next time, raise your irons–your stirrups– Don't let them bounce on her like that."

Emily stepped on the top step of the mounting block. She gathered the reins in her left hand and mounted. She rode to the outdoor ring that Mark had built between the two largest paddocks. He had a load of cinders delivered and spent the better part of the week raking them smooth until there was an even four-inch footing in the ring. He had set up jump standards, but had not added any cross rails yet.

Mark watched Emily's weight shift from leg to leg as she walked out on Abbey. The most ordinary looking woman becomes a raving beauty when on a horse. Mark recognized this to be a fact, some unspoken contract with God between women and horses. When a woman of Emily's beauty took a horse between her thighs, she became a goddess. Mark remembered talking about this with Daniel. He agreed with Mark and added 'That's why men ride' and they both laughed in their best bar room man-bragging guffaws.

"Drop your weight deeper into your heels," Mark coached.

Mark stood at the gate as Emily trotted, then cantered Abbey around the ring. It was a large ring, almost fifty feet square. He listened to the rhythmic pounding of the horse's shoes on the soft, relenting ground. The landing of each foot was like a muted drum played in the foreground of branches blowing in the wind like violins in a subtle symphony. He watched as tiny clouds of dust eddied around each hoof in tiny tornadoes. He fine-tuned Emily's form, telling her to move her leg forward or back; moving her hands up or down on Abbey's withers. Emily was an attentive student. If she didn't understand what Mark wanted she asked him to explain. Towards the end of the lesson, Mark set up some cavaletti poles for Emily to trot and canter through. She studied him as he paced off the distance between each pole. Mark went back to stand and coach from the gate.

Abbey trotted, then cantered through the cavaletti poles as if they weren't there. Mark was pleased. He set up two small jumps, just cross-rails for starters. He set the poles up low so that the top of the X sat about a foot off the ground. He watched closely as Emily brought Abbey to the fence. Abbey took the jump long almost knocking Emily off. She grabbed a handful of mane and righted herself on the smooth brown saddle. Her whip dropped to the ground.

"You were too far forward," he said, "that's why you almost fell off."

"Why'd she do that?" Emily asked while cantering in smaller circles in front of Mark.

"You squeezed her side as you approached the fence."

"I was just asking for a jump," she said, slightly breathless.

"You don't need to ask with Abbey," he said. "She's a thoroughbred. Just bring her to the center of the fence and do nothing. She'll jump. Trust her Em. Trust me."

She looked sharply around as if she heard something other than what he said and she needed to verify it with eye contact. Mark hadn't moved when she was almost tossed over Abbey's head. She cantered around in front of him at the gate and said facetiously "I'm all right, Mark. Stay there. Don't worry."

She had passed him already and missed his smile as he said softly to himself, "She's a thoroughbred. Trust her."

Mark studied them again as Emily took Abbey to the cross-rails. She jumped effortlessly, without hesitation. He saw the powerful horse lift off the ground and he watched as a smile blossomed onto Emily's face as Abbey landed in full stride on the other side.

"She's on the wrong lead," he called to her. Emily either didn't hear or didn't care as she cantered past him radiant in the morning summer sun.

"That's enough for now. Walk Abbey out while I go tack Ohio," he called. "We'll head out to the trails if you're still willing."

"How can an hour have passed already?" she asked.

Mark looked up towards the sun, still in the eastern sky. "It's been longer than that," he said.

Lessons went well. Within two weeks Emily was taking Abbey over two-foot cross rails and fences. She did not shy away from Mark's watchful criticism, but seemed to seek it out, often asking for more information.

"Was I too far forward on that jump?" she'd ask. Or, "How was my leg? Did I keep it at the girth?"

Mark always knew. He had an uncanny ability to hone in on several details at once. Emily sensed it and quickly learned to rely on his faculty.

Just the night before she had told her father at supper, "He's ten times the teacher that Mrs. Smoltz is at the academy. Each lesson has a week's learning packed into a day. Come watch us, Daddy. Abbey is getting so fit!"

Mrs. Harrison looked up from her plate. A silent alarm had gone off in her head, although she couldn't seem to place the source.

"Today Abbey was approaching a jump. Mark was forty or fifty feet away. Before I even felt her slow down, he hollered to me 'Hit her. She's going to refuse!' I reached down and whacked her–not too hard–I just couldn't–and she just collected herself and took the fence as easy as could be. He knew from across the ring what she was going to do. He's incredible! I can't imagine how he does it!"

Her father raised an eyebrow. "Maybe I should come by to watch," he said.

"I hope you're not keeping that boy from his chores," her mother said. "I'm sure there's plenty of work to be done," she added vaguely although she couldn't, for the love of God or money, have pretended to know what it might be.

"Mother! Daddy already went over this with Mr. Lerner."

Austin looked up to his wife's face with an absence of expression.

"Well, you shouldn't be spending so much time with the help. People will talk," her mother said.

"Oh mother. Don't be so horrid. He isn't the help. He's–he's–Mark," she said lamely. "And besides, there are no people here to talk."

Lucretia jumped to agree if only to move the conversation away from the inappropriate dinner topic of animals onto something more suitable.

"Well, if your father wasn't so stubborn about motoring alone our guests might have come with us instead of having to wait a fortnight for their own motorcar. It's a wonder anyone agrees to come to this wilderness at all when your father insists on placing so many obstacles in their path."

Her eyes darted from Emily to Austin. She stiffened her back as if bracing for a challenge.

Emily, as usual, counted on her mother's self absorption to stampede subtle revelations that she might inadvertently drop into their conversations.

A lone maple shaded Mark and Emily as they sat high on a ridge looking down onto the river. Small rapids scratched white water V's across the surface but they were too high to hear the current ripping over the exposed stones. The plaintive hollow call of a dove broke the silence in perfect circles of sound from an upper branch of the tree, but neither of them could see it. Without apparent provocation, the dove sprang from the tree spasmodically flapping its wings in a whirring sound that seemed to have nothing to do with flight.

Mark leaned back on the grass looking at Emily. She sat fearlessly on a huge protruding rock that hung two hundred feet above the river. Abbey and Ohio were hobbled nearby trying to graze on the patches of grass that managed to peek out from the rocky soil. In the two weeks since they embarked on their lessons Mark had come to look forward to this part of the day. He loved to listen to Emily. He knew if they rode long enough they would arrive at her perfect stories. Sometimes if they neared the stable in the middle of her talking he would detour onto a longer trail to give her more time to speak. He couldn't imagine her opening up so much if sitting on a porch swing, or in a parlor wing chair. They rode to her stories as if to a destination, as if they were hidden under the dust of the trails and needed to be uncovered by the steady pounding of the horse's hooves. He learned that if he interrupted her recitals with his own comments she'd become distracted, and never finish the telling. But if he answered her stories with silence, she would continue endlessly. Mark loved the rhythm of her voice. It contained an optimistic energy that excited him.

"Isn't this the most splendid of times to be alive!" she gushed.

There was no pretense in her voice. Mark looked down at the river that formed a boundary to his world. Ice houses dotted the water edge.

Dead shad were visible on the surface, their spawning season over. He looked back to Emily silhouetted against the cloudless sky, but said nothing.

"So much is happening! Life seems to spread out into the past and the future at the same time. Admiral Byrd is at the South Pole, and did you read about archeologists uncovering the magnificent tomb of Tutankhamen. The horrible war is long over. Everyone is prospering."

She spoke of her days in Manhattan. He felt she brought the world to his door. She seemed to be in the middle of life, and he only on the periphery. People he only read about in newspapers passed her on the street. In one week she saw John D. Rockefeller and J. P. Morgan walking "downtown". She spoke of Lady Mary Bailey's six thousand mile flight as if it held some consequence in her own life. Talked of luncheons at the Roof Garden of the Waldorf Astoria. Teas at the Vanderbilt Chateau. She was at the American premier of Puccini's opera "La Rondine". Had been to the Ziegfield Theatre. Had met Mary Pickford.

Mark couldn't get enough.

She spoke of vast sums of money as if mere pittances. The President gave Mme. Curie fifty thousand dollars for research. Byrd was spending ten times that on fifty-six men and three airplanes for his expedition. Al Jolsen was paid forty thousand dollars for four weeks work. She had driven in three thousand dollar autos. Spoke of eight hundred dollar dresses from Paris. Foreign sounding names dropped from her lips like water from a fountain. Lanvin. Chanel. Vionnet. Patou.

Mark was mesmerized.

She described the places she'd traveled. Paris. Italy. Holland. She had such a memory for details that at times he could have sworn it was he who had been there.

He accepted her stories as gifts. Tiny Faberge eggs depicting a life he knew little about. But what surprised him was that he could also give her gifts. He would interrupt her sometimes to point out the way the grasses sounded in the wind. The smell of shade as they left a sun-baked field. Rays of sunlight horizontally streaking a forest trail. The sounds of crickets banging against the summer silence. And she seemed to take these gifts as greedily as he took hers, and they were richer to him for her acceptance.

He watched her eyes dance when he spoke. Her eyes so unlike Kristen's. So naked was her stare that he swore he would know in a second if she ever lied to him. Each day their morning trail ride was extended, until by June fifteenth, they weren't returning until after noon. By June 18th Mark knew that the best part of the day had passed when Emily left the stable and walked up the small hill to Pine Bluff.

June 19th, 1928 was the third consecutive day over one hundred degrees. It seemed there was no spring that year as summer bulldozed its way through the fully bloomed foliage. Mark had Ohio out for an afternoon ride. Emily was home entertaining Judith, or Sarah. He forgot who. He intended to ride hard that day but the sudden heat hadn't given man or beast a chance to get acclimated to its force. Ohio had started blowing after the first trot so Mark contented himself with a slow ride, moving into a canter only when the flies got too bad.

He walked Ohio through the woods filled with the unceasing chirping of the seventeen-year cicadas. The horse seemed unnerved by the din that echoed in the solitary woods. At their thickest nesting spots cicadas would blindly fly into them keeping the wary horse on edge. Mark sang to calm him with nonsensical words he made up as he went along. "Only cicadas," he sang. "Only cicadas come back again. Singing 'bout Emily. Emily, Emily." Ohio was quieted by the singing and although alert to the unfamiliar sound, kept walking under the canopy of trees that towered above them. It was cooler in the woods. Damper. The smell of wet dirt filled the air. Mark could barely hear the hooves planting themselves in the moist undercover of the forest floor.

"It's twenty degrees cooler in here," he thought. Then he said it aloud in his normal speaking voice to see if he could hear himself over the din of the cicadas.

He thought about them as he rode. His mother had told him about the cicada's seventeen year gestation period. Born in tree roots, they lived their entire lives, mated and died within three months. The cicadas made him feel like he was in God's church, under an apse of towering trees. Made him wonder about Daniel. About death. He gave Ohio his head and let the horse plod along wherever he wanted. The horse stretched its neck downward and continued down the trail in the woods that ultimately would circle back toward Pine Bluff and the lake.

At the midpoint of the trail there was an opening in the woods, as if someone had cleared a plot of land for a never built cabin. The heat intensified in the opening baking the air on its way to the ground. Mark saw the treetops stirring slightly in a breeze but it was a breeze that abandoned its journey before it reached Mark. Sweat rolled down his face and collected in the crevice below his Adam's apple. He hadn't shaved that day and the heat made his shadow of a beard uncomfortable.

Ohio crossed the opening and returned to the relative cool of the woods. Mark decided he would sit in the ice house when he got back He fell into a deeper wordless reflection and it seemed only seconds before Ohio passed through the woods and headed back to the stable. The horse picked up his pace as he neared the barn.

Mark heard the sound just as Ohio's ears pricked back.

"What was that?" he asked the horse.

A sad hum had reached his ears coming from the direction of Pine Bluff. It was a resonant sound that seemed to be riding an imperceptible breeze toward him, barely reaching his ears before dying out completely.

He halted Ohio and cupped his hand to his ear trying to identify the sound. The rattling of cicadas was behind him. The hum got louder and began to take on shape as he pressed Ohio forward to Pine Bluff. As he neared the front porch the sound took on words. A man was singing the saddest song he had ever heard although he couldn't make out the words. He edged closer to the house and heard the somber wail of violins and realized he was listening to a recording. Someone had pulled the Victrola to the front of the parlor. Music bathed the front porch through the open French doors.

Mark moved Ohio to the willow that flanked the porch. He opened the branches of the thirty foot tall tree like he was opening curtains on a window and entered its inner sanctum. The air was cooler under there. He could see Emily sitting alone on the porch. Her head was pressed back into the wicker chair and she was rocking back and forth slowly, her eyes closed. The song ended. Emily stood and reached through the window to begin the song again.

There was a richness to the music that he had never heard before. The words were not English but Mark felt their sadness without the benefit of translation. The voice seemed to reach him as if through a mist. The song started out quietly and quickly built to a powerful cry of unintelligible words. He watched Emily sitting under its cover. He could almost see the notes showering over her. She wore a wide brimmed straw hat with a sleeveless blue sun frock. She was crying.

The song was not more than three or four minutes long but his impression was that it would have ended too soon even if it played on for hours. He didn't want to break the spell it cast. He watched silently as Emily rose again to restart the song. He listened harder to the words as if a better listen would make the foreign language more intelligible.

"Two say pie yaccho," the voice sang. "Vesty la jubba...." Then later in a stronger pained voice, "Reedy Pie Yaccho...." and his heart rose in his chest.

As the song ended for the third time he moved Ohio out of the willow tree.

"Ah, Mark," Emily said softly. She didn't seem startled by his presence. "I was just thinking of you." She wiped a tear from the corner of her eye. The smile there belied any sadness.

"What is that?" Mark asked.

"Enrico Caruso," Emily said. She seemed to be returning to herself as she spoke. Mark felt like he knew where she had been.

"He's an Italian tenor," she added. "The song is the climax to Leoncavallo's 'Pagliacci'".

"It's the saddest thing I've ever heard," he said, afraid he was banally stating a too obvious fact.

He noticed a movement in her eyes. They never broke from his but seemed to shift like an auto engine and drive deeper into him.

"It is," she agreed.

"Do you know what the words mean?"

"Most of them. Pagliacci is a clown who has discovered the woman he loves is in love with another. The song is sung by Pagliacci to try to convince himself to continue to perform through his sorrow."

"What does the 'reedy pie yacchi' line mean?"

"It means, 'Laugh, clown' then he says 'and they will applaud. Make a joke out of your heartache and tears.'"

He sat on Ohio singing the line in English to himself. It was so much stronger in Italian.

"Doesn't it seem there are a million ways for lovers to be apart and just the tiniest chance for them to be together?" she asked.

Mark dismounted but said nothing. An old stormy conversation with Kristen flashed like lightning in his mind.

Emily seemed uneasy with the tenor of her own conversation. She cleared her throat and waved her hand as if attempting to dismiss an annoying insect. "It makes me think of my friends. Catherine loves Henry, but Henry loves her sister. Then Sarah–you met her last summer–loves William, but he doesn't come into his money for years and besides, he's only in love with himself. Then there's us," she said and halted abruptly.

The word resonated in Mark's ears as deeply as Caruso's. "Us?" he said to himself. "Is there an Us?" The word sounded as foreign as the words of the song. Emily's face reddened. Mark sensed that she had jumped a fence she wasn't quite ready for into a field she might not want to be in.

He watched her intently as she tried to right herself.

"Anyway, listen to me sounding so moody over nothing."

Mark saw her struggle to recover but would not take his eyes from hers and remove her discomfort. She tried to cover her slip with more conversation as if she could dilute the impact of her previous words.

"Daddy saw Caruso at the Met when he debuted in America."

"I'll have to think on that some," he said, belatedly answering her original question. None of his friends seemed to be in love with anyone. Not like in that song anyway. But then he thought of Kristen and how she described her husband. She knew a pool of sorrow deep enough to produce a song as sad as Caruso's. He felt certain of that now.

"It takes a lot of love to make that much sorrow," he said.

His own words surprised him as if they had come from someone else. Someone deep inside of him. Someone he hardly even knew.

"Oh, Mark," Emily sighed.

She looked as if she wanted to say something else. Her eyes scanned his face as if looking for clues. She stood and said, "I must go." Her head bent downward away from Mark.

She left him standing alone near the porch. He heard the needle scratching weakly at the edge of the record as he pulled himself back onto Ohio and rode back into the din of the cicadas. When he was certain that he could not be heard from the house, he sang loudly, "Reedy pie Yacci." But the sting had gone out of the words.

Agreements

The morning after Mark had interrupted Emily's Caruso, she came down to the stable for a lesson. She was usually there by six. Mark had hoped to see her but no longer expected her when she arrived at eight. He was lunging a new mare in the ring.

"Good morning, Mark,"

She looked stunning in her riding habit. Her reddish brown hair touched her white blouse shining in the sunlight. She wore no jacket.

"Hi, Em. Are we riding today?"

"I wasn't sure. But if you have the time–"

Mark wondered briefly why she wasn't sure.

"Could we skip my lesson today and just go hacking?"

"Sure. Where do you want to go?" he asked.

"I thought we could take the trail up the mountain. It's cooler there."

Mark noticed a quaver in her voice. It seemed tentative, almost frightened. Her hands were shaking slightly as she got Abbey ready.

They didn't speak until they were deep in the woods. There was nothing particularly unusual about that. They both had grown accustomed to their shared silences, settling into them like old people into arm chairs.

"Do you think I talk too much?" she asked.

The question seemed funny coming as it did after twenty minutes of quiet.

"No."

"Sometimes when I'm with you I say more than I intend to," she said.

"With words?"

Her head jerked to face his. Her mouth opened slightly as her eyes fixed onto his. He fought being drawn into her. He blinked consciously trying to break her spell.

"Whatever do you mean?" she asked.

She had recovered from the initial surprise of his question. He thought she knew exactly what he meant. In fact he knew she knew what he meant. He meant the way her eyes spoke and the things they said to him alone. The things they said when they stood close to one another. The things they told him yesterday on the porch.

"Oh, you know," he said.

"I don't believe I do," she answered, her voice cloaked in a mock indignation as if Mark's conjecture was an affront to her propriety.

"People don't only speak in words," he said. "That's all I meant."

"Oh." she said. And she looked at him again as if searching for him.

"Yeah, like that," he said and impulsively buried his heel into Ohio's side. The surprised horse sprang into a canter leaving Emily behind. Mark's head was spinning. He felt acutely aware of everything around him. The thistle tops of the long hay whipping around Ohio's legs. The sway of the grass as the wind snaked through the distant fields. The uniformity of blue in the almost cloudless sky. The sound of the hooves on the hard rain-starved dirt. The sound of Ohio breathing heavily up the hill. He looked back to Emily over his shoulder. She was cantering behind him, a smile covering her face. She was gaining on him. So Mark did something he had never done with Emily. He urged Ohio forward into a full gallop. The horse shot ahead excited by his own speed. Mark looked over his shoulder again back to Emily. She had raised herself into a two-point like a jockey and had stayed with him. Good instinct, he thought. He wasn't certain if Emily could maintain a full gallop but she seemed more than capable. They ran hell bent on leather for nearly a half a mile. Maybe more. Mark brought Ohio back down to a trot as the fields stonewalled into the woods, Emily right on his tail. The horses were both snorting excitedly. Abbey was in full lather. Mark patted the wet matted hair on Ohio's neck.

"We better walk them out some," he said.

She smiled a reply that had nothing to do with his words. They fell into an agitated silence and walked along sometimes single file, sometimes abreast. When abreast they rode close together so their irons would meet and clank and their boots pressed together between the two horses. Neither said anything. Both ignored the contact as if it meant nothing to either of them.

They crossed a small brook as they neared the top of the hill. Mark told Emily to let Abbey's head lower into the cool water to give herself a drink. Abbey seemed confused. She put her lips and nose into the water but did not drink. As they started forward again Abbey decided to jump over the small brook, surprising Emily. She dropped her whip.

"I'll get it," Mark said. "You won't be able to remount out here without a mounting block."

"Will too," she said. "I'll get it."

They dismounted simultaneously. Emily's whip lay on the ground between them like a line drawn in sand. They bent to pick it up standing inches apart.

Mark pulled her into him and kissed her. A brief kiss at first, but that one catapulted them into another. Then another. They held each other awkwardly one handed, the other mindfully clutching reins.

He opened his eyes. Whispered, "Yes."

"Yes what?" she whispered back.

"Yes, exactly."

He kissed her uncertain smile.

A deer jumped out from behind a thicket of a thorny shrub startling the horses. Abbey backed up, frightened, pulling Emily toward her, then reared in fear. Mark reached for her rein but couldn't catch it. Emily quieted her horse without his help.

"We should go," she said. Mark saw she was as jumpy as the mare.

"All right," he answered, although he couldn't imagine why he would choose to leave of his own accord.

Emily could not remount from the level ground. Mark moved to her and cradled his arm.

"Step on with your knee," he said, and he easily boosted her onto the sixteen-hand mare. He mounted Ohio and they rode off again. They said nothing about where they had just been. Except with their eyes. They rode another ten minutes barely speaking.

"Do you want to stop a while?" Mark asked.

"No," Emily answered.

They rode the hour back to the stable both seemingly content in each other's company. Both seemed wary of the line they had just crossed. Both were lost in their own thoughts about what it meant.

As they reached the stable Mark noticed a perceptible change in Emily. Her shoulders tensed up. Her arms did not follow Abbey's head as easily as they had before. As they entered the barn Mark hoped for an opportunity for another kiss. Emily tied Abbey to the cross ties and said, "Mark, I have to go. Can I leave Abbey to you?" She wore that same frightened look she had arrived with that morning.

"Yes," he said. "Sure." Disappointed, but not. The kiss still hard on his mind. He watched her as she walked to the house.

"We riding tomorrow?" he called as she was about to pass from sight.

She didn't answer. He could not see that she was struggling to focus with her eyes filled with tears.

The following day, Wednesday, Emily didn't ride and Mark found himself wishing they had set up a more definite schedule. He took the day to work his other horses in the ring. He had been neglecting them lately.

Thursday, Emily arrived at six. They schooled Abbey over jumps in the ring for almost an hour. No words were spoken except words of instruction and the necessary response. If Lucretia Harrison was watching, she would have been quite comfortable with her daughter's propriety. After the class Emily led them south in the opposite direction of their last ride. They brought a silence with them but it was not their own comfortable silence. It had a static within it that they both felt and that they both caused. They rode for forty minutes and returned to the barn. Their horses were always at least ten or twelve feet apart during the entire ride. Mark was dying to know what she was thinking but he refused to ask.

They stood together in the barn brushing their mounts. Emily was careful not to let Abbey sway too close to Ohio.

"Mark," she said finally. "This can never lead to anything. We can never– It's foolish to think that we can ever be together. Every day I come down here to tell you that, but I don't know– When I see you it all seems so possible. I care about you, Mark. I really do. You know that. But– But– We're just too different."

Mark admitted to himself that she was probably right. What could he offer her? Of course he had thought of them being together but only in vague daydreams.

He said nothing.

"This is all so beautiful," she said with a sweep of her arm that seemed to encompass all of summer. "But it's not real. Being with you every summer is just a dream world. Do you know every year I go home in September and I cry for days? I don't know why, but I've done it since I was a little girl. This is a fairy tale, a place in a bubble that Daddy made. You're part of the fairy tale, Mark. Do you understand?"

"Sure," Mark said. He understood all the words but he didn't think he believed what they added up to. He wasn't part of a fairy tale. His life seemed real enough though he had to agree his time with Emily was like that.

But her words contradicted so much that he had seen from her. He thought of her tears for Pagliacci. He wanted to ask her now why she cried. But he didn't. He thought he knew. He thought someday, she might know.

They each walked their horses back to their stalls. They stood across the aisle from one another leaning on opposite walls in the cool darkness of the stable, their eyes locked. They stepped into each other's arms. Emily's hands went to the back of Mark's neck, holding him tightly.

"I need you to help me with this," she said.

He stepped away and sat on a bale of hay, leaning his back against the wall.

"Not sure I can do that," he said.

She remained standing and leaned back against the opposite stall wall, her hands clasped behind her waist. Her chest heaved. Her face searched his. Her eyes darted to his eyes. To his shoulders. To his lips. Back to his eyes.

"Can't we go back to being friends. Forget that kiss?"

"Can you?"

Her eyes seemed to turn liquid.

"I have to," she said.

Abbey kicked her stall as Emily leaned against its outside wall. She stepped forward startled, closer to Mark.

He didn't reach for her though she stood a foot away.

"Are you angry?" she asked.

"Confused," he answered after a moment.

"Me too," she said.

He stood up and moved to her. He put his arms around her encircling her small back between his elbows. She sighed. He felt her full breasts pressing against his ribs and wanted her more than he could remember ever wanting anything in his life. They stood a long time that way. Barely moving.

"If we were just friends," he asked, "could we still do this?"

She hummed a sigh.

"Sometimes. Maybe. Yes."

"Would I be able to do this?" he asked as he raised her chin and lightly lowered his lips to hers. He kissed her gently like a breeze on a feather.

"I don't think so," she whispered.

"How about this?" and he kissed her again. This time a little harder, and ran his tongue lightly on her lips.

"No," she said. "We couldn't do that."

He might have believed her had she opened her eyes. But she stood in front of him, eyes closed, head slightly back. Lips faintly parted. Not a wrinkle on her brow. Barely breathing. He kissed her again. He ran the tips of his fingers softly across the outline of her ear.

"This, I suppose, I shouldn't do either."

"No," she said, eyes still closed, but smiling now.

"And this..." he said as he ran his fingers delicately down her neck and between the buttons of her blouse, feeling the moisture of perspiration through the white cotton "...would be completely out of the question."

"Completely," she agreed. Smiling fully now. Eyes still closed.

"I just wanted to be certain," he said and stepped back from her. He slammed his back heavily against the stall door behind him. Her eyes snapped open, surprised by his withdrawal.

"I'd hate to do anything out of line," he said.

"Good," she said. "That wouldn't do at all."

"Agreed," he said.

"Agreed."

He smiled broadly for the first time.

"And Mark," she said as she stepped to him taking his hand in hers. "Absolutely none of this should ever be tolerated." She stood on her toes to kiss him firmly on the lips taking his hand and pressing it to her breast, her nipple hard in the palm of his open hand.

"Definitely not," he whispered. "This would be wicked."

"Terrible," she agreed.

The coughing sound of Mr. Harrison's auto pierced the envelope of their conversation.

"Daddy's back from golfing," she said, instantly nervous. The tenderness in her eyes vanished. "It's late. I've got to run."

She turned and walked to the approaching auto.

"Hi, Daddy," he heard her say. "We had the most wonderful ride."

He watched her until she went out of his view. She never looked back as she took her father's arm and walked him back to the house. He sat back down on the bale of hay glad they were able to agree on something.

Summer

For the rest of June into July, Mark and Emily expanded the borders of what was not allowed in their "friendship". By the fourth of July, Emily had initiated a practice of taking a nightly walk. She met Mark at different spots along the way, each night setting up a different rendezvous in case they had aroused suspicion. It was not enough. If they spent twenty-five minutes together, they wanted another twenty-five. If seven hours, then they wanted seven more. She had enlisted the confidence of Judith, who often helped her with an alibi. Emily began arriving at the stable before dawn. She awoke, fully alert and rushed into her clothes hoping to reach him before he awoke. They sometimes lingered an hour in his bed or until nerves got the better of them. And they were all nerves. Everything they did or said had to be weighed beforehand lest they speak out of turn and expose their secret.

"What would your father say if he knew we were together?"

"I can't imagine. He would be so disappointed in me, Mark. It would kill him. He would probably send me back to Manhattan. We really must stop."

"You stop first," he said.

"Tomorrow," she answered. She thought a moment. "There's a speakeasy downtown on Seventh Avenue that hangs a sign that says, 'Free Beer Tomorrow'. That's us. 'No Mark Tomorrow'," and they laughed and forgot for a little while longer the implications of their meetings.

July went by in what seemed like eleven days.

On August second, Emily resumed her stance that they should "break it off". By then Mark simply did not believe her. How many times that summer had she insisted, for a hundred and one valid reasons, that they break it off only to return the following day carrying a new intimacy that not only negated her words, but took them further into the maze of one another. Three days earlier, Emily canceled her riding lesson and told Mark that she simply could not continue to see him. She cried as she told him. This time she was serious, she had to do "the right thing". Mark tried to vocalize support. He too, was opposed to the theory of them. Of course they were a bad idea. Of course they could never be together Of course, he could not lead her anywhere except to drag her down into his own unadorned lifestyle.

And, of course, she would ultimately resent him and learn to hate him for it.

But the reality of them was outside and separate from the theory. He knew she loved him. She told him as often as the summer sun reappeared from behind the clouds. She couldn't keep her hands off him and resented any physical distance initiated by him. But it was her eyes that told him everything he needed to know. Her eyes showered over him and her words were as superfluous as the words of a weather forecaster predicting fair weather to a man standing in a drenching downpour.

That night he went to the ice house hoping she would come despite her avowal earlier in the day. They often met beside the ice house as Emily could return to the house with ice as an alibi for her absence. She was there when he arrived. They embraced in a silence punctuated by the vague hum of conversation coming from the house.

"What are we going to do?" she asked. "I can leave you today as long as I know you'll be here tomorrow to comfort me for my loss. I do nothing all day except wonder when I will see you again."

He hated to see her this way and at the same time he loved her need and her desire. He kissed her tears.

"Pretty exciting life, isn't it?" and she forced a crooked smile.

He told her what Daniel had always said. "There's nothing more boring than a man in love."

She laughed. "I agree entirely. What could be more boring than dragging my weary body out into the night to meet a silly man?" She stood on her toes to kiss him.

"I'm so bored," he said. He reached for her breast.

"Oh, stop for a moment, Mark. I must yawn."

And so it went.

"You're ridiculous," she said laughing.

"I'm the only rational one here. You're the ridiculous one."

And they laughed again, their laughter coating the pending bittersweet departure of another illicit meeting. Their lighthearted words led them down a trail into weighted silence.

"Mark–" she said in a barely audible whisper. She stood hesitant before him as if searching for the right words.. He had no words for the intimacy he felt. Words, if fashioned expertly, might represent what he

knew of her but only the way a painting might represent a person. And again he knew that all he wanted from Emily was more. He wanted her to tell him her life, and he didn't want her to leave anything out. He watched her as the very space between them changed. The air itself seemed to weave them together holding them in a soft yet unrelenting grip. They had arrived at an intimacy that resided on the outskirts of words.

He thought he could see individual light particles bouncing off her in the still, vacuous quiet of the summer night. "I feel like you're raining all over me," he said. And he knew then, that regardless of what happened to them, his life would be divided between the time before Emily and the time after. He wanted to remember her always the way she looked then. The smile in her eyes. The desire. He blinked his eyes as if he could somehow take a mental photograph. She drew him into her embrace trying to bury herself inside of him.

"I must go," she said after several minutes.

He stepped back from her as light from the half moon sparkled on her face.

"I think I have loved you every day of my life," she whispered to him. She kissed his lips lightly with hers, kissed them again with her fingertips, and left.

As she ran back to her house, he stood motionless in the residue of her departure. She lingered with him the way heat on sunburned skin lasted long into a dark cool night. What they had become had nothing to do, in his mind, with the theories of dissolution that confronted Emily. The impact of her oaths of departure had grown so weak that he could no longer hear them over the roar of blood in his ear.

Mark sat on the ground letting the breeze seeping from the ice house cool him. "This is bigger than me," he said softly to her open bedroom window fifty yards away. "This is bigger than the two of us." He felt them swimming in an ocean of warm water that threatened to drown them both when the wave they rode inevitably came crashing onto the shore. But he would worry about that tomorrow. Or maybe the next day.

And so on August second when Emily again said, "No more," Mark shed no tears. On August third he saddled Ohio and headed west alone intending to cross the Delaware into Pennsylvania. Ohio took to the water well. Mark thought of the day years earlier when he and Phil first took Ohio into the river. His young horse halted in midstream and pawed at the current with his front hoof. Mark allowed the horse to stop, thinking Ohio was acting out a harmless curiosity. With the suddenness of a lightning bolt, Ohio flipped into the water sending Mark headlong into the river and soaking his saddle and tack.

Phil chuckled and spit a wad of brown tobacco into the clear water. "What you doin' boy? We swimmin' or we ridin'?" He laughed that peculiar laugh of his that served only to draw humor away from any situation.

"I reckon I forgot to mention 'bout that," and he laughed again loudly.

Mark smiled at the memory and wondered how he tolerated the man at all.

He walked Ohio along the bank looking for a suitable crossing. He rode north a hundred yards, then returned south until he found an area that Ohio could step down from without jumping and that they could cross without having to negotiate river rocks or fallen trees. As Ohio stepped into the slow current of the river Mark turned to the sound of a horse galloping down the unseen path. He continued across wary not to let Ohio stop, looking often over his shoulder at the shoreline. Emily came into the clearing as Ohio stretched himself out of the water. He thought it odd that Judith had so pointedly asked him where he was going, and now he saw the reason behind her questions.

He stood Ohio in the sun of the western shore and watched as Emily took Abbey into the river. Abbey was almost a full hand shorter than Ohio and her girth dragged the water top as she plodded warily along. Water lapped on Emily's black boots. Her hair was pinned up revealing a summer's harvest of freckles on her neck. A smile shone from her face. Mark said nothing as she crossed to him. He was not surprised she had come, nor would he have been surprised if she hadn't. She reached Mark and raised her palms into the air and with a shrug of her shoulders that seemed to dismiss all responsibility for her actions, said "I lasted twenty hours without you. That's enough for one day."

He laughed at her without judgment. Merely happy to see her.

They spoke no more of departure that day. Mark rode hard. It was weeks since he worried about Emily keeping up with him. All summer her riding had improved and at times it was she who took the lead. As he cantered down a dusty path he sensed more than heard Emily's distance. He halted Ohio and turned to stand the wet horse. He waited several minutes until Emily appeared around the bend at a slow trot. He was not sure what first caught his eye, the devilish sparkle in her eyes or the exposed nipples of her breasts. The starched tails of her shirt flapped helplessly behind her in the breeze of her movement. She had unbuttoned her blouse, and wore no foundation garments. She trotted to him with a wordless smile brimming with desire and halted alongside him. Mark reached across Ohio's mane to touch her, but Abbey decided he was too close and nipped at Ohio's flank. As his horse wheeled around to avoid Abbey's assault, Mark's right foot flew out of the stirrup and he swayed hard right, almost falling from his startled horse. Emily dug her heels into Abbey's sides and bolted into a canter. Abbey's sudden departure started Ohio spinning again, and Mark found himself lying on his back as Emily disappeared down the wooded trail.

Mark remounted and followed after her at a canter ducking the larger branches and fending off the smaller ones with his arm as they whipped around his head. He rode hard for a mile but didn't catch her, and brought Ohio down to a walk. His head spun at this playful side of Emily. She surprised him daily. His brother's image flashed before him like a dark cloud on a summer's day. He found himself wondering what Daniel would have to say about all this. He spurred Ohio forward trying to outrun his brother's voice. They were ridiculous.

He rode forward, but never caught up to Emily. He circled to a couple of trails where he thought he might find her, but resigned himself finally to returning to the barn without her.

As the afternoon heat reached its peak, he arrived at the barn in time to see Emily and Judith leaving. Judith was wearing a flimsy summer frock and she waved enthusiastically to Mark.

"I just got back from a short ride," Emily called to him. She blinked at him. She had unpinned her hair and it hid the naked whiteness of her neck. Her hand moved to fasten the top button of her blouse, and she blinked again. A smile he couldn't interpret crossed her lips.

"Too bad I missed you," she added as he walked Ohio over towards the two of them.

"He's so sweaty," Judith said.

"Mostly wet from the river," Mark said.

"You crossed the river?" Emily asked so convincingly that Mark almost believed her charade. "No wonder I couldn't find you. What did you see? Anything interesting?"

Mark looked quickly at Judith who showed no recognition of the play being acted out before her.

"No," he said calling and raising her poker face. "Nothing out of the ordinary. It was pretty boring out there."

"Hmmm," she murmured. "Well, I'll see you later. Judith is driving me into town."

Mark smiled as they walked off. The girls turned towards the house. Mark didn't see Emily whisper to Judith, but he did hear Judith squeal with delight and watched her spin around quickly to look at him. He turned to bring Ohio into the wash stall. As he passed Abbey's stall his eye was caught by a flash of white on dark wood. He turned Ohio in the narrow walkway and stuck his head into the opened top half of the door.

Emily's camisole hung from a rusty nail. Its satin whiteness as starkly out of place against the hay and wood of the stall as her exposed breasts had been against the rich green of the woods earlier. And yet, nothing ever looked more at home.

"God-dammit, Daniel," Mark said aloud. "You should see what you're missing!"

The days of August burned by like newsprint on fire. Emily and Mark no longer spoke of separating and Emily fell into whimsical musings about marriage and a life that extended beyond the fences of summer. One day she sang Mark a song she thought would "be perfect" for their wedding song. It was a Celtic ballad, something about his blood flowing through her veins, but he was unable to focus on the words, his thoughts derailed by the subject of marriage.

"Do you think that could ever happen, Mark? Do you think we might ever marry?"

Her idle musings hit him like large rocks scattered into a still pond. The ridiculous notion of marriage that invaded his bed each night seemed so tantalizingly possible in the light of day with Emily at his side. Like jabs from a boxer, the steady torrent of her speculations was beginning to take their toll on his realistic misgivings about the possibility of joining their two very distinct worlds. The well founded diffidence he felt when he first saw her home in Manhattan or the extravagance of her mother's party was undercut by her optimism. He fought to hold onto the cynicism taught him by his brother. It was his last line of defense, and he felt almost certain she was unaware that she was eroding that cynicism and replacing it with unrealistic hope.

That evening she followed him from stall to stall as he made the evening feed.

He asked, "Did you mean what you said yesterday about getting married?"

"Oh, Mark, I always think about it. But what would we do? How could we?

Where would we live?"

"New Jersey," he said, and his spoken answer brought them out of the hypothetical world they played in and made it all seem so starkly real. "Peapack, New Jersey. Where you went for the wedding. I drove to Narrowsburg today in Dani– In my car and telephoned Andrew Bryant from the private booth at the drug store. He's asked me a million times to consider coming to New Jersey to run his stables. I told him I'd like to come down in the fall and talk to him about it. I thought I might work for him now and maybe later start up my own place once I get the lay of the land."

"How are you going to do that? It will take you years to save enough."

"I have some money."

"Mark, you'll need thousands of dollars for a venture like that. More than the few dollars you've made from your horse sales."

He frowned and exhaled heavily as he threw bales of hay into the stalls. His lips were tightly closed and he did not look at her.

"I have thousands."

She laughed. "Mark, I declare, this is so unlike you to be fooling me like this."

"I'm not fooling you. I do have money. I'm in the market."

He paused to see what effect these words would have. Words he had repeated pridefully to himself time and again. They had none.

"I'll go see Mr. Bryant next month after you leave. Find out what things cost down there. Maybe I can buy a place right away. Maybe work both places for a while. I don't know. I'll have to see."

"You are serious, aren't you?" Her eyes darted back and forth to each of his.

"Dead serious."

She put her hand to her heart. "This is so sudden," she said. "Why didn't you ever tell me about your money before? How much do you have?"

"I never told you because it isn't much money. I mean, it's a lot for me, for a fellow like me, but for you– Heck, your mother could spend every Indian cent on a few grand parties." He paused wondering if he should continue and searched her face for instructions. "I never told you because you never mentioned getting married before. Not so directly, anyway. I never thought you were really serious."

Mark finished feeding. He put the empty bucket on a hook by the door and they extended their walk down towards the lake. Emily grabbed at branches as she walked, mindlessly tearing pieces of leaves and tossing them behind her leaving a trail back to Pine Bluff. Her eyes flashed constantly back to the manor house. The sun was setting in the bowl of the lake and the sky was the unrealistic red of a bad painting

"I always daydreamed of marrying you," she said. her eyes darted up the rise to Pine Bluff. She sighed deeply. "You've taken my breath away, Mark Lerner."

None of Emily's reactions were ever what he expected, and this was no different. It was always Emily who introduced marriage into their conversations and his foray had created a huge space between them, larger than the two feet that separated them as they walked side by side along the lake shore. They cast no shadows as the sun dropped below the tree line. Mark watched as darkness seeped from the woods like fog obscuring and blending the individual trees. They heard Judith's voice calling from behind them.

"I'm over here," Emily called, and then quietly said to Mark, "You're a bag of surprises this evening. Enough to give a girl pause."

Judith appeared at the top of the rise. "Your mother is looking for you," she said breathlessly. "I told her I thought you'd gone for a walk, and she was coming to find you. Hello, Mark," she said as an afterthought before turning back to Emily. "She wants to speak to you. I thought I'd better find you first."

"Thanks, Judith," Emily said. She turned to Mark. "I'll talk to you tomorrow," and she ran up the darkened path after Judith.

"Damnation," Mark said when she left. He began his solitary return to his stable. "Why did I think she'd ever–? Dammit all to hell." He paused a moment and sat on a rock looking at the dusty trail. In the shadows, it suggested the view of the East River he'd seen from the grandeur of her Manhattan apartment. He thought again of the splendor of her home there. The view of the barges floating by her window. The steady stream of trucks and automobiles on her street. Of people scurrying about. Important people. Men in suits. People doing important things. What would he have her do? Muck out stalls in New Jersey? Talk to the chickens? Dammit. He was such a fool. He returned to the barn and mucked out the stalls and for the first time in his life, he saw his surroundings as something other than splendid. What could he offer Emily? The light she shined on his life accented only the shadows.

And yet what were they to do? He threw clean shavings on the stable floor. They couldn't keep on the way they were now. It was up to him to find a way for them to be together. He was the man, and that's what men did.

The following morning Emily arrived at the stable before eight. Mark met her by the door and greeted her tentatively. He put one of his boots on the mounting block that rested on the ground between them. She put her boot on the block one step below his. He wondered if she would bring up their conversation of the night before. If it weighed on her mind at all, she showed no signs.

"What did your mother want last night?"

"Nothing, really. She wants to have the Kinslow's back the last week of August."

Mark decided to back off his offer. It was absurd of him to have said anything.

"Listen," he said. "About last night–"

"Oh, Mark. That was sweet of you to think of that. At least now we have a choice. I feel so much better somehow." She took his hand and placed it on her knee under her own hand.

"You know that Daddy will disinherit me if I married you."

Mark couldn't hide his surprise. He expected resistance would come from Mrs. Harrison and he thought Emily was overstating her father's position.

"Your father likes me."

"Of course he likes you," she said, "but he doesn't intend to have his stable boy marry his daughter. I can assure you of that."

"I'm not his stable boy," Mark said.

"Oh, Mark. Listen to us. This is the type of thing we will have to deal with everyday. Everyone will talk. They'll think you were just marrying me to better your position. Daddy will too."

"Is that what you would think?"

Emily looked down to the ground. "It is something I have needed to consider. I was raised to question men's intentions, Mark." She lifted her eyes trying to lock onto his. "You have to understand. A fellow once asked me if he would get a window in his office at Daddy's company if we married. You must try to understand. We're Harrisons. We have a name to live up to. We have a President of the United States in our family. People write about what we do in newspapers. Mother would be dropped from the Social Register. It would kill her, Mark. This is not just about me being in love with you."

"You didn't answer my question," he said. "Do you think I'm here to better my position?"

Emily looked around her as if searching for a place to hide.

"No, I don't, Mark. I don't. But that's what scares me so much about you. I'm so in love with you that I fear I would be blind to any evil in you. I don't think straight when I'm with you." She laughed. "Far from it."

Mark thought a moment.

"Let me ask you this," he said. "If you had no money, no name, would we marry?"

"Of course," she said. "Tomorrow."

"Well then." and he held his palm upwards as if showing her something held in his empty hand. They had arrived at a dead end of their conversation where he thought his point was made by his argument and she thought it only served to prove hers. He looked at his upturned palm as if noticing it for the first time and put it in his pocket sensing suddenly that it held nothing she wanted.

"Are we going riding today?" he asked, seeking relief from this strain.

"It's more important that we come to an understanding about what is involved here, Mark."

She let go of his hand and took her foot off the mounting block. She drew him to her. "Do you know that I love you?" she asked. She turned her head and rested her cheek on his chest. "That I will always love you?"

Mark was quiet a moment until his silence caused Emily to release him. She studied his face.

"I shouldn't think you would need to think that long for a response," she said, her voice breaking in her agitation.

"No," he said slowly. "I know you love me. I'm just not certain what that means to you."

They stood precariously, as if in a canoe.

"I've changed my mind," she said. "Do you still want to ride?"

She reached behind her for the mounting block never taking her eyes from him as he disappeared into the barn. She sat on it gently as if she was afraid it might move beneath her.

Mark hurriedly tacked their horses and within minutes they were out on the trails. They rode in silence, not even speaking to ask or give directions. They just rode. If Emily felt like trotting or cantering, she did. Mark followed or didn't. An hour passed that way. Walk, trot, canter. Sometimes together, sometimes apart but always within view of one another. The muffled thuds of horse hooves as they pounded hard ground interspersed with the clacking on loose stones spoke to them in an exotic code of dots and dashes. They listened to these sounds as if they might hold secret answers to all their questions. The horses mirrored their moods and rode alert and controlled. Neither one skittish. Neither one too forward. Mark watched the back of Emily's blouse darken and then become transparent as it clung to her moist skin in the hot morning sun. He ran his hand through his short hair, brought it down wet with sweat and wiped it dry on his chaps.

They rode until they passed the entanglements of that morning. Past the brambles of money, through the thorny thickets of other people's opinions until they arrived at their propinquity. They found it in the field where Mark had led Emily over the hedgerow the day she first jumped Ohio. He marveled at how she magically took all the places he had known his entire life and branded them as her own. Her log. Her garden. Her hill. Mark felt the tidal pull of Emily's eyes and looked up to see her smiling at him. He edged Ohio forward until he caught up to her. They rode close, the occasional clanging of his iron stirrup banging against hers the only sound. Emily let Abbey's reins run long and put her hand up to Mark, fingers spread apart. He dropped his reins and put his hand to hers. Barely touching. Her slender white fingers shadowed his brown callused hand. She smiled and continued to say nothing.

Mark circled from east to west and they arrived at the ridge where they first picnicked with Judith a year earlier approaching the ridge from the back end of the valley. Mark watched Emily for any sign of recognition. After a moment, she breathed a small "oh," and her eyes danced to Mark's. They wordlessly dismounted and collided into each other like magnets to steel. They kissed passionately tearing at each other's shirts until standing bare-chested, Emily said, "I don't know what it means either, but I don't want it to stop."

It had been more than an hour since either had spoken, but he knew exactly and immediately what she meant. They lingered in the field letting the sun toast their naked skin. They hadn't bothered to tie the horses, just loosened their girths allowing them to graze. Mark spread his shirt on the ground and they made love with total abandon. Emily recited a litany of breathless "I love you"s that wove in and out of the silences covering Mark like a net. Afterwards, they lay side by side letting the reeds cushion their backs, until Emily moved and put her head in his lap as she had a year earlier. This time naked.

"You'll be gone in two weeks." Mark said finally.

She raised her arm over her head and blindly touched his lips.

"Shh," she said. "I'm still here now."

They made love again and still made no move to leave. They took turns cat napping until finally they stood and stretched. Emily gathered her clothes hidden among the tall grasses. Mark rolled his shirt and brushed strands of meadow grass from her back. Her naked body seemed to direct the swaying reeds like a maestro's baton leading an orchestra. The brilliant sunlight was her spotlight. He thought of how she had looked so flawless at last year's party in her elegant gown, pearl earrings and necklace. He remembered her hair done up so perfectly and he looked at her now. The sunlight on her face her only jewelry, her hair disheveled, her body glowing in an unabashed nudity and he was filled with pride that she chose to dance this dance with him.

As they dressed, Mark thought he heard a horse's whinnying from far off, perhaps down in the woods, and was certain of it when Abbey neighed back. He glanced at Emily, but she paid it no attention. They dressed and mounted and rode languidly back giving the horses long rein most of the return trip. As they neared Pine Bluff, Emily said "How do you do that? How do you bring me there?"

He looked at her and smiled, "I thought you were leading."

They walked their horses around to the front of the main house. To their surprise, Mr. Harrison stood on the porch. He closed the door on his pocket watch as they approached and returned it to his pocket.

"Hello, Daddy," she said.

"Mr. Harrison," Mark nodded.

"Emily, give your horse to Mr. Lerner and come into my office immediately. He turned on his heel and went into the front door letting it bang noisily behind him. He never glanced at Mark.

"What is it?" he whispered.

"I don't know," she said as she raised her irons and loosened her girth. Her voice trembled as she handed Mark her reins. "Look for me later. Half past eight at the ice house." She ran up the stairs and was swallowed by the large white house.

Mark walked the horses back to the stable. He had never seen Mr. Harrison so tight lipped or his eyes so narrowed. As he put Abbey in her stall he realized the root of the problem. Emily's camisole was gone.

"Oh damn," he said aloud. They had developed a blind spot to the idea of anyone going into the sanctuary of their stable except themselves. Why had they left the camisole hanging there the past two weeks? They never once mentioned it or the day Emily had opened her shirt to him in the woods. The silk undergarment hung as a silent talisman and both took pains not to acknowledge its existence. It was probably not the most foolish thing they had done, but suddenly it led the parade.

Mark's fingers massaged his forehead. How could they have been so careless? He started to shiver in the shade of the barn although the temperature was well past ninety. His hands shook as he undid Abbey's girth. As he walked past the end stall on his way to the tack room he saw Mr. Harrison's saddle still on Piper. He entered the stall and put his hand on the horse's chest. He was still warm. Had Mr. Harrison followed them?

He put the horses in their stalls and went to his room, laid on his bed and waited. He waited in a terror made acute by a lack of information. Did Mr. Harrison see them? What was he saying to Emily? What was she saying to him? Should he go to them and defend her? Or would his defense be nothing but an admission of guilt. He waited a long time while running through a thousand possible scenarios, but not one of them neared the truth that was unfolding before him. None of them remotely considered the possibility that he had just seen Emily for the last time.

He went at six hoping to meet her at the ice house. He went at six-thirty. He went at seven. Seven-thirty. Seven-forty. At eight he found a note stuck to the door with an ice pick.

Dear Mark,

Daddy found my camisole. I told him I didn't know why it was there. Deny everything. Give me a few weeks to straighten things out. Don't try to contact me. I leave tomorrow.

Emily

His shoulders sagged. He reread the letter sifting through the words like a miner searching for gold in a tin sieve. Some clue of her feelings. Some hint of her love. Why hadn't she signed it "love, Emily?" Was she going to "straighten things out" so they could be together? "Deny everything" he read again. It hurt to read the words. The most intimate moments of his life were contained in those words. Deny them to whom?

He put his arm down and the letter scooped dirt as it scraped the ground. He did not remember sitting and looked at the wooden bench a yard away, but he did not have the energy to move to it. He looked up to Emily's darkened window hoping to see at least her shadow cross in front of him. He picked up the letter and read it again. The remaining light of day glowed weak as candlelight and the words were all blurry. He swiped at his eyes and brought his fingers down wet. He dug his heels into the ground and pushed himself back so he could lean against the ice house wall.

Mark awoke several hours later under a starless sky. His back was cold and stiff from leaning against the ice house. His mouth tasted of dirt, and a tiny patch of mud lay directly under the mark in the dust made by his face. There were eight or nine seconds where he did not remember the events of the previous day and they turned out to be the best part of that day. He stood slowly and walked back to the stable. He turned backward looking up at the ghostly curtains blowing gently from Emily's window.

Although he missed last night's feeding, he threw his clothes on the floor of his room and collapsed into his bed letting the soft mattress surround him. He fell asleep again, a deep dreamless narcotic sleep, until he awoke to the sound of a far off auto.

He leapt from bed pausing only long enough to throw a pair of shorts on and ran through the stable barefooted. Ohio whinnied and kicked at his stall as Mark flashed by. He reached the driveway just as the auto turned out onto the dusty street. Mark could see the silhouette of Otis' cap in the front seat and Emily's shape in the back. He thought she turned to see him, but he couldn't be certain.

He returned to the stable, filled the horse's feeders with scoops of pellets while still dressed only in his shorts. He didn't bother mucking the stalls and returned to his bed again not expecting to fall asleep. Not expecting anything. Not expecting anything at all. He awoke some time later to an eerie silence that he could not place. His horses were gone. He jumped out of bed and opened his door to the empty stalls. He threw on his pants and shirt and his boots without socks and walked outside as his mother returned to the barn.

"I didn't know who went where," she said, "so I just put them each in a separate paddock."

Mark looked at her as if trying to place an old familiar face.

"You were sleeping so I– Mark, honey, are you all right?" She reached to him and brushed a stick from his short hair.

He nodded. "What time is it?"

"Almost noon," she said.

He shook his head unable to understand. He understood the word. Repeated it aloud without inflection. But noon never meant awaking to his mother turning out his horses and noon never meant a gaping hole that threatened to swallow him alive.

"Come up to the house. I'll fix you something to eat."

"I'm not hungry."

"Mark, we need to speak. I'll go fix something now."

As his mother walked up to the main house, she passed Mr. Harrison on his way down to the stable. Mark watched her wring her hands in her apron as he spoke to her. From time to time she glanced down to Mark. Nothing seemed to move on Mr. Harrison except his lips. Mark watched as he touched the brim of an absent hat to his mother and continue down the hill to the stable.

He stopped in front of the young man, but made no move to shake his hand.

"Mark."

"Sir."

Mr. Harrison expelled a deep sigh. He stood nearly eye to eye with the boy.

"I wanted to come to you to hear your story before I decide what to do about this matter. Emily has told me everything."

Mark blinked.

"There is nothing to tell, sir."

Austin frowned and crossed his arms in front of his chest.

"Why was my daughter's camisole hanging in your stall?"

Mark had a prepared answer for that inevitable question.

"It blew off the clothesline, sir. I hung it there a few days ago but we, I kept forgetting about it."

Mr. Harrison's nostrils flared, and he spoke through barely parted lips.

"So the sight of my daughter's undergarments is so commonplace that it does not merit consideration?"

Mark wished he knew how much Mr. Harrison had seen yesterday. If he had seen Mark and Emily naked in the field wouldn't he have confronted them at that time? "Deny everything," Mark said to himself.

"Sir, with all due respect. You are posing a question in such a way that any answer I give will be unsatisfactory. There is nothing to hide here, sir. Surely Emily has told you so."

An almost imperceptible change in the corners of Mr. Harrison's eyes flashed a signal to Mark that Emily had told him nothing.

"I would never do anything to hurt your daughter."

Mr. Harrison's expression turned to disdain. "It is rather late to make that claim, young man. You already have."

Mark's shoulders sagged. He was right. Mark had hurt Emily just as he had hurt his brother. He wanted them both near him and just as his proximity to Daniel cost him his life, so had he hurt Emily by his inappropriate proximity to her. He had not understood that love resided such a short distance from pain. How incredibly and foolishly naive he felt.

"I never meant for anyone to be hurt," he said in a voice so low it cut Mr. Harrison's wrath by half.

"A gentleman must learn to obey a woman's refusals," he said.

Mark frowned. He had no idea what Mr. Harrison was alluding to.

"Sir?"

"I told you, Mark, that Emily has told me everything. She told me you mistook her friendly manner as an unintended invitation and you made unwelcome advances. I can't help but think this incident with the camisole is part of your plan, although I confess to not having a clue about what you hoped to gain by stealing it. This entire matter is oppressively distasteful."

Mark's knees buckled. It took all his energy to remain standing. Was the man just fishing for information? Or had Emily actually suggested that to him. The words were hard to think. They sliced like razors through his brain.

"It is so far removed from the behavior I have come to expect from you that, that– I am quite speechless. I did not think you capable of such sordidness."

Mark stepped back from Mr. Harrison and leaned against the barn. He had slept fourteen of the last eighteen hours and yet was overwhelmed by the most debilitating fatigue he had ever experienced. He could not make out Mr. Harrison's words. He didn't seem to have the energy to open his ears. He tried to focus on what he was saying.

"...before I leave, I will let you know what that decision is."

As Mr. Harrison wheeled around, Mark felt an immense gratitude toward him for leaving him alone. He slid his back down the rough wall of the barn landing in a sitting position. He buried his head in crossed arms on his upraised knees and closed his eyes trying to force Mr. Harrison's words from his ears.

What was Emily's plan? "Give me a few weeks," she had written. Was this part of her plan? What did she hope to gain by saying such a thing to her father?

The same questions spun around and around his head and he felt he was on Mr. Ferris' Carnival wheel with no way to get off. His mother appeared with a sandwich wrapped in a linen napkin in one hand and a bottle of milk in the other. Sweat from the bottle glistened in the sun and Mark realized he hadn't eaten since before yesterday's ride, almost nineteen hours earlier. Mary Lerner handed him the sandwich and milk.

"Come. Sit here," she said and pulled bales of hay from the stack inside the door tossing them to the ground with a strength camouflaged by her small frame.

She sat silently watching her son wolf down his food. She produced an apple from her pocket and shined it on the front of her apron. She unfolded an old pocket knife of his father's and quartered the apple handing him three pieces. She kept one for herself and bit into it while studying her son.

"What did he tell you?" Mark asked.

"What he told me makes no sense. Do you wish me to tell you what I know?"

Mark nodded.

"I know that girl is in love with you and you her. I have known it for months. Maybe years. I should have done something about it a long time ago, but– I didn't."

Mark looked at her trying not to confirm or deny anything by his expression.

"I know she sneaks down here at dawn to be with you. I know that sometimes you are out on your horses six and seven hours at a time and the horses come back almost dry even on the hottest days. I know that you meet her at night and that drunken friend of hers alibis for you both."

Mark could no longer hide his surprise.

"I also know that her camisole hung on that nail for damn near two weeks and that it was an invitation to trouble. How it got there is none of my business, but if she were my daughter, I would have paid a little more attention to what she did and less on throwing ridiculous parties."

"How do you know all this?" he asked.

"Oh, Mark. Was I born last night? You are my son. My only son. Do you honestly believe I do not know what you are doing with your life? We live a hundred yards apart, for goodness sakes. I have always made it my business to know what you boys were up to. Do you think a mother would let her thirteen-year-old son run a stable if she did not know he was capable and competent? Do you think Daniel was subtle enough to hide his carousing with every girl in town?"

She paused a moment as if building energy to jump over her dead son's evoked memory.

"Daniel I never worried about. He kissed the girls and forgot them. But you, Mark. You, I have worried about for years. Your fascination with the Scott woman– Was I supposed to be foolish enough not to see that?" She waved her hand dismissively. "Give me some credit."

"Why did you never say anything? Why didn't you stop us?"

She sat quietly for a moment and closed her eyes.

"Because I saw in your eyes that you were in love with her."

Mark sighed deeply.

"And she with you."

"I didn't know you were such a Romantic," he said, trying his best to adopt his brother's scornful tone. He didn't know why, but her words generated anger.

"That is because you only see me as a mother. I was never a breathing, living woman to you. No mother ever is. But I was not always just a mother. I was once a woman in love."

"Yes," Mark said impatiently. "But this is not like you and Dad–"

She cut him off. "I did not say anything about your father." She held her hands together as if in prayer and closed her eyes again. "I was in love with a man as you are with Emily. I denied my love for him and turned him away. I have regretted it every day of my life."

Mark heard her words but was unable to fully assimilate them. His head was like a full bowl of water sitting under a running tap. Her words entered the already-filled bowl, and some of what she said mingled with the contents, but most was spilling over far in excess of the bowl's capacity.

He sat staring at her. A partially formed thought cracked on his horizon like far away lightning. Who was Robert Scott's "M"? it whispered. He was unable to fully form the question let alone speculate on the possibility of his own–

"Were you married?"

She frowned. "I fear this conversation goes beyond the things a mother should say to her son. I'm not comfortable with this, Mark. I tell you this only to show you that I see your pain. I thought it might help. But listen to me–"

Mark's eyes stared at the bottom of the stall door.

"Listen to me!"

He looked into her eyes.

"She is gone and she isn't coming back. No woman would make these..."

"She is coming back," Mark interrupted. "She needs to figure things out. We want to marry, Mother."

Mary's eyes filled with tears. She lowered her voice and continued, "...no woman would say those things to her own father about a man she intended to marry. She will find an excuse, Mark, to try to ease your pain, but she will not come back. You must believe this, Mark."

"But she loves me–"

"This has nothing to do with love," Mary said. "Mark, listen to me. Please listen carefully–" Tears fell from the corners of her eyes as she begged him to heed her. "You have eaten all the fruit of that love. There is nothing left. That is all that we get."

"But she's the one who brought up marriage. She–"

Mary stood and raised her voice to her son. "Don't be a fool, Mark. It is over. Trust me. It is over. She cannot marry you. She will hate you if you marry her."

"Why?"

"Because of her children.."

"What are you talking about. She has no–"

"Because one day she will be watching her daughter playing on your pony and she will remember that she had already been to Europe when she was her age and she will think of all the things she gave up for her so she could be with you, Mark. And she will hate you for that child's unwitting sacrifice."

"But–"

"Would you give up your horses for her?"

"Why would I have to? I make a living with my horses. Without them, I'm– I'm– I don't know who I am."

Mary did not wait a second to pounce.

"And she will not know who she is without her money and fancy friends and her parties. If you are not willing to give up your horses, you cannot ask her to give up hers. It's over Mark."

Maybe it was the overwhelming logic that made him so angry. Maybe it was the fact that his love was so defenseless against all her arguments that so enraged him. He stood and threw the half-filled milk bottle against the barn.

"You don't know what you're talking about," he said. "You don't know us. You have no idea how much she loves me."

He stormed off to the paddock. He grabbed Ohio's halter as he entered the gate and with only a lead line, he climbed his horse bareback and rode out towards the mountain.

Mary Lerner closed her eyes, releasing tears stored in their corners. "Why," she said aloud, "can't we teach our children about fire without burning their fingers?"

She sat back onto the hay and watched as Mark disappeared into the shadows of the woods. She started to pick up the pieces of broken glass, but changed her mind and turned to go back up the hill to Pine Bluff.

Mark rode slowly around the lake and up the mountain to all the places that had become Emily's. He tried to remember what everything looked like before she started riding with him, but every trail led only to her. When had she done this? When had she come into the woods and made every tree hers? When had she ridden into his head and made all his thoughts of her? He rode in a vague circle unaware of time passing. When Mark returned to the stable, his mother was gone. There was a note on his door that he glanced at without reading as he walked past the door of his bedroom. He assumed it was from his mother, and he couldn't listen to her any more that day.

He went to the tack room and began cleaning the tack. He didn't know why, but it had become essential that all the tack be cleaned. He polished his bits and stirrups. He saddle soaped his leathers and saddles. He took all his bridles apart and cleaned them thoroughly, even the creases under the buckles of the throat latches. He scrubbed the girths and polished their chrome buckles. Abbey's tack he cleaned last. He was so meticulous that he even stuck an awl into the buckle holes in case some dirt might have collected there. He re-hung the saddles on their racks. Emily's saddle was on the lower tier, next to his. He even cleaned his father's saddle though it hadn't been used in years. Mr. Harrison's. Daniel's old saddle that Judith used all summer. He put saddle covers over all but his and Emily's. He hung all the bridles in a neat row so that they all hung down exactly the same length. It looked like it had never been used. He lit a cigarette, but smoked it outside the tack room not wanting the smoke to cloud his work. It took him all afternoon.

He tended to his horses and returned to his bedroom picking the note from his door as he passed by. It was not from his mother, but from Kristen.

"Before Judith leaves, tell her that Emily can call me at any time and I will get a message to you. Give her my number."

He frowned. He hadn't seen Kristen in weeks, though it seemed like months. He hadn't even known she had returned from New York. How could she be aware of anything? He had never said a word to her about Emily. The implications of her offer were exhausting and in his blunted state of mind, he accepted it for what it looked like. An offer of help from a friend.

The following morning Mark was awakened by Judith shortly after he had tossed and turned himself to sleep. In morning's first thought, born half of dreams, he thought she was Emily come once more. His heart leapt, but like a man on a trampoline in a room with a low ceiling, it came to a crashing halt against the hard reality of Emily's departure.

"I'm sorry, Mark. I'm sorry to startle you, but I need to speak with you."

"It's all right," he said. "What time is it?"

It was still dark. Mark looked to the window wondering if dawn was near although he had barely slept. Judith carried an old candle lantern and she placed it on the table by his bed.

"It's almost five," she said.

"How is Emily? Have you spoken with her?"

"Yes. Last night. She's at her Uncle Stephan's. She feels terrible about all this."

"What's going to happen?"

Judith shrugged. "I'm not certain. We're leaving today. After lunch, I think. The Harrison's stayed up half the night packing. Mrs. Harrison cries, mostly. They're both quite upset."

"What do they know?"

Judith frowned. "I'm not certain. May I sit?"

Mark moved over to make room on his bed. He pulled a sheet over his naked leg. The candlelight from the lantern flickered on Judith's face sending it in and out of shadow.

"Emily is concerned that you will say something to ruin her reputation."

Mark blinked, unsure of what Judith meant. Surely Emily did not think him capable of betraying her like that. He shrugged his shoulders dismissing the very idea. The question was insulting.

"I suppose I could do that in one sentence," he said. "So could you, for that matter. What would be the point?"

Judith's back stiffened at Mark's words.

"Indeed," she said.

"Did she say anything to you about us? About New Jersey?"

Judith frowned again. "I think she's just concentrating on trying to smooth things over with her father."

"What did she tell him?"

"Mark," she said. "I love you like a brother. I truly do. But Emily is my best friend. Please don't ask me to get in the middle of this."

What was she talking about? The middle of what? he wondered.

"What will you do if she doesn't come back?" Judith asked.

"I'm certain she will come. I just wish I knew when. I wish I knew her plan. Can't you tell me anything?"

Judith lowered her eyes. She outlined a square in his sheet with her finger and smoothed the wrinkles inside it as she thought.

Mark did not wait for an answer. "Tell Emily to call me at Kristen's. I've written the number on this paper." He reached to the table, the bed sheet sliding from his waist. "I'll go there every night at seven until I hear from her. Don't forget, Judith."

"What will you say to Mr. Harrison?" she persisted. Mark thought she took the paper reluctantly, but he didn't dwell on his impression.

"I don't suppose I'll say anything. He spoke to me yesterday and I told him her camisole flew from the clothesline–"

"How could you both be so stupid to leave that there?" She scolded Mark with genuine anger. "What were you thinking? All summer, you both kept being more and more foolish. I told her weeks ago this was bound to happen."

"What did she say?"

"She dismissed my concerns as if I was a doddering old woman."

Mark smiled at the picture she summoned of Emily laughing and carefree.

"Did Emily tell you...?" He exhaled looking for words to ask his delicate question. "...about us being in the field yesterday, or when was it? Monday?"

"Yes."

"Does she think her father saw us?"

"She thinks he might have from far away, but she obviously couldn't ask him."

Light began to creep into the room. Mark reached over and blew out the candle.

"I didn't say anything to him about that," he said.

Judith stood abruptly and reached for her candle. Mark grabbed her wrist.

"Is that all you can tell me? Didn't she leave you a message for me?"

Judith's face darkened in the weak light of dawn that reached into the room. "She told me she loves you," she said and pulled her arm from his grasp. She turned and left. Mark wanted to run after her to ask a thousand more questions, but he was naked and couldn't leave his bed to chase her. He sighed deeply and crashed backwards into his mattress, the springs squeaking loudly below him. His blood was pumping furiously. A return to sleep was not a possibility. He got out of bed and dressed for another day without Emily.

The Sentence

Mark didn't give a moment's thought to why Kristen would offer her phone to him, but he hadn't given thought to much of anything all week. It took four days for Emily to call. Sunday at seven, Kristen's phone rang two longs and a short. Mark jumped. In all the days he'd spent there, he never heard her phone ring. Kristen went to the kitchen.

"Hello?"

"Hello, dear. How are you?"

His heart pounded against his skin threatening an escape.

"Why, yes. He is here right now."

Mark was on his feet and had the receiver in his hand by the "now".

"I can't believe you've finally called! How are you? Are you–"

"What is the sentence?"

Mark was puzzled. He barely recognized her voice. It shook and, if anything, sounded angry!

"I don't know. I miss you? I love–" The lightness in his voice was disappearing quickly.

"What is the one sentence that can ruin my reputation?"

He stopped with the suddenness of a boat running aground.

"Emily, what are you talking about?"

"You threatened my father by saying you could ruin my reputation in one sentence. He is beside himself in rage!"

"Em, I never threatened your father with anything. I barely spoke to him. I denied everything, like you said." He raced through his memory trying desperately to find the antidote for this unexpected poison.

"Mark. You can never know how devastated I was when he told me. I absolutely refused to believe him at first. All the blood ran from my body as if I'd been cut. I refused to believe you would betray me like that."

"Emily. I did not betray you. I never threatened anyone." His voice was shrill, unfamiliar even to himself.

Kristen looked at Mark and gave him a sardonic smile that he did not even see.

"I'll go for a walk. Be back in a while," Kristen whispered, leaving him alone to Emily's wrath.

"Did you not say that you could ruin my reputation in one sentence?"

Mark dropped into a wooden kitchen chair. He had said those words. To Judith. But he didn't mean them as a threat. Now it was his turn to be rocked. He felt like a skeleton devoid of all blood, all tissue, all muscle.

"I remember saying those words to Judith," he said, "but I did not mean it as a threat."

"Why would you say them at all? To prove what a man you are?"

He deserved her anger. He hadn't thought.

"I said it as a way of saying how ridiculous it would be. She asked me– Oh Christ, Emily. You have to believe me."

He floundered in her silence.

"Emily."

He spoke her name as an attempt to conjure her up. As if this entire conversation had taken place with a cruel impostor. Someone who did not know him.

"Did you think if I was ruined I would come running to you? Did you plan all this?"

The weight of her words pressed him into a defeated silence. "How can I ever believe you again? I have never seen my father so upset. I'm surprised he didn't leave that moment with a gun to shoot you dead." She paused. "You knew exactly how to hurt me. You knew how important my name–"

He heard her sob. Even had she spoken French, the strain in her voice would have translated her pain.

"Emily, I don't know what I can– What can I do to make you see? I never intended to– I would never betray– My God, Emily. How can you think me capable of this?"

"I loved you, Mark. I was willing to give up everything for you."

The finality of those words hit him with the violence of a strikebreaker's club. Thoughts raced through his head so fast that even had a good one presented itself, it was gone before he could utter it. He had said those words. But not like that. Not as a threat. A long silence followed. Mark clung to it like an exhausted swimmer clings to a raft in the middle of a lake.

"Emily," he asked. "How can you let six or seven words destroy everything you know to be true about me? How can you believe I would ever hurt you?"

"You have hurt me, Mark. That's how I can believe it. You have hurt me. I have to believe it."

"Let me come to Manhattan. I'll–"

"Daddy will have you arrested the moment– It's too late, Mark."

"I love you, Emily. I love you. That's all I can say. The rest is just–"

He was interrupted by her unrelenting silence.

"Good-bye, Mark. In time I'm sure I will remember you well." He thought he heard her sob. "I'll remember the sweet things. Remember how perfectly you loved me. But now I need to repair my life. I need to move forward. Good-bye, Mark."

She rang off.

Mark held the phone and stared at the wall. He didn't cry. He wasn't angry. He didn't know if there was a word for how he felt, as if all his emotions were trapped in a phone wire someplace between here and Manhattan. He held the phone until Gertrude came back on the party line. He could tell from her tone of voice she had heard the entire conversation.

"Are you going to place another call, honey?"

Mark put the receiver back on the hook without saying anything.

She was gone for good. He knew it. Most of him knew it. And she was gone because of something he'd said. He sat back down, then stood again and went to the phone. Suddenly he was cold. Freezing cold. His clothes felt damp on him, but felt dry to his hands. He lit a cigarette and started coughing on the first puff and tossed it away letting the embers splash in Kristen's tin sink. She thinks I betrayed her, he repeated to himself. Part of him was angry that she would believe him capable of that. But it was a very small part. Part of him wanted to run all the way to Manhattan to prove to her how wrong she was. Part of him wanted to hide. Part wanted to die. Part did. He felt it in a very real sense; could feel the weight of it floating inert inside him like ice in a glass of water.

He looked to see Kristen sitting across from him on the divan. He hadn't heard her return.

"I said, 'Is everything all right?'"

He searched for the part of himself that answered questions like that. He couldn't find it. He searched again for the part of himself that empowered him to stand and leave. After several moments he found that part, but it worked poorly and he staggered out of Kristen's front door almost falling down the porch stairs.

The dynamite contained in the phone call had scattered him into pieces that surrounded him like dozens of planets around a sun. But he felt no connection to any of them. He needed to go see Daniel. Started walking home to do so until after a hundred yards he remembered that Daniel was dead. He sat on a rock and made crying sounds. He thought that's what they were but he didn't recognize them at first, didn't know they were his own. He thought if he could cry for the first time in his life, he might feel better. He tried to cry but there were no tears. She had taken them, too.

The remaining days of August joined together and advanced as inseparable from one another as a pile of wet newspaper. Every day Mark hoped for word from Emily, and every day his heart was slammed against the wall of her silence.

The heart is related to reason like a retarded cousin the rest of the family struggles to hide in the attic. A simpleton who returns every day to the site of a long-departed circus unable to comprehend its absence. And so Mark's heart stood at the edge of an enormous field, the string of a deflated balloon still in his bewildered grasp. He could, if he closed his eyes, still see the colors of the remembered circus flash before him. He could hear the laughter, be dazzled again and again by the blood pounding excitement of the event. Every day his heart walked to the empty field that once held that circus. He watched as tumbleweeds of litter blew proof of its ephemeral existence by him. Each day seeing another colorful moment that he had forgotten before, and then opening his eyes again onto the vast emptiness of what once was. After a while his heart returned no longer anticipating the circus, but content, in a downward spiral of expectation, with the ghostly memory of it.

Two weeks after the phone call, Mark decided to ignore all reason, and make one more attempt to win Emily back. He had to fight his brother's remembered admonitions on the day he died, "No one ever comes back." He ignored his mother's warnings of the day Emily left. He ignored all those words, although he knew them to be true. He ignored them because he could not find anything else to believe in. If not what he shared with Emily, then what? And even though he might be wrong, even though he probably was wrong, he decided the slim chance of being with Emily was enough to warrant the effort.

Mark bought the paper and checked his stocks. Last June he had called Mr. Harrison's broker from The John Muir Company and bought twenty shares of American Tobacco stock at $157 a share with the money from his brother's insurance policy. A day later he bought twenty shares of the old Wells-Fargo company, now called The American Express Company, for $195 a share. He pulled out a writing tablet and found a stub of a pencil to try to figure how much he had. He should have been checking all along. His broker told him to check every few days but Mark hadn't even glanced at the financial section in three months. He scanned down the agate type. American Tobacco was up to $164. He had made $140 on that already. American Express closed on Friday at $236 a share. According to his figures, he already made $820! He ripped a new sheet of paper from the tablet and started the complicated process all over again certain that he was mistaken. There was no error. In a little less than three months, Mark had made over nine hundred dollars!

Propelled by his financial success, he went to see Andrew Bryant in Peapack on the fifth of September and agreed to come work for him in the spring after the ice harvest. He went to a real estate broker and found a house with six acres that he could buy for $8000. He would need to build a barn. That would cost him another fifteen hundred. While he was on the train back to Pine Bluff, he searched the Travel section of the Times until he found a first class cruise to Italy for $660 on the Regina d'Italia. He remembered how much Emily had loved Italy. He remembered how she told him that she would gladly give up every trip she ever took in exchange for one month in Italy with him.

When he returned home, he went into Mr. Harrison's office to use his desk. He did not want to sit on the corner of his bed with his papers as he usually did. He sat at the desk with the impotent indolence of a child making faces at a departed playmate. He sat and spun around in his chair flicking the ashes from an imaginary cigar into the air. He took Mr. Harrison's pen from the inkwell and scratched his numbers on paper. He needed $11,800. He included in this wish list a thousand dollars for furnishings and curtains and the like. He had no idea what those things cost but assumed that they could not possibly cost more than that. He wanted their house to be as nice as what she was used to. He included a savings account for their children, a fund that he could contribute to for traveling, and for all the things his mother had warned him that her children would need.

He scratched these numbers on his tablet. He needed almost four thousand dollars more. A staggering sum, but hadn't he already made nearly a thousand dollars in three months? He thought of all that had happened in those three months and it hardly seemed possible that it wasn't three years. He scribbled more numbers on his pad and tried desperately to do the complicated multiplication and division that would render him a sum. As best as he could figure, if things kept up the way they were now, he would need a year to make that much money. He wondered if Emily would wait, and then he laughed at himself. She wasn't waiting now. By September or October 1929, he could have $12,000 or more. He started to fantasize about how he would call Emily and tell her the news. They could be in Italy for Christmas. He pictured the delight in her face as she threw her arms around his shoulders. He would call her next summer and say, "Emily, will you join me in Italy for the winter?" If she was still around–if she still loved him– But she must. Surely by then she'll see that he never meant to betray her. Surely she'd see–

Mark buried himself in his work as the fall of '28 brought the year to a merciful close. He went to every horse auction he could buying and selling in a ravenousness frenzy. By December first, he sold eleven horses, traveling as far as Newton, New Jersey to sell one for a eighty-five dollar profit. He was relentless. He summoned all the tricks he'd learned but never used from Phil to make a horse seem less or more desirable to suit his needs. He bought them with his own money so he wouldn't need to split profits with Mr. Harrison.

He returned to Kristen's regularly. He went in the hopes that Emily might call again although he would not admit that to anyone. Not even himself. Kristen seemed content for the most part to having him around. She took to fixing him dinners, and in his dulled state of mind, he didn't mind her cooking. He went there mostly to drown out Emily's voice that resided permanently in his head. He didn't care what Kristen talked about, as long as she covered the silence. He marveled at how banal she sounded and wondered if she had always been this way, or had he just never noticed. He bristled at her touch, and would never sit on the divan lest she felt compelled to join him. He caught himself at times talking curtly to her, and when he did, he'd apologize. But most of the time he was unaware of anything about her except the fact that she wasn't Emily.

One night in November, they got drunk together. Stupid drunk. He didn't remember how or why they started drinking, but he took to it with a vengeance. The next morning he awoke in Kristen's bed unaware of anything that had happened after the first four inches of whiskey. His throat was raspy from a hundred cigarettes. An empty bottle lay on the floor in a puddle of spent ice. He remembered singing songs and how happy Kristen seemed. He recalled repeating limericks of Daniel's and laughing over and over at the punch line. He repeated part of one to himself, "She doesn't drink, She doesn't pet, She hasn't been to college yet..." and tried to figure out what seemed so funny a few short hours ago.

The air was stale from smoke and loveless sex. His head was throbbing as he staggered to her water closet to pee. He looked at himself in her mirror, saw his bloodshot eyes and his unshaven face. He stuck his finger down his throat to force himself to vomit. He rinsed out his mouth and took some of Kristen's tooth powder and rubbed it on his teeth with his finger. He ruffled his short hair in the mirror and turned his face from side to side. "No wonder she threw me over," he said.

He went back to Kristen's bedroom and covered her sprawling naked body with her quilt. She immediately curled into a ball, and a smile crossed her lips in her sleep like a shadow. It made him feel badly that he could make her smile so easily when his actions grew from weeds of indifference. She seemed so vulnerable to him at that moment and so damn far away. He hurried back to her toilet afraid he might get sick again. He looked at his eyes in her mirror. They reminded him of someone else's eyes and he wanted to run. Run from the person who he saw in the mirror and run all the way back to who he was when he was with Emily.

Ice

On December twenty-second, Mark returned to Pine Bluff along the same route he and Emily had taken the last time he saw her, arriving at the front of the large empty porch. The wind that blew across the gray boards was no colder than the memory of that day. He took Ohio out to check the footing, trying to decide if the ground was slippery enough to begin shoeing the horses with winter borium shoes. Ohio did not slide around more than once or twice so Mark decided to wait for the next regular visit from the farrier. He rode with his head down, partially as a way to keep his neck warm as the wind blew off the lake, but mostly out of an unconscious habit he'd developed. He didn't see Mr. Harrison's parked car until he was right on top of it.

He stood frozen for a moment until Ohio danced sideways impatiently. A girl's laughter trickled through the closed front door and Mark dismounted immediately and bounded up the porch stair. The door opened. To Judith. It was Judith's laugh he'd heard.

"Oh, Mark. There you are. I was afraid we'd miss you."

"Is Emily with you?"

"No," she said. "I meant Otis. Otis and I are here."

"Why?"

"Well you needn't be so happy to see me!"

"I'm sorry, Judith. Of course I'm glad to see you. But– I'm just surprised," he said though the monotone of his voice displayed neither gladness nor surprise.

She looked at him and frowned. Otis came through the front door with a large crate and placed it in the trunk of the car. He greeted Mark warmly and returned to the house rubbing his hands together.

"Emily wanted me to pick up some of her things. She–she won't be coming this summer."

"She needn't stay away on my account. I'm moving to New Jersey after this year's ice harvest," Mark said with all the bravado he could muster.

"It's not that," Judith said. "She's going to Europe in the spring."

Mark groaned.

"The Harrison's might take a year off, too. Mrs. Harrison wants to visit people this year. She's tired of playing hostess all the time."

Mark had heard that rumor from the butcher who was lamenting the fact that his best customer would not be placing orders this year. He insinuated the blame was Mark's, as did Mr. Stilson whose deal fell through on the sale of his house to one of the people who had been to the Harrison party a year earlier. It seemed that everyone in town owned pieces of Mark and Emily's story and they put them together like shards of a shattered mirror that issued no clear reflection when glued together.

Mark said nothing for a moment.

"How is she?"

Judith knitted her brow. "Oh you know Emily." She tried to sound lighthearted, but it didn't play.

"Why did you tell Mr. Harrison I threatened her?"

Mark hadn't meant to bring that up. Had every intention of letting it die.

"I never–"

"I saw you speaking with him the day Emily left. The afternoon after you came to my room." Months of anger rose in his voice.

"Oh, Mark, I don't know what I told him. I can't be responsible for every little word I say, can I?" She did not look him in the eye. Wouldn't even look at his face for more than a second at a time. "Why are you interrogating me about this? It's over. She always said you could never be together– She told me she told you that– Didn't she tell you again and again? Didn't she?"

Mark could not fight this fight.

Judith gathered confidence from his silence.

"She's moved on, Mark. She's with Tom DeSouza now. She's been with him since Halloween."

Mark closed his eyes in a defensive wince. He remembered Emily's comments when he asked her about that man the day after the party. That day on the swing.

"I don't believe you," he said, his eyes still closed.

Judith put her hands on her hips and glared at him.

"When did you become so horrid?" she asked.

Mark stood before her empty and defenseless.

"About four months ago."

He turned and walked down to his stable. He didn't pick up Ohio's reins, but the horse followed him down the hill towards home like a dog.

"I'm sorry, Mark," Judith called.

He didn't answer.

"Do you want me to tell her anything?"

Mark slid the door open and let Ohio in behind him. He closed and locked it with the slide bolt he never used before. He pulled Ohio's saddle and tack and hung it up on the way to his room. He put two large pieces of coal in the stove in his bedroom and waited for the room to warm up before removing his coat. He turned Judith's words in his mind like burning embers in the stove. Two months gone, he thought, she has "moved on." He saw his pile of figures stacked under the advertisement for the Regina d'Italia. He considered burning them, but the gesture didn't merit the effort.

He lay on his bed, surprisingly calm. He didn't feel the anguish he felt when she left in August. He didn't feel anything, really. He looked around his room, moving his eyes and not his head. Soot blackened the ceiling above the stove and hung over him like summer storm clouds. He thought of his grandfather and of tall-masted ships sailing to exotic ports. He thought of how the man spent his entire life carrying fragile shipments of ice around the world. His mind did not linger on any particular thought. It drifted to his mother. For Christmas, he bought her a little glass pitcher for milk that was shaped like a cow, and he hoped she would like it. He watched thoughts flicker through his head in a detached sort of way as if he was watching a newsreel. He remembered his first ice harvest when he so proudly rode the shine sleigh like a boy king. He thought of Billy's father's broken telescope. He thought if he had it with him now he would turn it backwards and everything would be as small and far away as Emily's love. He wondered about what Phil was going to do for Christmas dinner, and realized for the first time that he didn't even know if Phil's wife was still alive. Imagine that, he thought. I've known him my entire life and I don't have a clue. He remembered he needed to change the oil in Daniel's old car. He wondered what his mother did with Daniel's old winter coat and if Meghan still thought of him. He thought of Ray Radclay, and tried to remember if he died or was still in a coma. Abruptly, he jumped from bed and tore at his shirt. It felt heavy on his chest and threatened to suffocate him. He ripped it off half buttoned and threw it to the floor. He heard one of his buttons clatter along the bare wood floor as he laid back down again. He listened as his breathing slowed to a normal pace and he thought of all the sweet things Emily had said to him over the past summer. All like warm droplets that he drank so completely and so passionately and he watched as they instantly turned to tiny ice balls at the apex of their flight and scattered around the floor of his room like miniature misshapen marbles.

Secrets

Kristen couldn't remember when she initially felt it was wrong. It seemed harmless to her at first, a girlish impulse innocently acted out. One thing she did know was that she had stopped trying to figure out why she did it. For that question she had no answer. Any restraint was abandoned once she surrendered responsibility for her inexplicable wanderings as if not being able to explain her actions gave license to them.

She knew when it started. Not last summer, after Lindbergh. Not the June night her radio tube blew out when she woke Mark and crawled into his bed. That was just an innocent contretemps. The night it really began was the Thursday before the Harrison party last July. That was the first night she did not let Mark in on the secret. Having read that walking was good for insomnia she wandered outside for a midnight stroll. If she didn't pay close attention to where she was going, her steps always brought her to Pine Bluff. To Mark's stable. To Mark.

It excited her all over again just to think of that night. She remembered seeing the huge party tents set up around Mark's paddocks billowing in the night wind. The canvas snapped, alive and angry. Her blood percolated in an agitation that flirted with fear. Alternating currents of dread of being caught and her heart's pleading for exposure set her nerves rippling anew. She shivered but the chill seemed to flow from inside of her and the sweater she wrapped across her chest only insulated her from warmth. She thought it strange how a remembered feeling was so tangible, like a remembered smell. It revisited accompanied by all of the original sensations, so unlike the memory of an event recalled in the flat grays of a photograph.

When she reached the Harrison tents, she veered down along the lake past the ice house. There was always, it seemed, a light burning in the Lerner apartment and Kristen did not know if it was lit for someone like herself, a reluctant fugitive from sleep.

She lifted the latch of the bottom half of the stable door and entered the darkened barn. With each trip the foreign noises of the horses became less threatening but on that early trip last July, they electrified her senses. She walked through the tunnel of darkness towards his door, her eyes adjusting to its cover as she passed the silent white eyes staring at her from the stalls. She remembered there was no moon that night, and after that she always tried to go when she could count on the moonlight to provide an outline of her surroundings.

She pushed Mark's bedroom door open an inch at a time prepared to stop at the hinges' first squeak. She pressed through the narrow opening sideways, her breasts brushing the wooden door like cat's whiskers measuring sufficient clearance. She stood at the foot of his bed unmoving. Her own breathing sounded so loud that it took three or four minutes for her ears to measure the degrees of silence in the black room.

Mark was not there.

She patted the empty mattress frantically as if she might find him yet in a condensed form. Beads of sweat grabbed her fingertips as she put her hand to her forehead. Her own laughter escaped from her and bounced off the whitewashed walls. She threw herself onto his bed landing on her back as if jumping into a deep pool. The springs wrenched out a loud protest as Kristen luxuriated in a release of fear. She would not be caught that night! She lay on his bed and pulled his pillow to her chest in a tight embrace rocking side to side in the opulence of unexpected solitude spent in a forbidden place. She inhaled the pungent smell of his shirt that hung from his bedpost laying perfectly still on his bed for a long time as her mind careened around the room. She felt the linen of her own shirt scratching gently on the erect nipples of her breasts as she tentatively unbuttoned her trousers and touched herself until the springs sang out a muted release below her. She spent the final installments of this unexpected solitude riffling through his clothes. She took his shirts from the drawers of his dresser, unfolding and refolding them carefully, trying to duplicate the original uneven folds of his housekeeping.

Kristen made another secret sojourn two weeks later the night before she returned to Manhattan for her annual stay there. It was drizzling lightly as she sliced through the darkened path of the woods. The sweet smell of ozone filled the air. She fluttered between hopes of his being there and hopes of his absence, recalling the excitement of her previous visit. She stole into the barn confident in the effectiveness of her furtive movements and heard his bedsprings ooze out a soft moan as she opened his door. She stood at his footboard listening to his breathing. Listened as it intermingled with her own. If breath came in colors, she wondered what shades theirs would make blended together. She stood statue still, her hand resting on her breast. Her heart stretched out in excitement and beat hard against her fingertips. She left after several minutes giddy with inexplicable excitement.

When she returned home in August she stole back to his room again and again like a cat burglar. On each visit she became more brazen. She lost track of how many times she went but noticed after a time that she only paid her secret visits if she went a week or two without seeing him, and she learned to forgive herself because of this. It was his fault. The visits clustered together in a corner of her mind. She made no note of them and, in fact, refused to acknowledge their existence in the light of day. Mark spent much of the summer of 1927 doing whatever it was he did with the Harrison girl's horse and she saw him too infrequently for her liking. She held the minority opinion of wishing for summer's end.

In September of that year, after the Harrisons left, Kristen crept into Mark's room again. She sat on his hard wooden chair in the corner watching him, with her shirt partially unbuttoned, as he tossed and turned himself in an entanglement of sheets. She froze as he suddenly shouted "Emily!" and sat upright in his bed. She held her breath trying to come up with an explanation for her presence foolishly unprepared for its possible solicitation. But an explanation was not summoned. He lay back into his mattress and she watched his sheets flutter to the floor as he returned to his naked sleep. As her breathing quieted, she sat straitjacketing her impulses to touch him until spent from the effort, she returned to the sanity of her own house.

Mark's visits to her house increased in the fall of that year, and Kristen recalled only one secret sojourn to him. In light of her clandestine journeys, it seemed silly to try to conceal his trips to her bed. They seemed so normal juxtaposed with hers.

On the full-mooned night when snow first arrived in December of '27 Kristen was on her way to Mark's room. She was absorbed in the sound of snow arguing beneath her boots when she realized in a panic that her footprints would expose her secrets. She turned and walked home through crusty puddles of disappointment.

He came to her house on Christmas eve. She had quilted him a comforter and he bought her a book that she had already read. But she saved the red ribbon he tied around it.

After his accident in January of '28 she felt too ashamed to even admit to herself that she had ever snuck into his room at all. Her shame was superstitiously compounded by a belief that Daniel could see her and the thought inflicted enough disgrace to thwart her impulses to trespass. At least for a while.

Three months passed without Mark except for her visit to him while he was recuperating in February. He was still in his cast at the time and she involuntarily flinched when she saw him.

"They told you about the accident?" he asked when his mother left the room leaving them alone.

She nodded.

"It's my fault that he's dead."

"Oh, no, Mark. You mustn't say that. You mustn't think that his–"

"If I wasn't so close to him, he'd still be alive." Tears welled up in his eyes matching hers.

"We can only hurt those we're close to," she said, but she didn't think he understood.

"You cannot let Daniel's death destroy your life. It is God's will."

She wanted to hug him, or kiss him or both, but his lips were still swollen and his face raw where it wasn't bandaged. His one arm in a sling and the other in a cast left her no room to embrace him. She reached under his sheet and squeezed his good thigh. She saw him through a prism of tears. He reached up to her face and caressed her cheek to comfort her. Imagine that, she thought. He is trying to comfort me! He seemed distracted and uncomfortable with her in his brother's room, especially when his mother returned to offer tea. Kristen left hurriedly taking an uneasy dissatisfaction with her. She asked him to visit her when he felt up to it and watched his lips flash her a smile that contradicted the steely look in his eyes. She ignored the discrepancy.

By March, Mark had returned to his room and by the ides of March so had Kristen. She told herself on her way to his stable that she would wake him and tell him that she missed him terribly and needed to be with him again. But she did not wake him that night. She stood watching him sleep letting bits of partially-formed thoughts fall from her, thoughts like broken-glass chimes she had seen in a shop. Like the chimes, the individual thoughts were pretty but left no independent impressions. Together they softly melded into a wordless song. She leaned over him as if her thoughts might drip into his dreams. Kristen breathed in his smell and hoped that hers being inhaled by him would trump the other sensations of his dreams and make them hers. She lingered in his room for nearly an hour before leaving.

Her return trip home was filled with the usual self-reproach made no less troublesome through repetition. She should have wakened him, she thought as she climbed the stairs of her house. The inevitable feeling of guilt and regret met her at her door as a mocking silence shouted through the stone arches of Turtle Rock.

Mark's visits to Kristen in the tameness of daylight, though too scattered for her liking, sometimes made her think that they had reached a plateau that rivaled what she had with her husband. She let herself confuse his sexual appetite for something else. Something that might last longer than an hour at a spell. Kristen stumbled through those days fighting flashes of absolute clarity that told her exactly and precisely to abandon her relationship with Mark. Her role with him went no further than the bedroom, and it went there with a dwindling frequency. Yet, the more clearly she saw the starkness of their relationship, the more she clung to Mark's romantic accidents. The night they quarreled and she ran into the rain–when was that? Ten months ago–? Wasn't he there waiting for her when she returned? Didn't he hold her all night to comfort her. She fell in love with him that night. She promised herself she wouldn't and yet–she saw the two empty wine glasses he set on the table and she fell–not like with Rob. She would never love anyone like that again and she could not see Mark except through him–she didn't compare them–she didn't mean that–their similarities, if any, were incidental–but in the sense that she could only see Mark through the gauzy curtain of pain Rob left her.

Only a lake can be frozen and thawed and frozen again without scars. Kristen saw her heart grow smaller with each freeze, a perimeter of ice remaining like a shell protecting the inner warmth. Somehow Rob's memory tempered what Mark was. She didn't blindly trust the sweet things Mark said. She would get just so close to him, and then tread no more. She was a different person when Rob left, and although she gave Mark everything she could, there was less of herself to give.

She defended Mark during the silent arguments in her head rationalizing his occasional indifference. She liked being with him and that was enough of a reason to continue seeing him. She deserved the pleasure he brought her. She deserved it. She did. Didn't she? Besides, Mark had become an intelligent and thoughtful companion. She applauded herself on her contribution to that and he acknowledged her influence often. He read at least two newspapers a day and was always in the middle of a novel. He had at least a passing knowledge of the Viennese doctor Freud, Zelda Fitzgerald, George M. Cohen, Max Bohr, Texas Guinan and most of the famous names that provided a distant backdrop of their lives like a vibrant ever-changing wallpaper.

As to the future– She didn't want to think of the future. It loomed before her like a vulture ready to feast on whatever survived the present. A coldness filled her. She rose and went to her looking glass and began to brush her hair. She put the brush down and raked her fingers through her scalp burying the intermittent gray hairs under the blond. She again brushed it, holding her head from side to side in the mirror unable to settle on a style that she was happy with.

The spring of '28 brought several more secret excursions and an intermittent trickle of Mark's less secretive visits to her house. When Mark came to see her she devoured him greedily, slaking the assembled passions of her nightly sittings in a nearly religious lust. She tore at his clothes and raked his skin with her fingernails. She often bit him until he flinched during lovemaking and afterwards while he slept she searched his skin for marks. Through sheer youthful strength he kept pace with her but she sensed he treaded lightly in these pools of her passion. She knew he was completely unaware of the depth of the waters.

Then came June. Then the Harrisons. Mark all but disappeared. He explained his new responsibilities training Emily for the hunt, and maybe that was all it was, but Kristen struggled mightily with the summer of 1928.

As Mark came to her less and less, she increased her nighttime visits and had begun to leave clues of her presence. She knew the days he went into town and the days he went to the granary and she tried to accidentally run into him. He always greeted her warmly and she was certain he would have kissed her when they met if they weren't in public. If she saw him, she searched his face for any indications of suspicion of her invasions. Had he noticed any of the clues she left?

His shirt turned inside out and placed on his chair? His shoe kicked far under the bed? Mark had his own secrets to defend that summer and Kristen had long ago forgotten her father's words, "You'll never get caught by someone with more to hide than you".

The innocence of her encounters, if they could be said to contain any innocence at all, was obliterated when a July sojourn was aborted by the arrival of Emily Harrison. As she sat on top of the clothes he had thrown on his chair Kristen heard the click of the latch of the stable door. She was lifted by a jolt of panic and sprang to the bedroom door in one step. She left Mark's door ajar and stepped into a recess where brooms were kept. She tried to hide herself in the rags of shadows but felt that all the lights of Broadway shone on her. She stood pressed against the rough wall struggling to disappear into the woodgrain as Emily passed and entered Mark's room. Kristen blinked relief as Emily flew by. She watched through the narrow crack between the hinges as the girl awoke Mark with a kiss and proceeded to act out all of Kristen's fantasies in a wanton and unladylike manner before her prying eyes. Everything changed for Kristen in that moment. She tore herself from the pull of the private events with the difficulty of a witness to an automobile accident, but she was unsure who the victim was in this wreckage.

Almost drunkenly, Kristen left the barn leaving the door swinging open behind her. A sea of emotions rose and crested again and again rising to a nauseating peak before plummeting to a shameful nadir. She strained her eyes to see through the remaining darkness as if she was peering through a rain-splattered windshield. That hussy was–was–doing–only what she wanted to do. That whore had the temerity to–to act out all of Kristen's passions. Mark was hers! Didn't that insipid little girl know that it was she who taught him to touch like that? Why, he was merely a clumsy boy when she first pulled him into her bed and now that little tart was stealing her Mark with all her father's money and purchased charms. She would have none of it. This time she would fight back. She would–she would–do something. She clenched her fists and spun away. This time she would not let her man fly away without her.

Kristen fortified herself with an arsenal of caustic remarks that she intended to toss Mark's way when next he came around. Sentences that, she was certain, would cut him to the quick while letting him know she knew all about his empty fling with the Harrison girl. Lines that would make him see that he was wasting his time on that girl and that contained the words powerful enough to bring her prodigal son back to her bed.

But he never came that summer. She updated her barbs so often, that they lost their cutting edge. They were rubbed smooth by her constant reworking until they sounded merely like pathetic little pleas. She ultimately tossed them aside leaving herself completely unarmed to the assault of his indifference.

She went to Manhattan as she did every summer, but returned after four days unable to relax or to think of anything but Mark. In daylight hours she read feverishly, often skipping lunch in an absorption that bordered on compulsion. If a book had no love interest, she cast it aside. She pored over every word of the lovelorn characters. She cried when Hemingway's Lady Brett Ashley told Jake Barnes that "It was pretty to think so," and she felt as if she was living in the cottage at Wuthering Heights with Catherine sharing every poisoned emotion.

She studied at the altar of her bookcase searching for hidden flaws in all of the heroines seeking instruction for her goal of a happy ending. Weren't all book characters the same? One pathetic lover always blind to the love of their counterpart. But love always carried the day. Love was like that. Wasn't it? Love conquered all. Didn't it? Perseverance. Belief in love beyond all odds– That was the key. Wasn't this so? This is where she erred with Rob. She let him walk away, her pride wounded by a handful of silly words scrawled on a piece of paper. Her pride was the culprit. She saw that clearly now. Didn't the Bible say that pride cometh before the fall? She would wait for Mark to feel the heat of her love. Then it would be–then he would be–then everything would be just perfect.

Kristen had heard forever what a patient woman she was and she took the compliment as condescension. She was not a patient woman. What others recognized as patience was only ambivalence. She did not care if she had to wait in line at the butcher for her weekly order. She did not care if spring flowers bloomed this week or next. But of those few things she truly wanted and thought essential, she had no patience. She wanted Mark and he wanted her although his reluctance to see that was becoming annoying to her. She decided to watch his situation carefully and to be prepared when opportunity arrived. She continued her nighttime visits, sometimes as often as twice a week, but sat watching him now with less lust and more like an impatient hen waiting for a reluctant egg to hatch. Some nights. Other nights it was only about the physical.

Kristen was careful to leave long before the hour that Emily might appear, but on a night in mid-August their paths crossed again. Kristen was leaving, was halfway down the aisle between the stalls, when the cannon shot of the latch clicked into the darkness. How could Mark sleep through this deafening sound? She ducked into a vacant stall until the whoring Harrison girl passed and Kristen started home. It ripped at her heart to know they were together but she could not walk away from her self-induced pain. Before reaching the ice house, she circled back and walked around the barn to sit under Mark's window. She listened to his and Emily's giggles and whispers. The few words that reached her through the intermittent squeaking of bedsprings pummeled her heart but she stayed and listened more. As their breathing quickened, Kristen touched herself roughly. She did not want to. This, she knew, was wrong by any standard. Like the illusory relief of scratching poison ivy, she let their words scratch at her heart until it was raw and she stopped only when she could tolerate the pain no longer. When all sound halted inside Mark's room, Kristen sat still. The three of them were separated only by a thin wall. Contented unintelligible sounds hummed through the open window above her, a different language, it seemed, from the one screaming in her head. Kristen closed her eyes tightly until her head ached. She felt as low as the dirt she sat on. A grown woman in her mid-thirties reduced to a revolting pantomime of love. She wanted to slither away. The smell of her own wasted sex disgusted her. She could drop no further in her own eyes. She could feel her lowness more than see it like an obese woman who could no longer see her knees.

Kristen walked the long way home around the lake not arriving until after dawn, the entire way arguing to herself that what she had just done was not so terrible, but she could not get herself close to believing that. She felt the violation of the raped stacked precariously atop the guilt of the rapist. The first birds of dawn soared and sang so far above her that their song died out long before the music reached her inner ear. Robert Scott's wife was incapable of such a loathsome act and she cried in mourning for her. She entered her house and removed her soiled undergarments stopping only to burn them in the fireplace. She scrubbed her hands red with rough soap powder, and without pausing to dry her hands she pulled the paper shades, closed her sheer curtains and draped her bedspread over the rods to completely shut out the harsh daylight. She rolled and turned in bed and prayed for dreams. In dreams she was a whole person. In dreams her actions made sense. In dreams love cast no shadows of pain.

She slept through all the inevitable daylight hours and woke reluctantly only after all sleep had been wrung from her body like water from a sponge. A sense of loss hovered over her like humidity. She turned thoughts over in her mind carefully, distrustful of what might crawl out from under them. She reached for a match on her nightstand and, without watching, struck it on the wall above her headboard and lit a candle. She looked softer than she felt in the flickering light. After nearly half an hour, she rose and pulled the bedspread from the window. Hot air rushed in. She stepped past her dressing mirror, but refused to look at her image, afraid to find that there might not be one. She felt a hunger that was so far down in her hierarchy of need that she almost missed it. This was a hunger she could assuage, and she went to her garden and pulled ingredients from the moist black earth that might nurture her back into herself. She fixed a meal of carrots, string beans and cold chicken and poured herself a glass of wine uncertain if she was having breakfast or dinner. She flipped through the pages of Collier's until she found an article about the Yale crew team that held absolutely no interest to her and she read it twice.

She vowed that she would not go to Mark's again. She promised herself, and she kept her promise faithfully some nights wrestling with temptation minute by minute. Eight nights after her humiliation, she walked around the far side of the lake, again a sentry of sleeplessness. She stepped slowly because there was no moon and the stars were covered by a low cloud cover. She could barely see her own hand in front of her face and felt safe in the cocoon of darkness. The sound of the water lapping softly on the shore helped pilot her aimless stroll. From across the lake every light burned in Pine Bluff. The house shone like a lone star in the black sky. She thought she should investigate this unusual occurrence and decided to return to Mark's room, but she would not crawl in secrecy. She would wake him this time and see if there was an emergency that she might help with. No more of–of that other thing. She marched down the dirt path towards Pine Bluff like a reformed alcoholic towards a liquor store.

As she approached the barn, she heard the door of the main house open and she instinctively ran to the cover of the ice house. She watched as the Harrison's Negro loaded the car with a woman's valise, several hat boxes and a huge steamer trunk. Kristen stood immobile, her heart beating out seconds. She edged closer to the house hiding herself behind the cover of the black walnut tree that guarded the front porch. On the cusp of morning and night, Emily Harrison emerged from the house, her hair disheveled and clothes askew. Neither of her parents were there to see her off, nor had Kristen heard any farewells from inside the open front door. Emily turned and looked at the stable, a desperately sad look on her face that Kristen could not pretend was anything else. Kristen watched as she boarded the idling car. She slumped into the rear seat covering her eyes with her trembling hand and Kristen watched the spasmodic shake of her shoulders as the car coughed blue smoke and drove off. She stood frozen as Mark ran from the barn in his undershorts too late to see the girl. Kristen was invisible to him although she felt exposed in the new light of day. Her heart went out to him. It genuinely did. Didn't she know what he felt at this moment? Her chest rippled and snapped like a wind-blown flag at the thought of Mark and her together, but she heard a faint voice inside her daring to express an opportunity for victory. Kristen was certain that she was perfectly situated to ease his pain, and she stole away reverting to the stranger she had become that summer.

Kristen knew every earthquake had its aftershocks and she was careful not to wander too far from the epicenter of this one. A crevice had swallowed Emily and perhaps another would follow. One that she and Mark might fall in together. She walked home as the morning pressed on, stopping to steal a dozen apples from the Harrison's orchard. She busied herself in her kitchen rolling dough and pinching the crust around a tin pie plate. Her radio was tuned to "The March of Time", and she listened absently as the sound of one hundred musicians filed innocently through her kitchen. The rich radio voice of Howard Barlow could barely be heard over her own unflagging voice as she discussed, sometimes aloud, the state of affairs as they looked from her prismatic vantage point.

Kristen was dying to know the details of Emily's apparent exile. She packed her questions into the apple pie like soldiers into a Trojan horse hoping to unleash them within the gates of the Harrison home. She rolled and placed a thin cover of dough over the stolen apples as she planned her subtle invasion back into Mark's life. She carefully vented the soft crust of her pie with the tines of a fork in abstractedly set patterns of holes that precisely encircled the sweet apples and cinnamon. Coincidence would have her pay a visit to the Harrisons after lunch, apple pie in hand, in a neighborly gesture to celebrate the end of their visit. Or whatever. She'd think of something.

She could not remember how much time was needed to bake the pie so she pulled a kitchen chair in front of the oven to monitor the progress. A second later, she jumped up knocking the chair backwards as she did and hastily scribbled a note on a scrap of paper. She put the note in her shirt pocket, peeked into the oven at the pale dough, and ran out of the house and down the path with the single-mindedness of a Pony Express rider. She ran almost all the way to Pine Bluff, pausing only once when she got a stitch. She pressed the note onto a rusty nail on Mark's door and was gone from the barn before the note completely settled from the rush of the air behind her. She saw no one along the way, and assumed no one saw her.

Her calves were screaming a taut complaint as she reached her house. Her shoes thumped along the floor boards as she kicked them off at the door. She collapsed against her icebox, her lungs searching for air, eyes tightly closed. She opened one eye and noticed red streaks across her floor. Her foot was bleeding and she pulled a tiny piece of glass from her big toe. Her shirt was darkened by sweat and the oven seemed relatively cooler than the sun's heat that had stalked her as she sprinted the mile long round trip. She crawled to the oven, unable to convince her aching legs to stand. The pie was brown verging on burnt and she pulled it from the oven and placed it on a cooling rack. Kristen was suddenly hit with a wave of fatigue and the realization that although it was past noon, she had yet to sleep from the previous night. She walked into her bedroom collapsing into her mattress as her clothes hit the floor. The aroma of apple pie filled the small house creating a facade of normalcy that her senses embraced before they blurred into the shelter of sleep.

Kristen awoke as an evening thunderstorm ushered in a cooling reprieve. Like a newborn infant, she had her days and nights confused adding to a disoriented melange that had replaced the mundane structure of her daily life. She staggered from her bedroom on aching legs and walked to the front porch. The sun was perched just above the tree line and she rocked gently waiting for the remnants of sleep to fall from her. She absently massaged her calves, still in rebellious shock from her sprint earlier that day. She had dreamt heavy syrupy dreams that, although unremembered, left a troubling shadow on her mood. She needed coffee but was unwilling to leave the comfort of her chair to make it. Her toe still hurt and she touched it again to find it still seeping blood. There must still be glass left in it, she thought and fell into a daydream of Mark arriving up her path with coffee and his smile just like he used to. He would take care of her. Clean her cut foot, bandage it and pamper her as she sipped hot coffee, filling all her needs at once. She stared at the picture projected in her mind until she could squeeze no more pleasure from it and watched it burst like a soap bubble. Her toe ached for Mark's curing hands.

She frowned silently at the realization that she had slept through her opportunity to speak with Austin Harrison that afternoon. Her pie had cooled into the transparent attempt to steal information that it was and she couldn't think of what she might say to him that he wouldn't see through. She fretted over her new sleeping schedule and wondered how she was going to switch her days back into nights or how she would be able to get to sleep that night.

The evening loomed before her daring her to fill it. She finally went inside to make coffee and whipped the last of her eggs into an omelet filling it with onions, peppers and ham left in her ice box. She needed to shop, but of course, had slept through that opportunity too. She walked down the porch stairs to her milk box hoping the milkman had come and gratefully pulled a warm bottle of buttermilk from the tin box. She could not remember what day it was but hoped the bottle was delivered only that morning. She pulled the cardboard top from the smooth neck of the bottle and sniffed at the contents carefully. It did not seem sour. She skimmed the cream from the top and poured a tall glass that she chilled in the ice box for a moment. She used to derive pleasure from such simple acts, but now was mired in an unrelenting discontent. Whatever she was doing reminded her only of a desire to be doing something else. She sighed. She would give anything to have him run up her path, eager in his lust, the way he used to. He will, she said soothingly to herself. He will. Soon.

Kristen forced herself into bed around midnight and spent half a candle reading before finally falling asleep. She awoke at four-thirty in a darkness the color of her dreams. She knew she was up for the day but was content with her progress towards normal hours. She decided to go see Mark and wait for him at the paddocks until he turned out his horses. He was usually tightlipped about anything involving the Harrison girl, but she thought he might leak some news if caught off guard. She no longer cared what anyone might say if they saw her at his room. It seemed laughable that she ever cared.

She bathed and dressed and did something that she hadn't done in recent memory. She put on a dress. It was a floral printed sun dress with narrow shoulder straps. The gas light flickered as she twirled in front of the wardrobe mirror trying to evaluate her appearance. She tied a blue ribbon in her hair and left to wait for Mark. As she walked, she rubbed the goose bumps on her arm wondering what he might say when he saw her. She had never worn a dress for him before.

She still would not let herself walk all the way to the stable but waited instead on the bench in front of the ice house for Mark to wake and come outside. The moment of silence that broadcasts the arrival of dawn arrived. The peepers and crickets of night were ending their shift and the birds were still in the wings. As she waited, Emily's friend Judith ran from the main house into the stable. She thought it amusing that his room had all the privacy of a train platform, and she shook her head quickly as if trying to erase the notion from her mind. Kristen marched to Mark's window with her head held conspicuously high blocking out all the unpleasant reminders rooted in that spot like weeds.

Kristen listened to their conversation through the open window. Heard every word. She heard, too, what Judith did not say directly and understood the meaning of each of her pauses as she sidestepped Mark's questions about Emily. When she heard Mark say he could ruin Emily's reputation in a sentence, she knew she had just been given all the weaponry she needed to assure her victory. It was suddenly so simple.

Clearly, Emily was not coming back to Mark. It's not like Kristen caused that. She just wanted to be certain that all the bridges between them were destroyed. For Mark's sake. A clean break was always best. She felt like a prisoner who just turned the page on the calendar marking the final month of his sentence.

She turned towards home as Judith began her farewells, with more information than she could have dreamed of gathering. Kristen regretted that he did not get to see her dress, but was certain there would be many more opportunities soon. She was filled with the nearness of his return.

Kristen did visit Austin Harrison later that morning. Brought him the day old pie that outlived its usefulness the moment Mr. Harrison opened the door and reluctantly invited her in. He nervously adjusted his sleeves while looking at her as if she was an apparition. He could never allow himself the luxury to be rude but was clearly unwilling to entertain visitors. Kristen could hear Lucretia weeping in the front parlor. For a very long moment, neither waded into the uncomfortable silence between them.

"Is everything all right?" she asked finally.

"Yes. Well, yes. We must return to the city early. Hmmm. Something came up and we, uh, we will leave. Now. Today. I'm sorry to not invite you to stay."

"Yes," she said. There was no ramp to help her slide into what she had come to say. "Mark has told me of the–well, the unpleasantness, and I wanted you to know that he said he would never say anything to anyone to damage your daughter's reputation–although he might with one sentence–if he was less of a gentleman."

She watched as Austin put his hand on the wall to steady himself. She hated to use him like that, he had been so generous to her. She knew she would never be able to speak to him again. Knew instinctively that he would eventually see, if he didn't already, that her knowledge of anything between his daughter and Mark compromised their relationship and would make even the most banal exchange of pleasantries distasteful. She felt a trifle sad about that.

"Maybe if this is a bad time–" and she backed out the front door with her sorry pie leaving a stunned Austin Harrison unable to extend even a gesture of farewell. The head dominos had all been knocked over, and Kristen only wished that she was in a better position to hear the clicking of the others as all the obstacles that stood between her and Mark toppled before her.

The phone call she brokered between Emily and Mark a week later went better than she might have hoped. She had no way of knowing how sensitive Emily was about her reputation and the strength of her anger yielded a finality that Kristen could read clearly in Mark's expressions. Mark returned to Kristen, as she knew he would, but was, admittedly, sometimes a little distracted and distant. By November, he was almost all the way back to her. She just knew it.

Emily Harrison did call Kristen again trying to reach Mark. Once in October. Once in November. Again a week later in December. Kristen tried to explain to her that Mark was just upset and a little angry–you know how men get when things don't go their way–and yes, yes, she did tell him she called and no, he didn't really say if he would call back and well–these things are never easy and, yes, sweetheart, she'd be sure to tell him and maybe–yes–maybe, she thought to herself, perhaps one day she would. But for now there did not seem to be much sense in picking scabs off pink wounds.

Frozen Channels

Mark spent the final days of 1928 in near isolation. Not so much by design, but from a failure to make other arrangements on an hour-to-hour basis. Some days he spoke to no one save his horses. He thought of Emily so often he wore ruts into his brain so that soon it became impossible to go anywhere in his thoughts to escape her. She was the salve that could cool his burned skin, and yet she was also the burn. He rode his horses hours on end, brought one back to the stable, cooled him down and went back out again on another. He ate erratically, sometimes not having dinner until midnight when he realized, after tossing and turning for an hour, he hadn't eaten. He had never been able to sleep when he was hungry and made a mental note to pay more attention to meals. His mother had long ago stopped expecting him for dinner, but she sometimes brought food down and left it on top of his wood stove. Occasionally he went to Kristen's.

The first gray days of 1929 hardened together in a frozen clump. Mark read the papers daily, but had to restart a novel on three separate occasions unable to get beyond the first few pages before giving up on it entirely. The boom in Florida had ended. Mark read all the news reports trying to figure out what went wrong. All the speculation of the previous year had collapsed and the price of Florida real estate had plummeted faster than it had soared. Hundreds, maybe thousands of people had lost vast sums of money as the last man in paid the piper in a ruinous game of musical chairs. Overnight, speculation became a dirty word. The poorer inhabitants of Sullivan County seemed to take an inordinate amount of satisfaction at the idea of the rich losing money. They all "knew all along" that speculation was a fool's game, and congratulated themselves on not falling prey to the hysteria that sent prices skyward to begin with, choosing to forget that it was merely a severe lack of money that prevented them from joining the short-lived party.

The vibration from the tidal wave that hit Florida spread across the entire country. Mark had read that even in Tennessee real estate prices were plummeting, although he couldn't imagine real estate ever being valuable in such a place to begin with. He didn't know of anyone personally who lost money but he had heard that three separate contracts to buy land along the Delaware River had been canceled. The boundless optimism of 1927 had been reined in and the papers were filled with debate between the nay-sayers and the boom riders about the state of the economy in general. It amazed him that things could change so suddenly and that somehow events here were connected to events a thousand miles away. He wondered if the Harrisons had lost any money, but decided that Mr. Harrison was too smart for that. He remembered a group of people at the party in '27 talking about the "sure thing" in Florida and assumed some of them lost money. He wondered how many of the people in attendance that night lost everything. What would they do? Would they move to the Lower East side with all the immigrants? He thought it must be worse to have had everything and lose it than to never have had it at all. It confused him to try to figure these things out and made him more tired than he chronically was.

His confusion did not prevent him from moving forward. After Christmas he sold most of his stock keeping only thirty shares of American Express. He went again to visit Andrew Bryant in Peapack to finalize their working contract. Mark was to begin work on February first. He toured a new stable capable of housing forty-eight horses that was nearly completed in anticipation of his arrival. He would have two full time stable helpers to muck stalls and do the more mundane chores leaving him free to train and sell horses. He conceded that this move would do him good. There would be valleys and forests that would not remind him of Emily. Fences they hadn't jumped together. Fields they hadn't cantered through. Mr. Bryant had signed Mark and himself up for the current hunt season at the Essex Hunt Club. Mark would meet new people, and although it seemed a cumbersome burden, he knew it was what he needed.

With the money from the sale of his stocks he bought a small cottage on two acres on Highland Avenue, less than a mile from Bryant's horse farm. Ironically, his house was adjacent to Blairsden, the estate that held the wedding Emily and Judith had attended a year ago. Mark had mixed feelings about the house purchase. If he kept his money in the market, it would likely double by the end of '29. But he didn't care anymore. The money meant little to him without–well, there was no need to go through that again–he didn't care about the money.

He told his father about the house. He wasn't certain what his reaction would be, but his father was elated. He called Mary Lerner into the kitchen and disappeared into the Harrison wine cellar returning with a dusty bottle to celebrate.

"To the first Lerner to ever own a house," he toasted jubilantly.

The significance of the purchase hit Mark for the first time as he watched his parent's joy slip past their usually guarded gates. His mother grew misty eyed as they discussed a visit south. She wanted to come and help him set up house. She could make curtains, help clean. She was more excited than Mark. Mary assumed he earned the money through horse sales and investing and Mark did nothing to dispel the notion. He told her he had a small mortgage note, but in truth, he paid cash on the barrel head.

After the excitement of his announcement waned, Mark watched as early winter snows layered tiers of silence over the rolling landscape. The days of January passed slowly as he kept largely to himself until the ice harvest forced him out of his rut. The night he rowed the channel, he realized he could not spend another day harvesting ice. As morning broke, he decided to tell his father he wasn't going to help finish the harvest, but did not take the opportunity when he saw him the following morning on the shore. Mark rowed his boat to greet him.

The sky had brightened quietly announcing the arrival of a new day without the fanfare of a sunrise. The black sky turned to gray, then reluctantly to blue gray but refused to brighten any further. The dark thoughts that accompanied Mark all night dissipated quickly in the light of day the way a herd of deer scatter when spooked. His father had a steaming cup of coffee for him.

"How did it go?"

"Fine."

Mark looked behind him at his own wake slapping against the white walls of ice along the perimeter of the dark channel. He had spent a good portion of the night thinking about Daniel on this, the anniversary of his death. Mark had never shared a very vocal relationship with his father, but they spoke less than ever since Daniel's death. He felt certain his father held him at least partially responsible, and if he didn't, Mark still did. He shouldn't have been so close.

"Are you bringing Ohio with you when you move?"

Mark nodded.

"And the others?"

"I sold all but Abbey. I wrote Mr. Harrison and asked if I might buy her."

His father raised his eyebrows and Mark wondered how much his mother had told him about the entire Emily affair.

"He agree?"

"In a way. I got a letter from his secretary saying that Abbey could be sold to a prospective buyer for not less than eight hundred dollars."

"Eight hundred! She's not worth three. Four tops!"

"Yes, I know."

"So you're going to leave her here?"

"No," Mark said. "I sent him a draft for eight hundred."

Michael whistled, his breath visible in the cold air.

There was little else to say, somehow. It made Mark glad to see his parent's pride, but he felt uncomfortable all the same. He wished Daniel were there. He would be proud of his little brother and Mark wished he were there to rib him about being an "estated gentleman". He shut the door quickly on the nagging thought that if Daniel was alive there would be no money.

Mark looked around him at the barren lake where he spent his entire life. It was time. The past year had not only changed him, but had changed Pine Bluff. He noticed the paint chipping off the eaves of the great house. Some of the shakes curled under years of oil. Without Emily it was–maybe it was always like that. His father might fix things but without Daniel–Mark sighed unwilling to go down any of those roads.

At times he was convinced that years had passed since that January day twelve months ago when Daniel disappeared into the ice. He often felt guilty that he suffered almost no repercussions from the accident save for a twinge in his shoulder on cold days. What a year. The first two months were gone, surgically removed from his life like the amputated arm of a war veteran. March was a blur of pain and bewilderment and April and May were recalled through a gauzy ether. He returned to his horses like a sailor to the sea. Kristen provided him with physical comforts while kneading his battered psyche into a soft acceptance of his brother's death.

Then came June. Then Emily. He couldn't help but feel that he climbed to the highest point of his life in those days of summer. It seemed that everything he had done in his life to that point had prepared him only to be with her. He learned to ride horses that he might ride with her. He read every word of every book so that he might quote a line to her. The minutes of those days flowed through his fingers like gold coins and jewels. But nothing in his life prepared him for her departure. And still he wallowed in it. The remainder of the year was a void that swallowed him nightly before spitting him out each morning onto a new day without promise.

He hated his sadness, detested his melancholy. Anyone could see how lucky he was. He was fortunate to have lived through the accident. He had the company of a good woman in Kristen. He was wealthy beyond his wildest dreams, was about to start a new life in New Jersey. He could see all the happiness in his life. He just couldn't feel it.

"What?" he said, aware that his father had spoken. He wondered how long he was lost in his reverie.

"I said, 'Are you tired?'"

"Yes," Mark answered.

"Maybe you don't want to be drinking that coffee if you plan on getting some sleep."

Mark silently agreed and handed the steel cup back to his father.

"You all right, son?"

Mark attempted a smile.

"Just tired."

Men were arriving in groups of twos and threes some bundled in long wool overcoats, some in short jackets. They greeted Mark and patted his shoulder in silent congratulations for a job well done. Mark watched as they entered the shanty and pulled out saws, breaking bars and pikes. He walked tentatively across the frozen path to his room, his legs stiff and cold, as the sounds of the harvest faded behind him.

He entered the warmth of his room and dropped his coat onto his bed before turning to see Kristen asleep on his chair. Her presence startled him and he spoke her name.

She awoke with a snap of her head and jumped to her feet smothering him in her embrace.

"Oh, Mark. Where were you? I was so worried."

He looked at her and frowned.

"Why are you here? Is everything all right?"

She released him from her embrace and sat on his bed. "Yes. I was just worried. I haven't seen you in days and days and I was so– Are you angry that I'm here?"

"No," he said. "I'm just tired. I worked the channel last night. I thought you knew."

He sat on the bed next to her and started to remove his boots with his frozen fingers. She stood to help him, setting his wet boot on the thigh of her britches while working the laces.

"You're frozen! Your feet are icicles," she said taking them into her warm hands and massaging them. He felt embarrassed by her attentions vaguely aware that he could not return them.

"Will you come by for dinner tonight?"

"All right," he answered in a monotone he had never noticed in himself before.

She walked to him and hugged him. He put one arm around her shoulder.

"I miss you, Mark," she whispered.

"I'll come by later," he said, releasing her shoulder.

"We'll have fun," she said.

Mark nodded again unconvincingly and watched her leave the barn. She stopped at the door, turned and waved. He nodded imperceptibly in her direction and watched her spend a smile. It was a pathetic uncertain smile and it made him oppressively sad. Not for Kristen, he could barely see her from where he stood, but because he recognized it as an expression he'd seen in his small hand held mirror and of the expression he'd seen in his mother's face when she told him of her lover. He stepped back into his room and laid on his bed. He wondered if he was wrong in going to Kristen's house when his mind was so far away. She clung to him like a leech as that winter took hold, but he thought that maybe it might be good for him to be bled like that. Sleep took him in her maternal embrace, smoothing all the wrinkles from his brow.

Mark awoke mid-afternoon and walked down to the lake looking for his father. He wanted to tell him that he was quitting the harvest, but he couldn't find him. He watched the men determinedly pull the large cakes of ice from the lake slowly revealing the waters containing the dormant promise of spring. He listened to the clanging of bars, the intermittent laughter that hung visibly above the working men in swirls of steam. He walked to Kristen's following her footprints in the snow.

They sat through dinner dealing out hands of conversation like old married couples. He spoke of Daniel, the Florida crash. He needed to tell her he was leaving at the end of the week for New Jersey, but he thought the conversation would require more energy than he brought along. He had first mentioned it a month ago but she stared at him vaguely. "Maybe I'll come with you," she said.

He smiled at what he assumed was her joke, and his leaving was never mentioned again until now.

He had not yet told her of the final arrangements or the house. During dinner, she watched him as he spoke, but said little. Mark felt exposed under the spotlight of her stare. He picked at his meal, unable to identify the meat concealed under a lumpy gravy. Maybe venison, maybe rabbit. Kristen silently took his plate to the sink after nearly finishing her own. He rose and went to the divan, opening the newspaper in front of him as she washed the dishes. He watched her over the top of the pages, and she glanced at him over her shoulder repeatedly as she worked. He tossed the paper aside, unread, and stepped to her window looking down at the frozen lake. The north end of the channel was visible to his left.

"Did I tell you I'm not going to harvest ice anymore? This is my last day–"

"You don't want me to come with you, do you?" she interrupted in a small voice that confused him with its simplicity. He hadn't even told her he was leaving.

He exhaled a great breath surprising himself with its force, and finished his original thought: "...I rowed the channel all night. Let it freeze over from here on in for all I care."

They were both standing now, facing each other from opposite ends of the room, her question still suspended between them. She walked toward him, but stopped halfway. He looked at her and, for the first time in months, he looked into her eyes. He recognized something the way you recognize someone on a crowded street who is wearing the same coat. He averted his eyes from her relentless stare and looked out her window onto the ice. He thought of the way she looked through the telescope on Turtle Rock so many years ago.

"You'd miss the lake," he said.

He took her coat from the brass hook behind the door.

"I'm going for a walk. Do you want to come?"

She walked to him tilting her head as if he'd said something else. As she walked to the window, light sparkled in the moisture of her eyes.

"I love you," she said.

He frowned, puzzled by the motive for her statement. She tried to coax a smile from him as she extended her hand to him, fingers outstretched pointing upwards in a way that reminded him of Emily on the last day they rode together. He didn't want to be reminded of Emily anymore. He was tired of being reminded of her every minute of every day. He wanted to be more like Daniel. Shrug her off. Move on. He was wrong about love, about what it meant, what it was worth. He was ready to admit that now to whatever invisible judge ruled on such matters and meted out such heavy penalties for believing otherwise. He wanted a pardon for his foolishness.

Kristen's hand stood suspended in the empty space between them, outstretched and needy. He wondered what she would say if she knew he had been to a place where a man needed merely to think a smile and his lover's skin would quiver a reply. He closed his eyes for a moment.

He handed her the coat forcing her to take it with her extended hand. His gesture made her frown, but he pretended not to notice as she took it and threw it over her shoulders.

"Yes," he said. "I love you, too."

The words came from no deeper inside of him than his own throat. They left a metallic taste in his mouth. His voice sounded like Daniel's, not the words, but the cadence. He did not look for anything in her eyes as he looked through the listless space between them.

Spending the last few coins of his youth, he assured himself he was a safe distance from love.

Lawrence Cirelli is a Seton Hall University graduate residing in Basking Ridge, New Jersey. He is the father of two daughters and a son. He has been a self-employed wallpapering contractor for nearly twenty years while waiting to begin this, his first novel.

Acknowledgments

I would like to thank the members of my writing group at the Palmyra Tea Room: Anne Wolfe; Jonathan Fleishmann; Michael Hanson; and in particular, David Shaw and Diane Jones-Wallach. Their critiques and encouragement during this long process were indispensable.

I cannot count the many contributions of Dee Maltzan. In the very least, everything Mark knows about horses, he learned from Dee.

Thanks also to the people at the Hanford Mills Museum in East Meredith, New York for allowing me to participate in their ice harvest as part of the 1998 Winter Festival, and for their gracious hospitality and patience in answering my many questions.

Renowned author, David Markson of The New School in Manhattan provided (unwittingly, I imagine) a catalyst with his encouraging comments in the embryonic stages of this novel. The entire New School experience was an important and enjoyable prelude to the writing of this book.

Though she believes the most terrible things about me personally, I would be criminally negligent if I did not thank author Andraya Simpson. I learned most of what I know about writing from her and I am eternally grateful for her contribution.

Thanks to my friends and family, and especially Dan and Patti, for tolerating my ramblings about Mark, Kristen, and Emily as if they were real people.

And finally, a heartfelt thank you to Ruth Cochrane, wherever she may be. She believed many, many years ago that I would write this novel. Her kind and encouraging words were never forgotten, but merely stored in an attic room in my mind waiting for the story to unfold.

Lawrence Cirelli

Basking Ridge, New Jersey

June, 1999

LCirelli@townbookpress.com